El Cid

Also available in this series

El Cid

Mío Cid Campeador

Vicente Huidobro

translated from Spanish by
Warre Bradley Wells

Shearsman Books

Second Edition.
Published in the United Kingdom in 2019 by
Shearsman Books Ltd
50 Westons Hill Drive
Emersons Green
BRISTOL
BS16 7DF

Shearsman Books Ltd Registered Office
30–31 St. James Place, Mangotsfield, Bristol BS16 9JB
(this address not for correspondence)

ISBN 978-1-84861-628-8

First published as *Portrait of a Paladin*
by Eyre and Spottiswoode, London, in 1931;
first U.S. edition published by H. Liveright, New York, 1932.

Originally published in Spanish as *Mío Cid Campeador*
by Compañía Ibero-Americana de Publicaciones, Madrid, 1929.

Notice
Every effort has been made to trace the representatives of the
translator's estate but we have had no success. We would be pleased
to hear from anyone who controls the literary estate of Warre Bradley Wells.

Contents

DEDICATION
TO DOUGLAS FAIRBANKS

Dear Mr. Fairbanks,

One evening last summer at the Hôtel Crillon in Paris you talked to me about the Cid Campeador, and told me that he was one of the historical personages who most interested you. You asked me to collect some notes about him and send them to you in the United States. You spoke with such enthusiasm that it communicated itself to me, and then I conceived the idea of writing something about the Cid.

To you, therefore, I partly owe this *Hazaña* of *Mío Cid Campeador*,[1] and so I would like your name to stand at the beginning of its pages and there remain as long as this work endures. It was born for me out of all the documents which I started studying for you. If anything in it is of service to you, if any single phrase of mine helps you to feel more deeply for our great hero and understand him better, I shall be content.

Your sincere admirer,
VICENTE HUIDOBRO

---

[1] This may be translated, more or less, as 'The Exploits of My Cid, the Champion'. A footnote on p.65 goes into greater detail on the definition of 'Campeador'.

AUTHOR'S PREFACE

I owe it to the truth to say that I had already thought before of writing a new romance about the Cid Campeador, but I abandoned the idea. This was after having read some pages of A. García Carraffa in his *Enciclopedia Heráldica* about Don Alfonso X., 'the Wise,' who, as everybody knows, was the great-great-grandson of the Cid. I noticed here that Señor García Carraffa, following up the descendants of this King, traced one line which went to Chile and numbered among its latest scions my maternal grandfather, Domingo Fernández Concha.

Alfonso X did not attract me, but the Campeador certainly did. I make no concealment of my preference for men of action and adventure. I felt myself a grandson of the Cid. I imagined myself sitting on his knee, stroking that noble great beard of his, which was so imposing that nobody dared touch it. Whether my grandfather was a descendant of Kings or not did not concern me. I may say, however, that I have never met a man with more of the bearing and manners of a King than he. He was the quintessence of Old Spain. What greatness there was even in the humility of this Galician grandfather of mine from Mondoñedo! Someone has said that the Spanish race is a race of princes. So I think myself, and, if I speak here of my ancestors, it is because I cannot hide the pride I take in my Spanish blood. Through my ancestors I am Castilian and Galician, Andalusian and Breton. I am Celt and Spaniard, Spaniard and Celt: an aboriginal Celto-Iberian, impervious and hard-headed.

I propose to offer here some explanations regarding the form and content of this *Hazaña de Mío Cid Campeador*. The reader will find in this book some Gallicisms and (Latin-)Americanisms, both in turn of phrase and in individual words. I make no excuse for these. I employ them simply from caprice. I prefer to write *el volantín* (the kite) rather than *la cometa*, because I find this Chilean word more beautiful than the Castilian word *cometa*, and more natural than the colloquialisms *pandorga* or *birlocha*. Similarly in regard to some Gallic turns of phrase, it pleases me to use them, and I use them.

Besides, it seems to me a very good thing that languages should invade one another as much as possible—should fly like aeroplanes over frontiers and customs-houses and land in anybody's territory. Perhaps, thanks to this mutual invasion of languages, we shall arrive some day—a thousand years hence—at one international language, and then the only disadvantage which literature suffers among the other arts will disappear. Moreover, it is not to be denied that the pure Spanish of Castile is a somewhat stiff and stilted language, and that a little nimbleness and flexibility will do it no harm.

With regard to the content of this book, I ought to warn the reader that, whether the *Hazaña* is an epic novel, or a novel set to song, or an expression of the exaltation which a great life produces in the mind of a poet, it has in any case nothing to do with 'novelised lives' of that genus which is so fashionable today, and received its first impulse from the famous *Life of St. Francis of Assisi* by Johannes Jørgensen.

Since the *Hazaña* is essentially a means of poetical expression, it is natural that the author should choose lives out of the ordinary, which best lend themselves to his purpose, and offer him the most fruitful field of poetic imagery. The *Hazaña* is the novel of a poet, and not the novel of a novelist. There are some poets who write novelists' novels. Let them go their ways. I will have no share in this bad habit. I am concerned only with poetry, and I am concerned only with the truth as the poet sees it.

To avoid possible misunderstandings, I should also warn the reader that, in my data about the Cid, I have sometimes followed the old legendary romances, ballads, and *gestes*, and at other times history. For example, poetry tells us that the Cid killed Jimena's father, Count Lozano, and history teaches us that this is false, since Jimena was not the daughter of this Count, but of the Count of Oviedo, Diego Rodríguez. Here I have made a little compromise between history and legend, and Count Lozano is presented as the godfather and guardian of Jimena. Why not? Further on you will see that the daughters of the Cid are not called Doña Elvira and Doña Sol, as legend would have it, but Doña Cristina and Doña María, which were their real names. Nor are they married to Counts of Carrión, in accordance with legend, but to Kings: Cristina to Don Ramiro of Navarre, and María to Ramon Berenguer III of Barcelona, which is the historical fact.

Moreover, I have treated the story of the outrage of Corpes as false, in the first place because we know it to be false historically, and in the next place because it is incredible that anyone would have dared to strike the daughters of the Cid, or that the Cid would have tolerated it and not exacted a much weightier vengeance than legend asserts. I do not see my grandfather the Cid suffering my aunts María and Cristina to be whipped without knowing the reason why from their husbands. The thing is false; I swear it is. If it were true we should know it in the family, and you would see how I would have made mincemeat in these pages of such a pair of scoundrels. The fact that I barely mention them will prove to you that this insult is a fantastic lie. I invoke the learned testimony of the noble Don Ramón Menéndez Pidal.

At various other points I have corrected both history and legend with that right which the call of the blood gives me, and I have also assembled some episodes unknown even to the learned, which I have encountered in old papers of my ancestors. So do not argue with me about them, but be grateful to me for handing them on to the public. Here you have the true history of *Mío Cid Campeador*, written by the last of his descendants.

V. H.

TRANSLATOR'S NOTE[2]

I have preserved the original form of all Spanish proper and place-names, because (as in the case of other countries) the variety of their English renderings is anomalous; because the originals are more euphonious; and—what good is a translator if he cannot strike the note of his author?— because it pleases me.

W. B. W.

---

[2] See note on this edition at the end of the book, for further information on this subject.

BIRTH

It was night—a Castilian night of mid-August in the year 1040. The sweltering heat of the day had died down a little, thanks to the breeze which, since sundown, had blown steadily for three hours, bearing with it the scent of the fields and the rustle of poplars. All day long the sun had smitten down with all its force upon the poor parched earth, beating on heads dizzy for a breath of pure air. The night had brought a truce, and all created things lay in heavy slumber, the brute sleep of exhaustion.

The house of Diego Laínez, in the town of Vivar, half fortress, half country seat, an enormous pile which seemed to strive for coolness by sheer weight of stone, reared in hard, rigid lines its austere majesty of dreaming stones. Stone upon stone, stone upon stone: such was the house of Diego Laínez—a dwelling of the dreams of stone, of the silences of stone, of the speech of stone, of the nobility of stone, of the emotions of stone (how wrong they are who say that stones cannot feel!), of the energies of stone, a dwelling of men of stone: a dwelling marked out by Destiny's finger of stone.

Diego Laínez, the great warrior, the man of victories, the pillar of the throne of his Kings, heir to the blood of Laín Calvo; Diego Laínez, veteran of that battle wherein Count Fernán González vanquished Almanzor, was home from a council to which the King had summoned him; and sleep would not come to his wooing.

A thousand cares possessed him. Stripped upon his bed, he tossed in vain from side to side. The deep breathing of his powerful breast smote upon the walls like the blows of a prisoner. The fancies of the sleepless formed and refashioned and fused and crowded in his brain until it was on fire.

Spain took on for him the likeness of a patchwork coat, tattered and torn and tortured into a thousand elements separate and incongruous—provinces, cities, fortresses; here a kingling, there a count, there again a Moorish general proclaiming himself lord of a conquered territory; Christians at grips with Christians, Moors with Moors; medleys of Christians and Moors fighting with other medleys of Moors and Christians; treaties broken the day after they were made; the allies of today tearing themselves in pieces tomorrow, so that at the very moment when he took up his arms none knew against whom he was about to fight.

Such was the picture in the fevered brain of Diego Laínez. More than three hundred years previously the Moors had invaded Spain, and the

Empire of the Visigoths crashed with King Rodrigo into the waters of the Guadalete and was swept away down to the sea. The great Empire of the Moors reached its zenith, and all Spain submitted to its power—all except Don Pelayo. Then it, too, had suffered the decadence of supremacy, and began to break up in civil war. Of the Caliphate of Córdoba, once of an Arabian Nights' magnificence, there remained as broken pieces, as fragments of a fallen star, the Moorish kingdoms of Granada, of Seville, of Murcia, of Dénia, of Valencia, of Badajoz, of Toledo, of Zaragoza.

And Don Pelayo, swooping from rock to rock out of his lair in the recesses of Covadonga, had begun the reconquest. Diego Laínez thought of him with admiration not so much as a man as a flood, an avalanche; or Don Pelayo seemed to him like a dragon issuing from the caverns of Destiny, with fire flashing from his eyes, crunching Moors between his teeth, trampling fortresses underfoot.

Thanks to Don Pelayo, the Christians now held their reconquests from the Moors—the counties of Barcelona, of Aragón, of Castile; the kingdoms of Navarre, of Galicia, of León. The thoughts of Diego Laínez brooded with the pride of love upon Castile. He thought of the prowess of her counts, vassals of the Kings of León. The deeds of those Castilian counts who had bequeathed to their country an eternal memory of poetry and blood filed through his mind. Castile had made herself a living force, a personality; she was already a motherland. Diego Laínez was moved to speak his thoughts aloud: 'Give us another Don Pelayo, let there be born another unifying force, another unconquerable will, another man of Destiny!'

By his side his sleeping wife awakened in surprise at the sound of his voice. 'What ails you, Diego Laínez?' she asked; 'are you sick? Why are you not asleep?'

'I am thinking,' the man replied.

'And of what are you thinking?'

'What I think is no matter for a woman.'

'I know—politics and war.'

'The salvation of Spain.'

The woman fell silent, filled with pride in this man to whom she belonged. The thoughts of Diego Laínez, she knew, were high and noble thoughts. She had that instinct of all women for the thoughts of those near to them, but never in his thoughts had she heard the velvet footfall of betrayal. And she loved the integrity of her man—she who was daughter of a man noble as himself; she, Teresa Álvarez, daughter of Rodrigo Álvarez of the Asturias, a mighty warrior, conqueror of the castle of Ubierna, a nobleman of wide lands, powerful alike through his fortune and his own prowess.

'It is hot,' she said at length; 'it would be well to open the windows.'

'Go to sleep.' Diego Laínez rose and opened the windows. The silence returned, but still he wooed sleep in vain.

That simple gesture of opening a window, which seems so trivial, so unimportant, is a grave matter. For to open a window is as if to open the soul, and to expose the body to the soul's influence. Through the open windows flowed in the night, and with the night came Castile, and with Castile Spain. Millions of stars streamed through the windows like a drove of cattle that had been awaiting the opening of the gates of a corral. Thousands of dispersed forces, drawn as if by a magnet, pushed through the massive window-frames. All the heat and all the straying sap of Nature were impelled towards this channel opened in the wall of that room, making it the spear-point of all their energies, all their aspirations. Countless currents of electricity converged upon the room, focal point in the chart of that night.

Diego Laínez felt all this swarm of profound activities converge upon him like something tangible. An immense vigour seized hold upon his body; his breast swelled, expanded, overflowed into the night. The world is a factory of forces, an accumulator of stimulating energies, a laboratory of hydrogen. He breathed, he drew in through every pore, all this richness which flowed towards him and offered itself to him like the elixir of life.

What outlet, what destiny was it seeking, all this concentration of life's essences? Diego Laínez felt a vague disquiet. His flesh crept, and the blood tingled in his veins. Outside, the night was once more soft and languorous. A gentle breeze, born in some hidden garden, wafted in the caress of flowers, the softness of grass. A nightingale sang to his mate, and the night folded itself around him like a woman's hair.

Diego Laínez looked at the woman sleeping by his side. Beautiful, buxom Teresa Álvarez was a true daughter of the country, with the noble blood of her descent running strong in her veins. Beautiful, desirable, fruitful was her body, apt for caresses, ready in love. Her firm, rounded breasts, redolent of orchards, rose and fell to the beating of her heart with the serene rhythm of the sea. To look at this woman was to grow young again, to see life sweet and clean for all its problems. Vice and intrigue and the wiles of forbidden pleasures became unmeaning. Only love was direct and logical—love consummated in the embrace of man and woman, fulfilling an imperious and supreme law of Nature.

Diego Laínez took her in his arms and caressed all the sweetness of her. She raised her full, ripe lips to his. He thrilled at every touch, and she died at every kiss. It was a solemn moment, a moment in which the world seemed to pause and listen, to hold itself in readiness for a coming festival. The man was all male, and the male no longer resisted his need; and the woman was all female, ripe as a rose for plucking. Diego Laínez clasped his wife with the rough vehemence of a boy, strove with her with all the energy of a warrior refreshed, eager for battle, impatient of victory. The earth obeyed the rhythm of their panting, and the mountains sighed with them. Infinity was emptied; the universe halted, the stellar system stopped for a moment, and God smiled as He looked down through the keyhole of the sky.

'Ah, Diego, dear husband, never have I thrilled so before! I thought that I should swoon.'

'I, too, my Teresa; it seemed as if we had never loved before.' Diego Laínez was near tears for joy. I do not know what this may be, dear wife; but it seemed to me that it was not simply I who accomplished the act of love, but all the universe accomplished it through me. I feel that in me is fulfilled a design.'

'Something miraculous is abroad this night.'

Again the thought of Don Pelayo possessed the soul of Laínez. Don Pelayo, Don Pelayo: a work interrupted, unfinished, cut short half done. The shade of the mighty warrior marched through the dreams of Diego Laínez, and the night was full of strength and heroism. The night was Don Pelayo, and outside the nightingale sang of Don Pelayo. Truly, something miraculous was abroad this night.

* * *

Nine months had passed since that night pregnant with miracle. All was activity in the great house of Diego Laínez. Teresa Álvarez felt the first pangs of birth, and the house was making ready for him who should be born.

Simple in those days were the preparations for a birth. There was no German-trained doctor, no noise of instruments in a surgeon's case, no anaesthetic—nothing but the ancient midwife, with her age-old, undying wisdom. Nothing could be imagined beyond the wisdom of the midwife— she who had known the secrets of so many wombs, she who had held in her hands so many little lumps of life, heirs of the future.

The ancestral home of the heir of Laín Calvo had changed its aspect of austerity and sternness. Its stones were instinct with hope, hope solid as themselves. They were warmed by a heat peculiar to itself, that warmth of tenderness and longing souls, the smiling anxiety that rules a house where a child is to be born.

There were noiseless movements in the birth-chamber. There was a silence of expectation—a solemn silence, because unconsciously they awaited something great, something new, something never seen before: the unexpected, almost monstrous phenomenon of a child issuing from his mother's womb to greet the world with a malediction upon his lips.

The house was steeped in the scent of herbs cooked in olive oil, the scent of the secret preparations of the midwife. Its whitewashed walls were full of ears, and in the great entrance hall, where the friends and relations waited, the heads of wolves, of wild boar, and of bears hanging from the rafters seemed to watch for any disturber of the silence to leap upon him with snapping jaws. Voices went soft-footed. Only the mother had the right to groan or to complain. But from Teresa Álvarez there came no groan and no complaint.

'What is the news?' someone asked a servant who went by with a water-jar.

'Nothing yet. Patience. It seems the child is very big.'

The mother, lying on her bed between the white sheets, felt herself to be the centre of Spain and of the universe. Diego Laínez paced back and forth with soldierly step, his stern eyes full of a child-like mixture of self-reproach and paternal pride. Crouching like a beast in ambush, the midwife waited beside the bed. Her probing hands disappeared under the clothes. 'Soon. Be patient a little yet. He is coming...'

Teresa Álvarez uttered not a sound, she hardly moved, but her eyes closed, and she bit hard upon her lips. Then, 'What are you doing, boy?' she exclaimed suddenly; 'why do you not come? Be quick, my man!'

Outside the twilight sky was tinged with the colour of a mother's blood. The evening died, robed like an archbishop in crimson and purple. The overcharged clouds barely moved. The birds flitted by in silence. The flocks came down from the pastures noiselessly. Castile anointed herself in silence, waiting.

'Come, child, why do you tarry?' The mother writhed bravely in her pangs. All Spain shared the pains of the birth. The whole peninsula twisted like a body, contracted itself, bore down to ease the birth of the child.

'Come! Now, now!'

As if he had heard the imperious voice of his mother, the child turned in her womb, seeking the best way to present himself to life, to face the issue. He had, so soon, a strategic mind. The womb bore. Spain trembled, and a low groan ran through her. She was moved to her depths. She raised herself up. Not a fly stirred in all the peninsula. A head appeared. Now, at last! Hastily, quivering like a fish, a plump child sprang into History.

Spain sighed, half opened her eyes, tearful and anxious: 'A boy or a girl?'

'A man child.'

'Diego... I love you. What a relief!'

There was no cry from the child who had descended upon History; instead, he shouted, he bellowed. The mother smiled to hear him, and closed her eyes once more, worn out, as if she had given birth to an Olympian. Diego Laínez looked at his offspring, seeking to discover in him his bravery of the future, his muscles, feet good for hard marching, a strong hand for the rein. He sought to find in him all his line of ancestors. He recalled the names of his lineage, and he drew himself erect, growing taller until his shoulders touched the roof beams.

The child bellowed and stirred. Born of a great family, of a valiant race, shed by an illustrious genealogical tree, he dropped into the world like a ripe fruit, at his due time—a fruit in which all the excellences of other fruit had concentrated themselves, into whose fashioning had gone generation upon generation of natural selection of good fruit: the fruit supreme, the fruit peerless.

'Let us call him Rodrigo, after my father,' said Teresa Álvarez.

'No, not Rodrigo,' replied Diego Laínez; 'do not forget that a Rodrigo lost Spain.'

'On the contrary, let us call him Rodrigo for that very reason. How do you know that God does not wish another Rodrigo to save her? God is a lover of epigram.'

'Rodrigo, Rodrigo is born.' The wind carried the news on its way, and tree told it to tree, and star to star. 'Rodrigo is born,' the earth whispered along the roads of Spain, 'Rodrigo is born.' The clouds gathered in the overcast sky, black clouds heavily charged with electric current. The storm blew up, the storm fated to attend all great happenings. Stripped leaves fluttered to the ground, leaves mat were blessings shed by all the trees of Spain, messages of joy, letters of congratulation.

Rodrigo was born, and all things centred themselves in the new-born, all things followed the vital rhythm of that rosy, chubby body. Spain was born again with Rodrigo. Spain opened his eyes. Spain began to suck at the breast of Teresa Álvarez. Spain shouted and kicked for them to bring him orange-water to break his wind.

The eyes of a whole people, all their aspirations, all their anxieties, all their longings were fixed upon that cradle. All these fused in it as in a crucible, and aspirations, anxieties, and longings seethed and sang in it until the cradle grew, and grew, and waxed enormous. The cradle of Rodrigo was bounded on the north by the Pyrenees, on the south by the Pillars of Hercules, on the west by the Mediterranean, on the east by the borders of Lusitania and the Atlantic. And he was Pyrenees and Hercules and the sea, a being of mountains and waves, strong and tempestuous.

Stretched in his cradle, the child bellowed and stirred. The midwife approached to wrap him in swaddling-clothes. The indignant Rodrigo protested, kicked his feet, waved his hands. Like one condemned to death who puts away the bandage with which they would bind his eyes, so Rodrigo, condemned to life, put away the bandage with which they would bind his loins. 'No, no, no!' he seemed to say. And in the midst of his agitation, with a sudden movement, he fell from the cradle. Aghast, they flung themselves upon the little body which lay as if lifeless on the ground, and then Rodrigo, caught up in his father's arms, burst into uncontrollable sobs.

At the same moment a violent tempest shook the firmament, filling the air with trembling, shattering the windows of Heaven; and a blinding flash of lightning shot across the sky, writing across the clouds in great letters of fire:

CAM
P
E
A
DOR.

YOUTH

THE child grew. How he grew! It was as if all Nature had concentrated upon him, to the neglect of all else. The vital juices of the plants, of the herbs, of animals and birds, all the sap of living things flowed into him as if he were the favourite of creation. One would have thought that they had put saltpetre under his feet, the marvellous nitrate of Chile at his roots. Rodrigo was fifteen years old, and he was already a redoubtable athlete. He was massive, but massive without fat, rippling with muscles, with bones well plenished with lime, and nerves supple and sound as those of a machine. Rodrigo had the power of forty horses, 40 h.p., and they called him Rodrigo Díaz de Vivar.

How I worship you, light-hearted, leaping boy, rude and untamed, ingenuous and virginal! You were the forerunner of all the sportsmen of today, and by how much their better! You were the unsurpassed inventor of the Yankee youth, the football player and the cowboy.

His lungs were so capacious that, every time he breathed, he drew in half the oxygen in the world. The other people might share among them what was left. All day, from dawn, Rodrigo roamed the country, running the roads, scaling the hills, swimming the streams, taming colts, taking milk at his will from heavy-uddered cows, eating fruit off the trees, riding hard for the horizon, dominating the landscape with his smiling eyes, large and lustrous as pears or figs.

A violent urge to movement possessed all his being. Quietude is death, and Rodrigo was life, the archetype of life. This feverish need of action, of outlet for his superabundant energies, was the mark of the man. The richness and variety of his resources clamoured for the intoxication of continual activity. If he were not roaming the country, it was because he was sporting with his brothers in the courts of his ancestral home. He played at fighting, learnt the art of warfare, was trained in the niceties of fencing, the deadly slash of the two-handed sword, the usage of the lance.

'Attention, men! You are the Moors, and we the Christians. Charge! No quarter!'

His brothers, Hernán and Bermudo, were his elders, whatever History may say to the contrary. They were his elders; so my story demands. He must always be the third—the third, naturally. It would be a nice thing if my story must give way to History! The third is the hero, because that introduces the quality of hope, which is a fundamental element of our affair. It is required by the slow development of the emotion which leads up to the climax. He was the third, I say. Where should we be if the first settled everything, leaving the other two no time to fail? The thing is absurd.

Rodrigo, then, was the third, the third son of Diego Laínez. That did not prevent his vehemence, his spirit of initiative, and his driving force from making him the first, not only among his brothers, but also among all his comrades. He consorted, more than with his brothers, with his cousin Álvar Fáñez and his friend Martín Antolínez, because they were strong, bold and daring, full of guile and cunning. He was fond, too, of his other cousins, the four sons of Arias Gonzalo; but they were younger, and so—though his uncle Arias spurred them on in play, bidding them 'Play the man, boys!'—Rodrigo put them always on the other side, with his two brothers and as many other older boys as would make the balance of forces even.

'What would you have, uncle?' he asked Arias Gonzalo; 'I love my sport, and I have no time to play the instructor. Your sons are still very young, but I foresee in them great prowess and a glorious future.'

His uncle smiled his delight; he, like all the boys, was conscious of the influence of Rodrigo, of that power of inspiring an admiring affection which attached all men to him. Rodrigo was so open-hearted, so loyal, so much the knight. He was a gentleman savage.

* * *

In a corner of the courtyard Martín Antolínez, Álvar Fáñez, and Hernán Díaz were competing in jumping. Martín Antolínez had jumped a length of nine metres and a half, Hernán Díaz a little less than seven, and Álvar Fáñez, in a great leap, almost eleven metres. What have the champions of today to say to that—and all without spring-boards, or tricks, or fairy-tales?

'Let's see what you can do, Per Vermúdez, and you, Rodrigo Díaz,' Álvar Fáñez called to the others; 'two duros that you can't beat me!'

Per Vermúdez leapt, and achieved only eight metres. Rodrigo's turn came. 'Here goes for your ten pesetas!' he said, and prepared to jump. He thought of the romances, the ballads, and the *gestes,* he thought of Guillén de Castro, of Corneille, and of me; he drew himself together, took off, and launched himself into the air. He had far outleaped them all. They measured the jump: twenty metres!

'May I be cut in ten pieces!' exclaimed Martín Antolínez; 'twenty metres!'

'It is not quite twenty,' declared Álvar Fáñez; 'it is nineteen and a half, but it's more than enough to beat us all. Here are your two duros.'

'Not quite twenty? Look at the impress of my foot; I took off half a metre behind the mark, while you all took off touching the mark.'

'You are right, Rodrigo,' Álvar Fáñez conceded, 'it is exactly twenty metres.'

'Three cheers for Rodrigo!' shouted Martín Antolínez; and everybody responded: 'Hip, hip, hip, hurrah!'

The girls, relations or friends of the boys, who often came to the house of Diego Laínez, attracted by the cheers, ran up and joined in the applause for the winner. That day Rodrigo beat the world's record of the Olympic Games, and his record has never been touched since. Three cheers for Rodrigo!

'Take the two duros,' Álvar Fáñez insisted; 'you are unconquerable.'

'I don't want your two duros; give them to the first beggar you meet on the road.'

The girls had joined the champions, drawn to them by that attraction which women feel towards a man trailing clouds of glory, a man of strength, vigour and potency. It is a sexual attraction of maternal selection, an attraction unconscious and involuntary. It is a sacred impulse, sleeping in the heart of the species, the secret desire for perfection latent in women's inmost souls.

Among all these girls one stood out by reason of her bearing and her beauty: Jimena Rodríguez, daughter of the Count of Oviedo, Diego Rodríguez, and niece of King Fernando I. Her father at his death had left her in the care of her godfather, the Count Lozano, the Court favourite and at this time the King's right-hand man in arms, the military leader of the day. Jimena felt herself drawn to the great house of Vivar, and whenever she was abroad her feet led her automatically towards it. When her godfather's duties at Court kept him for days away from home, Jimena loved to go and spend hours of gossip in the protective company of Teresa Álvarez. Her hostess had so motherly a way with her that the orphan felt a wistful sadness, and with half-closed eyes she would drift into spacious realms of dream, until she almost lost herself to view, and dwindled to a mere speck on the horizon of her solitude. How she loved to get away from herself, to escape from life, sitting there in one of life's armchairs, listening to Teresa recounting the exploits of her son!

Every time she heard in the distance the voice of Rodrigo she awakened with a strange shudder and came back from the horizon, came back and returned to herself more rapidly than a kite that children pull down from the air, when three children's hands seem to do the work of a hundred. That one word, 'Rodrigo,' was the clue that led her through all her dreams. It was the motive force of her voyages among the starry latitudes through which her soul roamed. Her heart beat as though it would break the cage of her ribs and fly away for ever.

Was this love? She did not know; but it was a sense of profound disturbance, a flinching from happiness, an anxiety for the future. It was the defensive dread which every human organism experiences in the presence of something capable of changing it radically, of shaking it out of its rut, of breaking its accustomed rhythm.

Rodrigo, for his part, could not behold Jimena without feeling himself thrown completely out of gear, and suffering a sort of trembling at the knees and a wild desire to flee—to flee up hill and down dale and hide himself behind the back of night, away behind all those nights which await their turn in that far-off place where nights are fashioned. The boy felt his heart wriggle like a hooked fish, eager to break the net and leap to death and be done.

Was this love? He did not know; but it was a profound shock, a flinching from happiness, an anxiety for the future. It was the defensive dread which every human organism experiences in the presence of something capable of changing it radically, of shaking it out of its rut, of breaking its accustomed rhythm.

Love is like death not only in its mystery, not only in the swiftness of its coming, but also in the stealthy and sudden agony of its realisation—a sigh or two, and then the final sigh. They would be but two more victims of the mortal game, two more victims who would go unnoticed among the crowd of those who pass every day to that infernal heaven of love, if it were not that he was Rodrigo Díaz de Vivar and she Jimena Díaz Rodríguez.

Something in him drew her, something in him repelled her. So, when the boys shouted and she heard Teresa Álvarez saying, 'Hasten, they are cheering Rodrigo,' at first she could not move. But then she saw the sister of Martín Antolínez and the two sisters of Álvar Fáñez, together with the sweetheart of Per Vermúdez and several other girls, hurrying towards the courtyard; and she could resist no longer. She approached the scene of triumph, hanging back a little behind the others.

'He ought to have a prize!' the admiring girls cried. Jimena kept silent. She was the only one who made no sound, but her long eyelashes, fluttering in time with the beating of her heart, seemed to applaud louder than anyone else. 'He ought to have a prize, he ought to have a prize!' went on the sing-song voices of the chorus of girls. Suddenly one of them, the boldest or the simplest, proposed: 'Let's all take hands. We'll dance round him, and he shall kiss one of us for his prize.'

Jimena shrank back, but, caught in the midst of them, she had no time to speak, or even to think. The circle danced around Rodrigo. He went red, and there was a buzzing in his ears. Then he went white, and felt the ground opening beneath his feet. Red and white, white and red—his face looked like a lottery. The human wheel kept turning, and the evening began to turn with it, and finally all Spain swam around until Rodrigo closed his eyes to keep himself from falling.

Then another girlish voice cried: 'Let's have a round dance uphill. We'll dance up that hillock there. The first who reaches the top without getting giddy shall have a kiss from Rodrigo. The winning boy ought to have a winning girl for his prize.' And the revolving circle danced on its way, singing as it turned.

Rodrigo had mastered himself, and achieved a smile. But Jimena was very pale. She seemed to follow the game like a sleep-walker. They started up the hill. One of the girls, turning giddy, broke the circle and tumbled to the ground. Amid peals of laughter the circle formed again, and went on mounting. Rodrigo looked anxiously at the pale Jimena. His look conveyed a wish to transfuse to her all his own bodily vigour. She followed the round without knowing how, or why. She was an automaton in the hands of Destiny.

Another girl tumbled down. The diminished circle went merrily on. The hill seemed to grow steeper, as if taking part in the game and wishing it to continue indefinitely. The girl who had proposed the game, perhaps expecting to win it herself, let go of her companions' hands, and dropped like a rose from twilight's garland. Then two more fell. Only three remained, with the last lap to the summit before them.

Rodrigo followed Jimena with his eyes. He knew that they were saying: 'It is you, you only, that I love.' Why had he lost his fear? Into what trap, what snare of love had he stumbled? Perhaps the aspect of the affair as a game had made him forget its meaning, and all that might follow upon this harmless play of high-spirited, innocent children.

Jimena was at the end of her strength. She was not used to such exertions, and she obeyed only a blind impulse, an unknown force, the *motif* of this tale. Only from these did she draw the strength to keep on. Finally the third girl tumbled, and only two remained, Jimena and another. They had climbed so far and whirled so fast that she had forgotten the other's name. They were only ten metres from the summit. But they did not know how nearly the climb was over, and the dancers went on their reeling way—Jimena and the other: Destiny and nothingness.

Suddenly Jimena made a gesture as if of defeat. Rodrigo looked at her aghast. No, no, he did not want to kiss anybody, or be kissed by anybody, but Jimena. She read Rodrigo's thought and plucked up heart. The other, who had thought herself already the winner, sensed the new energy in her rival and felt herself falter in her turn; but she fought against her failing nerves, her tottering legs, against Destiny, and kept on and on. The two girls were red in the face, gasping for breath. The sky reeled above their battle of wills, and they could do no more. There was something at once pathetic and solemn in this climax of the contest.

Jimena stumbled again, and at the self-same moment the two girls swayed to the ground, one on either side of Rodrigo; but, before Jimena's body touched it, he caught her in his arms, and in two bounds set her on the summit. Her fallen rival lay half-conscious, unknowing whether Jimena had failed too or had not failed. She knew not what had happened, except that her reeling senses seemed to be plunging at full speed down the winding stairway that leads to the underworld. As if in a dream, she heard the jubilant shout of Rodrigo: 'Jimena wins, Jimena wins! So I have won again. You are not going to kiss me, my Jimena, but I am going to kiss you!' And up there, mark you, on the peak of Spanish poetry, Rodrigo kissed Jimena on the forehead. Jimena sighed, and was one with the infinite.

That was the first kiss of Rodrigo and Jimena. Many months, many happenings were to pass before it was repeated. But how that kiss re-echoes down the centuries, softening the story of the soldier, humanising the legend of the hero! The attention of the world was fixed on that summit, where their kiss was the focus of all its eyes grown luminous. Below, on the plane of everyday life, they were starting to cheer when someone bade them be silent.

The next day how many centuries had passed? Rodrigo was another man. He was languid, ill at ease. All his gestures had the gravity of melancholy, the weariness of meditation. His energies were dissipated in some vague realm of happiness. He walked like a man in a dream. He shunned society, and seemed to be afraid to speak, or even to smile, lest his lips should lose the savour of that beloved brow, the form of that unforgettable kiss. Silent and thoughtful, he went his way, his hard, chaste spirit mastered by that kiss. The champion had taken a knock-out.

Many days passed before Rodrigo was himself again, before his body, made for movement, for violent exercise, for running and leaping, lost its air of a sleepwalker. His comrades were astonished, but they dared not trouble him. Rodrigo inspired in them the respect due to a master, and even in their *camaraderie* they felt him a certain distance aloof, a distance measured by many metres of stature; and, as they loved him, they waited patiently until he should be restored to them as before.

This came to pass with the arrival at his home of Don Sancho, eldest son of the King, or rather the Emperor, as Fernando I called himself, and the heir to his crown. The Prince held Rodrigo, to whom he was drawn by his fame as a sportsman, in especial affection. A feast was held in his honour, and the youths were at a loss for invention. Something spectacular was wanted to follow the sports and the tourneys.

Then an idea of genius came to Rodrigo. He summoned all his companions and addressed them. This is what he said:

'Boys, let us release the wild bull whom they have just brought down from the mountains into the courtyard and play with him.'

'Splendid! A great idea!' cried Álvar Fáñez.

'Are you mad?' exclaimed one more prudent. 'How can you play with a wild bull? He will gore us and rip the guts out of the lot of us.'

'Who's afraid?' asked Don Sancho.

'In any case,' Rodrigo cut in firmly, 'Don Sancho will be excluded from the sport.'

'The idea! Why should I be left out?'

'Because it is not to be denied that the sport will be dangerous,' Rodrigo explained, 'and our future King must not expose his life foolishly. If the Prince insists, we shall not let out the bull.'

'Oh, let him out; I promise you I will not take part in the sport.'

'That is not enough; you will have to mount that wagon over there and resign yourself to sitting there quietly with the household and merely watching.'

'Very well; I agree.'

Martín Antolínez questioned Rodrigo: 'And how are we going to play with the bull? I have never heard of a bull allowing one to play games with him.'

'Everybody allows games,' replied Rodrigo. 'What is a tourney? It is a game. What is a battle? It is a game, in which it is a question of being victor and not vanquished—a question of killing your enemy and not being killed by him. You can play with a bull by trying to prevent him from killing you. That is the first part of the game. Then you can try to kill him; that is the second and last part.'

'What ideas you have, Rodrigo! But still I don't quite see how we are going to play.'

'We shall see; we shall act as necessity suggests. In the first place, we must make the enemy attack, because if he does not attack there is no sport. When he attacks we have to find a means of baffling him. To begin with, let us get to horse, release the bull, and see how the horses can defend themselves.'

Within three minutes the band of crazy youths were on horseback, and, with lances in rest, awaited the enemy.

'Let loose the bull!'

Álvar Fáñez and Per Vermúdez ran to the door of the courtyard, a door which opened upon a stable, dark and soft with hay, where the savage bull had been shut. They opened the door, and the bull emerged from night into day. An enormous black bull and the moist savour of the stable leapt into the arena.

Here was the epic bull—the first bull of the first verse in the heroic and brutal poem of bull-fighting. He tossed his head three times as if to shake off the darkness of the stable, then stood glaring in all directions, as if still blinded by the light of day. A brave spectacle! Here you have the bull who founded all the race of fighting bulls, the first link in the chain of the bulls of death. I turn my gaze back into the past, and I see a long line of dead bulls stretched across Spain, and far away, at the last range of vision, this great black bull, the bull of Rodrigo, the epic bull, the first bull of all future tragedies, father of all the horned beasts who have strewn their corpses to make a Spanish holiday.

That great holiday is the traditional festival of a people male, hardy, and rude; a people of hazard and of sport, of sport with Death, with Destiny; a people of ups and downs, of high fortunes and deep disasters. Their history is like a game played on a card-table. They draw an ace, or they draw blank. They draw America or Trafalgar, Góngora or Núñez de Arce, Cervantes or Echegaray, Picasso or Beltrán Massés—a people of dice, of lotteries; and of friars.

There he was, the epic bull—the first bull for applause and for tears, halted at the outset of Spanish bull-fighting history, pawing with his restless hoof the first page in that bloody story that is told week by week in the sunlight. Life is the game of life and of death, a game played in silence and obscurity, hidden in the depths of the human organism. But the Spanish people, realistic, avid of sensation, must see and touch this game every Sunday, seated in sun or shade, on the tiers around the arena where Life, tricked out in tinsel and tatters, falsified by a cloak which hides its weakness, pirouettes before Death, Death in the shape of a great block of hoof and horns, hide and hatred. Ah, those four 'H's'; and the people drunk, mad drunk with excitement!

Let us leave them, stretched across the peninsula, those two parallel lines, bulls and bull-fighters, and return to our spectacle. A brave spectacle, I say! On the one side was the bull, immense symbol of a catafalque gorged with dead, snorting in anger, seeking his prey; and on the other side was Rodrigo, mounted on his sorrel colt, with his lance couched, watching his beast. Beneath a shady awning sat the Prince Don Sancho, Arias Gonzalo, the smiling Diego Laínez, turned into a stone of watchfulness and pride; the trembling Teresa Álvarez, turned into a marble statue of anxiety and dread; and the motionless Jimena, more dead than alive. The other horsemen, behind Rodrigo, watched his movements and awaited his orders.

Suddenly the bull fixed his eyes on Rodrigo, and placed the life of our hero between the parentheses of his horns. He backed a few paces, lowered his head to clear his horns from the sky, drew himself together like an accordion ready to burst into a death-song, and launched himself behind his horns in a charge to cleave his enemy in twain.

Rodrigo gripped his lance, tightened his rein, and drove his spurs into the flanks of his horse, who reared on his hind legs, with his front legs pawing the air; and, just at the moment when the bull was upon him, he swung his mount aside out of the line of the beast's blind charge, driving his lance down between its shoulders. The weapon splintered into the air ringing with the onlookers' applause of the feat.

'Quick, another lance!' shouted Rodrigo, reining in his horse at a safe distance. The nimble mount obeyed his master with incomparable agility. Rapidly the bull swung in his tracks on the turntable of his back hoofs, and, blowing bloody foam in his fury, charged again at his attacker. In vain the other horsemen shouted at him and sought to distrait his attention to themselves. The bull was after Rodrigo; he meant to avenge his wound on his wounder. Under the shady awning the men applauded, Teresa breathed a sigh of relief, and in the eyes of Jimena started a tear, which, trembling a moment, fell on this story; and if it stains the page I cannot help it.

Rodrigo, equipped with a fresh lance, pranced forth again upon his sorrel to the fray, galloping back and forth in front of the bull to provoke him to the attack. The bull returned with blind violence to the charge, but Rodrigo, with incomparable skill, avoided it and saved his horse from scathe. The bull began to use his brains; he learnt cunning, he grew astute. The terrible black bull pawed the ground, he sidled up with catlike tread; then he drove in like a hurricane. Rodrigo clapped spurs to his horse and leapt aside. He was all but taken by surprise. The poor horse had a narrow escape. A horn grazed the buttock of the sorrel, but the ready lance skewered down again into the flesh of the fevered, infuriated beast and leapt again in fragments in the air.

'Now give me my sword,' shouted Rodrigo, 'and bring me a cloak!'

They gave him sword and cloak. To the dismay of the spectators, Rodrigo dismounted, and with firm tread advanced towards the bull. He called him, he enticed him, he stamped the ground with left foot forward, in that gesture which today is classic in the bull-ring. What was going to happen? All hearts had ceased to beat. Not a fly moved in the universe. The bull looked at him. The beast could not believe his eyes. What! His enemy afoot! Now we should see. What a joke! He licked his chops for glee, he opened wide his jaws, he roared with laughter. But vengeance is the food of gods, and the food of bulls is grass.

The beast drew himself together and glued his eyes, his terribly fixed eyes, upon Rodrigo. Fire flashed from them towards the heart of Rodrigo, and like a shooting star he launched his horned bulk at his prey. Rodrigo made a masterly swerve. Madly the bull came again in search of his elusive body. Who had said that you cannot play with a bull? Our hero stroked his crown, and slipped away, darting to left and right, rebounding from side to side on his rubber-shod nerves.

Look at him now, how tired he had the bull, resigned never to land a blow upon his body! With the death-stroke hovering over him, the beast fought on, for he was brave, and to fight was in his blood, but he fought now without hope; and when the sword, driven with all the weight of Rodrigo's powerful arm, slid as easily as through butter into his heart, the bull fell upon his knees before his slayer, as if giving thanks, ready to die to escape the nightmare of these blows, these parries, these leaps, executed by a being unattainable, fantastic, obsessing. Do you see him, where he lies dead; for no one yet has dared to bury him, and there he lies to the end of time?

Nobody applauded, because as yet nobody realised what it meant. Only an 'O!' of wonder floated down upon the air, and many rounded lips uttered that 'O!', which spread and spread in concentric circles until it assumed the size of a halo above the head of Rodrigo; and then assumed the size of the round table of the Knights of the Round Table, and then the size of the circle which the bull-rings form in finite space, and then the size of the Equator, and then the size of the earth's orbit round the sun; and now no man knows what size it has assumed in the depths of stellar space.

My dear bull-fight fans, why dispute about Pepe-Hillo, Lagartijo, El Guerra, El Gallo, Gallito and Belmonte? There are no such things as followers of El Gallo or of Belmonte. There are only followers of Rodrigo.

That was how Rodrigo Díaz de Vivar invented bull-fighting. For in this man there was everything of his race—everything good and everything bad. The the present, and the future of Spain found in their synthesis, their germ, their endemic condition. To approximate to him is to be truly Spanish, to touch the roots of the Spanish race: hard, rude, primitive, perfect. To recede from him is to become foreign: civilised, polished, subtle.

BEAR, CHIEF, AND BOAR

Rodrigo was sixteen years old. The fame of him had spread already over all Castile, and even in the territories of the Moors rumours ran that a marvellous boy was growing up among the Christians. Loved by the King and the Royal Family for his feats, and for the promise of his future held out by that perfect balance between vigour and boldness of body and nobility and poise of mind which was the mark of the man, Rodrigo was not puffed up to find himself the centre of all eyes. Simple of soul, busy with the activities of the day, he went his way with no vanity, no braggart's insolence. He did not seem to know that his brow was marked by Destiny, that he was the Hope.

During his childhood and youth all Nature had hung upon him. Thinking of Rodrigo, the crops were richer than ever before, the rains more plentiful, the beasts had a power of nourishment which they have never regained in any part of the land to this very day, the fruits doubled their savour. Vitamins and calories worked for Rodrigo, dreamed of Rodrigo. His grateful body repaid their favours one hundred per cent. He disappointed neither the efforts nor the hopes of his motherland.

Upright upon the keystone of the arch of Castile, he heard the murmurs of all his race, the clamour of all Spain. All his bodily functions were fulfilled with the naturalness of a perfect organism. He ate, as became a man who had to nourish a country, with a national appetite. He digested with the regularity of a machine which expels all waste products after extracting from them the utmost of life-force. He trod the roads of Castile as if he were treading upon a part of himself. He ran to tire himself and train himself to fatigue; he slept to rest. Admirable example of the harmony of a man's body and spirit—excellent lesson for the athlete whose honour should be worthy of his strength!

Supper was over, and his father gave thanks to God for His provision for wife and children, a pious thanksgiving for the bread and the water which are life and fight and blood and bone. 'Our Father, hallowed be Thy name, Thy will be done on earth,' the old man's voice recited. Evening was falling, and Rodrigo sat and dreamed of devouring all the Moors in the world. Jimena, sitting on a stone outside her castle, was eating blackberries, with stained lips smiling in the twilight. The sun died, serene in the know-ledge that it would be born again tomorrow. Night stole softly down its stairway, and Rodrigo went on dreaming.

This hour of digestion is propitious for dreams and adventures of the spirit; the tired body yields to the marching army of imagery and memory. The voice of Diego Laínez was speaking: 'Yesterday I discussed affairs of State with the King and Count Lozano.' Rodrigo raised his head and changed colour as he heard the name. 'This Count Lozano,' Diego Laínez went on, 'is prouder than any King, and it pleases him to insult me on every possible occasion. He seems to want to make me feel that I am old, and that he is the first man in the palace.'

'Father,' said Rodrigo, 'if your years no longer suffer you to be the first warrior arm of Castile, the Count should not forget that he is today what you were yesterday.'

'My son, when a man's arm no longer serves him, other men soon forget how well it once did serve him. That is the law of life.'

'But, Father, services should be rewarded, if only from self-interest, so that others may be drawn to serve too. If you have served your King, it is his interest, in order that others may serve him well, to show that he has not forgotten you and that he will allow no one to affront your years.'

'My son, no man serves thinking of what he may gain. He serves thinking of his own soul, and his own soul rewards him. Sometimes after we have left this world men repent of their injustices, and reward us with a monument. That is the law of death.'

'Father, you know that I, too, would serve with no thought of reward; but suffer me to think of your reward, if I do not of my own.'

Silence fell again, and their thoughts flowed out on a still, green tide. Rodrigo looked at his father. He was really old. His arm no longer served him in battle, his legs, that had marched so many years, had grown feeble, perhaps his eyes had lost their command of distance: but the memory of his glorious deeds made him more apt than another for counsel.

Rodrigo thought of that night in the mountains when he had gone hunting with his father and his brothers—his first hunt two years ago. The memories crowded in his mind, and his eyes, unseeing their surroundings, looked far away. He dreamed and he remembered. This is what he remembered. Up there between two peaks, hunting the bear, they had been overtaken by the great, shaggy bear of night. It was a night of tempest, a night of opera, of thunder and lightning, lightning and thunder. 'Father, here's a cave; let's take shelter.' The blackness of the cave was even darker than the night under the open sky.

'You know the bears are this year more bold than ever.'

There was snow on the mountains, and somewhere in the distance they could hear the rumble of an avalanche. Stalactites hung from the roof of the cave like *ex-votos* to winter—beautiful candles of ice which had dripped for three months and hung there turned into keys of memory, like those rusty keys that awaken thoughts of far-off days and scenes in houses left desolate. It was cold, and his brothers, Hernán and Bermudo, blew upon their hands.

Shivering with exhaustion, his father drew close to the torch that lighted them. The old dog Nero, who never left his master's side, sniffed and growled. Suddenly they heard a noise, as of heavy steps. The dog growled again. Diego Laínez, who was sitting on a stone at the entrance to the cave, peered outside under frowning brows. Rodrigo listened intently. No, it was nothing—perhaps the wind. They had left their arms on the rocky floor.

What a delight it was to the boy to spend the night up in the mountains, to listen to Spain, to scent Spain, in the silence of the high places; to talk with his father about Spain and the problems of Spain down there below them! He drank a glass of anisette, and his throat intoned a silent hymn of praise to this liquor of Spain. He leaned his head on his hands and dreamed. Spain must be freed, she must be restored in all her integrity to what she had been before the invasion, she must get back to the path from which the Moors had turned her aside.

But why was the dog growling again? Again there was that noise outside, and they had a sense of something watching them from the darkness. They waited with tense faces—for what? Again the noise sounded, this time a little nearer. The dog growled, raised his hind leg, and made water. What was he afraid of? Diego Laínez recoiled instinctively. At the same moment an enormous black bear appeared at the mouth of the cave, swaying his head like a pendulum. The dog stood with his one leg poised in the air, hung between two worlds like an angel with his open wing covering a dream of earth while he listened to the melodies of heaven.

None of them blinked an eye, none of them stirred an inch, for they all knew that this was what they must do in such a case. The bear shuffled his feet and kept on lolling his head like an idiot child. His slavering mouth dropped spittle. Have a care! The head stopped like a watch, the eyes fixed themselves upon Diego Laínez, and the great bulk, wrapped in its shaggy coat, hurled itself upon him. The old man reached for his knife, but it was too late; he rolled to earth, the bear on top of him. Quick as a flash Rodrigo flung himself into the *mêlée*. A kick in the stomach rolled the bear off his father, but he had hardly time to sit up when the beast was upon the two of them again, and, hugging them in his arms, pressed them to the ground.

Of his two brothers, fled to the back of the cave, nothing was to be seen but their eyes starting out of their heads. Hand to hand Rodrigo fought the beast, exchanging hard blow for hard blow, striving to free his father, who aided him as best he could. They rose and fell, fell and rose again. They beat against the walls, stumbled upon the stones, in a medley of arms, legs, and breaths. It was an epic fight, staged there over the night, in that cavern more than three thousand feet above the world. Neither could succeed in reaching a knife, and things looked ill for them. Suddenly Rodrigo caught himself up from a fissure in the rock, and, swinging his body through the air, kicked the bear full on the snout. The beast fell backwards, and Rodrigo, following up his master-stroke without giving him time to collect himself, seized a knife and slit the beast's belly from top to bottom like a wine-skin.

Diego Laínez, bruised and hardly able to breathe, lay with closed eyes and parched mouth, the blood throbbing in his veins. He could not speak, not even to say 'My son, you have saved all our lives.' He was old. All the same he had given the bear some blows like a mallet, but his breath and his strength had soon failed him. Rodrigo's father was old; but how strong the veteran must once have been! What a figure of a man! Cleverly as a surgeon the boy cut off the bear's head and gave it to his father—his first trophy, to which so many more were to be added.

Diego Laínez coughed loudly, and Rodrigo came back from his dreams, descended that mountain of memory, and fixed his eyes on the head of the bear, that first trophy, presiding like a symbol over the dining-table. The head was the mascot of the house, its luck-bringer. His father guessed his son's thoughts, and looked at him proudly.

'Do you remember that night, my boy? To think that if it had not been for you that head there would have crunched me in its teeth!'

'You are strong, Father, and you could have freed yourself. Why, you gave him some blows that made the mountain ring!'

'Every night when I look at that head I remember your first feat, and thank God who gave me such a son, and...'

'Help! Quick, hasten! The Moors are coming!'

What were these shouts, this clamour in the courtyard? 'Quick, to arms, to arms! The Moors are coming!'

A goatherd in his leather jerkin, with his crook in his hand, burst noisily into the room, stumbling over the chairs and his own words. 'Sir, over there, the Moors are coming over there, towards the bridge! I chanced to see their advance guard. They were coming stealthily, taking cover behind the trees. I saw them from the top of the hill. They are trying to take us by surprise. I should have given the alarm in Burgos, but they had cut me off that way.'

'You have done well to come first to Vivar, my man,' said Diego Laínez.

'God has guided your steps,' added Rodrigo, and strode out shouting to the courtyard: 'To arms! Ring the bells and call all the men of Vivar to arms! Everybody in the saddle!'

The bells rang out, and men came running up. There was clatter of bells in the air, clatter of men on the ground.

'What's the matter? What has happened?' 'The Moors! They have nearly reached the bridge. Follow me, all, at full speed!'

Rodrigo, armed to the teeth, sprang on his horse. Behind him hurried Diego Laínez and his two sons, Bermudo and Hernán, and behind them all the vassals of the house and lands of Vivar. The little force rode as if the Devil were after them. Afire with courage and enthusiasm were the men of Vivar. The twilight earth was alive with armed men, and the air was full of the dust of their going. A voice shouted: 'Tell Ruy Díaz not to leave us behind!'

But Rodrigo had galloped ahead off the road and reined in at the summit of a hill. There he waited for his father and the vassals of Vivar. He had espied the Moors, and quickly devised a plan. Soon as he sighted his father on the road he galloped down the hill again to meet him and explain the position of the enemy. Followed by thirty men, Rodrigo rode at full speed for the bridge. They reached one end of it just as the Moors reached the other, and crashed into them in the middle, drinking their healths in blood.

Sheering through lances and opposing breasts, Rodrigo drove into the midst of the enemy. The fight was desperate, but the onset of the Christians was irresistible. Horses and riders toppled into the stream. The Moors, surprised by the sudden attack, began to give way. Rodrigo had fought his way to the Moorish chief and disarmed him with two passes of his sword. The chief sprang into the river to swim to the bank and the main body of his followers. Rodrigo tore off his body armour and flung himself into the river after him, swimming like a fish.

The river was full of hands. Rodrigo overtook the chief and seized him by the throat. They grappled in the water with fists and feet and teeth. Soon Rodrigo had the better of his enemy. He plunged his knife into his breast. The wound filled with water, and the river with blood. 'Spare my men,' groaned the dying chief; 'there are no crops in our land.' 'Those who are hungry may drink first,' replied Rodrigo.

Dragging the body of the chief, he swam to the other bank. He clambered out, held up the corpse, and shouted to the Moors: 'Here is your leader!'

At the sight of the body the Moors fell into confusion and broke into flight. After them rode the men of Castile, and stopped only when the night had swallowed them.

With tears of joy Diego Laínez and his men, who had hardly taken part in the fight at all, embraced Rodrigo. 'You are a hero, Ruy Díaz!' a voice shouted. A group came up, carrying by way of banner the head of the Moorish chief. 'Send that to the King,' said another; 'this day will have done more than many years for the honour of Vivar.' 'Bear to your mother the sword of your first victory,' added Diego Laínez.

Silently Rodrigo rode back home beside his father at the head of his men. His sweating horse trampled on laurels and its foaming jaws champed as if they were snatching roses in the air.

Don Sancho, heir to the throne, was the first to congratulate Rodrigo on his victory. Ardent and bold of soul as Rodrigo himself, the Prince hastened to embrace him and bear him the felicitations of the King. The whole Kingdom was stirred by the news, and then began the days of warm applause from the generous, and secret jealousy from the envious. Between the one and the other Rodrigo went his way serene, following his star.

Two days later King Fernando, in honour of the triumph of Rodrigo, commanded a chase and a feast in the forest. All was bustle in the courtyards of the Royal palace of Burgos. Horses whinnied and pawed the ground as if in search of treasure, after the manner of spirited steeds. Leashes of hounds, ardent for the chase, strove tugging at the thongs until they nearly burst their collars. Falcons roamed the sky with their eyes from their masters' wrists. All was set for a fine chase after hide and feather.

The sun was hardly risen when the grooms and beaters were in readiness, awaiting the arrival of the King, the Princes, and the great lords. Noisiest of all was the pack of Don Sancho. They were hounds all picked by himself, a great lover of the chase. They leapt and barked and lolled their tongues, with eager ears listening for the voice of their master.

The lords arrived. Knightly upon his horse came Rodrigo, curvetting on his sorrel mare, his favourite mount. With him came Diego Laínez and his brothers Hernán and Bermudo. Next appeared the Count Lozano, accompanied by Jimena and her cousin, Count Per Ansúrez, who was the tutor of the two younger Princes. Behind them followed their vassals and their dogs, rivalling those of the King.

In another group stood Álvar Fáñez de Minaya, fast friend of Rodrigo, laughing with Martín Antolínez and jesting with the Count Arias Gonzalo and his sons, still children. Near them waited the Count García Ordóñez. Many other nobles and their sons and gentlemen swelled the chorus, but I shall not name them here, for they served only to form the background of the picture.

Silence! In that respectful silence the King came down the staircase, followed by his children. Don Sancho was in the centre, between Don Alfonso and Don García, and after them came the Princesses Doña Urraca and Doña Elvira. The lords bowed, the King returned the salute, and the grooms brought up the Royal horses. Jimena dismounted and went to greet the Princesses. Count Lozano, Diego Laínez, Rodrigo and the other cavaliers surrounded the King and the Princes.

Then Arias Gonzalo held the bridle of Doña Urraca's horse and aided her to mount. Count García Ordóñez rendered the same service to Doña Elvira; and, on the other side of the courtyard, Rodrigo came up to Jimena's horse, knelt with one knee on the ground, and with his other knee made a step for her to swing into the saddle. When all were mounted and all in readiness, to creaking of girths and neighing and barking the cavalcade set out.

The chase, the chase! It was the great festival of that age of war and men of war. The chase was the relaxation of warriors. Mountains and forests re-echoed to barking and neighing and creaking of girths. The voice of the horn ordered and led the way. All the Middle Ages are full of pictures of the chase, of towers and drawbridges, of armed knights, of fools singing behind the grating of their lutes, of dames spinning between the two long braids of their hair, while in the distance flees a deer, with a pack of hounds behind her, and behind the hounds an arrow, and behind the arrow a warrior. All the Middle Ages are a battle, a joust, and a chase. The three are the same sport.

A cross, a virgin, an *ex-voto*, a battle-axe, a girdle of chastity—these are the marks of the Middle Ages. In the north dies Siegfried, in the west dies Tristan, in the south dies Roland. South and west and north Poem weeps for them. In the midst of so much bustle of arms and hunting-horns, the voice of the few men who think is heard not at all, and hardly is heard the voice of those who sing. The chase is a kind of training for war, and gentlemen make light of its perils and compete in tests of boldness and valour. Ladies sometimes accompany the cavaliers, but they hunt only the bird with their falcons and their goshawks.

Hunting a great and savage boar were the party of the King, with the three Princes, the Count Lozano, Diego Laínez, and the Count Don Fruela. Rodrigo went from party to party with Álvar Fáñez and Martín Antolínez. Further behind the Count Arias Gonzalo and the Count García Ordóñez rode with the Princesses Doña Urraca and Doña Elvira. Near them rode the party of boys, the four sons of Arias Gonzalo and the two sons of Diego Laínez, who, though older than Rodrigo, took but little part in these sports; for the one was too much of a dreamer and the other something of a weakling.

The King's party stopped; they had lost the hot scent they were following in the dense undergrowth. Back and forth the hounds ran, sniffing among brambles and bushes. They doubled on their tracks, but the scent was lost. Don Sancho, boldest and most fearless of the party, swung himself from his horse, and with spear in hand plunged into the undergrowth. Hardly had he gone twenty paces when through an opening in the bushes the boar appeared, and with lowered head charged the intruder. 'My God!' cried the King. The rest of the party turned cold as ice, and their souls sank into their boots. Their hearts stood still, as with starting eyes they stopped at gaze. There was no time to do anything.

Don Sancho, unperturbed, flung his three-cornered spear. It stood quivering in a tree. At the same instant two arrows whizzed through the air and drove into the two eyes of the beast. He fell in his tracks, and rolled dead almost at the feet of the Prince. A single 'Ah!' of relief went up from every throat. Then all looked round, seeking the saviour. Leaning against a tree, on a fallen trunk, stood Rodrigo, with his bow in his hand and a glad smile on his lips.

King Fernando ran to embrace him, and the Prince Don Sancho wrung his hand between his own. 'I knew it was you,' he exclaimed; 'I had heard that you were practising the shooting of two arrows from one bow, and that you were a master of this shot of your own invention.' He took a ring off his hand and placed it on Rodrigo's finger. 'Thanks, Rodrigo; wear this ring in memory of what you have done for me.'

The King shouted to his huntsmen: 'Cut off the head of the boar, and give it to the vassals of Vivar!' Diego Laínez pressed his son to his breast with paternal pride. 'Blind so, my son, whoever dares harm to your King.' 'A marvellous shot!' exclaimed Don Alfonso and Don García in chorus;

'you had a narrow escape, brother.' The Princesses looked at Rodrigo as if he were a giant, and his uncle Arias and his comrades Álvar Fáñez and Martín Antolínez as if he were their hero. The Count Lozano said nothing. Only the heart of Jimena spoke for her.

The next day, after supper, Rodrigo, sitting in his chair of dreaming, looked at the wall where hung the head of the bear, the scimitar of the chief, and the head of the boar. From the first he had saved his father, from the second his land, and from the third his King. So much in so little time! It may be said that there are men to whom life hastens to offer chances of distinction. Is it not truer to say that there are men who at every turn find distinction for themselves?

JIMENA

Two weeks had passed. Jimena sat in a room in the castle of her godfather, the Count Lozano, busy with her embroidery. At the window stood her foster-mother, gazing away into the distance. Jimena's mother on her death-bed had bidden the woman be a mother to her, and so she was; and when the Count Lozano, in accordance with his oath to Jimena's father, as he too came to die, took her into his care, the foster-mother went with the child, so young then that she had but just begun to prattle.

The Count Lozano, a man of haughtiness and gloom and solitude, had not guessed in what affection he would come to hold the child, or that his heart could be so tender. Soon Jimena was as his very soul to that proud man, childless and a widower for many years. But, given up as he was to the intrigues of the Court and the business of war, he left her in the care of her foster-mother, well knowing that she was one of those good Spanish souls, loving and self-sacrificing almost to excess, who would lay down their lives for those they serve.

The Count had no eyes but for Jimena, and the foster-mother no eyes but for these two. He read the thoughts of Jimena, and the foster-mother read the thoughts of them both. Jimena took small pleasure in going abroad, and visited few but the mother of Rodrigo. When her godfather took her to Court she consorted with the Princesses, her cousins; but towards the Princesses she felt a certain jealousy, especially towards Doña Urraca, whose admiration for Rodrigo was undisguised. In this admiration Jimena thought she saw a secret love, nor did she forget that the Princess often visited Zamora, as fellow-guest with Rodrigo of Arias Gonzalo, who was chamberlain to the Queen and the Princesses, and held his nephew Rodrigo in great affection.

'Rodrigo would not dare to look so high,' Jimena reflected, 'but if he knew that Doña Urraca loved him, perhaps he would dare, and then… Dear God!' she said aloud, smitten at the thought.

'What is it, child?' asked her foster-mother, turning her head at the sound; 'what is the matter?'

'Nothing,' replied Jimena; 'I pricked my finger.' She raised it to her lips.

'How beautiful you look!' exclaimed her foster-mother. 'I wish Rodrigo could see you now. I would wager something that you were thinking of him.'

The room was full of scents of Spain and Cyprus. Beautiful beyond doubt was Jimena, with all the beauty of a woman; and what would you have more lovely than a lovely woman? Jimena was like a Greek statue. Her body was straight as a palm tree, her throat graceful as a swan's, her hands like lilies, her nose was perfect in its profile, her lips like coral, her eyes deep and dark as two lakes under the night. She fulfilled all the requirements of men's poetry. She was beautiful, I say.

(Here the shade of Rodrigo appeared beside the author's table.

THE SHADE OF RODRIGO. 'Poet, you are wrong. Jimena was not a Grecian beauty, she was a Spanish beauty. Nor had she a body like a palm tree, a neck like a swan, hands like lilies, a nose perfect in its profile, lips like coral or eyes like midnight lakes. What fools you poets are! Why do you compare a woman with all these things? Have you ever seen anything more beautiful than a beautiful woman? Then why do you not compare these things with a woman? That would be better. Say that a palm tree is like a woman's body, talk of a swan's neck beautiful as the throat of a woman, talk of a piece of coral like a woman's lips.'

THE AUTHOR. 'It comes to the same thing.'

THE SHADE OF RODRIGO. 'It may come to the same thing, but the other way round is less inane. I who am dead tell you so. I was familiar with poetry in my lifetime, but, now that I am dead and live among dreams, I see more clearly than you; for only in dreams can men see clearly.'

THE AUTHOR. 'As you will; but what you say seems to me poor stuff.'

THE SHADE OF RODRIGO. 'I could understand that it might seem poor stuff to you if you were anything very much yourself; but, seeing what a poor thing you are, it is only your vanity which makes you so self-satisfied. Now, listen to me. Don't argue with me about Jimena, and above all don't lie about her. If you lie in a poem about me, I do not care; but about her I will not stand it and I will not let you do it.

'Jimena had the body of a beautiful woman, wide-hipped and with breasts firm but not large, and with none of your marble or amphora about them. They were flesh, the beautiful flesh of a woman with milk in them for her children; and her womb was as it should be in a woman who was to be the source of a race great with thrones and destinies. Her throat was warm as if all the songs of love had warmed it. She had the hands of flesh and blood of a beautiful woman, little hands which smoothed away my cares and calmed my warrior fevers. Her lips were flesh, full and soft—lips for kissing, full of ardent kisses, ready for the man, for her own man only—for me. She had the eyes of a wife and mother. She was all beautiful, with the beauty that I love, the beauty of Spain. When I came to her she opened her arms to me wide as the gates of dawn. So now you know what Jimena was.')

Standing at the window, the foster-mother watched the distance. She was a countrywoman, of middle age, devout and fat. In a word, she was a foster-mother. She had ample breasts, made for pillowing heads at evening, when heads begin to nod. Jimena went on embroidering—or spinning. I cannot see, at this distance of the years, whether she was embroidering or spinning. She worked at a piece of stuff, and she waited. All her life was to be spent so: spinning and waiting.

So, while in the foreground Rodrigo gallops madly back and forth from one high deed to another, swinging his two-handed sword, I see her in the background of the tale, behind a distant window, waiting and spinning. Jimena is the lady of the Middle Ages, the heroine of the cycle of the knights. I have seen her somewhere. We have all seen her somewhere.

I remember a window of stone where the world looked in through three poplars and a vine. A bird came, perched on the sill, said something secret, and flew away. I remember a hill neatly clad in green, sloping down towards a plain which offered it a garland of flowers. I remember a castle, ancient, massive, dominating the fields and the roads of Destiny, an island set in a sea of silence. I remember a forest of embattled arms; and I remember pain in eyes soft as a dove's.

Yes, I remember her eyes; and she did not wear her hair in two braids. She was the only woman of that time who wore but one tress, one long tress bound around her brows above those eyes, long, fascinating as a snake. I remember a night which fell like a tress of hair unbound, the flicker of a smile which broke like a mirror, and the whiteness of a body, a wraith of foam. I remember a clear voice, clear as a carving on the violet arch of evening. I remember a tint of flesh translucent, shining with the strange light of some boding star, and a hand which was the key of spring.

I remember how a radiance grew like fruit about her footsteps— those footsteps which rustled in the grass as if they walked upon some calm, mysterious waters. I remember a gesture of forbearance in a star-lit silence. I remember a form framed in the door of a garden, poised as if with wings about to open upon the startled air in a flight from the burden of the flesh. I remember a flame of fire which ran along light fingers on a lute. I remember that the world was lost in a holy magic. I remember that there was a void in space, a vacuum which drew in all things, all ideas, all thoughts, all memories.

I remember that she was ready to let down that tress of hers, and to set free the last of all dreams and share it with me before it vanished. I remember that to see her I made a long journey, a long voyage over the sea—the sea, that word to frighten ships. The waves surged from their amaranthine bed, and my ship tossed like a bean of bitterness in the solitude. I remember that every time I looked at her I felt myself born again. I remember that she was on the shore when I came up out of the wet shadows of the sea. So I saw her, so I still see her; but the mirrors of memory-maze in my mind, and I can remember no more...

JIMENA. 'Who is coming over the fields, foster-mother? Someone is coming. I feel it in my soul.'

FOSTER-MOTHER. 'No one comes. Not a leaf stirs in the wind.'

The anguish of waiting set a heart beating like the throbbing throat of a bird about to burst into song, and the air was full of the stuff of dreams come true.

JIMENA. 'Tell me, foster-mother, do you see no one coming?'

FOSTER-MOTHER. 'I see a shadow which glides across the fields, a shadow like a Cross.'

JIMENA. 'It is he, it is he who comes. Secretly he comes, jealous for my fair name.'

FOSTER-MOTHER. 'It is not he. It is the shadow of an eagle flying high in the air.'

There was a span of silence, broken only by the fingers of Jimena, spinning dreams and hopes.

JIMENA. 'Tell me, foster-mother, do you see no one coming?'

FOSTER-MOTHER. 'The fields are empty. There is not a shadow, not a sound.'

JIMENA. 'I will go on waiting. He said that he would come, and if he said so he will come.'

There was a longer silence, and Jimena's fingers stumbled over her work as the night began to fall. 'It is getting dark,' said the foster-mother, 'and I can see the horizon no longer.' But leaping from ledge to ledge, his face muffled in his cloak, someone was gaining the window opposite, behind Jimena's back. Leaning into the room, the figure stretched out his hands, and gently covered the girl's eyes.

'You, Rodrigo?' cried Jimena, jumping up from her work; 'how came you here?'

'I came to the back of the house, so that none should see me,' replied Rodrigo. 'Listen to me. We have not much time; your godfather may return at any moment. He was summoned to Court on a matter of importance, and so was my father. I went with him, and saw them enter together. Then I came here at full speed, but I lost time through avoiding the roads, lest I should be observed. Next month, on the day of the Virgin, my father is coming to ask for your hand. What say you, Jimena?'

'My Rodrigo!' She gave him her hand, as if her heart went with it, and he kissed it. The foster-mother made a warning gesture. With a hasty 'Good-bye!' Rodrigo slid down to his horse awaiting him below. There was the sound of a horseman galloping hard along the path of Love. He leapt the horizon, headed for Vivar, as if he vanished in Love's infinity. Jimena closed her eyes lest hope should vanish with him.

INSULT AND VENGEANCE

WHY did Diego Laínez tarry in his homecoming? He had gone in the morning to Burgos, to the palace, at the King's summons. It was night, and he had not returned. The supper-table awaited him. Teresa Álvarez moved restlessly from her chair to the window, from the window back to her chair. Hernán, Bermudo and Rodrigo looked at one another in silence. Never had their father kept supper waiting so late. He was two hours behind his time.

'There is no need to be alarmed, Mother,' said Hernán; 'something of importance must have kept him in Burgos.'

'Father is a man of resource,' added Bermudo,' and no ill could befall him either at Court or on the road.'

Rodrigo was thinking of Jimena. A week hence it would be the day of the Virgin, the great day when his father would go to ask her in marriage from her uncle and godfather, the Count Lozano. The Count would surely agree to the marriage, for he must know that the bridegroom would be a man of worth, first among his peers. He smiled, for he was sure that Jimena was thinking of him too. There in her castle she was thinking of him and of the day of the Virgin.

Rodrigo had not as yet been anxious about his father, what could happen to Diego Laínez? But still a certain disquiet invaded him as he noted how late it was, and, even as he said to himself that nothing could happen, a trace of anxiety showed itself in his eyes. The pale, drawn face of his mother distressed him beyond all else.

Another hour passed. The air was heavy with their anxiety. Why did Diego Laínez tarry in his homecoming? It was full night. In that oppressive darkness the mysterious hour had come when frogs croak to the stars. Why was all so silent? Were there not ponds enough around them? But not even a cricket chirped. Then, from high up in a tree, an owl hooted. The omen dropped from his beak like the cheese of the ravens. The one sound that none desired to hear had broken the silence. The owl stared into the night, nodded his goggle-eyed head, and, pleased with his sense of the dramatic, hooted once more.

Gipsy bird, vile vagabond of the forest, may the Devil fly away with you and your message of misfortune! Off from that branch, harbinger of death, or here and now, here at my writing-table, I will seize a gun and fire it into your body, that body of yours full of bile and augury!

But what had become of Diego Laínez? It was not possible that ... A dog's long-drawn howl went up to heaven. Another howl answered it, then another nearer, then another in the house, then another on the other side of the house, then another further away, then another barely heard, then more and more not heard at all—a chain of howling that encircled Spain.

Galloping hoofs approached. Some ran to the window, some to the door. That was the gallop of the horse of Diego Laínez, of their father, of their master, of their lord. Everybody knew it. They hastened to light cresset and candle.

The gates of the courtyard opened, and he came in— how he came in, the father, the master, the lord! God in Heaven I what could have happened to him? His face was haggard, his eyes were moist and red as if he had been weeping, his hair and beard uncombed and his dress disordered.

'Are you ill, Father?' asked Rodrigo; 'what is the matter?'

'Ay, of a sickness that pollutes,' answered Diego Laínez. 'Keep away; don't come near me!' In three bounds he was up the stairs.

His wife came forward to embrace him. 'My husband, how terrible you look! Your eyes! What has happened?'

'Keep away. Don't come near me. I have a sickness that pollutes.' Diego Laínez strode on, with his family after him, grieving and wondering. At the door of his room he turned and said roughly: 'Everybody go to bed. I want nobody, nothing. Tomorrow God will decide.'

He closed the door and locked it. Behind it they heard a sob. Teresa Álvarez turned trembling to her sons. 'Let us go to bed. We must obey him. God rules in the universe, and your father in this house.'

But that night all beds were beds of sleeplessness. Bodies turned from side to side under the coveys while thoughts turned back and forth in their brains; and all night long they heard the steps of Diego Laínez, marching as he fought with his pain.

At dawn all were waiting in the great hall until Diego Laínez should come forth or summon them. Finally the door opened and he appeared on the threshold. How that night had changed him! His grey hair had turned whiter, his shoulders stooped as if under the weight of a rock. His cheeks were pale, his eyes sunken. He could hardly speak. 'Hernán, Bermudo, Rodrigo, come in,' he said. Then, as his wife approached too, he added: 'This is men's business. Wait a little, wife; have patience.'

His sons were no sooner in the room than he locked the door again, and turned his tortured face to them. Then with firm step he advanced upon the eldest. He seized the youth's right hand in his own and squeezed it hard, staring him in the face. 'So this lump I have in my throat presses on me,' he said.

'Ow, ow, Father!' groaned Hernán, and his eyes filled with tears. 'Enough, Sir, enough! Ow, ow!'

'Away with you; be off to your mother,' said the old man. 'The place of a man who weeps for any pain which is not of the soul is among skirts.'

He seized the hand of his second son and squeezed it hard, looking him in the eyes, with mingled rage and hope. 'So this weight I have in my breast presses on me,' he said.

'For God's sake, Father, you're killing me!' cried Bermudo, striving to wrench himself free. 'Enough, Sir. What are you trying to do?' and he fell upon his knees.

'Begone with you too,' said the old man, 'and learn how to die in silence and without cracking at the knees.'

He seized Rodrigo's hand. He concentrated all his strength, like all his hopes, upon him. He squeezed and wrung his hand, staring deep into his eyes. Rodrigo felt a pain which ate into his marrow. The old man squeezed harder and harder. 'So this pain I have in my heart gnaws my vitals,' he said.

Rodrigo glared him in the eyes, his hair rising on his scalp, and shouted angrily: 'Have a care, Father, let go in good time! If you were not my father, with my free hand I would tear your heart and guts out. Have a care, I say: my other hand is itching, and I cannot control it.'

The old man released his hold and embraced him with tears in his eyes. He swallowed as he spoke.

'Your hand is freed, my son; I need it free. Your anger gladdens me, your rage is a consolation and a hope for my soul. My Rodrigo, you shall show your manliness by cleansing my honour, my honour which is lost if you do not save it.'

'I do not understand, Father. What are you saying? Who has dared to smirch your honour? And to think—that, if you had not been my father, I would have given you a slap! Forgive me, Sir, forgive me!'

'You would not be the first.'

'Are you mad? What are you saying? Who has smirched your honour?'

'He who yesterday struck me in the face.'

'You—did someone dare to strike you in the face? Impossible, Father; you are raving.'

'I would swear to you on my honour, if I had any; but this blow broke my honour in two.'

'And the man lives? And I live! His name, tell me the name of this madman! Tell me, who is he?'

'Listen, Rodrigo.'

'I have no time to listen. His name!'

'Rodrigo, my son, listen to me.'

'I have no time, I say. His name! Give me his name and your sword.'

'Listen to me. Are you going to challenge him to fight?'

'By all the laws of honour, I will kill him, or he me. I ask you for his name.'

'He has many friends in the mountains of Asturias.'

'His name! I ask you for his name!'

'He is a power at Court; he has the favour of the King.'

'I will avenge you even if the King hides him behind his throne.'

'It was before that throne that he dared insult me, taking advantage of my years.'

'And the King suffered this insult? Does the King think so little of you?'

'It was because he had done me too much honour and named me tutor to Don Sancho that the quarrel began. The other claimed this honour, and thought that he alone was worthy to instruct the heir.'

'But the King permitted this outrage?'

'He had no time to intervene. Then he desired to hush the matter up and let no man hear of it, for it happened in his own chamber.'

'Father, silence cannot erase the deed. You know of it, and that suffices.'

'That is why I would be avenged.'

'But still you do not give me his name.'

'First you must swear not to turn back until this stain is purged.'

'By the Christ who gave me to you when I was born, I swear to you. Now give me his name and your sword.'

'Listen once more.'

'No more words; his name!'

'The Count Gómez de Orgaz, he whom they call the Count Lozano.'

'My God!' Rodrigo recoiled and turned pale. Jimena's godfather!

'Does the name frighten you? He has done great deeds. It is for you to do them too. Are you afraid?'

Rodrigo hung his head. 'Jimena loves him as if he were her father,' he said; 'he has been a father to her these fifteen years.'

'Would you draw back?' asked the old man, trembling. 'And without honour would you dare to raise your eyes to hers, would you dare to ask her hand?'

'Father, I do not hesitate for a moment; but you will understand that, when I heard this name, I trembled for that other name which stands behind it.'

'Forgive me, my son, for setting you a task so painful; but you know well that without honour there is no love, no life—there is nothing.'

'Say no more, Father. You have given me his name; now give me your sword. No man may insult the race of Laín Calvo.'

'Kneel down, Rodrigo. I am going to give you the sword of Mudarra; it is old and rusty, but it has the habit of victory. From its old wielder you descend, and the sword must feel that in the arm which bears it now runs the blood of that dead arm, heroic and bold, which knew its mastery so well.'

His father took down the old sword from the wall, and Rodrigo bent his knee to the ground. At the touch of the sword the old man had grown more erect, almost more young. He bore the sword to Rodrigo, placed it in his hands, and laid his own hands on his son's head: 'Heaven guide you, my son; and may God strengthen your arm.'

Rodrigo rose to his feet and ran his hand along the blade. 'A good steel,' he said. 'Good sword of Mudarra, another arm holds you, and I swear to you that the second shall make you remember the first. If I come not back a victor may you cleave my breast, may the weight of my shame drive you into my body to the hilt.'

'Tarry not in your vengeance, my son. Take Babieca, the best horse in my stable. I give her to you; for a young knight a young horse. Remember your honour, remember your blood, remember your father, my son.'

'My father, my father, good-bye!' Rodrigo went out at a run, fixing himself upon has horse, and sparks struck from the mare's hoofs as he burst out of the great gates like the Devil himself. From the distance there came the sound of a horseman galloping hard along the path of Honour.

Giving his horse free rein, Rodrigo reached the castle of the Count Lozano. In the grove around the castle Jimena's foster-mother was busy with hens and turkeys. Jimena, sitting on the stone staircase, rose to her feet at Rodrigo's approach. 'Foster-mother,' she said, 'Rodrigo is strangely changed of countenance.'

'And there is rage in his eyes,' the woman replied.

Rodrigo dismounted before them. 'Where is the Count Lozano?' he demanded.

'He is not here,' the foster-mother answered him; 'he has but lately left for Burgos.'

'For Burgos? Then I am for Burgos too.'

Jimena looked at him with eyes grown desperate.

She had heard already what had happened; the Count had told her all the night before. She knew her Rodrigo, and she sensed tragedy in the air. Rodrigo swung into the saddle, but she called after him: 'Rodrigo, what are you going to do? Think of me!'

'Think of my father!' replied Rodrigo.

'Think of my love!'

'Think of my honour!'

Man and horse were gone at full speed. The road slid giddily from under the galloping hoofs. Rodrigo disappeared under the moving roof of a cloud of dust between earth and sky. Jimena gazed motionless after that vanishing cloud. Stricken, but helpless, she blinked at its going, as if she wished her eyelids might be shears to cut the road before him. 'All is lost,' she sighed.

Near the gates of Burgos, in the first streets of the city, Rodrigo came upon the Count Lozano. The Count's proud body rose and fell with arrogant grace to the slow trot of his sorrel. Rodrigo reined in his sweating horse. 'Count Lozano!' he cried.

'Who calls me?'

'The voice of Laín Calvo, Rodrigo Díaz.'

'What do you want of me?' asked the Count Lozano.

'Your life.'

'What do you say, bold boy?'

'Get you down from your horse as I from mine. What, do you think to prove your valour by striking an old man in the face? Come and strike me in the breast. So shall you prove it better.'

'Begone, insolent, or by God's life I will dismount and give you a kick to match the slap I gave your father yesterday.'

'That is my desire. Down from your horse, and let me roll your arrogance in the dust.'

'Out of my way, I say; begone and learn to use a sword.'

'Coward! Coward you are, like all who are bold before an old man. You forget that I am the son of this old man. You have raised your hand against one whom no man may strike while I am his son. You have clouded his noble face with a cloud of dishonour. I will sweep away that cloud.'

'You, boy? And with what?'

'With the sun of this sword. See how it shines!'

People had flocked to their doorways at the sound of the voices. From a window the nose of an old woman of Valle Inclán peeped like the spout of an oilcan.

'Go your way, boy,' said the Count Lozano; 'there is no honour in beating a novice.'

'There is more honour than in striking an old man,' cried Rodrigo. 'Enough of words! Get down from your horse. The hand that insulted my father shall this night serve as a knocker on the gates of Vivar.'

'We shall see,' growled Lozano as he dismounted. 'On your own head be it, boy.'

The two stood face to face, with swords drawn. 'On guard!' cried Rodrigo, 'and have no pity for my years.'

'I shall have no pity, poor fool; for what you lack in years you make good in insolence.'

The swords clashed, their edges cleaving the air. The two men leapt back and forth, advancing, retreating. The two swords were like ten, a hundred, tracing circles and rings in space, fashioning arches over their heads, and the air whimpered as they sliced it. People had flocked around, and with eager eyes watched the two men hedged in by the circle of their blades. 'Let them be!' a voice cried; 'let no man interfere. It is a fair fight, man to man, face to face.' Another named the combatants. 'That is the Count Lozano. The youth is he of Vivar, the son of Diego Laínez. A shrewd hitter!'

'Not bad for a beginner!' There was anger in Lozano's taunt.

'And getting better!' answered Rodrigo, parrying a blow and giving back two.

The laboured breathing of the Count Lozano filled the street. All Europe heard the beating of Rodrigo's heart. Back, forward, left, right— the flickering of the blades dazzled the eyes. The Count lunged furiously. Rodrigo made a masterly parry, leapt and lunged like lightning in his turn, and his sword buried itself in the breast of Lozano. Like a sack the Count fell to earth, with the blood gushing from his wound, and as he fell he flung up his hand instinctively to guard his head. Quick as a cat Rodrigo slashed at the uplifted hand, and it flew through the air like a bloody rose. As the Count breathed his last Rodrigo wiped his sword, and the spectators backed away, crossing themselves.

Rodrigo galloped along the road to Vivar. The hand of the Count, tied to his saddle-bow, left a trail of red tears. Behind, in a street of Burgos, a smell of blood and voices in prayer went up to the sky. Ahead, in a great house at Vivar, an old man paced up and down like a lion behind bars, waiting and waiting. Without eating a mouthful, without seating himself for a moment, Diego Laínez had waited all day long. And away in her castle, seated at a window, motionless in her anxiety, Jimena, with her eyes of the Middle Ages, looked at a landscape grown sombre.

Midway between these three points on the map of the world's pain, Rodrigo rode his way, with heart at once lighter and more heavy. The evening fell, and from the distance there came the sound of a horseman galloping hard along the path of Fate.

But as the rubber of night erased the roads, Diego Laínez felt his anxiety ever growing. Had the Count Lozano vanquished Rodrigo? Had his son died without cleansing his honour? Or had Rodrigo not dared to challenge him, for love of Jimena? Like a lion behind bars, Laínez marched his dread to and fro. His pacing resounded through the house. The ears of the mansion followed the sound of his steps. What had happened? What fate awaited Vivar?

Destiny held hidden under its cloak the issue of the enterprise, and anxious eyes turned towards it in vain. Destiny, gloating in its dumbness, drew on the night to make their dread the heavier. A bell tolled. The sound hovered on its wings of iron, flew for a moment along the branches of echo, from branch to branch, echo for echo, and fell dead far, far away on the road. From the spot where it fell rose the sharp sound of the hoofs of Rodrigo's horse on the stones. One noise goes, and another comes, one man dies and another survives, one man is sorrowful and another merry.

At the sound Diego Laínez stopped like a broken spring, the night stayed its onset, the great house raised its head. 'Rodrigo!' cried the old man, and ran out lightly as a boy. All the family leapt to their feet, made way for him, and followed him, too stirred to speak.

The horse stopped at the gates. The old man waited breathlessly in the midst of his family. There came the sound of a stone hammering something to the gates. A star sprang into sight at every blow. There was a silence. Then the hinges of silence creaked, and the gates opened. On foot, grown gigantic in the frame of that silence, appeared Rodrigo.

'My son!' breathed Diego Laínez; and voices echoed him—'Son, brother, brother!'

Rodrigo entered with slow steps. His mare, faithful shadow of her master, followed him of her own free will. 'Father,' said a voice, the voice of a Rodrigo grown to manhood, 'see hung as a knocker upon our gates the hand that smirched you.'

The old man embraced him, and his voice trembled as he spoke: 'Rodrigo, from today you are master of my house. The hand which brings me such a hand can hold better than any other the reins of my domain.' They entered the house, and in the old man's room the two of them alone, father and son, embraced again with tears.

'Why do you weep, Father?'

'I weep for joy because Heaven has blessed me in you. And you—why do you weep, my son?'

'I weep because that hand which I have nailed to our gates tears at the heart of Jimena,' said a voice, the voice of a Rodrigo once more a child.

'Do you regret what you have done?'

'No, Father; I have done my duty, and if need be I would do it a hundred times again. Honour has rights that the heart does not understand; but the cry of the heart may still be heard.' Rodrigo stood there like a little child, dwarfed in the frame of his pain.

'Let your heart weep,' said the old man, 'and seek in other deeds forgetfulness of your grief. Jimena will pardon you. After all, you have but avenged the honour of your father, in fair fight, with no treachery. And the Count was not her father.'

'He was her uncle and godfather, and he was like a father to her; and, as she knew no other, like a father she loved him.'

'But he was not her father.'

'Still did she feel for him the same love that she would have felt for her own father, or even more. Do not seek to deceive me, Father. Jimena is lost to me, and all that is left for me...'

'All that is left for you?'

'...Is to go and fight against the Moors and lose my life in battle. Since without her I am dead already, what matters one death more? Five Moorish Kings have invaded Castile, and none has gone to meet them.'

'Go, my son. He who goes to battle seeking death bears a charmed life. When are you minded to go?'

'At dawn tomorrow. And so, Father, I ask you to assemble the men of Vivar, and let me summon them to action and tell them what I would do.' The bells rang out calling the men of Vivar. When the courtyard of the house was full from door to door with jostling men and boys, Rodrigo stepped out upon the balcony that gave upon the courtyard. Leaning upon the balustrade, he spoke to gentle and simple: 'Noble men of Vivar, a month ago you won a glorious victory over the Moors. The name of Vivar was blessed upon all lips, and a crown that we may not surrender encircled our brows. But in the camp of the Moors there is movement of war, their crops have failed, and hunger drives their arms once more against Castile. They have threatened Burgos; they have taken Montes D'Oca. Neither the King nor any other has sallied forth to give them battle. They are wasting our crops, raiding our herds, carrying Christian men and women into captivity.

'And so I say to you: let Vivar again be first in the field, and first in victory. Nobles and men in your degree, let all be mounted here at dawn. Quit yourselves like men, and by my father's grey hairs I swear to you that we shall return in triumph, with much booty and great glory.'

One shout went up from all throats: 'Hurrah for Ruy Díaz! Hurrah!'

RODRIGO RIDES OUT TO WAR

The next day—the next day was a day to make creation hold its breath, a day to fly the epic feather. Spain awakened, Spain shook off her sloth. She launched herself upon that dazzling whirlwind of a thousand battles which should regain her freedom. So loud at this point of history sound the trumpets of Epic, so deafening is the beating of its drums, that all others are muted. This was the great day. I call for a moment of silence in honour of this day—one moment of silence, and ten centuries of admiration. Stay in your courses, ye planets! And let the sun rise not yet; for this is a chapter to be finished by the light of dawn!

Spain awakened at the voice of Rodrigo. She came to him with open arms, and Ruy Díaz, he who had lost a bride, threw himself into those arms, strained her against his despairing heart, felt the warm sweetness of her ripe bosom, and fell her victim. 'Ah, if you can but make me forget the other!'

From that day forth the two of them, Rodrigo and Spain, went forward shoulder to shoulder, hand in hand, each trusting the other, to make History and to astound the world with Chronicle and Legend. Always they went together, from battle to battle, from day to day, from voice to voice, from verse to verse. Today those two lovers are no more of this world. They have entered the realm of fantasy, they have set sail for the land of dream, they have floated on the sea of marvel, coasted the capes of sublimity, passed beyond miracle.

Rodrigo was the lover of Spain, and Spain was the lover of Rodrigo. The one was fused in the other. He, like all lovers, was for setting his beloved above the stars. He created his beloved, fashioned his beloved, gave her a soul, and made her splendid. And as men tell of Paolo and Francesca, Abelard and Héloïse, Romeo and Juliet, so let it be told of Rodrigo and Spain.

It was barely day. The gates of dawn opened wide, and through them two by two, with Rodrigo at their head, rode the warriors of Vivar. Three hundred lances were all his host. The wind of dawn arose. The sky was luminous with rays of violet, electric with rays beyond the range of vision. The fields had borne a crop of beards and manes and tails.

Rodrigo stopped a moment. He let History picture him there, at the head of his men, on this day when he stood at the outset of his deeds: a moment for a snapshot. The dawn behind him served him for halo and for banner. His mare Babieca whinnied, pawing the ground, scenting that dawn. One moment, and they were ready. They spurred their steeds, and one and all, following Rodrigo, galloped into Romance.

JUSTICE AND INJUSTICE

On that same evening, three items of news became known throughout Castile, and there was talk of nothing else. Rodrigo Díaz de Vivar had killed the Count Lozano. The Moors had seized Montes D'Oca, and only Rodrigo had gone to meet them. A *nuncio,* sent by the Pope, had arrived at Burgos on an important mission. While tongues gave free rein to the national pastime of discussion and argument, Rodrigo and his three hundred spears advanced upon Montes D'Oca by forced marches.

Let us imagine for a moment that this yesterday were today. Away with Time and Space—if they have ever existed! Oh, marvellous Einstein! Long life to the fourth dimension and brains *à l'allemande* with mist and potatoes!

The *cafés* of the Puerta del Sol are full of people. In the Café de Levante there is not room for a pin, unless it be a tie-pin in the pocket of a pick-pocket. The evening papers come out with their capital letters, those capital letters which batten upon all surrounding life, swallowing up people and motors, houses and tramways. The great capital letters have made a Sahara in which newsboys are shouting:

COUNT LOZANO ASSASSINATED
MONTES D'OCA CAPTURED
CRISIS BETWEEN KING AND POPE

'Suspicion of guilt for the assassination of the Count Lozano centres upon Rodrigo Díaz de Vivar. The alleged assassin is reported to have returned to his home, and gone over, with a company of relations and friends, to the enemy.' Shame!

'The body of the Count was horribly mutilated, having one hand cut off, and from certain bruises on the body it is to be inferred that the assassin trampled the victim on the ground.'

Shame!

Happily in those barbarous days there was no Press, no *cafés* at the Puerta del Sol. The world as it revolves through chaos now goes on printing, with all the weight of its presses, the long newspaper catalogue of the banal gossip of the day. In those days it traced upon its orbit the poetry of legend. … Let us go back to them. And let us shake their dust off us, for much dust was raised by the going of Rodrigo's host.

While Rodrigo advanced upon Montes D'Oca by forced marches, Jimena presented herself before the King to ask for justice. The King was with his sons and the great lords, awaiting the envoy of the Pope. Jimena appeared clad in mourning, with a black lace scarf over her hair and a cloak flowing from her shoulders. Very beautiful she looked, and when she spoke it seemed that all the birds of desolation had nested in her throat.

'King Fernando,' she said, 'I come to demand justice at your hands. Yesterday Rodrigo Díaz killed the man who had been my father since I was left orphan.'

'The Count Lozano, your uncle, your godfather?' exclaimed the King. At this moment Diego Laínez burst into the room, pale and out of breath. He raised his arm in salute to the King. 'Let me be heard too, Sire.'

'I only ask for justice,' repeated Jimena.

Diego Laínez spoke again, and his voice was the voice of a weary man: 'Rodrigo killed the Count Lozano, but he killed him in fair fight, face to face, each with his sword in hand. There were more than thirty witnesses.'

'He has done ill,' said the King, 'for he has robbed the Kingdom of a brain and an arm, and that is a grave crime.'

'But tell me, Sire, what law can punish him who kills in duel?' Diego Laínez insisted. 'Until now in Castile, King Fernando, honour came before all else. My son has avenged in fair fight the insult which Lozano put upon me in your own presence. He might have been vanquished instead of victor, the slain and not the slayer.'

White and motionless, a figure of Fate, Jimena stood listening.

'May God in Heaven give me counsel,' said the King. 'If I take Rodrigo all Vivar will rebel; and if I leave him free half Asturias will rise.'

Jimena drew herself proudly erect at the King's words, and from the height of her dignity she spoke: 'Sire, I know nothing of your reasonings of State; I only know that yesterday Rodrigo sought vengeance, and today I seek justice. And I have always heard it said that me King who does not dispense justice does not deserve to reign, or to ride on horseback, or to carry sword or spear, or to take his pleasure with his Queen, or to have an heir. Rather he deserves to die abandoned and to find no sepulchre.'

Don Sancho leapt hotly to his feet. 'Sorrow gives you much boldness, Jimena.'

'I only ask for justice.'

Don Sancho turned to the King. 'My father, it is written in our laws that he who, without guilt, makes a woman orphan or widow shall take her in his care, as her servitor or her husband. Rodrigo has not orphaned Jimena by crime, which would merit death, but in a combat of honour, without treachery or wrong-doing. In such a case, Jimena, justice can only condemn him to serve you or to wed you.'

'I want neither servitor nor husband who reminds me of the dead,' replied Jimena.

The King looked at her in pity where she stood, so pale, so sad. 'My child,' he said, taking her hands, 'you loved him, and I divine in your eyes that you love him still.' He turned to Diego Laínez. 'Bring Rodrigo before me.'

'Sire,' answered Diego Laínez, 'Rodrigo took the field at dawn with three hundred men to engage the Moors. He loves Jimena, and he has gone to seek death because a dead man divides them.'

Jimena bowed her head. Pride fell like a mantle from her shoulders, without a sound, unless it were the sound of a tear.

'If they love with so great a love,' exclaimed the King, 'then time will heal all wounds. You have done your duty, Jimena. Now let Heaven do what Heaven wills.'

A sob was all Jimena's answer. Like some pale priestess she turned without a sound, and left the room to hide herself in her grief.

* * *

The Crown Council was met together. Around the King were Diego Laínez, tutor to Don Sancho, the heir; the Count Per Ansúrez, tutor to the Princes Don Alfonso and Don García; Arias Gonzalo, tutor to the Princesses Doña Urraca and Doña Elvira; the Count García Ordóñez, finest flower of the kingdom; and with them were two Bishops, three theologians, and various men learned in the law.

The *nuncio* of Pope Victor had come to demand, in the name of the Emperor Henry, who ruled the Holy Roman Empire, that King Fernando of Castile should acknowledge himself vassal of Henry, like all the Christian Princes, and, like them, render him homage and pay him tribute. If it had not come with this support of the Roman Pontiff, no King of Castile and León would have listened to the *nuncio's* demand. But the King was Catholic, a good Christian; and he feared the menace of spiritual pains and penalties.

Rome, it was well known, was pleased to mix God in mundane affairs, with which God has no concern, and in political problems, which God despises. In these cases the Pope made himself deaf to the voice of God, and the dove, messenger of peace, went back and forth between Heaven and earth in vain. The Pope wielded God as a weapon, flung all the many-starred weight of God into the scales, and against this weight what could avail to redress the balance—except to break the scales?

Warm waxed the discussion. The fearful and the fanatical counselled King Fernando to submit. The bold and the logical would have the *nuncio* leave the King's territory at once and take himself back to Rome. The envoy held over their heads the threat that the Emperor Henry had a great army ready, and that he would launch it against Spain, with the Duke Raymond of Savoy at its head. He threatened also interdict, and all the other pains and penalties that the Pope of Rome could wield. For all his Italian flexibility the Papal envoy showed himself inflexible, and among these stout but simple Castilians, half lion and half sheep, he moved with the nimbleness of a lizard, the invisibility of an ultraviolet ray.

He was here, there, and everywhere; he walked round them, slid away from them, answered questions from the right, asked his own to the left. He vexed them with subtleties and sophistries; and most of all, that bald pate of his, as of some slippery reptile, hypnotised them. What should they do? Ah, if they were not among the faithful, simple believers in the Apostolic succession! My God! For the love of God! The Devil! To the Devil with all cowards!

'We must play for time,' thought King Fernando to himself. With lifted hand he called for silence and addressed the *nuncio.* Monsignor, you are the envoy of the Pope. Your mission is to make peace reign on earth among the Christian Princes and in their dominions: but your coming here has sown schism in mine. All this discussion is sterile. By our law I must consult the Cortes, and so I will do. Await, therefore, the decision of the Cortes.'

He raised the session. Need it be said that the King planned to delay the meeting of the Cortes as long as possible and then to deal as slowly as might be with the problem, in the hope that the *nuncio* would weary and go back to Rome unanswered?

Rodrigo was a man not of words, but of deeds, and he had lost no time. To do great deeds there is no need of many words. There is one right word, and all the rest are hindrances. Nor is there need of many wills; all are superfluous but one.

Desolated was Rodrigo by the desolation which the Moors had strewn before his march. To fire his host he pointed to the ruined fields, the burnt-out homes; and he marched forward. From the sweating horses a dense fume went up to Heaven. Behind such a leader not one of his men felt one dismay. All were seized with the same excitement. The troop was an electric current on the march towards Destiny.

Rodrigo rode at a gallop, and his thoughts galloped to the rhythm of his steed. 'Ah,' he thought, 'if I had but a few thousand men and there were no strife among the Christians, in how little time would I clear Spain of the invader! Spain, fair Spain, with your bare body pierced by so many swords—Spain, Spain, how I love you, how I breathe your agony, how I hear your cry! "Ruy Díaz, my hopes are all on you; you are my last, my only hope, the ultimate promontory of my hopes. If you achieve nothing I shall be for ever a fettered, bleeding captive. Ruy Díaz, my strength is you, my arm is your arm, my brain is your brain, my heart is your heart." Oh, Spain, my Spain.'

The thoughts of Rodrigo slipped from his shoulders, slid over the crupper of his horse, fell to the ground, into disorder, grew confused, then clearer, flickered out and leapt into flame again. 'And you, Jimena, what are you doing, what are you doing? Your anger against me cannot be sincere, nor can it endure. Ah, child, you who make life a madness, you who bewitch the light that touches you, you who set the midnight reeling!

'The world of your smile is the only habitable world. Laugh, laugh; my heart weeps for your smile as over a bird that is dead. My heart sings for the passion in your eyes—your eyes, the only navigable sea. Our lives are caught in the snares of Fate. Oh, monstrous spider of Fate, dark as a hurricane, that broke the mesh of a future of warmth and song! Jimena, Jimena, my lamentation resounds across the breadth of Spain—Spain, Jimena, Jimena, Spain!'

'Halt there, men; halt!'

A Moorish encampment was in sight in front. Beyond it Montes D'Oca flaunted Moorish banners in the air. A thousand white tents stood up like breasts upon the plain. A Moorish chief, sitting his white horse in his white mantle, with his sword shaped like the new moon's scimitar and hiked with gold and mother-of-pearl, stood sentry over that silent whiteness. Rodrigo contemplated that vision of snow and foam. He seemed to have escaped out of one fantasy into another. That Moorish sentry whose white turban closed the road in front of him set the Orient before his path, and cut short his dreams of Europe with another out of the *Thousand and One Nights*.

'Ho, there, one of you!' Martín Antolínez rode up. 'Go and tell that Moor to announce to his five Kings that they have half an hour to surrender the town and return to their own territory; or else we shall drive them back at the points of our spears.' Martín Antolínez rode off at a trot to fulfil his mission. There was movement among the Moors, agitation of arms and turbans, of banners and lances. Rodrigo, standing on the brink of battle, marshalled his men in due array. On the other brink, too, they were preparing for the fray. Half the time had gone, and the messenger had not yet returned. A river of silence ran between the two armies. Finally Martín Antolínez rode back across it. 'The Moors refuse your ultimatum, and admire your audacity.'

'Good,' said Rodrigo, and shouted to his men: 'Charge, men of Vivar, and let no man stay his hand until it has counted five dead! Strike like lightning with mad blades, that these madmen may be brought to reason!' Riding low, the column shot across the landscape and hurled itself against the phalanx of the enemy. The Moors gave way, and the men of Vivar pressed on—forward, forward! The air was like a field sown with swords and spear-points. Foot by foot, with a force there was no resisting, the men of Vivar drove back the Moors, until they broke and sought refuge in the castle of Montes D'Oca.

Rodrigo advanced to the attack. Finding their situation perilous, the Moors planned to escape by a postern gate. But he of Vivar had foreseen the manoeuvre. He left Álvar Fáñez before the castle with half his men, and led the other half at full speed round to the other side. At the sight of their coming the Moors sought to close the gate. It was too late. Rodrigo shot ahead of his men and burst through the leaves before they could close. The mail-dad breast of Babieca sent ten Moors rolling to the ground. The rude urge of the steed flung the gates wide open, and all Rodrigo's men pressed through.

Inside there was no more fighting. The five Kings, seeing their cause lost, preferred surrender, and yielded up their arms. Rodrigo took them prisoner, and set them captive in the midst of his men. He freed the Christian prisoners, and took a rich booty, which he divided among his followers. 'Well have you carried me, Babieca,' said Rodrigo, caressing his steed. The Moors looked at him with eyes dumbfounded. What manner of man was this who with so small a force had routed his enemy? Whence had come this thunderbolt of war, this Titan with his lightning speed?

Rodrigo strode among his men, watching the division of the spoils. The five Moorish Kings could scarcely believe their eyes. Overwhelmed by their fate, at the bottom of their Oriental souls they thought they must be dreaming, and then in the most Oriental cell of their souls awakened a holy terror, a superstitious dread which spread to all their men behind them, prisoners like themselves, awaiting the orders of this beardless boy, with lips fit for mother's milk and eyes of Hell.

Upright beneath the evening, the beardless boy watched the sunset burn out before his eyes, those terrible eyes in which shone the light of victory. His men looked at him with eyes of homage. The Moors looked at him with eyes of men bewitched, under the power of a magic spell, and felt a thousand enchantments weave around their heads. They spoke to one another in low voices, and like a ring from hand to hand passed the spell...

There came six months of absence, six months in which the world was empty because nothing was known of Rodrigo—six months in which life was lifeless, there at the very edge of Epic, because none knew what was happening but a few leagues away. Where the sun shines brightest it casts the deepest shadows.

Over the balcony of her eyes Jimena watched the evenings fall—the evenings of six months which one after the other came to die in tired waves on the shore of her long lashes. Wrapped in the velvet of her sorrow, she felt life pass her by for all she knew, or all she cared to know. There was no news of him who had gone out to war.

In the great house of Vivar silence waited with open arms. Twice the bird of Epic flew overhead, but new so high that none saw its passage. Diego Laínez waited anxiously, but behind his anxiety there was a sure confidence. Teresa Álvarez waited anxiously, but behind her anxiety there was an enduring pain. How long must they wait; and what might lie beyond this waiting? 'Have faith in me. That is all I ask; that is all I demand,' there seemed to say sometimes a voice which issued from every stone and every tree of Vivar. How like it was to the voice of Rodrigo!

A dot appeared upon the horizon—a dot which patted the distances in two, and stayed a moment prisoner between them. Then it moved and advanced, advanced and grew. The dot became a line, the line became a shape, cutting the air as it advanced, growing before the eyes. The shape took concrete form—the form of a man riding at speed.

The heart can recognise what the eyes cannot yet distinguish. It was a warrior of Vivar, one of the host of Rodrigo, one who came back— perhaps a messenger. People came running out of all the houses. A great crowd gathered in front of the home of Rodrigo, and before them all Diego Laínez stood out like some figure of heraldry. What news was the messenger bearing? Did he carry on his lips victory or defeat, life or death? And what if he were no messenger, but a survivor? No, it was not possible. He came on at the; gallop of a victor.

He came on and on. Only a few yards of doubt remained. And then a hand flung in the air cried: 'Victory!' 'Victory, victory!' An avalanche of men and women, old and young, a solid mass of heads and uplifted arms fell upon the messenger to tear the first word from his lips. 'We have won,' said the messenger, and, leaping from his horse, thick with the dust of Epic, he handed to Diego Laínez a letter from Rodrigo.

The fingers of the old hero tore it open, and he read in a voice that rang aloud through all eternity: 'Father, praise be to God. I came; I saw; I conquered. I bring captive five Moorish Kings. Come you and meet me at Burgos, where I shall arrive before midday tomorrow. I am a faithful vassal, and to my King must I first offer these captives. If the King will not accept them, I will proclaim you King of their lands which I have conquered, and to you shall the five captive Kings render homage and to you shall they pay tribute.'

So high soared the enthusiasm of the listeners that it burst only in silence, a silence of laurels and of marble. Then all embraced with tears of joy. Again the name of Vivar had risen up to Heaven on the wings of the lark of Destiny. Vivar separated to its homes, but its full heart was all one. Like sparks of joy the tears of Diego Laínez fell upon his wife, his sons, his people, and his lands. Upon her knees before an image of the Virgin, Teresa Álvarez was carried up from earth to Heaven on the wings of a prayer and a sob.

PALADIN PEERLESS

In Burgos the argument which the Papal *nuncio* had brought with him in the folds of his purple vestments, like an apple of discord, had made heads feverish and throats hoarse. The apple had burst in the midst of the assembly, and the worms wrangled on the floor and twisted among their feet.

Apple, wonderful fruit of dawn! From the time of Adam until today this fruit has brought us nothing good, and I am very much afraid that it may still hide within it more unforeseen disaster. For the apple is a fruit of snare and deception, a friend of serpents, an enemy of men. It held concealed inside it for thousands of years the universal law of gravitation, and it needed the audacity of a man of vision to wrest its secret from it. The apple is an equivocal fruit, something between fruit and vegetable, so much potato that the French language only distinguishes it from the potato by its position in space—*pomme de terre* instead of plain *pomme*.

I hate the apple, because I hate everything undecided. Either a fruit or a vegetable; one thing or the other, and be hanged to you! In my imagination I see the apple rolling the gates of Paradise shut against us with all the sleek rotundity of its shape—round as the world, as boredom, as evil-doing. The handle of the door of Paradise is an apple, a greasy, slippery apple, so greasy that there is no way of turning it. I am sure that, if we made a hole in an apple and looked inside through a microscope, looked hard through a very powerful microscope, we should still see Adam and Eve with their silly faces hypnotised by the Tree of Knowledge.

So there was nothing odd about it, but rather it was quite in keeping with its tradition, that the apple which the *nuncio* had brought with him to Burgos should set everything at sixes and sevens. The prelates wrangled, the theologians shouted, the lawyers bawled, the nobles grew red with anger; and every five minutes the word 'excommunication' dropped like a bomb, setting all knees knocking, from those of the King to those of the meanest scribe. Lowering was the atmosphere, heavily charged with entreaties and threats. The tempest was near to breaking, and sheet lightning played about the attitude of the *nuncio*. Forked lightning and thunderbolts were on their way, ready to strike in the midst of the assembly.

But happily at this moment a distant shouting struck all lips dumb. The shouting grew nearer, louder, deafening. Hotly the King darted out to the balcony. He left the room with an angry gesture; he turned back to the room a face lit with a kingly smile.

Outside the people were making way like two river-banks at the passage of a tidal wave. Through them Rodrigo and the men of Vivar rode up to the palace, with the very dogs barking for victory. All were clad in silk and gold, but Rodrigo rode in golden mail, shining like the sun. All other swords were sheathed, but Rodrigo bore a rapier of light. All carried lances high, but Rodrigo's spear was borne highest in his mailed hand. All hats were richly jewelled, but Rodrigo flaunted a cap of crimson above his casque tinted like the dawn. At that moment he was the most luminous spot in all the universe.

Diego Laínez, ahead of his son and his men, was already with the King. 'King Fernando,' said the old man,' I present to you my son, back from his campaign, with five Moorish Kings as his prisoners and a whole army captive.'

'Let him come to me,' cried the King, 'let me take him in my arms, this Ruy Díaz of yours, this lion-hearted devil of a warrior!' And, turning to the envoy of the Pope, the King added: 'See, Monsignor; this is what my men do against the infidel, while you come from Rome with talk of war between Christians.' Beneath a halo of admiration Rodrigo advanced towards the King and kissed his hand. 'I do not hold myself honoured to kiss a King's hand,' he said, 'but to kiss the hand of my King does me too much honour.'

'Come to my arms, Rodrigo,' replied the King; 'a vassal such as you is no vassal, but the pillar of a throne, the adornment of a Court.'

'Sire,' said Rodrigo, 'I have brought you five tributary Kings, for one Count of yours I killed.'

'Five tributary Kings,' repeated the King, 'at this moment when the Emperor Henry, supported by the Pope, sends me an embassy demanding that I do him homage and pay him tribute?'

'What do you say, Sire,' cried Rodrigo; 'Castile pay—and why?'

'The Pope declares that all Christendom owes homage and tribute to Henry. What is your counsel, Rodrigo? He who brings five Kings to his King has good right to give it. Speak your mind; what do you say?'

'I say that this land which our forefathers won with sword and spear is free, and a free land owes tribute to none. To render homage, to pay tribute, is to recognise another sovereignty, and that is slavery.

I accept no other King but you, as well I have proved to you. But, if you consent to pay homage to another, then I am your vassal no longer, and I will go and win my own kingdom from the Moors.'

'But the *nuncio*,' the King objected, 'claims that the Pope is ruler of the universe and King of Kings.'

'Of their souls,' replied Rodrigo, 'not of their lands.'

'The Emperor asserts that tribute was paid to him in earlier times.'

'Those who paid it in those times are gone with them. Let the *nuncio* tell this in Rome: Pope and Emperor are foreigners here, and none will pay them tribute.'

'Ruy Díaz is right,' pronounced the King.

The *nuncio* rose menacing in his anger. 'The wrath of Heaven will fall upon you.'

'The wrath of Heaven is not in your hands, but in the hands of God,' roared Rodrigo, crimson with rage. 'I am a Christian, I have fought for Christ, and tomorrow I will take the field again for Christ, and in His name I will offer the enemy my head; but this head which I give for Christ bows to no yoke. I am no man of argument, but I know that I was not born a slave, and a slave I will not be. I am no man of subtleties, I am a man of the field; I know my way in the field, and in the field I will defend my freedom.'

A doctor learned in the law arose, and his slighting words were like a glove flung lightly in Rodrigo's face. 'The youth confesses that he is ignorant of the matter we are discussing. He is not learnèd, he has no love of books; he loves to be in the field, he is a man of the field.'

'He is a man of the field.' The *nuncio's* laugh was loud enough to break the windows.

'He is a man of the field.' The word[1] went from mouth to mouth among the timorous who had no better defence than their irony. 'He is a

---

[1] Campeador. *The word is a derivative of* campear, *a verb of varied meanings in modern Spanish, the pun upon which here cannot well be rendered into English. Its original meaning is 'to be in the field, to pasture'. It has the further meanings of 'to frisk in the field' or 'to crop out of the field' and so 'to be in the field of battle' and especially 'to be prominent in the field of battle'. By special association with the name of the* Cid—*the title acquired by Rodrigo Díaz de Vivar as narrated and explained in the next few pages—*campeador *came to have the particular, and now almost exclusive, meaning of 'surpassing in bravery'. It is used above by Rodrigo as meaning simply 'a man of the field, a soldier', and by his detractors as meaning 'a man of the field, a rustic'.* (WBW)

The term is attested in an official document of 1098. A poem in Latin about the Cid, *Carmen Campidoctris*, written by a Catalan monk in Ripoll, is thought to have been composed around 1083. *Campidoctris* is cognate with *Campeador* and is a late Roman term meaning 'battlefield teacher', akin perhaps to a drill-instructor. Legend has it that the Cid was in fact Sancho II's *alférez* (often latinised as *armiger*), a role denoting a high-ranking knight who was effectively the ruler's military commander, and frequently also standard-bearer. (*Ed.*)

man of the field.' It slipped glibly from lips unctuous with envy.

'I am a man of the field,' cried Rodrigo, catching the jesting word like a ball hard driven, accepting the nickname with pride, and launching it into the firmament. 'I am a man of the field, and you, you race of slaves, what are you? I am a man of the field, and what that means I will show you in the field.' And on his lips the jesting word assumed a dignity, and sparkled and shone and flashed, and became a blazon and a star.

'He is a man of the field,' said the King, 'and for that he shall be the first in my Court.'

Rodrigo drew himself proudly erect, and his lips still seemed to savour that word of irony: *Campeador.* What a pleasing savour the word had on his palate! He looked gratefully at the King, and, with his lips still enjoying the epithet, 'King Fernando,' he said, 'send your doctors of law to the Pope to convince him of his error, and send me with ten thousand warriors to convince the Emperor of his. We shall see who does better, a man of the field or ten doctors.'

'You shall go against the Emperor—I give you your ten thousand men—and then you shall go yourself and reason with the Pope. You shall be man of the field and man of learning too. Man of the field, you have shown yourself surpassing in valour, and man of learning more than all these others. You have the science of the soul, the pure learning of the field, the wisdom of good sense, the only wisdom which always finds the right word, without intricacy or artifice, clear-cut as the stone of a monument.'

'Sire, my arm is yours; command it as you will,' replied Rodrigo. 'My sword shall uphold your honour and the honour of Castile against all the peoples of the world.'

One moment the assembly hung in suspense, and then suddenly enthusiasm caught all hands, freed them from the tyranny of heads, and broke in a single clap of applause, unanimous, united, blazing like a bonfire. The King and Diego Laínez embraced, as much moved as if they were both fathers of that son.

Rodrigo seized the moment to address the King. 'That matter is finished, Sire,' he said; 'God will soon say the last word. Now let us go down to the courtyard, where I would present to you the five captive Kings who will be your vassals, and all the Moorish prisoners who will kiss the ground before you.'

'Let us go down, Rodrigo. Come, my man of the field, let us see your spoils of war and share your triumph.'

At the sight of the King and Rodrigo descending the stairway, the crowd pressing about the warriors of Vivar and their captives broke into a shout of enthusiasm which lifted the sky a thousand yards above its normal level. Rodrigo presented his new vassals to the King, and the five captive Kings bowed down before him all the splendours of the Orient—their foreheads lined with the wisdom of the Koran, their eyes that had seen a thousand mosques, their crowns that had dreamed of a thousand houris.

'Long live the King! Long live Rodrigo! Long live Rodrigo! Long live the King!' And a strange voice was heard amidst the other voices, crying: 'Sidi! Sidi! Sidi Rodrigo! Long live Sidi Rodrigo!' It had been heard already in the camp of the soldiers of Vivar; they had heard it when they marched the captives home, heard it in the dust of the roads. Whence did it come? What did it mean? It sprang out of the stones, issued from the earth, and they repeated it without understanding: Cid Rodrigo, Cid Rodrigo. It had clamped to their hearts, grappled to their tongues, like creepers to the trees whence it was born: Cid Rodrigo, Cidi, Cid.

Who was the first to say it? No man can tell. None of them knew; it found itself suddenly upon all lips. Was it born from the earth? Did it fall from the sky? No man can tell. From earth and sky, from stones and trees, from the dust and the air—it was born from everywhere at the same time. It filled all space like light.

'What does "Cid" mean?' asked the King; 'what is the meaning of this word "Cid"?'

'It means "Lord." "Lord" in Arabic is "*Sidi*,"' some learned voice replied.

'Good,' said the King; 'since your captives call you so, and since such a name has the ring of triumph and good fortune, from today all men shall call you Cid. So, my man of the field, my pride, my captain, from this day forth your name is Cid.'

Rodrigo raised his head to Heaven as if to receive his baptism. He raised it high, so high that the clouds touched it, and a holy finger wrote across his brow: Cid.

'A good name for my man of the field,' the King repeated: 'Cid, Cid Campeador.'

From this moment Rodrigo Díaz de Vivar was called the Cid Campeador, and by this name he was to be known over all creation. And so one word born of irony and another from the womb of earth, from the dark, deep soul of Destiny, formed that name most strange and singular of Epic: Cid Campeador.

The heart of Spain expanded at the name and embraced the world. Anointed, transfigured, Rodrigo raised himself upon his toes to touch the tops of the mountains. The King kissed him upon the brow as if to consecrate the baptism, and the two raised their eyes and swept the heavens in a mighty sweep, There was a noise of palms, a murmur of verses. Rodrigo had entered at full speed into glory.

The multitude was but one throat, shouting: 'Long live the Cid Campeador!' All Spain was but one echo to repeat: 'Long live the Cid Campeador!' The name rose up, rose up into space, was charged and condensed and fell again in a heroic rain: 'Long live the Cid Campeador!' A flight of swallows flying overhead caught up the name on the wing, and carried it to all the corners of the world. 'My Cid, my Cid,' the swallows sang as they flew; and Spain grew by leagues as she heard that word.

So the name Cid issued suddenly from the pores of the earth and found itself upon all tongues, singing like a tree in the sun. It was born, and grew, and ascended into Heaven; multiplied, and was one with the forests, invaded the plains, crossed the mountains, covered Spain, leapt the frontiers and seas, filled all Europe, burst the boundaries of the world, and grew and ascended and stayed only at Hope's zenith.

History and Geography were obsessed with the name——Cid to the north, Cid to the south, Cid to the east, Cid to the west, borne by the wind like a rose. It passed above all banners and all birds, with a noise like a thousand banners, a thousand birds, while beneath a multitude, weeping for joy, followed its passage on their knees—a million heads raised in a branch of offering. Cid, Cid Campeador—that heroic name, garlanded with laurels, is an eagle's nest on the highest peak of History, sending through History a surge of song; and there it remains through all eternity, nestling in the strings of a lute.

A lark soared up like a rocket and burst singing over Spain.

FANTASIA IMPERIAL AND PAPAL

Duke Raymond of Savoy marched upon Spain. Such was the sequel to the reply which the *nuncio* carried back to Rome. The angry Emperor made ready an army of twelve thousand picked men, the best of his cavalry, the shock troops of his infantry, the flower of the German army, with that master of strategy to lead them, Raymond of Savoy. The Spaniards mustered nine thousand men, men of the King and men of the Cid. Rodrigo led the army, with Álvar Fáñez and Martín Antolínez as his seconds.

Singing '*Deutschland über alles*' the Germans advanced, and as they went new countries heard strange tongues. The Pope of Rome had sprinkled them with blessings and sent them forth with prayers. So the troops of Germany marched in good order, a machine of twelve thousand men marching upon Spain, shaking the earth and levelling the trees: one, two; one, two; one, two; tic-tac; tic-tac. The clock of Time, one might say, has marched since then to a rhythm Holy Roman and militarist.

On the other side the nine thousand Spaniards filled the countryside with spears and smiles. With hearts mail-clad and lips that jested over their sausages they went to meet the enemy—nine thousand Spaniards, nine thousand bad jokes to the minute; bad but better than good ones because those jokes were humble, unpretending, dropping from their lips like timid monkeys. So the nine thousand, jesting and all unconscious of the gleam of their heroism, advanced to the encounter with '*Deutschland über alles*' sung by twelve thousand throats with the gravity of an organ, the solemnity of a forest grove. You could almost eat the air with the smell of cured sausages and highland ham.

Ahead of his troops rode the Cid, thinking of Jimena. Before his departure he had sought to see her, and she had refused to see him. She sent him a message that she had forgiven him, but that they could never meet again. But he knew that she still loved him, and that she was suffering as much as he. Babieca, as if she guessed the thoughts of her master, turned her head and whinnied towards Spain.

The Cid shook himself out of his dreaming. He tossed his head, and tried to think of the coming battle. It was all in vain. Jimena stood in the road before him. He turned his head; Jimena was there in the road behind him. Jimena filled his eyes wherever he looked, and in no way could he free them of her. The conqueror was conquered. He bowed his head in resignation. The way had been long, many days of march lay behind him, but she had followed it without faltering. Her memory kept the rhythm of his pace with the fidelity of a loving dog—walking when his horse walked, at the trot when he trotted, at the gallop when he galloped.

The Pass of Aspa was hardly crossed when the two armies came in sight. There in the distance shone the strategic eyes of Raymond of Savoy in the midst of his hairy face and his twelve thousand men. The Cid, his heart heavy with love, reined in, and his archangel's glance met the glance of his rival mid-way. At the shock of those two glances, one cold with the science of strategy, the other warm with the passion of Destiny, the current was set in being and the thunderbolts struck.

Again between two armies face to face there ran a river of silence. On the one bank flaunted the banners of the Empire, on the other the standards of Castile, like two bands of fighting cocks with wings outspread. 'You, Álvar Fáñez, take command on the right,' said the Cid, 'and you, Martín Antolínez, on the left. I will lead the centre. And remember, above all, no movement until I give the word.'

In those days generals marched at the head of their troops and fought sword to sword, like the best of their soldiers, better than the best of their soldiers. It was not as today, when generals control battles from far behind the front, looking on death through field-glasses, giving orders by telephone, bending over a map and marking points with little flags, with a cigarette in their mouths and a bottle of brandy for their belly's good: a hellish smile unsheathed upon their lips, but their heavenly sword sheathed at their side. In those days men fought body to body in a phantasmagoria of shouting and of spears; those were wars of soldiers, not of chemicals, of brawn and boldness, not of calculation and geometry.

Shields and cuirasses German gleamed under the sun, and under the sun gleamed cuirasses and shields Spanish. Impartially the sun shone upon those two mirrors, and they shot up its rays again like a waterspout.

The two armies felt each other's pulses. Quiet and serene the Cid waited, hitching his heart to his star. The first German column deployed and marched forward, compact, mechanical. The Cid waited. The Germans advanced in column of fours. The Cid waited. The enemy column was scarcely a hundred yards away when he raised his sword and charged with his men at top speed. In a charge unbridled, sweeping, they crashed upon the enemy, and in a space of time no longer than a blackbird's song they undid them utterly. Not one remained afoot.

Back rode the Cid Campeador with his men, and took up the same position as before the encounter. Raymond of Savoy read this as a good sign that the Spaniards were in no great heart, and launched a second column. There was another charge of the Spaniards, another shock, another rout of the Germans. He of Savoy frowned over his bushy brows, and flung in a third column to a third attack, a third shock, a third rout. Strewn with corpses was the field, and the stones seemed like little islands in lakes of blood.

With the eye of a swallow the Campeador swept the opposing forces, saw that the mass of the German army was moving at a trot towards him, made one signal to Álvar Fáñez and another to Martín Antolínez, and hurled his right and left at full speed against the enemy. His wings caught them in the middle and hemmed them in. The Germans wavered. Too late Raymond of Savoy understood the manoeuvre. Attacked on both flanks, he was impotent to retreat.

This was the moment which the Cid had waited to launch himself with his men of Vivar into the midst of the furnace. Like a man possessed of demons, the Campeador dealt blows to left and right, cleaving through heads and arms, piercing the flesh of mailed breasts. Babieca reared and kicked, trampling on corpses, spattering blood.

Through the thick tangle of spears drove the Cid, pressing into the centre of the enemy's ranks, his eyes hypnotised by the Holy Roman standard which floated in their midst. He pressed on, and none could resist him. Babieca's mailed prow cleaved a way through the human waves. He reached the standard, and with one leap he seized it, and with another he flung the Savoyard to the ground, where his men made him prisoner.

The Cid flung up his head to the clouds. 'Victory!' he cried in a voice of thunder, and swept the enemy standard downwards in his hand. At the sight of their leader prisoner and their banner in the grasp of that Lord of the Lightning, the Germans threw up their hands in token of surrender: '*Kamerad! Kamerad!*' 'Victory!' shouted the Campeador again, drunken with the sound of his own cry, 'victory is mine!' He rode from the field with the enemy banner streaming in the wind like a tress of hair.

Aflame, shining, erect, taller by one more victory, he smiled at Romance. So generals in those days seized Victory by the hair and dragged her to their camp. They did not flirt with her or send her scented missives like the generals of today.

Scarcely had the men of Castile time to taste the savour of their triumph when the French in turn fell upon them. Allies of the Holy

Roman Empire, the French were come to lend aid to the Germans. But in their hearts they came unwillingly, only because a pact must be fulfilled; for the King of France was no great lover of the Emperor, and a deep rivalry divided them. Singing *chansonettes*, the French advanced, the leaders with spears in the right hand and a bottle of champagne in the left, the men with spears in the left hand and in the right a bottle of Château Margaux. The Spaniards were drinking a savoury must without a name. An odour of wine went up to Heaven, and the plains began to dance and reel in a rhythm musical and vinous.

At the sight of the Spaniards a shout went up from the French ranks. The bottles disappeared as if by magic into the mysterious recesses of haversacks, songs died on all lips in the middle of a verse, swords and spears glittered, and spurs drove home. Like a torrent of rock the French army rolled down upon the men of Castile and León.

'Here come the French,' cried the Cid, 'the sons of bitches!' Hardly had he time to send his prisoners to the rear under strong guard before turning his breast to meet the new shock. This sudden arrival of the French was almost his Waterloo. But happily so ill a jest of Fate went awry; the bird of innocence hovered over him, and that angel which guards the pure and primitive shielded the Campeador. He undid the French as he had undone the Germans. Like a madman he drove into them, and his men wrought a great havoc.

The leader of the French fought like a lion, but nothing could withstand the Cid. Barely had he begun to cry *'Merd...!'* when he fell with a slit throat, and the final *'e'* was spoken in the other world, in the presence of the Supreme Judge. So many German prisoners had the Cid already that he let go the French who survived the battle, and rode from the field waving another enemy standard in the air. Aflame, shining, taller by two more victories, he took his homeward way, and with him as his prisoner went Duke Raymond of Savoy.

When the Emperor and the Christian Kings saw the carnage which the Cid had wrought among their troops, they begged the Pope to write to King Fernando that he should recall the Cid to Castile. Irresistible was the might of the Cid; none could stand against it. It was better to bow the head and let fall the crown of hopes and ambitions.

The Holy Father convoked a Council at Rome, and summoned all the Christian Princes to attend or send their representatives. King Fernando, in obedience to this summons, sent the Cid, with a train of some of his highest nobles. They traversed Catalonia, crossed the Pyrenees, and galloped the length of the Côte d'Azur, between the perfume of classic flowers and the sea, so much sung by poets that the waves hold the rhythm of Greek poetry, as the flowers exhale a scent of Latin verse.

When hunger or the fatigue of their horses checked them, they called a halt, took breath, and rode on their way. In Barcelona they stopped to eat sausages, and in Marseilles a succulent *bouillabaisse* washed down with the rich wines of France—wines which made their eyes and their beards dance to the accompaniment of jokes worthy of the famous Musketeers; those jokes which are whip-cracks that the tongue gives to wine, to extract all its savour and drain out all its blood. Then they got to horse again, riding at walking pace for the first hour of digestion, then at a gallop.

Flights of birds wheeled in the sky over their heads, dropping from time to time little packets of excrement like wireless messages of good luck from the sky. They laughed and sang and filled the air with their French chatter, swooping in their lightness of heart as if on the long glides of well-oiled skates. Fascinated the Cid watched them, with his soul full of content, well-being, and love. What sweetness there was in Nature in these regions! Everything seemed like a happy omen, and he smiled with the birds and the trees and the stones.

When they reached the spot where Monte Carlo stands today there was a great concourse of people on the shore. A Greek sailing-ship had cast anchor off the coast, and three Athenians had come ashore, spread a green carpet on the shore, and invited the people to play at dice. The men of Castile approached to see what was afoot. The Cid watched everybody lose, and then asked for the dice himself. He shook them in his hands and flung them on the carpet. The three dice rolled with a noise of Destiny and of fortunes undone, and stopped dead: three sixes. 'Friends,' said the Cid to his comrades, 'we shall win at Rome; God is with us.'

And then he looked at himself aghast, growing angry over his own weakness, and kicked the carpet, the dice and the money-box far across the shore. Where was the sense of this lure to challenge fortune? Was this destined to be a vice of his race? He, who felt that he carried within his own body all Spain, trembled at the thought. 'Let us leave this foolish game to others,' he cried; 'come, friends!' The three Greeks looked at him dumbfounded, and something in the bottom of their age-old souls winged a word to Olympus.

Evening was falling, but the men of Castile rode on. Slowly, between rocks and trees as hard as rocks, they ascended the spurs of the Alps, and before the sun set they reached the summit. Erect upon his horse, enveloped in the rosy rays of sunset, the Cid loomed over Italy. He gazed a moment over the country spread beneath his feet, then he slid down towards Rome in the swing of a long gallop, raising a scent of Parma violets as he sped.

They galloped all night. There was no time to lose. Italy swayed like a bridge to the rhythm of their riding. A moon of Italy shone in the Pontifical sky. Until they were broken with fatigue they rode, then they stopped a moment and surveyed the countryside in ecstasy. A rooster sleeping in the hat of a Florentine soldier awakened and sang like a tenor. The Campeador shook off his weariness, wiped the sweat from his brow, patted Babieca, and rode slowly on, lighter in the confidence of fulfilling his mission. All night long, under a moon resplendent as marble, between a mandolin to the south and a lyric gondola to the north, were heard the hoofs of a horseman on the path of Duty.

After many days they reached Rome. From the first moment the Campeador felt himself ill at ease at this Court of flattery, fawning, and fornication. There was too much outward showing, too little inward meaning; too much appearance, too little reality—rich attire to deck poor bodies in this Court of comedy. Rather would he have the Court of Castile, a Court of men sincere, of rude, bearded knights, ready to risk their skins at any moment and for anything, not hiding their souls behind sweet, fermented phrases. There was no flattery, no flirting, about that Court. There men knew how to ravish, but not how to flirt or turn a polished phrase.

He looked, he understood, and he judged. Here there was no justice or love of justice, he thought; no reality or love of reality. Here there was only expediency and love of expediency. Here all was venal, and to feign worth was better than to possess it. It was true that in Spain all was not well either. Justice was far from realising the ideal. It was true that there were abuses, true that there were those who stole that to which they had no claim, those who usurped and flaunted titles which belonged of right to others, bringing the law and their own dignity into contempt. But, despite all that, at the Court of Castile there was more substance of reality, more of things real and not seeming. There one might at times feel indignation; but here one felt disgust.

A few days later, in the Church of Saint Peter, Pope Victor held Court, surrounded by his Cardinals and courtiers—a sacred, solemn picture, set in a frame of glass. Princes and nobles advanced to kiss his hand. It came to the turn of the Cid. Beside the throne of the Pope he saw the seats of seven Christian Kings; and he saw the seat of the King of France next to that of the Pope, and the seat of his own King one step lower. He paled at the sight.

He advanced to the Pope, bent his knee to the ground, and kissed his hand. 'This homage is to you, Saint Peter,' he said, 'from a knight to the King of Souls.' Then he stood up, moved aside the seat of the King of France, and set in its place the seat of King Fernando. 'This homage is to my King,' he said, 'from a vassal to his lord.'

A Duke approached him angrily. 'Curse you, Castilian,' he exclaimed, 'and may the Pope excommunicate you! You have insulted a King, the greatest and most glorious of all.'

The Cid looked him up and down. 'Leave the Kings in peace,' he said, 'and if you are offended let us fight out the quarrel between ourselves.' He gave the Duke a push which sent him reeling and left him silent.

The Pope was moved to excommunicate the Campeador, but the Cid prostrated himself before him. 'Pardon me, Holy Father,' he said, 'or Romance will censure you to the end of time.'

A wise man was the Pope, and within Rodrigo's boyishly impulsive and unruly body he sensed a simple, healthy soul. 'I pardon you, Rodrigo,' he said, 'I pardon you freely on the sole condition that here at my Court you carry yourself courteously and discreetly. Master your passions, and keep these barbarous impulses for your battles.'

Rodrigo withdrew, and smiled his satisfaction to the world. During the following days he bore himself more respectfully. Every time the Pope touched the sore spot of the Emperor Henry, or any other matter concerning Spain, the Cid replied simply: 'Without aid from any our forefathers won our land. Without aid from any we have fought against the Moors, and without aid from any we fight them still. What can one ask of us who has not aided us, who does not aid us, and who will not aid us?'

From this answer nothing could shake him. No other reply could he or would he make. He held to it so stoutly that, by force of repetition, it finally convinced them all; and, seeing that it was impossible to deny its truth, they ceased to try. So when, shaking from his feet the dust of the storied stones of Rome, he set out again for Spain, it was with his cause won—that cause which he would certainly have lost if he had entered into long arguments of law, learned discussion of doctrine, and the subtleties of theology.

And as he went the Cid Campeador thought to himself: 'Here perhaps is the throne of God, here perhaps are the keys of Heaven; but God is in Spain, and the gates of Heaven are beyond the Pyrenees. Rather for me

Saint James than Saint Peter. The one wept, but he denied Christ three times; the other did not weep, but neither did he deny Christ at all.'

And as he went the Pope thought to himself: 'I would rather have this boy, rude and violent, candid and subversive though he be, than all the lukewarm and the ornamental who surround me. Of him I might expect anything; but of them I can expect nothing.'

All who had profited by the bickering and fighting among the Christians were the Moors, but the time was coming when Roman ambition was to favour the sons of Christ. The Moors had returned to the attack. They invaded Castile, laying waste all in their path, plundering and burning.

When the Cid reached Burgos the news greeted him that the King was awaiting him so that he should sally forth against the invaders. The Court and the people received him in triumph. The King embraced him, and would not suffer him to bend the knee to earth when he saluted him. Thousands of hearts crowned him king, and wildly the people acclaimed their hero, the man who knew how to triumph not only with his sword, but also with his tongue. The people had found someone to stir them, someone who shook them from common things and gave wings to their spirit and their imagination. They adored in Rodrigo the marvellous fulfilment of their own desires, adored in him their own hunger for greatness, their own thirst for realisation. Spain needed no other spectacle than the Campeador.

Before he left the feast at the palace news met him like the thrust of a spear. The Moors were attacking the Castle of Lozano, and Jimena for two days had been defending herself heroically with a handful of men of the Asturias. Rodrigo shuddered from head to foot as he heard it. Quick as lightning he assembled forty lances. He called to his friends, Martín Antolínez, Muño Gustioz, Álvar Fáñez, Per Vermúdez, and leaping from the table on to horseback, sped with them towards the castle.

Word he sent also to his father and his uncle Arias Gonzalo to make ready more men in case he should need to call upon them. He prepared for everything, was forgetful of nothing, except himself. In his mad career he left all thought of himself behind. The anxious sun sank dying and plunged into the distant clouds with eyes reddened with weeping. A wind arose, and brought the clouds up on its wings. It blew softly, but with a keen edge—that treacherous wind of Spain, fitter for slaying men than for blowing out candles. It began to rain. The sky unbound its hair and let it fall in torrents into the evening.

Never had Babieca felt so sharply the spur of her master. How the little band of riders raced through the roots of the rain! They seemed as if suspended from the sky by skeins of silver. How long had they been riding? The Campeador did not know, but it seemed as if he had all eternity to cross. A century of breakneck speed had gone when they reached a height from which they could see the castle.

The castle was in flames. They rose up into the sky in a riot of writhing arms. The twists of fire embraced and clambered like bindweed round the rain stiff as cane stalks. It was a duel between two switches of hair—the switch of the rain, and the switch of the flames; the switch which streamed from sky to earth, and the switch which streamed from earth to sky.

As they drew nearer the horsemen made out shadows which ran among the flames—shadows of attacking Moors, shadows of defending Christians; a fight in a furnace. Rodrigo thought of Jimena, of Jimena desperate, unconscious, perhaps dead, somewhere in that enormous bonfire, behind that curtain of flames. Stung beyond endurance, he broke into a protesting cry: 'Saint James, what work is this? Sons of dogs, I swear you shall pay dearly for it!'

Cursing and thrusting, he drove like a whirlwind into the fight. Like men possessed of devils the Cid and his horsemen rode from side to side, cutting swathes of death between the flames and the rain. A great cry went up from the Moors: 'The Cid, the Cid! *Walí,* the Cid! The flames have vomited him forth to destroy us!' Terror and confusion seized them at the mere name. Back and forth the Cid hewed his way, and the sword of death gleamed in his hand. Into disorderly flight broke the Moors, jostling one another, stumbling and picking themselves up, boring into the refuge of night and the rain.

Rodrigo, in a fever of anxiety, thought of nothing but Jimena and saving her from the flames. Let the Moors go to the Devil for the moment! He would pay them later. From an upper window he heard the despairing cries of the foster-mother. Rodrigo sped up the staircase towards them. Caught by the flames, the staircase crumbled in blazing fragments under his feet. What was to be done? He went out at a run, and looked up at that sinister window whence came those cries. Ah, there was a tree, not far from the window, but higher than it, reaching almost to the roof of the castle—a way of salvation! Blessed be the hand that had planted that tree!

With a bound Rodrigo started to climb it—up, up. High in the air he swung from a branch and burst through the window. He was barely in time. The flames were licking about the room, and between fire and smoke he could scarcely see the foster-mother's outstretched hand. 'There she is—there!' In a corner Jimena, half smothered, was on her knees awaiting death. In a stride the Campeador reached her, lifted her in his arms, and bore her to the window. Jimena made a gesture: 'Her first. Save my foster-mother first.'

Rodrigo hesitated, and looked around him almost in despair. A curtain which was just taking fire caught his eye. He seized it, ripped it from its fastening, stamped the flames out on the floor, and tied it round the foster-mother. She, half dead, let him do what he would. In a moment he had let her down to his friends who waited below, gazing up spellbound at the scene.

Once her foster-mother was safe, Rodrigo took Jimena in his arms again, and with his precious burden held in one lowered himself out of the window, and leapt from sill to cornice, from cornice to balcony, from death to life—with her in the circle of his arm, light against his heart, until he sprang to earth beyond those walls of flame.

Under the trees, under the rain, before the blazing castle, the Campeador rocked Jimena on his knee; and Jimena, a little child again (Death makes new-born those who escape his claws), buried her head in his shoulder, and wept, and wept. The Campeador was no more the Campeador; he was just Rodrigo. His warrior soul was drowned in a wave of tenderness.

'Do you love me still?' he said; 'have you forgiven me?'

For all reply she strained him closer to her heart, her poor, hungry heart.

But he insisted: 'I have not saved your life to ask your pardon, but because I love you. Heaven has joined us one to the other, and in the eyes of Heaven we are already joined. If I killed the Count it was because my honour so demanded of me, and without honour I would not have dared to look you in the face. So it was a proof, not that I did not love you, but that I do love you. Try to understand the soul of a man.'

She turned her eyes upon him, and opened them so wide that all the sorrow of the world was emptied into the night, poured into the night on two rivers of tears. Rodrigo saw in her eyes the *Via Crucis* of hope, and he kissed her on the brow. 'You love me still?' She made no reply. Her eyes still looked at him, and all her body trembled. Her throat seemed clasped by a necklet of thorns.

SINGLE COMBAT

The King had called into council the first men of his Court. Diego Laínez, Arias Gonzalo, Per Ansúrez, and, youngest and most glorious of them all, the Cid, hung upon the King's words. The quarrel about Calahorra was in question. For some time past King Ramiro of Aragón and King Fernando of Castile had been at odds over this frontier town of their kingdoms. Fruitlessly had both Kings spilled the blood of their subjects to win or lose a town which, in truth, was not worth such carnage among Christian men; and so the King of Aragón had sent to King Fernando an emissary charged with the proposal that they should settle the strife by single combat.

'Cousins and faithful friends,' said the King Fernando, 'King Ramiro has proposed to me that a joust should end this old dispute over Calahorra, since it is not right that a long war should drain our Kingdoms, when a single man a side could represent the judgment of God. He charges me, if I accept, to name my doughtiest warrior and send him forth to meet his champion in the field.'

'To me,' replied Diego Laínez, 'there seems good reason that one should die to save many lives.'

'But I,' said Per Ansúrez, 'hold that it is perilous to hazard all upon a single spear. Army to army we of Castile shall conquer in the end.'

'Many years have gone,' Arias Gonzalo answered him, 'and we have not yet conquered. Who is the champion chosen by Don Ramiro?'

'Sire, what matters it who he be?' asked the Cid. 'He is Don Martín González,' replied the King, 'the same who bears Ramiro's embassy.'

'What,' exclaimed Per Ansúrez, 'has he chosen that giant—Martín González, he whom they called the strongest man in the world?'

'He is a mountain of a man,' added Arias Gonzalo, 'a bull for strength and courage.'

'The best lance in Aragón without a question,' Diego Laínez agreed.

The Cid looked at the King, and spoke straight as his glance. 'And is there no lance of Castile, Sire, which can withstand Martín González? Do you not know whom of your men to choose? Is there none who has proved himself a man above all others?'

'Against such a monster I fear for any of my men,' replied the King.

'I,' cried Arias Gonzalo, 'am ready to meet him.' 'No,' roared the Cid, 'not you. You have four children, and I have none. King Fernando, I pray you summon this ambassador of Aragón.'

'He awaits our answer in the hall below. Bid him enter,' said the King to a page, and the page went out to call the terrible champion of Aragón.

The door opened, and there loomed upon the threshold a man who could hardly enter it. His shoulders filled the portal like a rock, and his hands might have been the fins of a shark, were his arms not folded across the breast of a widow-maker. Martín González, with head held high, surveyed the company in his pride. He was no man, but a tower of arrogance. 'Greetings to the King of Castile,' thundered a voice, heavily charged with self-confidence and self-esteem.

'Approach, sir,' said the King; 'if there be a man in Aragón, his peer will not be lacking in Castile and León.'

'Such is the hope of King Ramiro, and in accordance with that hope is the proposal I bear you in his name. Name you a knight to face me in the field, man to man, sword to sword, and may Calahorra fall to that King who has the better vassal.'

'I have some difficulty in choosing the champion of Castile, since all would be chosen to defend the rights of my Kingdom.'

'So, Sire, your vassals who hold their lives in contempt grow in number,' began Martín González; but the Cid gave him no time to make an end. He leapt to his feet.

'To hold you cheap is not to hold life cheap, Don Martín González, and so I will show you in the field tomorrow.'

'You are he they call the Cid, he who has done great deeds against Moors and Germans? I am here to prove to you that it is not the same to fight against Moors as against men of the mountains and Christians of Aragón.'

'Be insolent as you will, man of Aragón; but keep your boasting for your spear. Tomorrow, face to face in the field, we shall see.'

'Until tomorrow, gentlemen. The lists, you know already, will be set upon the frontiers of Castile and of Aragón. There will be my King, and when the judges summon we shall come forth to do battle. We snail bring two hundred men, and do you bring as many.'

'Tell Ramiro that I shall be there with my men,' replied the King; 'until tomorrow in the field.'

* * *

The lists were set—a smooth field of shining sand; the table on which were to be staked the fate of a city and the fate of two men. On either side were the two companies: on the one side Don Ramiro, King of Aragón, with his men, and on the other King Fernando of Castile, surrounded by his nobles and escorted by his soldiers. No fear of trap or tumult had the gentlemen of those days in the case of such a combat. It was ruled by the code of honour, and the laws of the game were obeyed with all the strictness imposed by the nobility of knighthood.

Seated upon their dais, the judges awaited the hour of combat, the moment of judgment. Upon one side and the other the standards floating in the air flapped back and forth, tossing their heads to heaven like flights of restless birds. Armed from head to foot, with spear in one hand and shield in the other, the Cid approached the dais of his King. 'Ruy Díaz de Vivar, my Cid Campeador,' said the King as he blessed him, 'do not forget that in your hands I have placed the honour of my kingdom. May God be with you, as are all the hearts of Castile and of León.'

Rodrigo rose to his feet. 'My thanks to my King—my thanks, King Fernando.' Confident in his own strength and in the strength of all the hearts of Castile and of León, the Cid strode to Babieca and caressed the mare on neck and shoulders. Babieca felt a thousand hands in the hands of the Cid. Quivering with pride, she sensed that somewhere Poem was watching her, and drew in deep breaths of Heaven. Babieca was all devotion to the Cid, and the Cid was all devotion to Babieca—a fit horse for a fit rider.

Upon her back leapt the Campeador, and the two were one. Legend united them, and to separate them would be a crime to make Romance weep tears of blood. Without the Cid upon her back Babieca felt herself dead; without Babieca between his legs the Cid felt himself lifeless. The one without the other was a stanza cut short. Horse and horseman were one, a single piece of Epic.

Each was confident in the other. They loved with all the passion of *geste,* were linked with all the vigour of a verse. They knew that so linked together they were fated to pass into History, a knot of heroism, made for the marvelling of men, which nothing could unloose. Together until the end of time they would cross at a gallop the memory of mankind. And when the final trumpet sounds, the Cid will come curvetting on Babieca over the grass of the valley of Jehoshaphat.

There they were at the edge of the lists under the Iberian sun. With all the assurance of an equestrian statue they took the field, and at the other end appeared Martín González. Even more huge, more awful, he seemed today in his shining armour than on the day before. He was a tank which had come forth to fight against a man. But this man was as an angel of Destiny, and he bore the wings of Epic. Only so could he fight this fight. If one could have looked behind those visors, he would have seen a face ferocious, fierce, and frowning, the face of Martín González; and a face fresh and open and smiling at the sun, the face of Ruy Díaz.

Face to face the two took their stations, with their restless horses pawing the ground, and between them brooded Fate, an Unknown God. The currents of Destiny flowed through their spears. Silence drew its cords tight round every throat and strung up every gaze—a silence in which no fly dared to buzz. Every soul hung in suspense upon the judges' signal. It fell, and two men's fates flashed forth like streaks of lightning which should cleave Destiny itself in twain. Trampling underfoot that carpet of a thousand eyes at gaze, the horsemen crashed furiously together. The shock re-echoed over all the valley.

See them there, spear to spear, exchanging blow for blow—two steel-clad spirits of wrath and death to make day hide its eyes. Splinters flew from their armour as they hewed, and made the field a summer night of stars. Suddenly at a deadly stroke the spear of Martín González shattered in atoms into the sky. He reeled in his saddle, all but unhorsed. The Cid reined back. 'I do not fight an unarmed enemy,' he said; 'get you another lance.'

Quick as he was gone Martín González was back with another weapon in the field, and the fight went on, shock after shock, with neither man a whit dismayed. Drunk with the frenzy of all Spain, the Cid was a demon of fury mirrored in a glass of flashing strokes, a whirlwind of spears and shining splinters of armour. He smote and smote, and took back blow for blow. Not an inch did he yield before his monstrous foe, whose breathing filled all space like a bellows. The air cringed between them as eyes of Hell glared through the slits of their visors. Their horses slid body to body, rearing and turning on their hind hoofs, and battled together, borne out of horse sense by the madness of their masters.

A thrust of Martín carried away the spear of the Cid, and he felt the spear of his enemy wound his body. The blood welled forth, but he sat his horse as steady as before. Martín González in his turn waited until the Cid should arm himself anew. 'Get you another spear, Rodrigo,' he said, 'and see that it be of true steel. You are more of a man than I thought you, and your heart is high; but your boldness will not bear you out of this fight, and on this field will rest your severed head. You will not see again Castile

or Vivar; you will not see again Jimena who loves you and whom you love.'
'Martín,' answered the Cid, 'that you are valiant knight I shall be the first
to bear witness. But these your words are not those of a brave man; for this
fight shall be decided by the force of our arms, the strokes of our spears,
not by the strokes of our taunts and the force of our tongues.'

He flung himself upon his enemy as he spoke, an avalanche of blows
to strike him dumb, and sheared through his coat of mail and pierced his
breast. But Martín González budged no inch, giving back spear-thrust for
spear-thrust. The fight was like a bursting of stars in some commotion in
the depths of space, a tumult of thunderbolts and dust, as if a storm had
broken there in the field under the cloudless sky. Blood trickled from their
visors to their breasts, and from their breasts to their feet. The air was full
of fragments of their fury, and the breeze that stirred above their heads was
saturated with a hard sound, the sound of hard breathing that filled the day.

Facing each other across the lists, the two Kings watched the fight
and one another. When fortune favoured Martín González something sang
in the heart of Ramiro; and when the tide of battle swayed to the Cid
something sang in the heart of Fernando. An eagle, weary of watching the
motions of the stars, hovered above their heads looking down upon the
combat. The valley was full of a din like a wrecking sea, and the two spears
hammered on the gates of Heaven.

It was a dread spectacle of mystery and fate, this strife of two spears to
wrest His secret from God Himself, a spectacle to put men in fear of Him.
Nothing could surpass in tragedy and awe this fight for justice, in which
two peoples left it for two right arms to decide to which side God should
lean and show it had the right—two peoples full of faith that God would
speak through one of them and make His will known in a stroke of steel.

Eyes anxious for the miracle swept the sky for those threads which the
Supreme Judge was moving, those threads upon which hung suspended
the paladins of death, the instruments of His will, charged with weighting
the balance with their lives, and making the judgment of the Lord issue
with their life's blood. Watching the combat, the two Kings trembled as in
the presence of God Himself. None spoke around them until God should
speak. And when God spoke these simple people would bow their heads
before His word in resignation and go their ways with no hate between
them.

Silence! God was there. The fight grew ever fiercer, as if each combatant
drew new source of fury from the other's failing powers. Each had faith in

his star, and his star sustained him with its light, fired him with its heat. The blood of the stars spattered the ground with every horrid shock. The wind that turned the mills in the distance passed over them to turn the wheel of Destiny, to turn it slowly with the tireless rhythm of the spheres. God was about to deliver judgment. Were it not for the clash of arms on earth the combat might have been far away above the skies.

At last it could be seen that Martín González was beginning to lose ground. He still had faith in his Herculean frame; but the Cid had faith in his destiny and in Babieca. Fearlessly he unguarded himself and tempted his enemy. Martín González sprang at him like a tiger. The eyes of the Cid flashed fire. He dug spurs into Babieca and launched to meet his enemy all the weight of his own body and the steed's headlong charge. Parrying the spear of the man of Aragón, he drove his own full into his breast, cleaving through armour and flesh with a thrust that rocked the star of Aragón.

Martín González crashed to earth like a felled tree. The Cid leapt from his horse. He made a woodman's axe of his sword and held up to the judges the head of Martín González. 'Is there more to do?' he asked, 'that Calahorra should belong to my lord?'

'No,' replied the judges; 'no; for in this fight the right has abandoned Ramiro and his Kingdom.'

The Campeador wiped his sword and fell upon his knees on the ground. He held his hands high to Heaven and rendered thanks to God. 'I thank Thee, Lord of the Universe, that Thou hast given victory to Castile through this the humblest of Thy servants.' Bearing a Kingdom on the point of his spear, he sprang back on his horse and rode towards his King. A drum-fire of applause rained upon him from the camp of Castile. With outstretched arms the King met him, and drew him to him and embraced him. The King embraced the Cid; but the Cid embraced Babieca. He clung to the neck of his noble steed, leaping and laughing like a child in the drunkenness of his triumph. He hung by a thread upon eternity; and he was happy.

DOÑA URRACA

Beneath a sky of glory the Cid rode back to Burgos. An exaltation of nobility widened the arch of Heaven, a wind of heroism beat in waves upon the clouds, and earth and sky were one in the plenitude of their admiration. Every breast breathed in the greatness of this man who shed greatness on his way. Castile had no words for any but the Campeador, and his name was a prayer upon all lips. The soul of Vivar was a garden in which all the flowers were Rodrigo, singing 'Don Rodrigo, Don Rodrigo!' to the night and to the day.

The first who met him as he rode into the capital was the Princess Doña Urraca—Doña Urraca, woman of mystery, the silent heart, the hard enigma of this epic. Did Doña Urraca love the Cid? No one has ever known. There is a poem which pretends to reveal the secret of a great soul and an untold love. But was this inspired of God or of man? That is the problem. We have no right to speak.

She saw him pass in triumph before her eyes, from crown to crown, from laurels to laurels, and her lips smiled; but they said no word. She saw him linked to Jimena by the rays of his unseen star; she saw the ties that might have bound him to herself broken by destiny; and her eyes of a Princess clouded and cleared, clouded and were silent. A woman superhuman in her powers, with steel beneath the softness of her breasts, strong, skilled in government, subtle in politics, she sensed the magnetism of the future. She was bold, but she was prudent. She may have cried out in her pain, but none heard her cry. She sang, and she whetted her sword.

Did Doña Urraca love the Cid; and was the Cid conscious of that love? Was it perhaps he who, in some childish hour, there when they stayed together at Zamora, spoke to her of love; and then, aghast at his own madness, left the seed behind him and never returned to the field where it grew in silence?

Princess of fair words and dark shadows, of chastity and blood, I feel that a love weighed upon your soul. But fear not, I will guard your secret. Let your pride rest in peace, for I am a gentleman, and that word which you never spoke to any man I will not speak in my book. See him fight here in these pages, noble as a swift-sailing ship in storm, and go your ways into the darkness and let your heart weep in silence.

Did Doña Urraca love the Cid? Soul that was a stronghold, a castle sealed against all the winds that blow, was your pride wounded that another woman should dare to rest her eyes where you had rested yours, and, wounded, did you feign a friendly indifference? Was he, the favoured son of fortune, he who held five Kings vassal, not high enough for you? Did he not think that he was high enough, or did the love of Jimena make him forget all else? O Doña Urraca, woman of mystery, draw your starry mantle around you and go your ways into History, haughty and aching!

THE KNIGHTING OF THE CID

As the tides obey the moon, the Cid Campeador obeyed his destiny. The King Fernando was growing old, and he was weary of warfare, but he could not bring himself to die without realising the dream of his whole life—to carry his arms so far that they might round off his Kingdom from the Ebro to the Tagus, and from the Tagus to Coimbra. Did not the arm of Ruy Díaz offer him a Heaven-sent weapon with which to undertake this great campaign? Was not this son of Destiny he whom the Kingdom, full of a faith fortified by portents, had so long awaited?

Forward, then; for with the Cid in the van all walls were Jericho: the Campeador was in league with the trumpet of miracle. Money was short for the enterprise: but there were the jewels of his wife, the noble Queen Doña Sancha. Soldiers were few who could be counted upon for such a stern campaign; but there was the name of the Cid, and the enthusiasm which that name inspired throughout his Kingdom would make armed men spring out of the ground.

Forward, then: with the Cid Campeador at the head of six thousand men, King Fernando set out in pursuit of his old dream. There was a dawning over the world. Impatient birds flew into the east to tap the dayspring so that the sun should rise. The army was on the march. There was a dawning over Spain.

Marching from victory to victory, gaining battles and taking cities, making tributary the Kings of Zaragoza, Toledo, Badajoz and Seville, after seven months' campaigning the army stood at last one evening before Coimbra. The Cid set the camp of the King, and left with him Álvar Fáñez and Per Vermúdez. Then, taking with him Martín Antolínez, Galín García, and Muño Gustioz, he set out to survey the city and the country round about it. They rode around it. Well defended was the city, with stout walls and massive towers of stone, encircled by a wide moat.

Nothing daunted, at dawn the next day, amid shouting of 'Stand fast for Spain! Saint James the Apostle!' The Cid led the assault upon the city. A tempest raged upon the earth with a rain of arrows, an avalanche of stones spat by catapults, a battering of rams like mad bulls, a heaving of towers which rose and ladders which fell with human clusters clutching at the sky. But the Moors of the city were many and brave, and the assault was repulsed. One after another the attacks followed, in hard, tireless fighting day and night. But six months passed, and the city had not yet yielded.

The besiegers began to lose patience and the soldiers heart, and hunger grew among the Christians. They had consumed all their food, and there was no more to be had in the camp. Infected by the bad spirits of his soldiers, the King was for raising the siege, but the Cid would have him sanction one more attack the next day. In the midst of the argument some monks from the monastery begged audience of the King. In the name of their Abbot they came to offer him wheat and millet and vegetables which they had been at pains to grow. They besought him not to raise the siege, promising if he did not do so that they would give him food and all he needed in plenty.

The King thanked them, promised that he would not yet abandon the field, and distributed the food among his men. The monks withdrew, saying that the Abbot sent them his blessing, and that he was praying day and night to the Apostle Saint James, beseeching his aid for the Christians. 'I saw him smile upon his altar the other day,' declared a lean monk with gleaming beard and eyes that shone with a divine fever; 'how the good Apostle smiled! I was lighting candles to him, and I begged him in a low voice: "Protector of Spain, aid the Spaniards!"'

'Pray to him again for us this night,' said the Cid, 'and if he will not aid us he does not deserve to call himself Patron of Spain.'

'Tell him that we shall change our Patron Saint!' cried Vermúdez, reckless and bold as ever.

The monk backed away, crossing himself. 'Do not say that, for the love of the Saint!'

'Silence, Vermúdez!' ordered the King. 'What if the Saint should be offended?'

'He will not be offended, for he knows that we all love him, and that among soldiers he must uphold his reputation. He calls himself a soldier; let him show himself a comrade.'

Darkness fell, and a mystery brooded in the obscurity. The night was heavy with portent. Satisfied stomachs were ready to sing of victory, but anxiety kept all heads in a whirl. Nerves strung taut as a lute waited for a chord to relax them. It was about to issue forth. What was this something which soared above their heads? What was this murmur like a beating of wings far off in space? What spirit was moving in the womb of night?

Old and weary, the King had left all things in the hands of the Campeador. The Campeador looked at those hands heavy with responsibility, and he saw them shining—shining in the darkness. Whence came this strange radiance? And what was that noise of wings? What was this presage being written across the breast of Time? Rodrigo had his arm, his brain, and his high heart; and he sensed something more in this mystery that moved above him in the darkness. Feverishly, as if exalted above himself in his strategy, he passed the whole night long studying his plan of attack.

The next day the rising of the sun gave the signal for the assault. 'Stand fast for Spain! Be with us, Apostle Saint James! Santiago! Saint James!' Earth creaked beneath the weight of munition wagons, horsemen dashed madly from side to side, a forest of crosses waved in the hands of the Christians among spears and swords. Rope ladders grappled the air, and files of men swarmed up them as if they were ascending into Heaven; archers twanged their bows in the musical rhythm of death. Christendom swung upon a hundred battering-rams, belched from a thousand catapults.

Amid the hellish din of battle the Campeador roared orders, and between order and order he shouted into the wind: 'Santiago, Saint James! We fight in your name, Apostle! Saint James, Santiago!' 'Yago, Yago,' echo repeated; and some swore that they heard a cry 'Go! Go!'

At eleven of the morning the men of Castile had taken one of the towers. By midday they were forced to abandon it. They had made progress here, been beaten back there. One of the comrades of the Cid fell at his side with a gaping wound in his belly. Terrible was the killing. Like a flash of lightning the Cid darted from one gate to another, directing in person the manoeuvring of seven towers which were pushed up to the walls. The King himself took part in the fight. The soldiers, flinging their arms to Heaven, were one throat shouting madly: 'Saint James! Be with us, Santiago!'

With all his engines together, the Campeador assailed a gate, and hundreds of soldiers streamed towards it. They were keyed up to a pitch of frenzy. It was a phantasmagoria of men with the strength of madmen. They pounded at the gate, and the universe trembled. The Cid was in the forefront sitting squarely upon Babieca, cleaving the wind of battle with her breast. 'Forward, men, forward!' roared the Cid. 'Stand fast there! The gate is ours! Saint James, Santiago, Patron of Spain!'

And suddenly, splitting the sky, was heard a great voice which echoed round the firmament: 'Stand fast for Spain!' And there in the heavens, leaping from cloud to cloud, upon a white horse, shining in a mist of light which wreathed upon a mighty wind, came at full speed the Apostle Saint James.

A howl of terror went up from every dog in camp, and from all the frantic soldiery a sacred shout of greeting. A wave of madness swept the world, and the whole army felt itself shaken as by an electric shock into one great sob which burst forth in a flood of jubilation over the miracle. Renewed energy seized hold upon all arms, and every man's strength was doubled. Trebled were the blows of rams and catapults. An indomitable ardour blazed in all hearts, until each man had the strength of four. Splintered into a thousand pieces, the main gate yielded before that thrust, and the Cid burst through, the head of a seething water-spout. Coimbra was won.

In Coimbra the King installed himself to set his new conquests in order. Thither he summoned the Queen, Don Sancho, and the Princesses, under the care of Diego Laínez and Arias Gonzalo, together with the Archbishop of Oviedo and other prelates, who came to bless the mosques which the King had converted into Christian churches.

To crown the deeds of his Campeador, the King resolved that, after two days of feasting, on the third day, Sunday the twenty-sixth day of July, at the altar of Saint James in the great mosque, now consecrated as the Church of the Virgin, he would dub Rodrigo Díaz de Vivar a knight. On the evening of the day before, Saturday the twenty-fifth day of July, the Queen and the Princesses set about preparing the altar. The church was filled with a whole summer of flowers. Their warm perfume poured out of the doors in a flood and intoxicated the whole city.

The Cid had willed it that they should lay his arms before the altar on the day before, so that he might pass the whole night there given up to recollection and prayer, making himself ready for the solemn act of the morrow, the communion of the soldier with his duty, the reception of his Host of glory, the consecration of his life to his sword. So he was the initiator of that vigil of arms which later became the obligatory ritual of every, aspirant to the noble order of knighthood.

It was night. Diego Laínez accompanied his son to the church.

'My son,' said the old man, 'reflect upon the honour you are about to receive, think of all those things to which honour constrains you, remember your blood, venerate your ancestors, and never fail in the loyalty you owe to your country, to the King who has bestowed so many favours upon you, and to his successors.'

'All this will I do, Father. Fear not for the honour of your son.'

'No man so young as you has ever yet been dubbed a knight. No man of your years, it is true, has done so much as you have done.'

'The King rewards your loyalty in me. You, Father, were a mighty warrior and a pillar of counsel; that which the King does for me he owes to you.'

'Your modesty is kindly to me, but it is not so, my son. It is your own merits which the King is about to reward. And now I will leave you alone with yourself.'

'My thanks, Father; I would be alone.'

The steps of Diego Laínez rang upon the flags, and the Cid was alone, swallowed up in the half-darkness of the church. A great lamp burned flickeringly on high. The Cid approached the altar and knelt down in the silence. The Cid Campeador was alone, alone with himself, alone within himself, with his eyes turned inwards to search his own soul.

A moving spectacle! There was the man who loved the field, the man of tumults, the lord of armies, the leader of multitudes, the shouter of commands, alone in the darkness and the silence. Before the altar, on a silver salver, shone the sword which the King would gird upon him, and his golden spurs. Not a sound disturbed the quiet of the church, locked away from life, locked like a heart which has ceased to beat but yet preserves within it a beloved form. The Cid was alone, enveloped in himself, in his past, his future, his deeds, his days of light and his days of tears. Behind him moved a shadow of miracle, before him moved a shadow of Destiny, and above him poised an aureole of God.

O Cid, how I love you at this moment, when I can surprise you still and silent before me! It was the great night of your soul. You saw yourself so pure in your nakedness, so huge in your recollection, that you soared above your reflections, above space, above life and death, and showed your head above the ages. You come to me shining from beyond the bourne of death, you come to me across life over a wide sea beneath a sky of doves. The tide of battle surges upon the gleaming shore of your eyes. Your eyes are two bas-reliefs of your glory. Your hands, those hands which cut the path before the thirsty caravans of the Moors, are folded to offer up your heart. Clothed in a comet, you soar above Spain, above human history, into the infinite.

The tree of your deeds sheds its leaves upon the universe in an autumn shower of stanzas, a metamorphosis of verses into nightingales that sing of princes. The first poem of my race was bedewed with the sweat of your brow. Not like Attila, where your horse set its hoof flowers bloomed and from the soil sprang forth romances. Your fury of love and faith planted four crosses in the wind, and on them still hangs above the world the garland of the four quarters of the compass. The hurricanes of God conjure you above your battles. I see you dedicate yourself and arise out of your flesh, in a divine frenzy, drawn up towards the infinite in a mystic ecstasy, a celestial drunkenness. You are a tree which climbs and climbs to bear up once more the Christ who came down to visit souls.

There you are upon your knees, bent over a flight of thunderbolts, with your eyes fixed upon a journey. Whither are you going? In an immense sweep you soar resplendent up to the kingdom that is within yourself. He who now should seek to follow the march of your thoughts would lose his reason in dismay, would go astray in the abysses of vertigo. There are no limits to your soul. Stay; whither are you going? How can I follow you?

The courses of the seven planets are reflected in the mirror of your shield. Go your ways, go your ways. Leave your flesh behind and go your ways, clad in Epic. I will watch beside you as you roam the spaces of the stars, without form and void. Go your ways.

While you circle the ellipse of God I will keep vigil at the foot of your memory. Your heart leaves a wake of spreading deeds, and perhaps I can follow you with my eyes.

He is gone. The church is empty and the world is left desolate. Before my eyes, on its platter of silver, the sword gleams, and twists in a sudden blaze, and sprouts wings, two great wings of fire and flaming feather. The sword moves, it is lifted up, its soars, soars above my head, above the church, above the world. I hear a hecatomb of planets falling into chaos, I hear windows opening in space, I hear eternity rushing in my ears. Where am I? What is happening to me? A whirlpool of light sucks me into its centre, and I fall down, down, down.

Ah! At last I have returned to earth, come back to myself. Here I sit before a virgin page. It is dawn. The Cid is there at his prayer-stool, kneeling, pale, rigid as a statue, with his eyes fixed on his soul. He has spent all night long on his knees. I look at him in silence, and I see that this man was made for me to love him. I look at him, and I look at his history. I have seen his soul; and now I can leave him and follow more certainly the magical marching of his troops over the enchanted meadows of Romance. At the first stirrings of life in the city the Cid came back to himself with a start, raised his head, and rose to his feet. Outside the noise was growing. The Sunday bells rang out, pouring their melody in streams into the sky, making ready for the ritual. At the opening of the windows of the church the light rushed in like a drove of cattle. Shadows of monks came and went, gliding over carpets of sunlight, with their hands in their wide sleeves, in which the night lurking in the nave had taken refuge.

People had flocked around the church. In the square before the great door Christian soldiers jostled for the best places. There was a sound of music in the distance. Over the multitude fell the pealing of the bells. The company of the King arrived at the threshold. The door opened, and Rodrigo appeared between two pages. He carried no sword. The King advanced, and Rodrigo bowed his head before the King and waited.

Preceded by the Cross, followed by his prelates and his acolytes, the Archbishop of Oviedo moved towards the door. All Coimbra fell upon its knees. Then the King with his Queen, followed by his heir Don Sancho and the Princesses, went forward with the Cid and all the Royal company to the altar of Santiago. The Queen, Doña Sancha, was to be the godmother of the new knight, and the Prince Don Sancho his sponsor; and, to lend more lustre to the ritual, the King had presented the Cid with his own sword.

The church was full of people. Ten thousand admiring eyes were fixed upon the Campeador. Next the altar, in front of the Cid, stood the King. On either side of the Cid stood the Queen and the Prince. Behind them were the Princesses, Diego Laínez, Arias Gonzalo, and the other nobles. Finally came the lords, the friends and followers of the Cid.

The Cid sank to his knees, the Archbishop opened the Bible before him, and the King, with the solemnity due to a crowning moment of History, asked him: 'Rodrigo, would you be a knight?'

'I would,' answered the Cid, in a voice which still resounds through Spain.

'Then may God make you a good knight'; and the King repeated: 'Rodrigo, would you be a knight?'

'I would.'

'Then may God make you a good knight. Rodrigo, would you be a knight?'

'I would,' Rodrigo answered for the third time.

The King looked at Doña Urraca. 'Princess, give him his spurs.'

Doña Urraca took the spurs and fixed them to his heels. Reader, in vain you seek to read the eyes of the Princess; no smallest tremor will you find in them. You forget the character of that great woman, and you forget her race.

'My thanks, Lady,' said the Cid; 'with this sovereign honour that you have done me you raise me above the world.'

The King took the sword, and with it in his hand he asked the Cid again: 'Rodrigo, do you swear by the Cross to be true knight?'

'I swear,' answered the Cid.

'Rodrigo, do you swear to defend justice and the right?'

'I swear.'

'Rodrigo, do you swear to be faithful to God and to the King unto death?'

'I swear.'

The King touched him on the shoulder with the sword and girt it upon him. 'Take this sword,' he said; 'it has gleamed in ten battles faithful in my hand. May it gleam in twenty in yours.'

'Your example and my father's,' answered the Cid, 'will aid me not to dim its sheen.'

'May God our Lord and the Apostle Saint James keep you as a knight and may they guard your footsteps.' And to the clamour of a thousand trumpets which shattered the firmament at the same moment, the King kissed him on the lips and gave him no other accolade. In an avalanche of iron, a cataract of bronze, the bells crashed forth. The roof of the sky caved in above Coimbra. Outside the people broke into a frantic shouting. The soldiers tossed their arms wildly to the sky, and hung suspended above frenzy by the name of the Cid.

Upon his altar the Apostle Santiago, held in his tapestry, looked at the Cid with eyes of envy. The King smiled down from the height of his pride, the Queen and the Princesses trod upon garlands of glory, and Don Sancho felt a tingling in his soles as if wings lifted him. Diego Laínez was all one lonely tear in that emotion. Outside, beside the church, Babieca nibbled the arches of flowers.

Burgos had never known more festal days than those of the homecomings of the Cid. Every return of the Campeador was a triumphal entrance into the city. The nobility, the clergy, and the people kept special attire for these entrances of the Cid. The echo of the bells of Coimbra had not yet died away when the bells of Burgos began to beat the air. During this time of his life Rodrigo traversed Spain on paths of bells. He rode upon the bells of all the Christian cities, and the bells galloped behind him to the rhythm of his retinue.

He was the man of triumph. Triumph went tied to his saddle-bow, linked with him in some mysterious fashion. I do not know why; in presence of the fact there is nothing to do but bow the head. As in a pack of cards there is one ace of trumps, so is the habit of life; suddenly there emerges a man who is life's ace of trumps.

The Cid was no military genius like Hannibal, like Caesar, or like Napoleon. It was something else. Nor had he a military talent like Scipio, like Turenne, or like Wellington. It was something else. He was more, and he was less, I am wrong; he was more. Talent can rout genius—witness the case of Scipio and Hannibal, of Wellington and Napoleon.

Look at the Cid in battle. He was more than genius or than talent. He was a man of electricity. Genius may fail of inspiration, talent may fail in calculation, but the electric man does not fail in current. Higher than the inspiration of genius and a nicety of calculation is the discharge of a high potency, the current of irresistible voltage which a man can make pass from one pole of his army to the other. That was the Cid.

He was a fury of body and brawn and biceps. He was faith, ardour transfigured by faith, the unconsciousness of faith, the madness of faith which multiplies strength and knows no possible barrier. Wherever he passed there sprang behind his footprints mystic signs. I put it to the wisest to reveal the mystery, to solve the problem.

The truth is that the problem has no solution. He regarded himself, he contemplated his work, and he saw himself escape from all laws and enter into that region of the imponderable where things cannot be reduced to logic. So he was, and that was all about it.

Without a doubt the quality of the nerves, the blood, the bone and muscle of the Cid was superior to that of the men we know today. A perfect functioning of all his organs in an absolute equilibrium assured him that marvellous health which enabled him to concentrate in himself matchless energy and strength. His stomach, his bowels, his kidneys and his spleen, superbly endowed, permitted him to consume ten times more fuel than ten individuals of our time. He ate magnificently, with an appetite of quintessential gastric juices. His amazing digestion enabled him to transform into power all that was caught in his machinery, to extract from his food the oxygen, the phosphates, the carbon, the salts, the nitrogen and the arsenates in the perfect proportions necessary to create a human prodigy.

That was one thing about the Campeador, but it does not suffice to explain the whole man. There was, besides, his high voltage. His body was a stupendous factory which manufactured the imponderable. It was a factory which created the supernatural out of the natural, which created excess out of proportion. He broke with all logic by force of logic, because all this factory worked in the service of an exaltation such as has nowhere else been seen, and this exaltation made him sublime and made him illogical—so illogical that many think they see in his deeds nothing but the inventions and the exaggerations of childish minds. But all the deeds of the Cid were real, and assuredly we know but few among all those that he did. So it is, even though reason be offended.

It was not logical that the Cid should fight one against seven and that he should win. But so it was. It was not logical that he, at the head of a handful of semi-barbarous soldiers, should triumph over great armies of Arabs, cultured, brave, proud, and convinced of their own superiority; for these men who had founded in Europe a great empire, a civilisation higher than any in Europe at that time, held the Spaniards in an Olympian contempt—the same contempt in which the Spaniards of today may hold the Moors. It was not logical that the Cid should conquer against superior numbers, superior armament, and superior civilisation; but so it was. He conquered.

The reason was that the Cid rose out of the category of men and entered the category of the elements. The Cid was not a man. He was the wind, the sea, the tempest, the hurricane. The Cid was faith. One moment of doubt, and the Cid was finished, undone, crumbled to dust. But the hurricane does not doubt; it blows and obliterates. An earthquake does not doubt; it shakes, it uproots, it overthrows.

In the category of the elements was the Cid, but he did not cease on that account to be a man; he was a very human element. There was nothing in him of the warrior of Myth; he was no Siegfried. His sword had not been forged in a cave of the gnomes, or on the anvil of the gods of the mountains. He did not draw his strength from the wizards of the forest, nor had he plumbed the mysteries of the depths of earth, nor had he bathed in the blood of a dragon.

The Cid Campeador was a man who wept and suffered. He was a vulnerable element, a hurricane which was wounded and bled, but was not dismayed. He wept when life separated him from Jimena, he wept when a thankless King sent him into exile; he wept like any other man, salt tears from a man's eyes. He bled when an enemy spear or arrow pierced his flesh; he bled like any other man, red blood from a man's wounds.

But the people, under the impulse of that mystical necessity of all peoples, would persist in making a god of him. For peoples are essentially idolators, and it pleases them to make a Neptune out of the sea and an Æolus out of the winds. To enemies and friends alike the Cid transcended the natural. The one made of him a god, and the others a devil. Nothing could have been finer than this child of the Devil climbing up out of Hell on a rope, hand over hand, and falling upon Spain in the darkness of the night. Nothing could have been more marvellous and more fascinating than this child of the Devil placed in the service of God.

The people of Castile adored their god. They had a god on earth to whom they could render homage, a god tangible and visible, and they surrendered themselves wholly to the pleasures of idolatry. This idolatry of the Cid extended even to his horse. Babieca was a demigod. Tongues clicked telling tall tales of Babieca, and hands which had been lucky enough to stroke her back in the evening could not bring themselves to wash in the morning.

It was not strange, then, that when the Cid rode into Burgos this time there were no eyes but for him, nor was it strange that all hearts were bells wild with joy and all bells were hearts wild with joy. All the city streamed in the wind in thousands of banners, and every balcony was a cluster of heads. A fever fell from the clouds, and rose from the earth in applauding hands like startled birds. Emotion swept the city in magnetic waves. Vocal chords leapt in frantic outbursts, and fascinated eyes watched the Cid ride by at the head of his troops like an image of God.

Like the Red Sea before the miracle, the people parted before the horses with ears adorned with coloured ribbons. The bustle of folk and oriflammes blazed up in a mystic fire. The girls on the balconies would have torn out their eyes to cast them beneath the feet of the Campeador, were it not that if they tore them out they would not be able to see him. All were blushing like brides, as if all had a secret tie which united them to the idol, as if all felt themselves parties to his triumph. Whole groups went down on their knees as if adoring the company of glory. Others fell in behind the procession carrying crowns on the points of their spears. Four youths bore on their shoulders a kind of shrine, with an image of the Cid roughly carved in wood; and Babieca, too, in popular, rudimentary effigy, surveyed the world, superb in her magnificence. Some of the heart, some of the soul, of all Burgos gone mad was blown into the air on the blasts of the trumpets.

Night fell, and the multitude dispersed to their homes, but they had left the best of themselves behind them in the streets. In the Royal palace there was spread a feast for Legend, in a setting of state worthy of Chronicle and Song. A rustle of palms floated over History. The night, plunged in Lyric, seemed an embodiment of laurels and caresses. All the girls of the Kingdom dreamed with Rodrigo.

BABIECA

Babieca was a demigod. There was once a Roman Emperor who built a temple to his horse and accorded it the honours of a senator. The horse of Caligula deserved no temple; but Babieca did. I demand that a temple be dedicated to Babieca—a temple of the open air, a temple of sky and sun, with plenty of oats and barley instead of floral tributes. To offer Babieca the honours of a senator, however, would be to dishonour her.

The horse of the Cid was a demigod. She was a mare of steel and elastic, of nerves strung taut as the strings of a lyre, with a tail stiff in its stubbornness and wide nostrils that beat like a heart as they sniffed the air. When Babieca whinnied the wind preened itself and blew gusts of Epic, Spain awakened more swiftly than a sleeping army at the beating of the drums, and Echo proudly carried her neighings from verse to verse.

For my part I confess that I would rather have the whinnying of Babieca than all the famous speeches I know, and I believe that they wrought more effect in Spain and had more influence upon her history than all the polished phrases of her orators. Babieca was the Demosthenes and the Cicero among horses. She was greater than the Greek and the Latin, because there was about her also something Homeric.

Babieca was a demigod, and she grazes on Olympus until the end of time. Such was the idolatry of Spain for this horse of Heaven that many mothers flocked to their priests asking whether they could give their children the name of Babieca. The priests, of course, had to refuse their request, pointing out that there was no Saint Babieca in the Calendar.

Babieca was a demigod and a prototype—a horse more horsey than has ever been known before or since. Her body was healthy, robust, and strong, a perfect rippling balance of nerve and muscle, with the superb, magnificent lines of a horse and not the least likeness to any other animal, or to a man or a woman. There was nothing of the hybrid about Babieca. She was the ultimate achievement of horseflesh—the horse typical, pure-blooded, deep-lunged, strong-shouldered, firm-quartered—a creature impetuous, full of passion, charged with dynamic power.

Imagine the Cid transformed by some Muslim witch into a horse, and you have Babieca. Imagine Babieca transformed into a man, and you have the Cid. From that sprang the understanding of these two beings one of the other. Each was a part of the other, and they loved with each other's passion; Babieca loved the Cid with the love of a man, and the Cid loved Babieca with the love of a horse. They were inseparable. The principle of the universality of energy was synthesised in them both.

Babieca with the Cid upon her back forgot the world and its vanities and its oats, and neighed like a trumpet of heroism. She pawed the ground, taut and tense, with her flanks contracted in readiness for action. She felt beneath her hoofs the granite of the pedestal, and the pen of the poet stroked her sides. Square-set on her four hoofs, she seethed with decisive energy, but she controlled her nerves with the patience of a saint. Nothing disturbed the harmony of her being. This magnificent Arab steed, convert to Christianity, was the summary of the secret forces of Nature, of the blind laws of physics. Her body was a temple—the temple of her race; and it held within it more soldiers than the horse of Troy. She alone was worth a host.

Babieca, it matters nothing that you have neither temple nor the honours of a senator. You may laugh at Caligula. You are your own temple, and here you have its picture, painted with all my love and admiration. You know that this picture means more than the honours of a parliament. You, Babieca, would inspire any poet to soar higher than Pegasus. Babieca hears me and stamps her hoof. She is pleased with me. I thank you, Babieca.

There, on the topmost arch of Story, Babieca stamps, rears on her hind legs to nibble a star, lifts her tail and breaks wind over History, pours forth a stream of golden verse, and bounds away at a gallop to the other end of the world, shaking from her shining saddle-bow a stream of rubies for her idolators.

LOVE ON THE CROSS

It was a month since the King had transferred his Court to Zamora. The Queen and the Princesses also were well pleased to stay from time to time in that loyal and lovely city. Many of the nobles were accustomed to accompany them and lodge there too. The Cid had a great house at Zamora, and, although he would have wished to withdraw himself for a season to his parents' home at Vivar, the King had bidden him adorn the Court with his presence.

Zamora was pleasing to the Cid. The historic city held for him many memories. There was a savour of heroism in its sky, to which so many spears had been raised, and its square stone houses, firm based on their foundations, seemed like Royal Octavo bindings awaiting some future poem. The Cid felt himself at home in Zamora.

One day the King had summoned him to Court to discuss with the great lords the affairs of his Kingdom. Not a few were the complexities which still troubled the King, surrounded, in spite of his conquests, by so many little states. The Campeador was at the palace when messengers presented themselves from the five Moorish Kings, conquered in his first campaign, who recognised themselves as his tributaries.

'Sidi,' said the messengers, bowing low before the Cid, 'the Kings your vassals have sent us to pay the tribute due to you. Besides that which is your right, in token of good friendship we bring you also twenty horses white as ermine, and twenty furs of spotted minever, thirty ruddy and as many sorrel, all with the pelts sewn in gold and silver thread. For your lady, Doña Jimena, we bring two precious rubies and jewelled headdresses, and for the attiring of your gentlemen two coffers of rich silks.'

'My friends,' answered the Campeador, smiling his thanks, 'you bear your message to the wrong address, for in the presence of King Fernando I am no man's lord. All is his, and nothing is mine, since I am his most humble vassal.'

Well pleased with the modesty of the Cid, the King addressed the messengers: 'Tell your masters that, though their lord may not be the King, here he stands in the King's stead. All that I possess was won for me by Rodrigo Díaz de Vivar, and I am well content to have so good a vassal. Tell them that all the presents they have sent him are his by my command, and so shall it ever be.'

Rodrigo thanked the King Fernando, and withdrew to speed the messengers of the Moorish Kings with presents of equal worth for their masters. For the Cid was no man to accept a compliment without returning it, even though it should come from those more powerful than himself, even though he must strain his resources to repay it. The Campeador held himself on an equal footing with the highest, and he had no love for being in any man's debt. He was a very great gentleman.

The Cid was no lover of the quiet of the city, nor could he rest tranquil at the Court. The King, well knowing his tastes, knew well, too, how to turn them to account. For three months he had kept the Cid busy in studying the fields, the roads, and the mountains towards Valencia—Valencia the coveted. Towards that city turned the eyes of every man who held something of power in the peninsula. It attracted the eager eyes of all those who desired to be the first to attain it. But the enterprise was arduous, for Valencia was held in strength by the flower of the Moors, and its defences by land and sea were accounted impregnable.

That was no matter. The Cid came back to Castile, and already he carried in his brain and biceps his plans of conquest. He came back at evening at walking pace, dreaming and whistling. This task had been a stroll, the quiet, unostentatious stroll of an owner who takes a walk to survey his lands. And how the Cid loved to survey the lands of Spain—to let his soul pasture in her valleys and frolic on her mountains, to let his eyes roam the beloved peninsula, to watch her skies, to drink her waters, to breathe her forests and her fields! In the soul of the Cid grew all the flowers of Spain, and he felt that savour of his own soul rise to his head.

His eyes, ardent and innocent, surveyed the world drunken with the delight of simple things, and as they roamed he thought. He thought of his plans, he thought of Jimena; and he whistled over his thoughts. Babieca paced enchanted by that whistling of her master. She had a wild desire to be able to whistle too, and make a duet of that pastoral of his. Jimena had forgiven him, and, although discretion would not yet let him visit her as before, the day was approaching when his dreams would come true.

This quiet, peaceful return to Burgos, with no hubbub of triumph, though his soul was full of it, was in accord with his mood. He savoured the calm of the moment with deep content. Away in the distance he could see the city, where none yet knew that the Cid was on his way back from a long secret mission.

Labourers working in the fields doffed their caps as he passed, and blessed Heaven that had allowed them to see him on his way.

But hardly had he reached Burgos when news met him which pierced his heart. His parents were dead. Blessing his name they had sped from the glory of this world to the next, one following the other, within the space of two weeks. Arias Gonzalo broke the news to him. Pain transfixed him like a spear, and he grew deathly pale. He fell into the arms of his uncle weeping like a child.

Through his own tears the King bade him bury his parents in the Abbey of San Pedro de Cardeña, the city which he had given him in fief as the reward of his victories against the enemies of Castile. The King wept, and Burgos wept, and all Spain wept, Romance itself wept with them; but through all tears were heard the sobs of Vivar. Thither went the Cid, as soon as his duty to the King was accomplished. Like a second father, the King embraced him, and Rodrigo betook himself to his ancestral home to shut himself in his grief within those walls of memory.

There he was closer to them; there he could breathe the air which they had breathed for the last time. There he could see the stern figure of that dearly loved old man sitting in his chair, amidst his trophies and his arms, looking at his son with pride. There he could see the sweet figure of his mother busy about the vessels and the fruits on the table.

Diego Laínez and Teresa Álvarez were in every corner of Vivar and of the soul of their son. They had come into the world to give birth to Epic, and they would live for ever in all its deeds, hover above all its feats, be celebrated in all its songs. Diego Laínez and Teresa Álvarez slept the sleep eternal beneath the stone of Romance, the stone carved by their son. The Cid wept upon that stone. He wept as no man has ever wept, and as I alone have seen him.

Locked away behind his grief lived the Cid. That warrior soul of his felt itself shrouded in a cloak of dear memories, and he let himself be borne away on the tide of his sentiment. The days were calm at Vivar.

Jimena was moved at length to visit him. She had never ceased to love him, if she would, and she knew that at the last their lives were linked. She had come to realise that for the slaying of her godfather the Campeador was not at fault. Honour had compelled him, and he had done no more than avenge an insult. She knew that he had not sought to harm their love, and that he would have given his life could the man who insulted his father have been some other than Lozano. And besides, how could she master that heart which at every beat bade her go and comfort him who now suffered as she had suffered, and with more cause, since he had lost his true parents?

Rodrigo awaited her with his soul hanging bare upon the Cross. Into that soul, that soul which was a gulf of sadness, she came like a ship bearing a breath of blue horizons. She poured upon his wounds the sovereign balsam of her eyes. He felt himself live again beneath her hands in which the dawn nestled. In all his nights, whether of melancholy or of anger and blood, he had never ceased to see her eyes, which held for him all the wonder of the world. Now she was there before him, she of those eyes which were made for poems, of that hair which set hands trembling with passion; but now he hid himself beneath it to weep.

A stream of stars of love, of stars without a name because they bore every name, was born in the sky of renewal. The love that made them one was tinted with the colour of that Destiny which had driven them asunder.

* * *

It was some days since a Moor had shown himself in the lands of Castile demanding the Cid and hurling challenge at him. He penetrated into Castile, insulted the Campeador, and returned to his own lands. This Moor Abdala was a brave man, a great horseman and a great warrior, skilled as few in the usage of arms. He had been born under special astrological signs, and the wise men of his race saw in him a future Almanzor. So the stars had told the world, so it was written in great letters of the Zodiac.

The challenges and insults of Abdala came to the ears of the Cid. The idle impudence of the young Moor angered him, the affront shook him out of his grief, and he leapt from his chair of thought into the saddle, resolved to punish his presumption.

Through the valley of the Estacas the Cid rode upon Babieca, mailed and with spear in hand. Leaving the town of Constantina upon his left, he went his solitary way under the evening, fearless of ambush or of the beasts which lurked in the thickets of the woods and came forth at this hour to roam in search of prey. These, he knew, were the haunts of the proud Moor Abdala, whence he launched insults upon the wind, secure in that almost superstitious terror which his unequalled boldness inspired among the men of Castile. They thought they saw in him a species of demon evoked by some Eastern spell to avenge Mohammed and restore his kingdom.

Abdala dreamed that by conquering the Cid he would in one day acquire greater glory than all the Moorish Kings in ten years of warfare. In one bound, thought that ambitious man, he would spring to be the undisputed leader of his race; and once he was chief absolute he would put the Christians in their place. The Cid had heard of him, and sensed him to be a man capable of great things, a boaster, but a warrior worthy of his steel. That was why he rode in search of Abdala.

The sun struck full upon his armoured breast as he came to the summit of a hill. How the Cid blazed, shining across the world in the Paradise of his own element of arms! He dismounted and set himself to wait between two rocks, whence he could command all the valley. He had not waited long when he saw the Moor Abdala coming across the plain, richly clad and heavily armed. The Cid let him approach until he was within the carry of a voice; then he issued from the rocks, shouting: 'Await me there, Moor Abdala; stand, if you would not show yourself a coward.'

'Long have I awaited this day, good Cid,' replied the Moor, raising his head at the shout and watching the Cid ride full speed down the hill. 'Have no fear that I shall flee. There is no man born of woman before whom I hide myself. Only the coward flees, and I was born a warrior.'

The Cid drew up before him. 'Self-praise will serve you little, Moor Abdala, if your right arm will not serve you truly. If you are what you claim, the hour has come to use your valour and your strength.'

'At your service, good Cid; I am ready.'

They charged upon each other, and the spears met, measured and matched. The Cid smiled. Here was a good adversary; his man was bold and steady. The combat was worthwhile. The Cid smiled. Then he bit off the smile, swallowed it in one mouthful, set spurs to his horse, gripped his spear, and charged as if shot from a catapult. The spear burst the breast of the Moor and flung him through the air, and Abdala smashed upon the ground like a blinded bird. The Zodiac flew into pieces, the constellations rained down in bits, and all astrology's stock-in-trade was smashed to smithereens. The Cid dismounted, approached his enemy, and, under the sun which already dyed the evening blood-red, cut off his head with great politeness.

DON SANCHO

The King Fernando was very ill, and he felt death advancing upon him with stealthy tread. Today, as yesterday, the graveyard clock had gone forward a little. To his bedside, where all the Royal Family kept vigil in their grief, the King summoned the Cid and commended his children to him.

'Rodrigo,' said the King, with trembling voice, 'you are only twenty-four years old; but one year of yours is worth five of another, and so it is of you I think to watch over my children and over Castile. I have more confidence in your arm and in your brain than in those of any man of more years than you. Give me your promise, and I shall die content.'

'Sire,' answered the Cid, 'I am a man of Castile, and I swear to you that the King of Castile shall always be my King. I will watch over all your children, and I will do what I may that no ill should touch them.'

'I thank you, Rodrigo. I will carry your promise to Heaven and pray God to aid you.'

The King felt himself near death, and he bade them set a hair-shirt upon him, clothe him in a monk's habit, and bear him to the church. So the sad company set out from the Royal palace, with the King lying in a litter, the centre of Abbots and psalms. At the head of the procession the Cross was carried by his own son, the bastard Don Fernando, Cardinal of Castile, Archbishop of Toledo, and Lord of Santiago. The Royal Family and the nobility followed. Jimena walked with the Princesses. Behind them came Arias Gonzalo, the Cid, the Count Per Ansúrez, Álvar Fáñez, the Count García Ordóñez, Martín Antolínez, Per Vermúdez, Muño Gustioz, Galín García and many others. The minor lords and knights, and finally the people, brought up the rear.

Softly in the sky the bells wept for their King, and on earth the people wept softly for their King. Laid on a bed of ashes before the altar, the King took off his crown, and they set it at the foot of the Crucifix. With a taper in his hand, he heard the Mass and communicated. Lower and lower his voice sank as he made the responses. Death psalms filled the air with death, and the last sigh of the King rose up to God amid the hymns, so that none would have known that he was dead had not the taper fallen from his hands out of the other world.

The King is dead! Long live the King!

Unhappily the classic cry could not be raised on the death of Fernando the Great. At the end of his life the King had made a grave mistake of policy. He left his Kingdom divided among his sons—that Kingdom created with so many pains, so many wars, which drew its strength from unity, and, once separated, must lose its power. It was the unity of Castile, León, and Galicia which had given the Kingdom such strength that it could overawe the Kingdoms of Navarre and of Aragón, and subdue them to a kind of vassalage and tutelage. It was unity which had enabled it to extend its boundaries and penetrate the Moorish Kingdoms, which had no choice but to yield to its power and influence. Once that unity was broken rebellion might rise its head and the way was open to ambition.

King Fernando left his Kingdom divided among his children—to Sancho he left Castile, to Alfonso León, and to García Galicia. Doña Urraca inherited the lordship of Zamora, and Doña Elvira the lordship of Toro. The King is dead! Long live the Kings! But it is no easy matter for several Kings to live together on the fragments of a single Kingdom. And so the cry 'Long live the Kings!' was changed first into 'Death to the Kings!' and then inevitably into 'Long live the King!' Long live one King!

Such at least was the mind of Don Sancho, who, as the eldest, held himself defrauded by the partition of the Kingdom of his father among his brothers. He understood, besides, that only in unity could there be strength enough to give the Royal power real weight and to impose respect for it at all times; and that only so could there be realised that great dream which was the natural dream of his House—the reconquest of Spain, the union of the Spanish nation. With the Kingdom broken into three toy kingships Spanish dominion was set back a hundred years. Only in one hand was it a force that could make itself felt.

Nothing is so hard to surrender as a dream. A reality one can sometimes abandon; but a dream converts itself into an endless longing, an implacable obsession which grapples to our soul and masters our whole being; and there is no means of ridding oneself of it. Three great black clouds of tempest had formed in the Iberian sky.

Don Sancho II the Strong was a man stout of heart, restless and ambitious, but in his depths a man profoundly logical. When he ascended the throne of Castile in 1065 he found himself faced with the problem created by the death of his father: the recovery of the other Kingdoms and lordships shorn from his crown. Castile was the smallest portion, and if his brothers should unite against him it would go hard with him. So it was not enough for him to be a good warrior: he must show himself also a clever diplomat.

One of his first actions was to appoint the Cid commander of all his forces. Let us not forget in what admiration the new King Don Sancho held the Cid, let us not forget that the new monarch had been the comrade-in-arms of the Campeador, who had saved his life in those boyhood days when his name was but Rodrigo; for that day of the famous hunting of the boar Ruy Díaz de Vivar was not yet the Cid Campeador.

The King Don Sancho saw Spain as the bulwark of Christendom in Europe, and he held it necessary, cost what it might, to restore the unity of that Kingdom over which his father had reigned and which he should never have divided. But more than a year had he to wait before occasion came for him to seek the realisation of his hopes. He waited with what patience he could, silent and surly.

Then Don García offered him the desired pretext for intervening in his affairs. Don García, youngest of the three, but most belligerent of all, Don García, King of Galicia, decided one fine day to invade the dominions of his sister, Doña Urraca. All of a sudden he wrested from her the half of her lordship of Zamora. Don Sancho seized the pretext. His brother, so he deemed, had violated their father's will; and he resolved to attack him.

To this end he summoned the Cortes and announced his plans to all the great lords of the Kingdom assembled about him. The Count García Ordóñez openly opposed the will of the King. 'You have no right, Don Sancho,' he declared, 'to forget the will of your father. Your duty as a son compels you to respect it.'

'And my duty as a monarch?' retorted the King angrily. 'You forget, Count, that love of country comes before all else.' He seized the arm of the Cid.

'And you, Ruy Díaz, what do you think? Speak, give me your counsel.'

'Sire,' answered the Cid, 'to me it does not seem good counsel that you should go against the will of your father. You know that your father divided his Kingdom among you, and that on his death-bed he made me swear that I should advise his sons as best I might, and never give them bad counsel. And while I can do so, so I will.'

'Then you all desert me?' said the King bitterly.

'I do not desert you,' answered the Cid. 'I tell you what I think. It is for you to do what you will, and I shall be ever at your side.'

'And you, Álvar Fáñez,' asked the King, 'have you nothing to say?'

'Sire, you are the King, and it is for you to command.'

'I tell you,' said the King, 'that Don Alfonso and Don García make alliance against me, and that if I do not fall upon them suddenly, they will fall upon me when I am unready.'

'King Don Sancho,' asked the Cid, 'are you sure of what you say?'

'Yes, I am sure; for from sources sure it has come to my ears that Don Alfonso has made alliance with his cousins of Aragón and Navarre, and not alone with Christians, but also with the Moors of Córdoba and Toledo. Having made these alliances, he now seeks the friendship of Don García. Our lesson should begin with Don García.'

'Against whom are these alliances directed?' inquired García Ordóñez.

'That is easy to divine. They are not directed against the infidels, since these are included in them. They are not directed against Don García, for his alliance is sought too. There remains Castile, whose friendship none of them has sought.'

'God enlighten you,' said the Cid, 'and may He work upon your conscience. If you judge that Don García gives you cause to intervene, and that thereby you may begin to realise your hopes, God guide you, if your plans are good. I have but one counsel left to give you: if you would attack Don García, seek permission from Don Alfonso to cross the territory of León. Let us not have to deal with two enemies at one stroke.'

'Well spoken, Ruy Díaz. This I will do, and more. You, Álvar Fáñez, go and treat with Don García that he may surrender me his Kingdom willingly, and not compel me to make war upon him.'

'King Don Sancho, at your orders,' replied Álvar Fáñez.

'Gentlemen,' ended the King, 'you know my will. Let those who are with me follow my banner; and let the others do what seems good to them.' The King raised the session. Sadly the Cid remained behind, and silently the Count García Ordóñez went his way.

A Prince bold and impetuous was Don García, and it needs no saying that he refused the demands of his brother and committed himself to war. The first and second of those three clouds which we saw forming in the Iberian sky, swollen now to bursting point, crashed and broke in a thunderstorm of rolling dice.

Less bellicose than his two brothers, but more astute in politics, Don Alfonso of León freely gave Don Sancho passage through his territory. What could he ask better than that his brothers should weaken themselves fighting against each other? He kept no very strict ward upon his neutrality, nor did he withdraw his offer of friendship to Don García; but he made no move to take part in the struggle, or to forbid either way-leave through his lands.

In the first battle Don Sancho defeated Don García. Don García and his army retired, but they did not yield. Instead they offered battle again to Don Sancho, routed his troops, and took him prisoner. The men of Castile were in flight and Don Sancho captive. In vain he offered rich presents to the seven knights who guarded him that they should let him free. His offers and his entreaties were alike rejected. Hopelessly the King followed his captors. Then suddenly he saw the men of Galicia crowding towards one side of the valley and battling there.

A few moments later Álvar Fáñez dashed up with two knights. Spear in hand, they flung themselves upon Don Sancho's guards and unhorsed them.

'Quick, follow me,' Álvar Fáñez shouted to the King; 'the Cid has sent me to you. Let us hasten to his aid. The Cid has stolen a march and gives battle to Don García.'

'How many men has he?' asked the King.

'Three hundred only, but the best of his men.'

'Courage, then, gentlemen!' cried Don Sancho; 'and all speed into the fight; if the Cid has surprised them, then the day is ours.'

Swinging his flashing two-handed sword, the Cid plunged into the troops of Galicia and turned rout into triumph. With his own hands he took Don García prisoner. Don Sancho put fetters upon his brother and set him captive in the Castle of the Moon—a castle with a name well chosen, of white nights, propitious for dreams; a castle meet for the wandering minds of prisoners. Don García was to have moonlight until the day he died...

Victor over the King of Galicia, Don Sancho turned upon his other brother and sent to him to demand his Kingdom. 'Alfonso of León,' so ran the letter of Castile, 'the interests of the Kingdom call for a single crown; therefore let us settle this matter in fair fight, face to face in the open field. God will decide the issue and give judgment.'

The two brothers were of one mind, and battle was joined at Llantada. There the Cid turned the balance of the bloody struggle in favour of Don Sancho, but with the issue undecided the men of León held themselves ready for another reckoning, and during the night aid came to them from the conquered of Galicia to swell their host. Recoiling from rashness, the Cid persuaded the King of Castile that prudence counselled him to leave the field in triumph and bide his time, rather than risk the danger of defeat.

So Don Alfonso kept his Kingdom of León, and for a space the two brothers ruled side by side in peace. But Don Sancho did not so easily abandon his design, and finally he proposed to Don Alfonso another battle on the same terms as before. Confident of victory, Don Alfonso was nothing loath to accept Don Sancho's challenge. The two armies met on the frontier of Castile and León, outside the town of Golpejares. Here Don Sancho, headstrong in his folly, divided his army, and sent the Cid with his famous three hundred to cut off the allies of Alfonso. That folly cost him the battle.

The Cid came back to find his comrades in rout, with their camp abandoned in the hands of the men of León, and his King once again a prisoner. Fighting as best he could, attacking here, retreating there, in vain he tried to stem the flight of the fugitives. Don Alfonso and the Count Per Ansúrez, scanning the battlefield, rested upon their laurels. Far in the rear thirteen knights escorted Don Sancho into captivity.

Suddenly, like a vision, there appeared before them the Cid. His spear was shattered and his armour split. 'Gentlemen, release my King!' roared the Cid.

'We take no orders here but from Don Alfonso,' replied the escort. 'Go get his orders and we will release the prisoner.'

'Give me a spear, if you are men; among knights there is no order like a spear.'

The thirteen horsemen took counsel together and gave him a spear. So chivalry demanded, and in those days chivalry was law. The Cid flung himself upon them. Wielding his spear, manoeuvring his horse, he killed some and wounded others, strewing them on the ground until only one remained in his saddle, and he so tired that he surrendered. 'Take this and buy yourself sweets,' said the Cid, and tossed him a penny.

The King was free. He flung his arms around the neck of his deliverer. 'I thought you had deserted me,' he exclaimed.

'I never desert anyone.'

Back they rode at full gallop to join their men. Reunited to his nobles in the shelter of an oak grove, Don Sancho sank down disheartened on a fallen trunk, with his head between his hands, staring in front of him into the night. The heavy silence of disaster choked all throats. A frog croaked in a pond, and bit his tongue when he thought to catch a star. The fugitive King broke the silence. 'We have lost. What is to be done?'

'I warned you that it was not wisdom to divide the troops,' answered the Cid; 'my men have hardly fought at all.'

'I have paid dearly for not heeding your counsel. But now what is to be done?'

'First rally the fugitives, hearten the dispirited, and restore the army. My men of Vivar are intact, and eager to spill their souls for you and yours. King Alfonso thinks the battle won, and has withdrawn to Carrión, where his men are celebrating their victory. Until tomorrow they will not seek to invade Castile. Therefore let us take them by surprise at dawn, and triumph will yet be ours.'

So they did. Martín Antolínez, Per Vermúdez, Diego Ordóñez and Álvar Fáñez hastened to round up the troops. The Cid and Muño Gustioz set forth to survey the field. When all was ready the host of moonlit phantoms began its march. In Carrión the men of León held high revel. All night long they made very merry, drinking and dancing with the women of the town by the light of bonfires.

Holding its breath, the column of the Cid approached in secret. There came to it the sound of guitars, of tabors and bassoons—a sound of good augury. In the countryside all was silence, and night walked stealthy as a cat. It was a silence to affrighten anyone, and if in the camp of Don Alfonso there had been any but some sleeping, some drunken, and some dancing, one would surely have given the alarm—the alarm of stillness, of that stillness in which it seems that all Nature has frozen into an iceberg.

With the hose of silence drawn over their boots, the men of Castile advanced. Orders passed secretly from mouth to mouth behind crooked hands. They came to the hardest part of their march—the crossing of the River Cea. The Cid sought out the point where the stream might best be forded, and the foot-soldiers crossed clinging to the cruppers of the horsemen. Once on the other bank they followed the Cid, who led them by short cuts and through thickets. Carrión rose before them less than half a league away, high up on its hill. They left the horses in the care of a few men and went on, taking cover in the copses. The Cid strode ahead, leading the way. They climbed the hill on all fours, noiselessly. Castile scaled the night on foxes' feet.

Carrión danced and drank and slept to the tune of rounds of triumph. Carrión in its gaiety was very far from the enemy, an island of innocence set distant in the seas. In the council hall the King Don Alfonso debated with his knights and captains what should be done on the morrow.

The morrow was breaking through the windows of the sky when a frightful clamour rent the air. Like buds bursting out of the ground the men of Castile fell upon the place, flung themselves upon their startled enemies, and hewed them in pieces where they surprised them, without truce or quarter. 'Don Sancho! For Don Sancho!' a voice of blood went shouting. Don Alfonso and his lieutenants sprang to their feet as one man at the tumult, and laid hands upon their swords. There was no time. Doors and windows splintered into the air in a thousand pieces, and an avalanche of men yelling 'For Don Sancho!' burst into the room and struck their blades out of their hands.

Like a flash Don Alfonso glided among his men, and behind their shelter he was making his way to the door when a hand touched him on the shoulder, and a voice respectful but masterful fell upon his ears. 'There is no way out, Don Alfonso. I take you prisoner in the name of Don Sancho.'

The King turned his head and found himself face to face with the Cid. 'Let me go free, Ruy Díaz,' said Alfonso, 'and I will give you what you ask of me.'

'Ruy Díaz buys from none,' answered the Cid, 'and Ruy Díaz is not for sale.'

Breaking his way through the midst of the tumult, with his sword dripping blood, appeared Don Sancho, mad with fury. At the sight of his brother he hurled himself upon him with uplifted sword. The Cid seized the sword-hand, and his arm of steel held it rigid in the air. 'Let me at him,' foamed Don Sancho.

'He is my prisoner.'

'I buy him from you, Ruy Díaz. Ask me what you will.'

'Ruy Díaz is not for sale. Ruy Díaz sells to none.'

'I will give you for him…'

'Tomorrow you will give me thanks that I would not yield him to you.'

'I am your King.'

'You would not be if I had not twice set you free.'

'That is as may be. I am your King. Yield him to me. I command you.'

'I am against my King for my King. I would have no fratricide for my King.'

'Rodrigo, you have won this battle, you have given me back my crown. Do you not realise the danger that my brother means? You do not know it. Would you have me to be a fool?'

'I would have you be generous.'

'You make yourself responsible for him. Perhaps you are right.'

'Sire, victory has its duties. Don Alfonso is my prisoner. You may dispose of his person, but not of his life.'

'If he is your prisoner,' replied Don Sancho, 'let fetters be put upon him, and let him be cast into prison.' So it was done. The Cid had saved him from death, but not from captivity. Upon that point the violent Don Sancho would budge no inch.

With Don García and Don Alfonso imprisoned, no King remained but Don Sancho. Hearing of the fate of her brother Alfonso, who was very dear to her, the Princess Doña Urraca came from Zamora to plead with Don Sancho for him. To her petition was joined that of the Count Per Ansúrez, who had been tutor to Don Alfonso in his youth and was his chief counsellor in the Kingdom of León.

'Sire,' said the Princess to Don Sancho, 'Don Alfonso is no danger to you. In the name of our father, let him go free.'

'Our father, when he divided his Kingdom into three, made a grave mistake,' replied Don Sancho. 'A great Kingdom demands one King alone.'
'Don Alfonso will cede you his rights,' Per Ansúrez broke in; 'Castile will be great, and none will dispute your sceptre. Let him go free.'

'Free?' exclaimed the King. 'Never!'

'He will go into a monastery and become a monk,' insisted Doña Urraca; 'I swear it to you in his name.' Faced with so much entreaty and such an affirmation, Don Sancho yielded, and gave his brother his liberty. He was taken under guard from the prison to the monastery. In the monastery of San Fagundo, Don Alfonso one morning took the habit of a monk. From the monastery of San Fagundo Don Alfonso fled one night, and sought refuge in Toledo under the protection of the Moorish King al-Mamun.

ZAMORA

Now there was no King but Don Sancho. But two quarterings were still missing before his banner was complete—Toro and Zamora. For the lordship of Toro he sent to ask his sister Doña Elvira, and she ceded it to him for the sake of peace. There remained Zamora, and in Zamora Doña Urraca, strong of head and heart as her fortress.

In Toledo, at the Court of al-Mamun, Don Alfonso lived under the Arab spell of the Princess Zaïda, daughter of the King of Seville. Perhaps his day would come. Meanwhile to kill the time he drank deep draughts of the heady potion of beloved eyes. In all the palace gardens, under the Toledan moon, nothing was heard but sighs of love: 'Dear God, if only Zaïda were a Christian!' 'Alas, if only Alfonso were a Moor!' But between sigh and sigh Don Alfonso remembered politics. He had venom in his marrow. Shaking his head clear of Muslim dreams, he wrote often to his sister Doña Urraca, who waited anxiously at Zamora. For she knew her Don Sancho, and she knew that his ambition did not sleep.

Don Sancho did not sigh; instead he roared. He thought of Zamora as a nest of conspirators, and besides he needed that strong place more than any other in Spain for the vantage of its ground and its natural defences. Don Sancho must have Zamora at any cost. The Cid counselled him that he should try first to get it willingly, though he knew Doña Urraca, and he found it hard to believe that she would surrender the city

With a great army and the best of his train the King set out for Zamora. Arrived before it, he rode around the city—the city beautiful, the fortress magnificent. He seemed to have within arm's reach the dream of a thousand nights. Stoutly built it was on the sheer rock, with rude walls and many towers, and, as if this were not enough, defended by the Duero, which ran at its feet—a strong place, impregnable, though all the armies in the world should lay siege to it.

'If my sister Urraca will give it me,' said Don Sancho to himself, 'I had rather have this city than any other in Spain.' He sat thoughtful in his tent, with his eyes still full of that vision of stone and towers soaring into the sky. Then he sent for the Cid, and when he came at his summons received him with affection and flattery.

'Rodrigo,' he said, 'I have made you head of all my household, first among the first. I have given you of my lands more than a county, the best of all Castile. In the name of the friendship which has united us since childhood, I ask you to go to Zamora and treat with my sister that she yield me the city freely and for exchange. Tell her that I will give her for it her choice between Medina de Rioseco, Villalpando, Valladolid and Tiedra with their lands. But tell her that if she will not yield it I will take it by force.'

'Sire, I will gladly do your mission. Many times have I stayed in Zamora with Doña Urraca in the house of Arias Gonzalo, who played the guardian to us both. An embassy of words I can accept, but if it comes to war I cannot unsheathe my sword against the Princess. I have sworn an oath, and I swear to you that this oath ties my hands. Please God that the Princess accept your demand.'

'I trust in you.'

'I would stake my soul upon it, if I could but avert such a war.'

On the entrance of the Cid into Zamora, Doña Urraca and that good veteran her adviser Arias Gonzalo, her loyal commander and chief of her household, received him with all honour and courtesy. But, seized of his embassy, the Princess protested through angry tears.

'Don Sancho, against the will of our father, has usurped the Kingdoms of Don García and Don Alfonso, and now he would wrench Zamora from me. He thinks that I am a woman, and that I can do naught against him. But sooner or later he will pay for his injustices. Let him not be forgetful of Heaven. Now see you, Arias Gonzalo, you who are my second father, it is as I have told you many times; Don Sancho is not to be trusted.'

'Lady,' replied Arias Gonzalo, 'I beg you in all honour not to lose heart. Summon your vassals and tell them the demands of the King. If they consent, surrender the city. If they choose to resist, let us die together in its defence as our duty as gentlemen demands.'

Her knights came at the summons of the Princess, and, when they had heard her, they swore one and all that they would die to the last man rather than yield the city. The Princess turned to the Cid. 'Go and tell my brother that I will die with the men of Zamora, and they with me, before we yield the city.'

And as the Cid went back with this answer to the camp of the King, he heard behind him the shouting of the vassals of Doña Urraca: 'Long live the Princess! Long live Zamora!' And at the bottom of his knightly heart beat golden bells in honour of all true knighthood. 'God of Heaven, so may it always be in my Spain!'

With eyes inflamed with fury, Don Sancho heard the reply of his sister. He could barely speak, he roared, with clenched lifts in the air, bursting with threats. 'If Zamora were the citadel of Hell itself, if it were guarded by flaming rocks and abysses of fire, still I would take it. Ah, that old traitor Arias Gonzalo! His head and those of his four sons shall sate my vengeance!'

'Arias Gonzalo is no traitor,' said the Cid; 'it is but his duty to serve the Princess. Would that all our servants served you as faithfully as Arias serves Doña Urraca!'

'You set yourself against me, Rodrigo,' bellowed Don Sancho. 'Is it not enough that you have refused to fight against Zamora? Would you sow disaffection in my ranks?'

'I have never spoken of deserting you. I will abide with you, I will stay in your ranks; but I will not fight against Zamora.'

'You have no need to stay. Don Diego Ordóñez de Lara shall be my lieutenant. What if you should dispirit my army? Maybe it was you who counselled those of Zamora that they should not yield me the city.'

'I do not answer such insults. I withdraw.'

'Begone, then. Begone, I say, Rodrigo; and were it not that my father left me his blessing for you, you should hang upon the instant. Begone; and within nine days from now take yourself out of my lands for a year of exile.'

Quietly the Cid withdrew, with head held so high that it shone in the heavens, but, before he went, 'You exile me for one year,' he said; 'I exile myself for four.'

On the evening of that very day the Cid struck his tents and marched with all his men to Castro Nuño, whence he planned to set out for Toledo. 'Friends,' said the Cid to his followers, 'in Toledo is Don Alfonso, and there perhaps we shall find much to do. To Toledo, then—forward for Toledo!'

They set out well content, for these tireless warriors saw more worth in fighting against the Moors than in wasting their time in a struggle whose purpose was not clear to them and for which they had little heart.

But when the counts and the great men of Don Sancho's army saw the soldiers of the Cid set out singing on their way, they went to the King much disturbed over what he had done, and begged him to recall the Cid.

'King Don Sancho,' they reasoned, 'it is not well that you should lose a vassal such as the Cid for no' good cause. Reflect that you are losing the first warrior of the world. Sire, send after him, and do not let him leave you whom you can ill afford to lose.'

Now that his first anger was past, the unjust King realised the folly of his action, and he sent Diego Ordóñez de Lara at the head of an embassy to bid the Cid return, promising that he would bear no malice and that he would give him another county of his lands and hold him always the first of the Royal household. Diego Ordóñez overtook the Cid at Castro Nuño when he was on the point of continuing his march towards Toledo. 'Honoured Cid,' he said, 'Our King has sent me to recall you.'

The Cid listened to the words of the King through the mouth of his ambassador. 'As for his offer of lands and honours,' he made answer, 'tell the King that I thank him, but that I will not accept them. As for his request that I should return to his side, tell him that I will first consult my vassals.' The Cid offered entertainment to Diego Ordóñez de Lara, whom he held in high esteem, and sent him back to the King with this proud reply. 'Tomorrow the King shall know the decision of my vassals.'

Such was the bitter pill of answer that Don Sancho had to swallow. It made him better understand his own excess and the worth of the man he had offended, who set himself now as high as the highest, and showed that he would yield only of his own free will. A master-stroke of policy was the Cid's decision to consult his vassals, for it made them feel how far he ranked them his associates in the most vital moments of his life. Placing his future in their own hands, he could give them no greater proof of his regard for them, nor bind them more closely to him for that future.

When it was learned that the vassals of the Cid had decided to return to the King's camp, there was great joy among the lords and the soldiers of Don Sancho. The King himself, with an escort of fifty men, rode out two leagues to meet the Cid upon his way. As they embraced again in token of reconciliation, all the men of Castile clapped their hands together. There was gladness in the air, hope upon the breeze, and a flight of swallows blessed the camp.

Don Sancho drew his lines close around Zamora, squeezing, squeezing like a serpent of steel; but within the place the soldiers of Doña Urraca were undismayed. 'Long live Zamora! Long live the Princess!' Arias Gonzalo and his sons were everywhere at once. They ranged around the battlements with the speed of an electric current. In their fighting fury they multiplied after a miraculous fashion. They were to be seen everywhere at the same time. On every tower there was an Arias. How, since the towers were more than twenty? It is a mystery; the Devil only knows how. But wherever the men of Castile opened a breach, there appeared the breast of an Arias.

'Long live the Princess! Long live Zamora!'

'Long live Castile! Long live Don Sancho!' War cries and arrows flew from camp to camp. The besiegers flung ladders up, and the besieged flung them down. Zamora was a nest of eagles in a cloud of stone. Castile was a serpent circling on the golden sand. The eaglets swooped, but the serpent pressed his ring ever tighter.

Already in Zamora food was running short, and it boded ill for the defenders. But, if there was little to eat, there were brave men, and hunger spurred their boldness. There were two eyes of fever which flashed from side to side, two eyes of madness and a voice which shouted to the wind: 'Goad me not too far, Don Sancho, or I will not answer for myself!' His comrades looked at him with concern. 'What ails you, Vellido Dolfos? What is amiss with you? Calm yourself.'

Vellido Dolfos did not even hear them. Some force was tugging him by the hair of his head. Like a man in a trance, he rode to the gate on his thoroughbred steed.' Open the gate for me, men of Zamora,' he cried, 'and I swear to you that victory shall be ours!' He shot out at full speed, and at full speed he crossed the camp of Castile and made for the spot where Don Sancho, sitting his horse, with his lieutenants on foot around him, surveyed the movements of his troops.

At the sight of the horseman coming at a gallop the soldiers made way for him, wondering what might be afoot. The King himself watched his approach in perplexity. He might be a fugitive, or perhaps an emissary. Vellido Dolfos had reckoned with the effect of his boldness, and he was quick to take advantage of it.

He rode up to the King. 'At your service, gentlemen!' he cried. 'For Doña Urraca!' and swift as lightning drove his dagger with all his force into the King, piercing him through breast and shoulder, swung his horse around, and sped back towards Zamora.

A sudden shouting brought the Cid out of his tent. He saw disorder in the camp and a rider who raced towards Zamora as if the Devil were after him. Sensing some ill, the Cid mounted his horse, forgetting in his haste both helm and spurs. As if he would kill his mare he pursued the horseman, but he could not overtake him. The gate of Zamora opened to receive the fugitive, and crashed shut again before the very nose of the Cid's horse. 'Luckless is the rider who rides without spurs!' he cried in baffled rage.

The Princess leaned over an embrasure of the battlements at the sight of the Cid beneath her walls. 'Begone, begone, Rodrigo, proud man of Castile!' she called in that voice of Romance, but forgetful of all harmony in her anger. 'What would you here? You should take shame to fight against a woman, and you should remember that, when my father made you knight in Coimbra, it was I who gave you your spurs.' Stricken by the stanza of the Princess, the Cid rode back silently to camp, with his heart full of the sense of failure and as if soiled by remorse, yet ignorant of what had befallen. The camp was in an uproar. Don Sancho had been mortally wounded. Vellido Dolfos had stricken him to death. 'He killed him by treachery!' yelled Diego Ordóñez de Lara. 'By treachery!' took up all the camp of Castile. 'Not by treachery, face to face!' shouted back the men of Zamora. 'By treachery!' 'Face to face!' 'He is a traitor!' 'He is a hero!' 'He has killed the King!' 'He has saved Zamora!' 'Traitor, traitor!' 'Hero, hero!' 'History will pass judgment on him!' 'Your history will be lies!' 'There will be a reckoning!' 'To the Devil with your reckoning!'

Upon his death-bed lay the King Don Sancho, soon to breathe his last sigh. Around the dying monarch the flower of Castile made a wreath of tears. 'It is God's will,' murmured the King, in a voice broken by hiccoughs of agony; 'perhaps I have done wrong. Count García Ordóñez, come hither. You who among my vassals were the best friend of Don Alfonso, tell him to forgive me, tell him that I thought to act for the good of Castile. And tell him that I recommend to him my Cid, that he may treat him well and take him as his vassal. And you, gentlemen, in my name tell...'

Death cut him short. The name was never known, that name which stumbled on the tongue of the dying man, which his lips were in the act of forming, and which perhaps his soul fled repeating in space like the song of a bird. The King was dead.

The Cid rose to his feet and cried in a voice which rang over the corpse and the code of chivalry: 'Let a knight offer himself before this day's ending to challenge Zamora and avenge the King!' No one answered. Before the eyes of all arose a vision of Arias Gonzalo, old but still brave as the bravest, strong as the strongest, and of his four sons, already almost as famed as their father. 'You know,' added the Cid, 'that I cannot fight against Zamora, for so have I sworn.'

Diego Ordóñez, kneeling at the feet of the King, stood up. 'Since the Cid has sworn an oath which he should not have taken, I will challenge Zamora. I am of the blood of Lara, son of the Count Don Ordoño, and cousin of our King through the Royal House of León. I left my lands to serve him, and to serve him I will lay down my life.'

'You are brave,' said the Cid, 'and you are strong. You will not lose your life. Gentlemen, here is a worthy champion of Castile, a champion in whose presence none will miss me.'

Diego Ordóñez de Lara rode out from the camp to Zamora, hurling insult and challenge at the city and all who dwelt therein. 'Men of Zamora, I hold you all for false traitors. I defy you all, I challenge you all to fight, your dead and your living, your ancestors and your unborn, the bread you eat and the water that you drink, all that is in Zamora and breathes its air!'

Arias Gonzalo answered from the nearest tower: 'You are out of your senses, Diego Ordóñez, with your challenge to our dead and our unborn, our bread and our water. It is enough for you to defy the living. I accept your challenge; and, since you have issued a general defiance, you must do battle with five, for such is the law of chivalry. I accept your challenge—I and my sons.'

* * *

The lists were set and the judges named, and Arias Gonzalo and his four sons armed themselves for the fray. The veteran sought to be the first to fight. He knew that Ordóñez de Lara was a rude warrior and a master of arms, and he would rather die himself than witness the death of his sons. He thought, besides, that since he was more expert in this mode of combat, he might weaken and wound Don Diego before his sons were called on to give battle.

But the Princess Doña Urraca, with hair disordered, clung round his neck. 'My father, my second father,' she sobbed, 'I beg you not to take the field. You are old and weary, and if you are killed I shall be left alone in the world at this the hardest moment of my life.'

'Let me go, Lady; they have defied me and called me traitor.'

'Your sons will wipe out the affront. Come you here, Gonzalo, Diego, Pedro, Rodrigo. Do not suffer your father to go out to fight before yourselves. That would be for you worse than an insult.'

'Lady, they called me traitor.'

'We will avenge you, Father; and if we all are killed, then let you take the field.'

The other knights took the part of the Princess. All of them besought him not to be the first to sally forth. Arias Gonzalo felt himself tried more sorely than was one man's due, but to such entreaties he could do no other than yield. He called the eldest of his sons: 'Gonzalo Arias, take the field and avenge Zamora.' The Princess Doña Urraca embraced the old man in tears. 'I tremble for them,' she said; 'this Diego Ordóñez de Lara is a wild beast.'

'And I envy them,' answered the good Arias Gonzalo.

Gonzalo Arias, son of Arias Gonzalo, died at the hands of Lara. The old man called the second of his sons: 'Diego Arias, take the field and avenge Zamora.' And as the second breathed his last upon the grass, the old man called the third of his sons: 'Pedro Arias, take the field and avenge Zamora.'

'What a tiger is this Lara!' groaned the Princess. All around the veteran there was weeping, and many mourned to see these heroes cut down in the bloom of their youth by the deadly spear of the Castilian.

'Why do you weep?' asked old Arias Gonzalo; 'what mean these sobs? Have my sons died in taverns or at gaming-tables? They have died like gentlemen, with arms in their hands, to defend Zamora, to defend your honour.' Over the head of that great veteran Romance weaved a crown of verse.

Pedro Arias, third of the sons, entered the lists and hurled himself upon Diego Ordóñez, wounding him in shoulder and arm. Lara clove him through casque and crown. But the son of Arias Gonzalo, falling in his life's blood, wounded the horse of Diego Ordóñez in the breast, and the steed bolted with its rider from the arena.

Bitterly Diego Ordóñez de Lara cursed his horse. 'Let him take the field again,' shouted the men of Castile; 'he is unhurt.' 'He may not enter the lists again,' replied the men of Zamora; 'he is defeated.'

'The horse ran away with him,' cried the one. 'No matter; the fight may not go on,' cried the others.

The Cid was overseer of the field, and he took counsel with the judges. Arias Gonzalo approached. 'There is nothing to be said; my son has conquered.'

'How can a dead man win?' asked a judge. 'By driving the living out of the lists; and so he did.'

Don Diego Ordóñez would have the fight continue. Much as he loved the sons of his uncle Arias Gonzalo, the Cid too would have wished that Castile should triumph; but honour and chivalry bade him uphold the judgment of the majority of the arbiters. The duel was over. So ended that ill-fated siege of Zamora. Zamora remained impregnable as Doña Urraca.

The camp was filled with sounds of mourning. Five hundred knights rode bareheaded in the wind in which the red standards streamed. In their midst advanced a litter, and on the litter rested a covered casket. There lay the King Don Sancho, fallen from his raging into the quietude of death.

A murmuring of grief rose up to Heaven. On their shoulders and on their sorrow the men of Castile raised the body of their King. The sky took on the aspect of a temple, and the earth was all forlorn and solemn, full of ashes and of majesty.

In sad procession they bore the King to the monastery of Oña, and there they left him to the repose of stone, the sepulchre of forgetfulness, whither comes every mortal, to be a beggar for remembrance and for a prayer. May he sleep in peace! How little space he needed, for all that he had filled in life!

THE OATH IN SANTA GADEA

The King Don Sancho was dead; and the men of León and Galicia, whom only force of arms had held faithful to him, began to desert the field and return to their own lands. Assembled in Burgos, the lords of Castile debated the proclamation of a new King. Sorely it went against the grain for them to accept Don Alfonso, for he was not likely to have forgotten the rout he had suffered at their hands when he reigned in León. His crowning, besides, would mean the dominance of León over Castile, and they felt the same lack of loyalty towards Don Alfonso that the men of León had felt towards Don Sancho. But, since there was no other prince to whom to grant the crown, they had to think of Don Alfonso.

'We cannot accept him as our King,' broke in Diego Ordóñez de Lara in the midst of the discussion, 'for Don Alfonso is held to have been privy to the slaying of Don Sancho.'

'What proofs have you for such a charge?' asked García Ordóñez.

'There are no proofs, but there are suspicions. It is known that the day before the death of the King an emissary sent from Toledo by Don Alfonso to Doña Urraca arrived at Zamora; and it is said that he conferred long with her and that he passed the night in the house of Vellido Dolfos.'

The Cid rose to his feet, and silence rose with him. 'Then, gentlemen,' said the Cid, 'before we offer the crown to Don Alfonso we must make him swear that he had no part in the death of Don Sancho; and, if he will take that oath, then must we proclaim him our King, since there is no other prince to whom to offer the crown, and he is the lawful heir.'

All were agreed that, if the Prince would clear himself of suspicion on his oath, they could do no other than proclaim him their King.

At Toledo Don Alfonso, informed by a letter from Doña Urraca of the death of his brother, only watched his chance to set out for Castile. He feared that the Moorish King would seek to prevent him from returning to his own land, and he kept secret the news of the death of Don Sancho. Opportunity to shake the dust of Toledo from his feet was not long in coming, and one night, companioned only by the Count Per Ansúrez, he fled from the Court of al-Mamun.

With horses' shoes reversed, to baffle their pursuers if the Moorish King should give orders to follow them, by a path cleverly devised so that their tracks ran southwards, the horsemen rode towards Castile. Have a care! What noise was that? There was a country without a King, and a man who crossed the night towards a Kingdom and a throne.

Upon all the great lords of Castile, assembled again together on the day after his arrival in Burgos, Don Alfonso imposed his will. Don Sancho was dead, and he the second son of King Fernando, and to him belonged the crown. 'I demand of you,' said Don Alfonso, 'that you swear fealty to me and render me what is mine.'

To the winds went the agreement of the great lords with the Cid. One by one, with the prelates and the counsellors, they took the oath of fealty and kissed the hand of the King. Only the Cid stood fast, immovable and with head held high.

'What is this, my friends?' exclaimed Alfonso; 'since all of you accept me as your King, I would fun know why Ruy Díaz has not come to kiss my hand.'

'Sire,' answered the Cid, with that serenity of great souls which live soaring in the heights, 'all these men whom you see here, though none dared tell you, hold you suspect of being privy to the death of the King Don Sancho. But I tell you that if you will not clear yourself of this suspicion, as you ought to do, I will never kiss your hand.'

'I am well pleased,' said Alfonso, 'that there is one among you to tell me what the rest have thought of me. Tell me now, what must I do to wipe away this vile suspicion, which rumour has dared to set upon my brow?'

'You must take oath that you had no part, either by order or by counsel, in the death of Don Sancho.'

'And who will dare administer such an oath to me?'

There was a silence of intimidation in the hall. The Cid frowned and his words fell solemnly. 'I,' he said.

'Since no knight, though all agreed together, has dared aught before you this day, I will take your oath: I, Ruy Díaz, greatly honoured to represent Castile.'

The King mastered the anger which the high chivalry of the Cid provoked in him. He knew that the taking of the oath would be a good stroke of policy to win the men of Castile to him and avoid the traps which the ambitious might lay for him. So he humbled himself and yielded. 'Where must I take oath?' he asked.

'In the Church of Santa Gadea,' answered the Cid, 'where we crown our Kings.'

* * *

The hour of the oath had come, and the Church of Santa Gadea was transformed into a shrine of knighthood. Its flags resounded under the heavy tread of warriors, the people crowded it to the doors, the arches of the vaulting bowed down in solemnity, and the enormous columns, as if they had grown wings, raised the church high above all Spain.

There was the flower of the Kingdom, the Court with its nobles and its lords. This was the crowning moment when the Cid stood upon the peak of his life, the transcendental hour in which he showed the world the measure of his soul, the grandeur of his character. For the oath of Santa Gadea proved that the Cid was not only a warrior who knew how to conquer and defend his country, but also a man fitted to guard his own conscience and the conscience of his people.

Victor in battle, unquestioned leader in the realm of matter, the Campeador today became leader also in the realm of spirit. At one stride he took the place of the first man in his land. All the idolatry of Castile hung upon its hero. Castile was a necklace of eyes clinging around the throat of the Campeador. In him were incarnate at that moment the liberties and the rights of man asserted in the face of power, the independence of the spirit which demands that conscience be satisfied even against one who ranks himself higher than its claims. Spain felt at that moment that no man ever had personified her, ever would represent her, like the Cid; and she grew in glory, and was transfigured with pride, so that she broke the boundaries of the map and filled all the world. It was not a Spanish moment; it was a universal moment.

Moved despite himself, Don Alfonso waited at the foot of the altar— that altar at whose foot the Cid was the conscience of the world. The Cid took the Bible and opened it on the lectern of the moral judgment of mankind. The King laid his hand upon the Holy Book. An awful expectation seized upon all men. Suspense held all faces set, all eyes focussed. There was a silence carved deep in stone. The world might have hung upon a thread which was about to be cut.

Above the expectation of men and Chronicle thundered the voice of the Cid. 'King Alfonso, do you swear that you had no part by order in the death of the King Don Sancho, my lord?'

The King was deathly pale. 'I swear,' he answered.

'If you swear falsely,' said the Cid, 'may God will that you die at the hands of a traitor vassal.'

'So be it,' answered the trembling voice of Alfonso.

'King Alfonso, do you swear that you had no part by counsel in the death of the King Don Sancho, my lord?'

'I swear,' repeated the King, white as a winter.

'If you swear falsely, may God will that a vile hand stabs you in the back.'

'So be it.'

'King Alfonso, do you swear that you had no part even in thought in the death of the King Don Sancho, my lord?'

'I swear,' answered the King, livid as a corpse.

'If you swear falsely, may God will that he who slays you throws your heart to the dogs.'

'So be it,' cried the King; 'and that is too much already, Rodrigo, from a vassal to his lord.'

'I was not your vassal, but now I am. Yesterday I would not kiss your hand. Today, if you will give it me, I will kiss it.'

'No,' said the King coldly.

'King Alfonso, he who holds many Kings his vassals may keep his honour without kissing the hand of a King. I see that you do not understand all the loyalty I have shown you, all the favour I have done you, by forcing you to swear your innocence.'

'My soul and my hands are clean of the death of Don Sancho.'

'Then you should be grateful to me because through me the world knows it and History will attest it.'

The Count Per Ansúrez advanced to the Cid. 'The King will forget your presumption, though you have vexed him sorely.'

'Aye, sorely an oath vexes.'

'Way for the King!' Nobles and knights made passage, and King Alfonso VI strode lightly from the church, a man new-born.

That the new sovereign held him in no favour the Cid knew well, and rather than remain in Burgos he withdrew to his own lands. There he waited until time should make Alfonso understand who had been the most worthy of his vassals.

Very welcome was the Cid in his own lands. Long had his rich heritage and estates, Vivar, Silos, Cardeña, waited for their lord. Wide were his lands, and they needed the touch of their master. Hats in hand his people received him, shining in the sun of his glory. The great house of Vivar, strong, old, and dark, was radiant in the presence of its lord. There the Cid and his nearest comrades took their abode.

At the homecoming of his troops all the town made festival. Vivar was a fairground. Joyously the girls watched the passing of the soldiers who had fought with their lord. All were mirrored in heroism, all carried in their own persons something of the Cid. The evenings were one long tale of deeds around the braziers. Vivar dreamed battles, slept among swords. Epic was tangled in the hair of the sleeping children; Epic made them full-grown and the old young again. All were tameless, aflame, and virile. Their speech rang like steel. In the lands of the Cid was spoken a Spanish purer, loftier and more epic than in all the rest of Spain. They talked in poems, and their words held echoes of miracle.

A day came when they learned that the envoys of the Moorish Kings, vassals of the Campeador, had arrived to pay their tribute. As if it were the most natural thing in the world, the people watched them enter the great house of their lord. None was surprised at this procession out of a fairy-tale. They lived among marvels, and they of Vivar held themselves more proudly than those at Court, and felt themselves greater in the shadow of the Cid than in the shadow of a King.

With their mules heavy with riches, the fifteen Moorish messengers entered the courtyard of the noble house. At the other side of the courtyard the Cid was leading Babieca to a drinking-trough. 'Sir,' said the Moors, 'we seek the Cid.'

'I am he,' answered the Campeador, stroking the neck of Babieca.

The Moors looked at one another in astonishment. This man simply clad, without silks, or gold, or fine linen; this man busy about grooming a horse—was this the hero of the world, the terror of the Muslims, the idol of the Christians? The Moors looked, hesitated, looked again. The Cid smiled. The Moors spoke in whispers among themselves.

The Cid smiled, and his frank lips had the curve of soaring wings. 'When my arms are at rest,' he said, 'I am a simple labourer. A man of the earth, I return to her; she is ever loyal and ever generous.' He was a lord great enough to labour.

'Cid, here is the tribute of your vassal Kings: horses, mules, turkeys and hens, ivory, gold, silk and precious stones. They send you the best of their possessions with their greetings and their homage. At the same time they bid us tell you that great is the damage wrought by the cruel Abenamic, who wastes their lands and robs their cattle.'

'Who is this Abenamic?'

'He is the chief who has installed himself in an old castle in the pinewoods of Alcolea. He is a man bloody and terrible, who respects neither laws nor treaties.'

'It is well. Give my thanks to your masters, and tell them that I will deal with this chief. Spend the night here in Vivar. I will have you lodged, and you shall return tomorrow.'

In the courtyard of his house the Cid, as was his custom, divided the tribute equally among all his people, and that night they held high revel in Vivar. With shouts of glee, one showed to another the presents of the Cid. Every man bore to his house what he had received, and then they all came out again to sing and dance. Great flares were lit, and all was laughter and merriment. Eyes shone with firelight and with must.

The fifteen Moors were fifteen beards sitting on their heels beneath their turbans, thirty fascinated eyes peering from the depths of an Araby of incense and of dreams. The almonds of their eyes watched the dances go round, and evoked a Paradise of houris, of trees so heavily charged with ripe breasts that the branches bowed down above their lips. 'Ah,' thought the Moors, 'if we but had among us today a warrior like the Cid!'

Ten days later, in the calm of the evening, a horse ended his gallop before the walls of Abenamic. In that cavern among the rocks lived the monster detested by his own people, the tiger thirsting for bloody entrails, hated by all and loved by none.

The Cid dismounted from his horse, crossed the courtyard through wineskins and stolen jars fit for the Forty Thieves, and strode on with the resolute tread of an Emperor. In his eyes shone the supreme light of justice. He passed the threshold of the chief. As he saw before him this man of solemn, awful mien, Abenamic rose to his feet and drew his sword. 'Who are you?' he asked.

'I am Justice,' answered the Cid.

'What do you here?'

'Justice.' His terrible arm rose, and his sword fell upon the head of the monster. Abenamic collapsed in a welter of blood and brains, and the Cid turned with the same resolute tread of an Emperor.

Before that man of steel and blazing eyes, serene but grim, none had a word to say. The Cid passed on. The crew of the chief flung themselves on their faces, kissing the ground. The Cid passed, and wonder passed with him. The tread of the executioner of Justice re-echoed, and none moved, none dared to raise a head. The weight of miracle bowed down their turbans.

Only when the sound of a gallop grew fainter in the evening did the crew raise their heads and rub their eyes. 'Who was that?' one asked. An old man, white-bearded, full of years and lice and secrets, made answer: 'It was the lightning of God.'

THE NIGHT OF LOVE

At last the day had come when his white dream should be fulfilled, that dream which Destiny had interrupted—the day so long desired, the day of his heart. Its bells and its trumpets sang over all the world. It was the eighteenth day of July of 1074. The dawn rose up clad like a bride, Spain trod on orange blossom, and in the church turned into one great nosegay of white, white with sun, white with love, white with hope and happiness, the Cid and Jimena united their souls for all life, for all History, for all Song.

Out of the midst of the fire of battle the Campeador had snatched his heart, and he gave it unharmed, full as a ripe fruit, to Jimena, to Doña Jimena. The warrior had come back to his soul. Jimena before the altar, sheathed in a white lace veil which fell over her shoulders and flowed into a pool of silver, looked like a woman of the sea. Was it perhaps the presage of a stormy life, of a future in a galley of gold ever on the verge of shipwreck?

Two voices low with emotion, broken by tears of happiness, that murmured: 'I will,' made in the air above their heads a bond that grew in the light and echoed in the infinite. The air caressed that bond which linked echo to echo through space. Until the end of the world will be heard the echo of these voices merged in a single sigh.

None looked at the King, none at the great lords glittering in their attire of State, none at the beautiful ladies decked in fine linen, shining with jewels. The eyes of all were fixed on Jimena and the Cid—on Jimena without a single jewel, as who should say: 'My worth is in myself,' and indeed her beauty was all the clearer marked in the lines of that form without gaud or tinsel; on the Cid, soberly clad as she, showing his rank only in the rich simplicity of his dress. Jimena was the cousin of the King, but Spain spoke of the King as the cousin of Jimena.

The sky adorned itself to match the day—a sky deep with blue and with content. From time to time little clouds made over Burgos crowns of lace, diadems of blossom, and drifted away towards the lands of Vivar, smiling advance-guards of happiness.

When the Cid and Doña Jimena, with all the Royal wedding company, came out of the church, the people broke into cheers and songs for their idol. All Castile fell at the feet of the Cid in one great garland of flowers. All the city was decked with arches and banners. Rich tapestries hung from all balconies, souls from all eyes, adoration from all lips. At the sight of them coming from the church enthusiasm burst all bounds and ran in a flood of fire through the multitude to the utmost confines of Burgos. There was no corner of the city untouched by the sun, unwarmed by the heat of that great blaze.

The streets were in festival. Carefully the walls of the houses drew themselves aside to make room for all the people. Out came Pelayo, clothed in russet, masquerading in a bull's hide; there was dancing of lackeys; Antoño played the cavalier on a donkey; Pelaez the bladder-seller ran for his life; and a servant arrayed as the Devil scared all the women.

From the balconies handfuls of rice were flung at the bridal pair. And flowers fell as the company passed—flowers and flowers and flowers, a downpour of flowers. Nobody knew whence could have been plucked all those roses and carnations and orange blossoms and marguerites and lilies and violets. They must have fallen from the sky, for all the flowers of Spain together could not have made the half of those that flew through the air and lay on the ground like doomed butterflies.

The love of the Cid had wrought the miracle of turning every flower into many. It was a bombardment of blossom, a snowstorm of petals, and some in their frenzy flung with the flowers fragments of their hearts grown wild with fondness. All signs pointed to happiness, and the planet exhaled good fortune through all its pores. There in the centre of the universe Babieca grazed on four-leaved clover.

The world was an orange-grove in blossom. Burgos was a ship of perfume. The day was splendid as a Dreadnought illuminated. Life voyaged on seas enchanted with auguries. Castile weighed anchor for Story, Spain weighed anchor for Glory, and Earth weighed anchor for the Sun. Love took possession of all the people. The dykes of all souls burst their banks, all that passion of adoration overflowed, and a wild river of idolatry raced in a tidal wave through the streets, tossing high the spirits and the arms of that multitude which must at all costs give its emotion vent.

Spain was the bride of the Cid. Spain had named Jimena to represent her, and Spain beat in all the throbbing heart of that noble woman. Spain trembled with emotion, and her cheeks were touched with red and her candid eyes veiled every time she looked at her husband. Spain's timid hand crept out to surrender itself to the hands of that strong man, and Spain marched proudly at his side, safe in the shadow of her hero. The heart of Heaven was a mantle in which Spain walked...

No sooner were the marriage ceremony and the feast of custom in the royal palace over than the bridal pair set out for Vivar, there to seclude themselves in their own lands, to withdraw into themselves, far from the world, alone together.

Rounds of dancing and singing went out from Burgos to speed them on their way. Rounds of singing and dancing came out to meet them from Vivar and bear them back in triumph to the old house made young again. The road from Burgos to Vivar was a chain of nine kilometres of exalted souls. A thousand mouths sang, two thousand eyes wept, ten thousand hands applauded, and a hundred thousand stars slid from the sky into all breasts. All the girls had their hearts on their lips, their hearts in their eyes, their hearts in their hands. Here was the Cid re-clad in love. Here was the conqueror made human by tenderness. And there beside him was Jimena, the key to all this emotion, the woman of strength and beauty who thrilled him to his very soul.

Now in the solitary house the two, face to face with their love, could hide themselves in their happiness. Gone were the days of separation and bitterness, the nights of anguish and sleeplessness. There was the man of all those deeds, the man headlong but just, the man who fascinated Legend and made History reel, in the arms of love, his first night of love—a theme for the sighs of all the youth of the world.

O Campeador, again as in that memorable night there in Coimbra, you are about to pass out of Time and Space, beyond heat and cold! This night was the night of your flesh. But how like it was to that other night, the night of your spirit! For is it not true that all moments of exaltation free a man from himself and send him speeding through the Milky Ways of infinity; and the means of release are no matter, or at least the difference is imperceptible to our poor human vision?

In that terrible duel of duality, spirit and flesh, there is no way of knowing which is mastering the other until one or the other has conquered. Into what traps, into what snares of seeming, must fall the judges of the lists, for all their watchful eyes? Of the two eagles which soar fighting together, striking with wings and claws, who can say which drags down the other?

But to you, Campeador, there was something that said darkly that for you the spirit must gain the upper hand. You felt that the life of the flesh was less rich in marvels, less apt to enchantments and to the ultimate evasions. You were afraid of the material. Something in the flesh that your ancestors had handed down to you recoiled and trembled. What if too soon the flesh had won mastery over the spirit? You were but a man; and you could have been no other than a man.

Something in the depths of your being had said to you: the life of matter is a cancer on the soul. The soul goes wandering in the spaces of the Zodiac, on the long glides of dream, drunk with its own magic. Suddenly it falls sick, there grows a tumour, it develops rapidly, malignant in its appetite; and there you have Life. The tumour is man. The roving bird, flashing so lightly in the circles which all the riches of its imagination are free to weave, finds itself sluggish, anguished, poor, embedded and filthy. Like all sicknesses, the tumour has its time of appearance, of crisis, and of ending. The tumour dies, and the convalescent spirit breaks the barrier of fatted molecules and returns to win back its health again. For as the body sickens to enter into death, so the soul sickens to enter into life.

The Campeador was afraid of the flesh. But he loved with all the strength of his being this lovely woman who clung to him, a body of passion, dreaming on the verge of surrender. Man of purity, man almost a saint, how in the midst of licentious men, soldiers in rut, had you preserved this cleanliness of yours? There was indeed something strange about our Campeador. He was thirty and three years old, and his body had never touched a woman's. He was virgin.

You may laugh if you will; but I shall hold him worthy of all homage—— this matchless man who, in an age when even the clergy gave themselves up to every kind of licence, had kept his chastity for more than thirty years. And this for no reason of infirmity or abnormality: nothing of the kind could there be in that body of his, peerless in its balanced vigour; nor was it that the flesh made no demands upon him, but that he could master it and curb his desires. He was a man, I say, for homage.

And now there he was, a poor thing trembling on the edge of yielding. Of yielding, do I say? From what subsoil of our mystical heritage springs this foolish word where it is matter of love? The warrior shook himself free from the slavery of scruple, and it was enough for him that with his passion was intermingled all the ardour of his soul. Never had he been so fine as now, held prisoner in the deepest of all mysteries.

Within the circle of her arms Jimena offered him his consecration as a man, opened to him a new life in the passion of the flesh. The marvellous springtide of her body was a sacrifice on the altar of her love. There was a moment flashing like the Northern Lights in eyes anguished as those of lambs doomed for the slaughter, a moment that stabbed two breasts like the agony of stricken doves, and then death—the annihilation of two beings kneaded to death in love, the act of life, that jest of a jealous god. For a moment the world of flesh was transformed into a garden where bloomed a thousand flowers, and then it sank into the dank depths beneath that garden, into the sombre land whence spring all roots.

What matter? For no man ever yet has taken a fairer journey than this brief death of twain. The Cid put up his lips, and all was sweetness. Jimena half closed her eyes of the Middle Ages. Something broke in the misty depths of the world, and of that breach there was an echo in Paradise. Rodrigo, Ruy Díaz, the Cid, the Campeador, flung away his chastity, plunged into the cavern of human madness, fell into the whirlpool of the fever of the world. It was the night of his flesh, of flesh and blood, of the dear bleeding of the stars, when Heaven raised her veil, was pierced, and set herself to bleed for ever.

How heavenly are the delights of love, what magic poison it ingests into the veins, what celestial ambrosia it instils into the blood! The mortal rhythm of those bodies interlaced set the earth pulsing in harmony. All the lovers of Spain were one with the rhythm of their god. The whole world gave itself up to love in honour of the Cid, and all its offspring were sealed with his seal. All the lutes of the universe sang one strain: the woman has risen to the stature of the man, the giant has come down to earth in the stature of a man. Well may you sing, ye lutes, that night illustrious!

TWO VOICES

It is well known that all countries have a Fairy Godmother charged to protect them. The Fairy Godmother of Spain was ill at ease. For many nights she had not been able to close her eyes, those beautiful dark eyes, serene for all their long vigil, which no man yet has celebrated in fit song. From side to side of her cavern, whose walls are mirrors of things that pass and dreams not yet come true, she paced to and fro. Much she was troubled by the doubtful bearing of the new King towards the Cid. Grave fears oppressed her. At night, when the King was alone, she approached him and whispered in his ear.

But by day came Jealousy, and she approached the King and whispered in his other ear. It is well known that Jealousy is the rival of the Fairy Godmother. In all countries, opposite the grotto of the Fairy, you will find the cavern of Jealousy. The poor King Alfonso heard the two voices and, torn with doubts and hesitations, did not know which of the two gave him good counsel, counsel noble and disinterested, or at least interested only in the greatness of the country which he ruled and in true justice.

'King Alfonso, King Alfonso,' said the Fairy Godmother, 'the Cid is the man of whom you stand in need. Do not doubt his loyalty, and bear no grudge against him for an act which was your salvation and for which you ought to thank him. The Cid is the greatest man in Spain, and Spain has need of him.

Have confidence in him, and seek to win him back to you. It is not enough that you graced his marriage with your presence; recall him to your side, and in your Court let him be first among his peers.'

The King listened, then he rose up and was about to summon the Cid; but Jealousy approached him and spoke into his other ear: 'King Alfonso, King Alfonso, the Cid holds himself greater than you. Between him and you the people are for him. Do not suffer him to rise too high, for perhaps one day he will strike you low. He is a man of pride, and where he is there is none greater than himself.'

The King sat down again. He wrinkled his brow, he frowned, and he clenched his fists. The Fairy Godmother wept, and she spoke to him again: 'King Alfonso, King Alfonso, put no trust in Jealousy, nor in the Count García Ordóñez, whom you have set so high. The Cid does not know the uses of flattery, but he knows the uses of loyalty. Put no trust in your favourites, for their smiles mask much readiness in treason.'

But Jealousy came back and spoke again: 'King Alfonso, King Alfonso, García Ordóñez is your man. Put away from you Rodrigo and all those who plead for him—the Count Don Per Ansúrez, Don Diego Ordóñez de Lara, and that old Arias Gonzalo.'

It was the turn of the Fairy Godmother; 'King Alfonso, King Alfonso, those who plead for the Cid are the flower of your land; and those who speak against him are cowards and traitors. With one blow the Cid would make them sprout wings and send them flying over your mountains.'

But Jealousy said: 'King Alfonso, King Alfonso, if you do not soon clip the terrible Campeador's wings, he will fly away with your crown, and Spain will applaud him. He would rather live withdrawn in Vivar among his own people than bow before you. He defies your power, and does not fear your anger.'

THE FAIRY GODMOTHER. 'King Alfonso, King Alfonso, the Cid is more loyal than any, and he serves you better than any. But for him your crown would be at the mercy of any. He is not born of a race of courtiers, but of a race of warriors. While others fawn upon you, he takes fortresses, and wins battles and lands. What matters roughness in a man who tears down towers? He will not bend the knee, because his knees are of oak and rock, but he will make the knees of others knock in your presence.'

JEALOUSY. 'King Alfonso, King Alfonso, the Cid is foil of guile. He plans to tweak you by the beard, and he looks beyond one blow. This knight, who with the air of an Emperor walks the hillsides where the wolves themselves shrink from him, is too free in his gait about your lands. I warn you of the danger of this thunderbolt let loose.'

THE FAIRY GODMOTHER. 'King Alfonso, King Alfonso, where will you find bonds to fetter the thunderbolt? Do not match your wrath with his, but seek to win his love with yours.'

JEALOUSY. 'King Alfonso, King Alfonso, mark you how the man grows. Five times above the stature of your shoulder must you stand before the world can so much as see you; and five times multiplied you reach only to the height of the Cid's knees. Do you understand your peril? His will is stronger than yours throughout all Spain. Babieca inspires more dread than all your troops together.'

THE FAIRY GODMOTHER. 'King Alfonso, King Alfonso, the Cid puts this dread of him at the service of your cause. Summon him to you; you have nothing to lose, and much to gain.'

JEALOUSY. 'King Alfonso, King Alfonso, to the world he is Castile. And what are you? You are nothing. The Moors hold him in fear by the length of his lance, and you hardly by the girth of a horse. His name fills the world; and yours barely fills your own household.'

THE FAIRY GODMOTHER. 'King Alfonso, King Alfonso, the Cid has placed his name at the service of your country.'

JEALOUSY. 'King Alfonso, King Alfonso, if you do not clip his wings, when you least look for it you will see Babieca sitting at the head of your table.'

THE FAIRY GODMOTHER. 'King Alfonso, King Alfonso, the future will decide.'

Did the King hearken to the voice of the Fairy Godmother, or was it necessity that bade him call upon the Cid? However the case may be, the fact remains that he sent a summons to the Cid and charged him with the most important of his enterprises. Among these enterprises the King would have him restore order in Andalusia and collect the tribute which, since the time of Fernando I, had been paid by the Kings of Cordoba and Seville.

During the time of his retreat at Vivar the Cid had wrought for himself alone. His hands and the hands of Jimena had spent two years moulding their own happiness. In all this time he had seldom been at Court, and only once had he sallied forth to war. This was a short campaign against Cuenca, from which the Cid returned covered with blood and triumph to shut himself up once more in his own lands—the lands of his first dreams and his first deeds, where he was lord and undisputed master. His brothers Hernán and Bermudo had died in obscurity, in the obscurity thrown by the shadow of the giant. Since Epic has no need of them, we may let them sleep in peace, and we might almost say that they never existed.

In the old castle of the Laínez life had fallen into the rhythm of the hands of Jimena. Every morning the sun smiled upon the faces of two chubby children and into two pairs of enormous eyes which were the light of the Cid's heart. Jimena had given him two daughters, Cristina and María; and in truth dawn in Vivar appeared first not with the rising of the sun, but in the cheeks of these two babies.

The corridors of the old house were full of little, tottering footsteps, of laughter ringing over teeth scarce cut, of inconsolable cries bursting from small, downy heads. With their magnificent precocities the two tiny queens of Vivar made the mansion forget its age. All the severe gravity of its stones melted in the sea of those young eyes. Vivar doted upon them.

Tales of the doings of the children passed from mouth to mouth among the people, and that year the priest baptised ninety Cristinas and ninety Marías out of every hundred. Arithmetic—you say—may scout the figures as impossible; but what has arithmetic to do with the truth?

So it was natural that the enterprise entrusted by the King to Rodrigo was little to the liking of Jimena. Her beloved man was to take up once more his terrible life of the warrior. War was the rival of Jimena. It is necessary that every wife should have a rival. The Cid took farewell of his wife and children. Jimena noted that from that moment the pulse of war beat in his veins. Already he was attuned to battle. A surge of slaughter rocked Vivar to its foundations. Babieca stamped a warlike hoof, and shook stagnation from her shoulders.

The dawn had hardly broken in the cheeks of his children when the Cid and his men rode on their way.

To Andalusia they rode, there to be greeted by the news that Mutamid, King of Seville and vassal of King Alfonso, was at war with Abdallah, King of Granada. The two Moorish Kings had for some time had no love to lose between each other, and war had broken out as it must. In the ranks of the King Abdallah several Christian knights served for the cause of Granada. Chief among them were the Count García Ordóñez and Fortun Sánchez. These Christian nobles aided Abdallah with their arms and their wealth against Mutamid despite the fad that Mutamid was vassal to Castile's King. Angered at the news that the King of Granada was marching against the King of Seville, the Cid sent him a letter couched in these terms:

𝕿𝖔 𝕬𝖇𝖉𝖆𝖑𝖑𝖆𝖍, 𝕶𝖎𝖓𝖌 𝖔𝖋 𝕲𝖗𝖆𝖓𝖆𝖉𝖆.

'Sire, I learn that you are marching with a great army against Mutamid, King of Seville. Let me warn you that, since Mutamid is vassal and tributary to my King Alfonso VI, I cannot permit such an attack, nor can I witness with folded arms the devastation of his lands by the army of Granada. The duty of an ally bids me defend him and ask and demand of you the instant withdrawal of your troops.

'If you heed not this my request, I shall have no choice but to support the arms of Seville and enter into a state of war against Granada. I should inform you also that I have learned with no little surprise that among your officers is to be found the Count García Ordóñez, together with other Christian knights. Be good enough to inform these gentlemen of my surprise and desire them to reflect upon the possible consequences of their attitude.

'Trusting that you will give heed to my words,' I salute you.

THE CID RUY DÍAZ.'

A clap of thunder bursting the bounds of Heaven affixed the full stop to this letter, and the phosphorescent zigzag of a flash of lightning added a flourish to its signature. So the letter was sealed in the clouds. But Abdallah broke into a cackle of Moorish mirth as he read the message of the Cid, and amidst a chorus of bursts of laughter it passed from hand to hand among the Christian knights.

The King of Granada summoned the messengers of the Cid, and he still joked as he gave them back their answer. 'By way of reply to this Cid of yours, you may tell him that as yet we are but a few kilometres within the boundaries of the lands of Mutamid; but tomorrow we shall have advanced as far as the castle of Cabra.'

So it was. The next day, with blood and fire marking their path, the troops of Abdallah advanced to the castle of Cabra. There the Cid awaited them. No sooner had he heard from the lips of his envoy the haughty reply of the King of Granada than he told it to Mutamid, bade him make ready his troops, and with the united hosts of Christendom and of Islam he advanced by forced marches upon Cabra. 'Let us hasten,' said the Cid; 'for there I have a tryst, and they schooled me that it is bad manners to be late.' He kept the tryst, with time to spare. Nearly an hour had they waited when the hill before them flowered into savage shouts and thousands of turbans. Upon an Arab steed, with pride streaming loosely as his robes behind him, rode Abdallah; and beside him, mounted magnificently, barbarously bearded, appeared the Count García Ordóñez. Babieca looked at the two steeds and spat through her teeth.

Everywhere against the horizon stood out warriors. Over it surged the serried ranks of oriflammes and of turbans. Moors and Christians, as if they issued from some secret source of earth, peopled the countryside. Commands rang out among the neighing of the horses. It was the tercian hour, that tercian hour of Legend and Holy Writ, flavoured with Poem, steeped in happenings transcendental, terrible in its associations past and to come, the tercian hour which is among the hours what the number seven is in magic.

For a moment the two armies regarded each other. It was the solemn moment of all combats, affecting all created things from the very inserts through cocks and dogs to lions and men—a moment in which the world held its breath. All Nature sensed the coming battle, and in the space which separated the two forces the last rat disappeared into the earth. Face to face thousands of statues stared motionless at one another.

Suddenly there was movement among the statues. Like a meteor the Cid shot across the space which divided him from the enemy. It was the signal. Behind the Cid an avalanche of gleaming marble tore loose at full speed. The Cid thrust himself among the men of Granada, and how that Titan was used to thrust we know already. With him myth entered into reality. An immense Moor, a veritable Goliath, came forth to meet him. With one great stroke of his two-handed sword the Cid clove him in twain from top to bottom, and passed between the bloody halves of him, swift and unrestrainable, an intricacy of unerring sword-strokes.

Before the cataract that burst upon them the enemy army fell into disarray and began to weaken at the knees. A holy terror possessed their hearts and arms. Scattered in all directions, the hosts of Abdallah tried vainly to re-form, reconcentrate and resist. Dismayed, the chiefs shouted commands; their disordered men rallied here, but broke there. Wherever the ranks of the enemy opened, the men of the Cid flowed in like a raging torrent which had burst its banks. The Cid was lost amid the sweeping strokes of the windmill of his sword, which made a whizzing, gleaming panoply above his head.

Before midday the enemy were in hopeless rout. The sun had hardly reached its zenith and let fall the twelve burning strokes of noon when rout had become a fearful flight. Nothing could stay those feet through which flowed the current of panic. Abdallah fled with his men, and all that was seen of him was a white mantle streaming in the wind.

With his Christian knights and the Moors of Seville the Cid took up the easy task of pursuit. The great Castilian had his eyes fixed on a bearded horseman who fled before him. He paid no heed to Abdallah or any other; only this Christian cavalier held his gaze hypnotised. The bearded horseman spurred on, and the Cid spurred after him. Babieca sensed what was afoot, and her hoofs beat tirelessly, like pistons under full steam. In five minutes the Cid had overtaken his prey. He charged, and horse and rider rolled to the ground. In the twinkling of an eye the Cid dismounted and flung himself upon the fallen man. He seized him by the beard and wrenched him to his feet.

'It seems, Count García Ordóñez,' cried the Cid, 'it seems you make so bold as to adventure in wars against vassals of your lord. If you must seek booty or lands, seek them in fight against Moors who are enemies of Castile, but not against tributaries of our King. You are my prisoner, and you know why I have tweaked your beard. Laugh now as you laughed yesterday.'

The Count García Ordóñez said never a word. He gulped down his shame in saliva and bile. Shame is an indigestible mouthful, it sticks in the stomach, and there is no purgative for it but the vengeance which can sometimes dislodge it.

All the wealth and booty in the enemy camp the Cid ordered to be collected, and with it he returned to Seville. There he restored to Mutamid all that of which the men of Granada had robbed him, and let him choose besides among the spoils of the enemy. Generous man that he was, within three days he set García Ordóñez and his companions at liberty. Mutamid could not do enough to show his gratitude. He ordered five days of public festival in honour of the conqueror, and loaded him with presents; and on great arches across the streets he had written in letters of flowers: Cidi Campeador, Cidi Campeador.

Sealed to the Cid was the title of Campeador by the Battle of Cabra. It was united to his first title by rivetings of blood and glory. From that day the name Campeador assumed a significance even higher than that which the Cid himself had given it when he accepted it from the lips of irony.

On the evening of the fifth day the Cid took leave of Seville and its King, and set out on his return to Burgos with his trophies, his presents, and the tributes for his lord. He and his men rode singing on their way. Seville was a far-distant point behind them. The night fell. Above the dust of their going a beautiful moon played the coquette between two clouds.

* * *

The Cid was back in Burgos, and the King welcomed him with a triumph, and showed himself full of affection for him, satisfied with the accomplishment of his mission, and in accord with all that he had done in Andalusia. Well content with the swift and glorious issue of the enterprise, the Cid Campeador withdrew once more to his own lands and his own people.

But while he lived in peace and reposed upon the love of his household and the adoration of his people, Jealousy did not cease to work against him. Day and night she whispered in the ear of the King, and now, after his new triumph, she whispered more insidiously than ever; and she found an ally in the hatred of García Ordóñez. With what envy did the courtiers look upon the hero of Vivar! Above all the Count of the tweaked beard made himself the evil shadow of the conqueror. But the King would not yet let himself be persuaded. A shrewd man in politics was Alfonso, and he knew that it would not serve him to alienate the Campeador.

So the days and the weeks passed in truce between them. Ruy Díaz saw García Ordóñez become the great favourite of his lord, but he paid no heed. He knew that the relations and friends of the favourite were weaving all manner of intrigue against him, but he made no sign. The Cid listened to the nightingales singing at Vivar, and took his rest upon his honour and his own proper worth. The King, he thought, would learn to value him. He knew that every day his courtiers recalled to the King's mind the day of the oath and sought to paint in lurid colours the danger of a man so loved by the people; but he held that in their speech the King would hear the voice of Jealousy.

The Cid listened to the song of the nightingales. The spring came, and the fields grew green again at the touch of the sun; and the thoughts of the King grew green again at the touch of intrigue. But soon the flowers covered the green of the fields, and it seemed that a show of friendship covered the resentment of the King.

Out of a clear sky there came to Alfonso news of rebellion and war in Andalusia. At once he raised a great army, and sent a messenger to the Cid that he should come and set himself at the head of the troops. But the Cid was sick of a high fever, and Doña Jimena received the messenger and bade him tell the King that her husband was so weak that he could not leave his bed. More lustily than ever the nightingales sang at Vivar. The Cid could not take the field.

Doña Jimena retired to her room, and there she wrote in her diary. This is what she wrote: 'The thirteenth day of March. They have sent on behalf of the King to bid Rodrigo place himself at the head of a new expedition of war. My poor Rigo, as the children call him, is sick and cannot go. Dear God, almost am I content that he is sick! May Heaven pardon me; but there have been so many times when I have had to lament that he is so famed a conqueror.

'Often I ask myself, when will there be an end of these campaignings and these conquests? What Divine law suffers Kings to hold married lovers so long separated with their wars? The King has made of my sweet and tender Rigo a ferocious lion. By what right does he summon him to his side at any moment, by what right does he load enterprises upon him at his will, and leave him to me only when he does not need him? When he returns to my side his horse is covered with blood, and he himself so blood-stained that he fills me with dread. And even when he falls asleep weary in my arms he is restless and disturbed, dreaming of his battles. In truth I have no husband, and much I would like to know whether Rodrigo married me or Spain.'

Poor Doña Jimena! The Cid does not belong to you, nor does he belong to himself. The Cid obeys the obscure purposes of his race. He is moved by unknown forces which spring from the roots of his people and are realised in him. And there is nothing to be done against such forces, against the fate of a future which fulfils itself....

Since the Campeador could not lead the army of Castile and León, the King placed himself at the head of his troops and set out for Andalusia. But the Moors of the frontier, seeing the army on its way to the South, lost no time in seizing their opportunity when Castile and León were bare of defenders. They invaded the Kingdom of Alfonso, laying waste all before them, and boldly laid siege to the castle of Gormaz.

News of what was passing came one morning to the Cid. He was recovered, and he felt the ardent beating of the wings of his heart. He called for his arms, bade them saddle Babieca, and dispatched messengers to rally his men to go forth against the Moors. With but a few hundred men he took the field. His name rather than the number of his troops sent the Moors into retreat. None dared offer him battle, and after but a few skirmishes the enemy forces fled in all directions like a herd of buffaloes.

Following up the flying Moors, the Cid penetrated into their lands, and pressed as far as Toledo, sowing in the fields of the enemy what they had sown in Castile—waste and pillage. Seven thousand captives the Cid carried away, seven thousand men and women. It was a great triumph; but (there was a 'but' in the triumph) the Cid had attacked Toledo, whose King had a pact with the King Alfonso since the time when he had taken refuge at Toledo's Court.

Alfonso returned to Castile to learn that during his absence and without his leave the Cid had devastated the Kingdom of Toledo, and he was filled with fury against him. The enemies of the Cid did not let slip their opportunity to embroil him with the King. García Ordóñez, clinging like a monkey to the ear of the King, knew better than any how to drop words of hatted into it. His beard still tingled, and the words that issued through it were red as bleeding roots.

'Sire,' he said, 'in breaking the pact which you made with al-Mamun when he gave you asylum at Toledo, Ruy Díaz can have meant no other than to provoke the men of Toledo to fall upon you and all your friends.'

'Ruy Díaz seeks to set his voice above yours, and make you break your alliances at his whim,' dripped the voice of another courtier. 'Do not forget that he took you captive at Golpejares.'

'If you do not punish him and make him feel your power,' yet one more voice instilled, 'his pride will mount higher than your crown. Never have you punished his presumption in making you take oath in the matter of the death of the King Don Sancho; and now if you leave him unpunished he will feel himself stronger than you.'

The eyes of the King flashed with anger, with all the lightning that wrath can draw from human eyes, as the insinuating words of envy slipped into his ears. The oath of Santa Gadea, the capture at Golpejares, the apparent insolence and rebellion of the Cid against his King—all these fused together in the depths of the soul of Alfonso, all these awakened and inflamed again his sleeping rancour. What a gamut of evil passions and base emotions was run to bring down the giant whose gigantic shadow had grown too great! Hatred and envy and resentment flowed together in a polluted stream to issue in an order of banishment, in a letter which the King sent the Cid bidding him quit the Kingdom within nine days.

We have no record of this letter. With eyes moist with emotion the Cid read it, and then he flung it in the fire to save before posterity the memory of his King—supreme chivalry of the offended towards the person of his offender!

THE GATE OF EXILE

At the news of the banishment of the Cid there was a rallying to the old castle of Vivar. His friends and comrades came to learn what had passed and to seek his orders. Those were not lacking who counselled him to rise against the King. Not only that might the Cid have done. He might have marched against Burgos, taken the city and overthrown the King if he would; but his soul of a faithful vassal and the loftiness of a purpose unstained by personal ambition would not let him do it.

Not for a moment did the Cid entertain the idea of rebellion. The King had banished him from his lands. The Cid kept silence, and made ready to obey. The King had confiscated his estates and fiefs. The Cid kept silence, and bowed his head. You shall hear what he said to his family and his vassals, seeking always to excuse the King.

'My lord the King Alfonso has lent ear to my enemies and the traitors who surround him, and has banished me from his lands and barred his gates against the most faithful of his knights. Time will tell him who were his better servants. For the rest, my friends, we have nine days within which to leave the Kingdom. Let us obey. Those who will come with me God will reward; and with those who stay behind I shall have no quarrel.'

'None but the women and the old will stay behind, good Cid,' cried Martín Antolínez, 'we are with you to a man.'

'We will go with you, Cid,' Álvar Fáñez agreed, 'we will go with you whether by field or fell, and none of us will falter while strength remains. As loyal vassals, as faithful friends, we put at your service our horses and our mules, our wealth and our gear.'

'We will go with you, Cid,' repeated Muño Gustioz; 'in your shadow we shall lack nothing, and glory will go with us.'

'Long life to the outlaw!' cried Per Vermúdez, leaping to his feet and waving his hat gaily in the air. 'There is no lack of castles we can take to lodge us overnight. Cid, your standards shall float on ten thousand battlements, and every knight who has suffered injury will find refuge in your shadow, and come to swell your ranks.'

Deeply moved was the Cid, and his words went out to greet all his friends like a hand-clasp. 'From today you are more than vassals and more than friends; you are my brothers, and I swear to you that you shall not regret what you do for me. Summon our host and let us set out this very night; we have no time to lose.'

Then the Cid wrote a message to the King:

𝕸𝖞 𝖑𝖔𝖗𝖉 𝖆𝖓𝖉 𝕶𝖎𝖓𝖌, to-morrow, in obedience to your will, I shall set out to cross the frontiers of Castile. I leave your side; and from to-day I gain for myself, since for you I lose. My thanks, Sire; you open to me the gates of exile; but beyond those gates there is so much that I feel my wings stronger than ever. The gentlemen who take my service and follow me are proud knights and brave, and the four corners of the world seem narrow to them. So with them I shall increase your Kingdom, and the lands I conquer shall be New Castile.

'I blame you not for what you do with me, nor do I bear you ill will; I blame only your courtiers. May God forgive you as I forgive you, and may He soon make you recognise the loyalty of your

RUY DÍAZ'

In the house of Vivar they made ready for the departure of the banished. There was uproar of men and horses, mules and dogs, and a disorder of arms and provisions and gear to make the head reel. Question and answer were shouted back and forth at every pitch of the voice. Vocal chords shook with excitement, and oaths ran along them like 'Hallos' over telephone wires. Suddenly an oath too gross stayed like a swallow in its flight. Doña Jimena had appeared upon the balcony in displeasure, and all faces were abashed. She was their lady, the wife of their lord, and she was no lover of coarse speech. A flush tinted every cheek, and a moment of shamed silence fell upon the courtyard.

While his people gathered and his soldiers made ready, the Cid sent his wife and his daughters with their ladies under strong escort to the monastery of San Pedro de Cardeña. Thither he would go to take leave of them. So great was the indignation aroused by the banishment of the Cid that all Vivar was for setting out with him, and the hero found himself forced to refuse all the offers of his idolators. That was all the achievement of the King: to raise still higher the stature of the Cid, and deify the man he sought to punish. The outlaw entered more glorious than ever into the fervour of all souls.

The host was in readiness. From out of the houses poured the women and the old men to bid farewell to the soldiers who preferred exile with the Cid to staying in their lands without him. 'When we come back to Castile,' shouted a lad, 'we shall come back all rich and all honoured.' The women wept, and the ancients sighed, and the children raged. The Cid Campeador was going. Going was heroism, going were the evenings of Epic; and all the future was dark.

All great happenings are like islands surrounded by tears and applause, washed by the murmurs of envy and the wide waves of glory. The Cid was going, and the great sob that followed him silenced the noise of hatred. Sitting Babieca proudly as a King, the Campeador seemed an exile bound for Olympus. Around his head shone the halo of great destinies—such a halo as can be felt, inspiring confidence and enthusiasm, an electric aureole rich and warm as the Equator.

'Forward! For Burgos!' The column marched out of the town, and a great cry went up from a thousand breasts and broke in the sky: 'Long live the Cid Campeador!'

The lord and his knights were gone. His town stood at the side of the way gazing and stretching out its arms after him. Vivar sought to grasp its beloved so that he should not go. A crow passed flying to the right. Long live the loyal Castilian! Long live the Cid! The last little cloud of dust was lost to sight, and Vivar was left poor and desolate.

Folk flocked weeping to the windows as they passed through Burgos. Love and anguish were painted on all faces, but none dared offer the exile hospitality for fear of the anger of the King. From window to window passed a long-drawn sigh: 'God, how good a vassal; would that his lord were as worthy!' Many would have lodged him, but none ventured. Only from the windows was there a low murmur of prayer: 'God, how good a vassal; would that his lord were as worthy!' Only from some balcony bolder than another a flower fell at the feet of the Cid. Gratefully the Campeador looked up, and sadly smiled his thanks for this timid and nameless homage.

But when he reached his own house, the house in Burgos where he had lived in the days when the King had his ears closed to intrigue and his eyes open to worth, he could not restrain a shudder. The gate was closed. The followers of the outlaw shouted at the top of their voices; but none answered, none came to open.

The Cid could not control his anger. 'What, have they closed my own house to me? This is too much!' He spurred his horse, rode to the gate, drew his foot from his stirrup, and in two kicks flung the gate wide open.

Then, at the moment when he was about to cross the threshold, a little girl nine years old sprang out of Romance and approached the Campeador.

'Campeador,' she said, and her simple words had the savour of verse, 'my Cid, who in a good hour were girt with the sword, we may give you aid in nothing. The King has forbidden us under heavy penalty. If we open to you we shall lose our goods and our houses, our eyes and our bodies, and perhaps our souls. We may not lodge you, or even sell you aught—not corn, or bread, or meat, or any sustenance, however meagre. Cid, you have nothing to gain from bringing ill upon us. Go your way, for God will protect you and the world is wide.' So she spoke, and ran and hid herself again within her stanza.

'So be it,' said the Cid; 'we will do harm to none. Let us go our way, and since I may not enter my own house, let us camp in the sand-pits outside the city.' As they rode on they passed the Church of Santa María where he was wed. He dismounted and knelt down upon his knees, and all his heart came to his lips.

'Blessed Virgin,' he prayed, 'thou who knowest all things knowest that the King has banished me for no blame of mine. I obey, and I do not question. I leave the land in which I was born, the land that I love and that loves me. It is right that the King should command and the vassal obey. Blessed Virgin, to thee I commit my Jimena and my daughters Cristina and María. Shelter them beneath thy cloak, and may I soon call them to my side. Queen of Heaven, make my King fortunate, that he may not miss my sword and my arm; but let a day come when he may open his eyes to see how envy stains the breast of chivalry.

'And Thou, Lord Jesus Christ, exiled from Thy city, Thou who didst know all the bitterness of injustice, aid me with Thy glory and Thy blessing. Thou seest that I am poor, and that I have no food even for two days' march for my men. Protect me and them, for they are brave and they are loyal; and give me many enemies who are rich and powerful.

'Our Father Who art in Heaven, blessed be Thy name. Alas that Thy will is not done on earth! I commit myself to Thee, and with Thy aid may I make thousands of the infidel bow the knee at Thy feet.'

Rising from his prayers with his soul lighter and his body refreshed, the Cid leapt upon his horse, and at the head of his men rode out of the walls of Burgos, crossed the River Arlanzón, and ordered his camp to be pitched in the sands which surround the city. It was night, and a great moon smiled kindly upon the exiles. By its light the tents looked like beehives, and above them swarmed the honeyed standards of the Cid.

Burgos seemed besieged by an army—the ungrateful city besieged by love, with folded arms before his tent the Campeador contemplated those fields which were created so that he should be born in them and nurtured by them, and breathed in the breeze which blew to cleanse his lungs and passed on its way proud of purifying his blood. He looked at the rivers which ran to wash their tresses in the sea, the mountains which by all the pathways of the sky sought the feet of God, and upon their slopes the herds which grazed the Divine pastures.

Castile, Castile, how it searched your soul, that regard which loved you and understood you! Did you not feel that this man who looked at you was the eye of your universe and the peak of your life? What a burning sadness was there in that gaze which feared that it might look upon you for the last time! There were no secrets for those eyes purified by the passion of Nature. Countryside, beasts, birds, flowers and trees, surprised in their hidden laws, yielded themselves up to him with open hearts.

A free man, a conqueror whose hands injustice had tied, without aid from his King or his country he was about to launch himself to found Kingdoms and create a nation. Blessed be the hour of injustice! Blessed be the hour which opened the gate of exile! Through that gate Spain was to issue to become Spain. Blessed be the hour which should give birth to such a stave of Epic!

In upon the dreams of the Cid broke the stroke of a far-off bell, and out of the sound of it galloped Martín Antolínez with seven men. 'My Cid Campeador,' he said as he dismounted before him, 'here I bring you bread and wine for all your host. I did not buy them. I went to seek them in my own house.'

'I thank you, Martín Antolínez. Short indeed were we of provender. My thanks, faithful friend; if I live I will repay you twofold.'

'But now, my lord, let us rest and then set out as early as may be, for tomorrow the anger of the King will pursue me because I have served you. What I leave behind me here I esteem of little worth, and, if I ran win free with you, someday the King will account me his friend.'

'Listen, Martín Antolínez; we cannot start without the wherewithal to feed and clothe ourselves. Gold and silver must I have to furnish my campaign. I would have you go to Burgos and fetch money for me.'

'And whence am I to fetch it, my Cid?'

'Is the name of the Cid worth nothing? Go you to the Ghetto. I have here two leather coffers. We will fill them with sand, so that they may weigh heavy. Seek out those two good Jews whom they call Moses Roschil and Abel Vidas. Tell them that I am banished by the King and that I need money. Tell them that I may buy nothing in Burgos, and that I would have them make me a loan on two coffers which contain my treasure. I will make ready the coffers here while you go and fetch them.'

Martín Antolínez set off at full speed. The Cid summoned Álvar Fáñez, and together they dragged the coffers out of the tent, filled them with sand, and sealed them with all care. Before midnight Martín Antolínez was back in camp, with the two Jews mounted on mules beside his horse.

'Enter my tent, friends,' said the Campeador; 'my good Moses and Vidas, give me your hands. You know that I must leave Castile because the King has banished me, but the world is wide and I am a warrior. There is much for me to gain, and I shall not be forgetful of you. For the moment I need money, and since I cannot take with me these two coffers you see here, which contain a part of my treasure, I would leave them for security in your hands, but on the condition that you swear not to open them within a year. If within a year I have not repaid you double what you lend me, then alone may you dispose of them.'

In a corner of their beards the Jews took whispered counsel together. Then the elder replied aloud, opening wide his eyes, in which shone all the gold in the world: 'Who can refuse anything to the Cid Campeador? My lord, we will give you two thousand florins, and we swear to you in the name of the God of Abraham that we will not open the coffers within the space of a year.'

'Agreed,' said the Cid. 'Take the coffers and place them in safety; and have a care that none in Burgos knows of this. And you, Martín Antolínez, take two squadrons, escort them home, and bring back the two thousand florins. And hasten, for I would be gone from here before cockcrow.'

In high content the Jews kissed the hand of the Cid, and bore away the coffers. How light-hearted they seemed, though they were old and the coffers very heavy! The wind of night stirred the standards. The flaps of the tents pulsed with the rhythm of eternity, as if impatient to launch that great flight across the world. Away at the sources of the Almanzora a wolf bayed the moon....

The host of the Cid slept. He alone kept vigil in his tent, so sunk in his thoughts that he did not even hear the entrance of Martín Antolínez. 'Here I am, Campeador. I have fulfilled your mission, and bring you the two thousand florins. The good Jews gave me a hundred more for a present, because I had introduced the business to them.'

'Come to my arms, Martín, my faithful vassal and dear friend. Now we have the money to begin our campaigning. Give orders to strike camp.'

'You are in haste to go.'

'Yes, let us be gone. I would hear the cock crow at San Pedro de Cardeña.'

'My Cid, born in a good hour, I would return home to speak with my wife of those things which my people must do during my absence. If the King confiscates my goods it matters nothing. At dawn I will overtake you at Cardeña.'

'It is well, Martín Antolínez; go you to Burgos, and tell the other knights that all who would return home to order their households for the time that they are gone may go with you. I will await you at Cardeña until sunrise.'

The Cid mounted his horse and set off with his men at full speed. Outside the city groups of people had come to look, perhaps for the last time, at those who were driven forth by the anger of the King, and in the clear night the horsemen as they sped made out dim shapes which waved their hands in farewell. Babieca turned her head towards Burgos, and neighed into the moonlight. They galloped and galloped. The girths of the horses creaked, shedding epic stars by the wayside. A crow passed flying to the left. Now the noise of their going was barely heard in the distance; but Echo kept it to hand down as a heritage to the future.

It was near dawn. A nightingale burst into song. Out of its warm breast it poured forth all the best it had of memory for the Cid, weeping for the exile in a long ballad whose trills soared into the night that shuddered in its pain. At that moment the little nightingale represented Spain better than any. It was Castile, which could find no other mode of utterance. The soul of Castile gushed from its throat, and thousands of hearts wept in its notes. Spain fell from its beak in blessings and farewells to her Campeador.

In front of the host rose out of the night San Pedro de Cardeña, and with it rose the dawn. The horsemen pressed on, and over them a form without a name bathed itself in the sky. They felt themselves refreshed like the trees. Their hearts were full of trines. Dawn was an altar of the birds which rose to Heaven before any chalice. For a moment all the universe was a clamour of trines. Life ran up and down the gamut of a million scales, the world was caught in an infinite snare of chords, and Earth turned on its orbit through arches of song.

Suddenly there fell a silence. All those winged breasts calmed their fever and hushed their melody as if by common accord. It was the moment of which the cocks take advantage. Their bellies swelled in readiness, and they crowed to rouse the sun. Before the sun obeyed them the Cid had reached the Abbey of San Pedro and sprang from his horse. He knocked upon the gate. Within there was a murmur of Matins suddenly cut short. The monks guessed that it was the Cid, and came out to the courtyard with lighted candles.

The Abbot Don Sancho advanced to the threshold. 'Praise God that you are come, my Cid,' said the Abbot, 'and now that you are here you are my guest.'

'You are truly courteous, Don Sancho; here, if we may, I and my vassals will take food.'

'This house is yours to command, my lord Ruy Díaz.'

'Father Abbot, in this abbey, founded by my ancestors, and which is exempt from tribute to the King, in this abbey where my parents rest, I leave in your care my wife and my daughters. I leave them under your protection until I return in victory or send for them; and, if I die, I commit them to you and the abbey so long as they shall live. This day when I leave these lands I will give you fifty marks, and soon I will send you twice this sum; for I have no wish that the monastery should suffer any expense for me. For my wife Jimena, her daughters, and her ladies, I give you a hundred marks. If this money should be exhausted, grant them what is needful. This is my charge to you, Don Sancho. For every mark you spend for them I will give four to the monastery.'

'It shall be as you bid.'

At the end of the corridor appeared Jimena and her two daughters, each borne in a lady's arms. The Cid ran towards them. Doña Jimena flung herself weeping into his arms. 'My Cid, my Cid, must you be banished from the Kingdom through the intrigues of backbiters?'

'Jimena, honoured and blessed wife, I love you as my own soul. As long as we two shall live we are fated to separations; but in a little while, with the help of God and the Blessed Virgin, we shall be united once again, and with these hands I will win my daughters husbands and serve you till I die.' The Cid pressed her to his heart, and then he took his little ones in his arms and kissed them again and again, and looked at them as if his eyes would never tire. Always one sees so little of those one loves.

In the great refectory, with Doña Jimena and his children beside him and over against him the Abbot Don Sancho, the Cid Campeador ate his last meal in Castile, his last meal in the bosom of his family. Outside they served his vassals. The news of the banishment had spread far and wide, and many other knights came to join those who were setting forth. Groups of warriors arrived by every road from every city. Martín Antolínez came with a hundred and fifteen men. How the ranks of the Cid grew! How many had left their homes, their lands, and their possessions to follow him until death!

When the meal was over the Cid with Doña Jimena and his daughters and the Abbot withdrew for a space to the church. Fervently, stiff as stones in their rare piety, they prayed before they parted. On her knees at the left of the altar Doña Jimena prayed, with her eyes of the Middle Ages lit with the light of Beyond: 'Lord Jesus Christ, Thou Who art the guide of all, guide the Campeador, deliver him from all evil, and, if today we must part, let us live to meet again.' Kneeling at the right of the altar, the Cid prayed, with his warrior eyes shining like the armour of faith: 'Lord Jesus Christ, Thou Who art the guardian of all, guard Jimena and my daughters, deliver them from all evil, and let us all live to meet again.'

Between their father and their mother the two children, rosy and smiling as tender fruit, spoke to Heaven for the father who left them, and in their language of birds and flowers prayed God for their Rigo. Behind them the Abbot Don Sancho prayed in Latin.

Álvar Fáñez de Minaya burst into the church. 'It is late, good Cid,' he said. 'Have you forgotten the limit they set us? We must hasten on our way. The mourning of today will turn soon into gladness.' They left the church. Outside the horses were waiting impatiently. A knight held Babieca by the bridle, and at the sight of the Cid the good mare shook her head more happily than a dog wags his tail.

The Campeador embraced his children and Doña Jimena. The four made a bond of embrace that separation must unloose. Doña Jimena kissed his hands, and she could but weep and weep. She could not speak, but every tear enclosed a crystal word of love, and her sobs were whole sentences that fell translucent from her eyes and that shook the Cid to the depths of tenderness as he read them there. Neither could he find words; and around them no word was spoken. Pain cut them off from the world; pain makes them a phrase apart in this page of farewells.

Suddenly the Cid tore himself away from his own. His face was distorted and every nerve in his body shuddered, as if one of his members had been cut off at a stroke. Confusedly, clumsily, as if dazed, he found his saddle, 'Good-bye, good-bye; but it will not be for long. Don Sancho, my treasure is in your keeping.' The riders set out at full gallop as who should wrench themselves away from grief.

Álvar Fáñez lingered behind for a last word. 'Abbot Don Sancho, if more should come to join us, bid them follow our tracks and make all speed. Farewell—until we meet again.'

'Heaven have you in its keeping!'

'We leave our blessings with you.'

'You take our tears with you.'

'Farewell.'

'Farewell.'

The Cid looked back as the horsemen galloped away, and Doña Jimena waved a hand out of her agony. It waves still in the air of Spain, it waves still in the realm of Poem, that beautiful white hand that seemed to fly in benediction after the hero—that beautiful hand on the lute of the wind, on the lute of parting, that should play on absence and sound in memory for ever.

Banishment was freedom. Exile was the Cid lost to the King, but won for Spain, won for the deep hidden purposes of the race, won for himself, restored to the true reason of his being and committed to its design. The year 1081 shows us the Cid obeying the categorical imperative of his destiny. Tirelessly he was to gallop through the year, and leave it in the midst of history intertwined with prowess.

He was thrust out of the heart of the King, and millions of hearts opened their gates to him. As fast as he left Alfonso he entered into Spain, entered into the world, entered into Legend, entered into Myth. He left Castile, and all the roads of Spain offered themselves to him, came and licked his feet like friendly dogs. In all the forests and all the mountains the birds called invitation to him. 'This way, this way,' their cloud-drenched voices cried. Wherever the Cid went there came miracle and mystery, marvel and vision. Wherever the Cid passed by, wherever he abandoned, that place stayed shadowy and lustreless, and crawled into a corner of History to die.

Five hundred men went with him: five hundred men who had chosen to leave all to enter with him into Story. Five hundred men rode at full speed across Legend, scattering Ballad, enriching Epic with imagery, and leaving in the air a stream of strong language and strange oaths. With the Cid at their head they had no fear of anything. Stout braggarts as they were, when the Cid spoke they all fell silent. Among so many men of purity, with hearts of nobility and faith of chivalry, there must have been some bold adventurers, with eyes of fever and hands of rapine. It did not matter: all were blind instruments of the cause, and all obeyed him as they would have obeyed no other, and all adored him.

That fierce and unruly retinue were the slaves of Poem. Behind the man they adored they galloped and galloped towards the frontier. Not for a single moment did doubt or dread assail them. What did they care if they left the Kingdom, when this man alone was worth a hundred kingdoms? The Cid was leaving the land which had seen him born. He in whose soul sounded all the murmurs of his land was today expelled from her; but, as he went forth an exile, it seemed that it was he who banished the Kingdom which had cast him out. He banished it to obscurity, while he entered into light.

To follow him Chronicle almost forgot his enemies. They stayed behind, little, raging, unsatisfied in their vengeance; and over the carpet of injustice he strode majestically away. His soul was at peace, and that peace nothing could break. A great serenity streamed from his eyes and passed on slow wings over the heads of those behind him. Alfonso had thought to banish the Cid from Castile; and in truth he had banished Castile from the Cid.

So those who made up that column which rode away into the night had nothing of the air of exiles. They rode with song and laughter, full of enthusiasm and confidence in their leader. They knew that this man, whose head was hot but full of knowledge, of imagination, and of strategy, was a master of craft and skill like no other warrior in the world, who had discovered the secret laws of warfare, could sense the plans of the enemy, and seize the vital moment as it flew. After him to the pit of Hell!

And the Cid, if it had not been for Jimena and his children, would have laughed and sung with them. He was not afraid of life or of death. He followed his destiny, and he suffered only for his land and his lady. They galloped and galloped. An enormous gullet opened in the night, and Epic swallowed them.

Difficult it grows now to follow the doings of the Cid. During a space his way was sown with obstacles, and twisted and turned so swiftly among a thousand difficulties, passing from one battle to another, from a mountain to a plain, from a plain to a forest, from a forest to a river, that it is impossible for us to keep up with him.

Reader, to follow him in this dizzying course we must get a telescope of long—centuries-long—range and focus it on the year 1081. Here we are. Put your eyes to it and focus it. What do you see?

I see Cleopatra in a barque on the Nile.

You have made a mistake; you have gone too far back. Focus it nearer. Give it to me; I have the knack of setting it.

No, no, leave it to me.... Ah, now I have it right. I have got the year 1081—1081 on the roads of Spain.

What do you see?

I see the Cid Campeador, born in a good hour and belted knight in a better, with his noble great beard.... They have passed the night at Espinas de Can, then ridden on again at dawn, and they follow their path into exile. They have left San Esteban behind, and are passing by Alcobiella. Dear God, how gaily they ride! How eager they seem to achieve their liberty! Now they are approaching the frontier, they have almost finished with Castile. They traverse the causeway of Quinea and are crossing the River Duero at Navas de Palos on the massive arch of a verse mildewed with age.

Everywhere the shepherdesses come down from the mountains bearing them garlands of flowers. The shepherds offer them the best of their flocks. The eyes of the Cid are moist with gratitude. 'My thanks, children, for your flowers; some poet will speak my gratefulness for me. As for your flocks, why should I deprive Christians when I can so soon win them from the Moors?'

They march on. Babieca is covered with flowers, and there is a rush on the point of every spear. They reach Figueruela, and the Cid calls a halt for rest. From all sides warriors come to join them. They sleep under the banner of the night.

* * *

On the morning of the next day, which was the last of the days allotted them, they set out at a gallop faster than ever. Through plains and over mountains, with oriflammes streaming in the wind, they sped with the speed of the flicker of a film. At evening they halted to rest their horses in the Sierra de Miedes. They had reached the frontier. The Cid did not dismount. He rode slowly through the ranks of his men. He stroked his beard. He looked before him across the lands of Atienza, which belonged to the Moors.

The wings of nearby windmills revolved in the wind. The Cid felt a mad desire to spur his horse, charge the windmills lance in rest, and leave them speared to the sky, like evening moths. But he mastered himself, and I hear him say: 'Let us leave those gestures for others.'

Ah, Cid, everything of your race was in you. In vain you controlled yourself. You knew that others would come who could not master themselves, and that in time to be the gesture you would not make would yet be made, and it would not rest in that limbo where pile up the deeds that are not done. Why did you smile? O Cid, father of Poem, at the thought of Cervantes bells rang out in your heart!

Before he entered the lands of Atienza the Cid Campeador reviewed his troops. He had three hundred lances and two hundred men on foot. When there was need for haste the footmen mounted in relays behind the horsemen. When there was not they followed as best they could, at a brisk march or a loping trot.

The Cid smiled his content. 'Give barley to your beasts; let them eat their fill. To-night we cross these wild mountains, and the lands of the King will lie behind us. Look before you! There is the frontier! There the gate of exile opens!'

'Long live the Cid Campeador!' Long live the Cid! Hurrah! Hurrah!'

Those 'ahs' that filled all echo fill me with emotion. Reader, what do you see now?

It is night, and they are crossing the mountains. The moon, big with good augury, watches over them as they go, and her kiss anoints their brows. There at the top of the pass they traverse the gate of exile. Beyond the gate Poem waits for them with open arms. Song clings to the neck of the Cid and kisses him full upon the mouth. Ballad presents him with a magnificent sword—the sword Tizona.

TIZONA THE SWORD

You were a man of the sword, and by the sword must you live. For you, a King without a Kingdom, your sword must be your sceptre and your crown. Your sword was to create a country, to create Spain, and you could have no other country but your sword. How many monarchs were to render homage to that sword! In how many verses was it to shine brighter than a poet's eyes!

Deeply moved was the Cid as he received his Tizona, and his hands caressed it like a woman's body. Tizona felt at once the electricity in those extraordinary arms, the currents which ran through those hands. At once she was united to the Cid, like Babieca, for all the centuries. So was formed that invisible trinity in the infinite: the Cid, Babieca, Tizona.

Afterwards was to come Colada, also a good sword, but not to be compared with Tizona. Colada was to serve for minor deeds, for her name was not so noble and her steel was not so fine, even though she was superior to all the other swords in the world except Tizona. Tizona was the god of swords, the Babieca of swords, she was among swords what the Cid was among men.

It is false that Tizona was won from the Moors after the taking of Valencia: she was presented to the Cid by Ballad when he left Castile. Tizona crosses the darkness of the past like a meteor. Tizona with great blows carves the name of Spain in eternity. Tizona cuts human history in two. In the hand of the Cid, on the statue of Babieca, Tizona reigns in Epic over the world.

Tizona had a life of her own—the life of a bird and a dragon. The sword flew over the earth, changing her victims like the lightning of God. She knew the path through breasts and heads, all the ways of death; and she broke lives and shattered horoscopes and severed destinies without hope or chance of escape. Tizona had flesh and nerves; the nerves and the flesh of the Cid were prolonged in her. The hurricane was born in the milling of Tizona—a hurricane which snuffed out all the candles of life. The innumerable hands which were stretched forth to seize her caught nothing but her edge.

Tizona leaves a track of brilliance all down the ages. She is a zigzag in the night of Time. She goes preceded by prodigy, followed by miracle.

She brings forth a profusion of sorceries. Hanging from Space, Tizona still spatters drops of blood over this book and over the centuries which pass beneath her. Tizona, you are eternal as a swan whose song is drawn from it by death.

TRIUMPH AND TROPHY

W hat do you see now?

The Cid and his host are riding downhill, and a wind of presage goes with them. They halt in the woods before reaching the plain. The Campeador looks into the distance with his piercing eyes of fire, and his hand strokes his great noble beard. 'We shall ride all night, so as not to be observed, and at dawn we shall attack the town of Castejón. Let us prepare for a surprise.'

At the word 'surprise' all bodies are anointed in secrecy and silence. The world crouches down and lays a finger to its lips. They pass the rest of the night hidden among the trees.

Álvar Fáñez approached the Cid. 'My Cid, I have thought that, while you remain here with the main body, I might take two hundred men as an advance guard and make a raid through the country.'

'Well spoken, Minaya. Raid as you will beyond Hita. Let the vanguard range as far as Guadalajara and Alcalá.'

'You should be able to garner a rich booty,' said Martín Antolínez, 'while we take Castejón.'

'I shall stay with the main body,' declared the Cid. 'I shall keep Castejón, so that it may serve us as a refuge in case of need, and if aught befalls you send word back to us, that we come to your aid in good time.' Then he named the warriors who should set forth with Minaya, and stayed behind with the others.

The white of dawn was breaking. A sun of conquest rose at the steady pace of a soldier into the sky, shining more fiercely than any armour. The Cid smiled, with his lips wide with hope, and among spears and bucklers he reflected the furnace of his paradise of war. The gates of Castejón opened, and the people came out to the work in the fields. Seizing his opportunity, the Cid broke from his ambush and fell upon the town.

Moorish men and women huddled together with the herds which they had brought out to graze. The guardians of the gate fled in panic at the sudden attack. With Tizona naked in his hand the Cid entered Castejón. 'Have no fear, little Moors,' he said; 'we kill none when there is no need. But bring me quickly your gold and your silver, for I must follow my campaigning.'

Two days later Álvar Fáñez came back with the vanguard. They had advanced as far as Alcalá, and thence returned up the River Henares. Minaya brought in many cattle and sheep, attire of worth, a rich booty to add to that which the Campeador had taken. The Cid welcomed him in Castejón with embraces and felicitations. The riches conquered by both were assembled together, and the good Cid offered Álvar Fáñez the fifth part of the whole.

'I thank you much, Cid Rodrigo. With this fifth part of the booty the King Alfonso himself might well be content. But I take no wealth which belongs to you alone, since you have won it with your men. You may give me something on the day when I gain as much for you.'

'All that is mine is yours, Minaya, and you have but to ask for what you will.'

The Cid ordered that the booty should be shared, and that every man should receive his portion. To every one of the horsemen was given a hundred marks of silver, and to every one of the footmen fifty. The Cid kept the fifth part of the whole. Since he could not sell it in Castejón, and did not wish to take with him captured herds or heavy gear, he ordered his part to be sold to other cities richer and better peopled. The Moors of Hita and Guadalajara bought his fifth for three thousand marks of silver.

When he had received his payment the Cid assembled his men and addressed them. 'Listen to me, Minaya, and all of you; we must not linger here in Castejón. The King Alfonso is near, and he might come and attack us. Let us be going. I will not raze the castle. I leave it intact to the Moors, so that, for all I have taken from them, they may not speak ill of me. You have all been paid. Tomorrow at daybreak we march again. I do not wish to fight against my King. Forward, then, forward! Sleep well, and tomorrow we take the road.'

They left Castejón with the rising of the sun. They passed by the Alcarrias and the caves of Anguita, crossed the river, and entered the lands of Tarans. Everywhere they took booty. Now they lacked for nothing. They had provender, money, and clothing for many days. Well content they went in that good shadow of the Cid. They took their ease between Farija and Cetina, with life and death on either side of every man.

By way of Alhama, Hoz del Rio, Bubierca and Ateca, the host of the Cid arrived one day before Alcocer. The Cid planned to take the city, and pitched his tents on a rounded hill over against it. Another part of his camp he pitched on the bank of the River Jalon. Around the hill where lay the main body of his troops he ordered a moat to be dug to guard him against surprise.

Fast spread the news that the Cid had entered the country of the Moors, taken Castejón, and laid siege to Alcocer. None dared leave the city to work in the fields. But after fifteen weeks of siege the Cid Campeador, seeing that the city did not yield, decided to use his cunning in one of those stratagems of war which teemed in his brain. He ordered all his tents to be struck, all save one, which he left standing as if there had been no time to strike it, and rode at full speed with his host down the Jalon.

The men of Alcocer asked themselves what was happening. The Cid was in retreat. This was the moment to make a sortie from the city and fall upon him. Doubtless he had exhausted his supplies, or heard that another army was approaching. The Moors of Alcocer hastened after the Cid. 'Do not let him escape us,' they said, thinking of the rich booty they would win from the Christians.

When the Cid saw that his pursuers had advanced far enough from the city, he turned back with all his men and fell upon them in the open plain with all that speed and strength which he was wont to use. With Álvar Fáñez, Muño Gustioz, and some thirty of his best knights, he sped to cut off the retreat, while Martín Antolínez, Per Vermúdez, Galín García and Álvar Salvadores, with the main body of the host, attacked the enemy in front.

The Moors fell in pools of blood, and their bodies wrestled with death while hundreds of souls flew to the Paradise of Mohammed. Per Vermúdez entered the castle with the banner in his hand and planted it on the topmost tower. Over Alcocer floated the standard of the Cid. 'Now we have a better dwelling wherein to take our rest.'

But little rest was to be allowed them. In the life of the Cid there were many battles and few beds. Inns are rare along the roads of Epic. Disquieted by the advance of the Cid, the people of the district sought aid from the Moorish King of Valencia, who ordered the Emirs Galve and Fariz to lead three thousand men to attack him. The Emirs invested the castle of Alcocer, pitched their tents in the plains and cut off its water.

The Cid assembled his lieutenants and took counsel with them on what they had best do. 'You have seen that the forces which besiege us are too many for us to fight against them in the open field. We cannot escape by night. The castle is completely surrounded. They have cut off our water, and we shall soon be short of bread. What shall we do?'

'Let us attack them at dawn tomorrow!' cried Álvar Fáñez.

'That is the counsel I thought to hear,' answered the Cid.

'Let us attack them, let us go out and fight them!' shouted all together. So at dawn the next day the whole host sallied from the castle, leaving only two men to guard the gates.

'Per Vermúdez,' said the Cid, 'take my banner. I know that you are bold, but do not go forward unless I give the word.'

Per Vermúdez bowed before the Cid, and took the banner in hands of loving pride.

The Moors hastened to take up their arms, and their drums beat so loudly to rouse their troops that they broke Echo itself and cracked the ground in all directions. Then they advanced to the encounter.

'Let no man move!' shouted the Cid.

'Let no man break ranks until the Cid commands!' repeated Álvar Fáñez.

But Per Vermúdez, seeing the Moors advance, could not restrain himself. He spurred his horse, shouting: 'God be with us! I go to plant the banner in the midst of the enemy. Let those who may come to defend it!'

'Do not do it, for God's charity!' roared the Cid.

'I can do no other,' answered Vermúdez; and suited his act to his words. Before they were ended he spurred his horse again, and rushed like a river upon the enemy.

With the standard high in one hand the Cid saw him, while with the other he swung his sword among thousands of arms outstretched to seize it, in the midst of hundreds of swords and spears that sought to pierce his breastplate. At the sight the Cid flung away discretion. 'Follow the banner!' he shouted to his host, 'aid for my standard-bearer!' and launched himself to the attack.

The Christians set their lances in rest, bent low over their saddle-bows, and drove against the foe as if ten hearts beat in every breast. Spears rose and fell, bucklers were pierced, ruptured was the mail of cuirasses, blood ran to the elbows, shields shivered into the air, white pennons were dyed red, and in the midst of the tumult plunged riderless steeds. 'For Santiago!' 'For Mohammed!' 'For Christ!' 'For Allah!'

In compact band around Per Vermúdez fought the Cid with the best of his cavaliers: Álvar Fáñez, Martín Antolínez, Muño Gustioz, Galín García, Álvar Salvadores, Martín Muñoz. To see them fighting like devils burst out of Hell one would have said that this phalanx of madmen alone was enough to put all the armies in the world to rout.

The horse of Álvar Fáñez was killed and his spear shattered. He laid hand upon his sword, and though he fought on foot he dealt such blows that his arm might have been driven by a motor. At the sight of his cousin dismounted the Cid rushed upon a Moorish chief who rode a good horse, sheared him through the middle at one stroke, flung the two halves of him to the ground, and seizing his horse fought a way to Álvar Fáñez. At a bound Álvar Fáñez was in the saddle, and he went on fighting with such fury that every enemy who encountered him was a corpse in the twinkling of an eye.

Meanwhile the Cid had come face to face with Fariz. The three blows that he aimed at him! So blind was the Cid in his raging frenzy that the first two missed, but the third reached its mark through breastplate to breast, and the Emir fled from the field leaving a trail of blood behind him. Martín Antolínez for his part had left the other Emir Galve half dead. With helm splintered, and spear and sword broken, the Emir could do no other but turn in his tracks and quit the field.

With the flight of the Emirs the Moors broke into flight, leaving the Cid master of the battle-field, strewn with dead Moors and a rich booty. The Cid concentrated his men and counted his losses. He had lost only fifteen men. He fell on his knees on the ground. 'Praise be to Thee, O Lord, Who hast given us the victory in so rude a battle!'

He divided the prizes won among his men. Then he summoned Álvar Fáñez and spoke to him thus: 'Álvar Fáñez, you who are my right arm, I would have you go to Castile and take the King Alfonso thirty good horses, well saddled and bridled, with a sword hung at the saddle-bow of every one. I would have you fill a great wine-butt with fine gold and with silver, and bear it to Jimena and my daughters. Let them have a thousand Masses said for me and keep what remains. Take besides four thousand florins to those good Jews Moses Roschil and Abel Vidas. Take them also some rich fabrics such as they value and cherish as Christians guard their sight.'

'I will go to Castile, good Cid,' answered Álvar Fáñez, 'and willingly will I do all wherewith you charge me.'

'If it should chance that we are not here upon your return,' said the Cid, 'follow us wherever we may be. By sword and by spear must we live; and here the lands are poor, and soon must we march on. We go to Barcelona to offer our services to the Count Ramon Berenguer.'

From all sides more warriors trooped to join the Cid. Triumphant as a flight of thunderbolts had been his campaign. It was not a campaign of men, but a campaign of devils or archangels. Every day he embarked upon a new adventure as if on a swift-sailing ship of dreams. Headlong and bold, in the time for three stanzas of Ballad he took a castle, won two battles, and made four Moorish chiefs captive. He sold Alcocer for five thousand marks of gold. Calatayud, Ateca, Terrer, Daroca, Molina, all paid him tribute. Celfa, which would not pay him, he took; but Teruel he pardoned because his romantic heart foresaw that there two beings were to love romantically. All his race and the history of his race were within him!

Álvar Fáñez entered Burgos to fulfil the mission with which the Cid had entrusted him. Opening a path through the curiosity and the admiration of the townsfolk, he reached the palace of the King.

'King Alfonso, King Alfonso, the Cid sends you by me thirty horses richly caparisoned and the homage of an outlaw. May God will that your battlements do not fall without the aid of his arm. He has conquered many lands, and goes his way winning battles and extending your Kingdom. So the Cid repays the King who forbids him his own lands.'

'Álvar Fáñez de Minaya,' answered Alfonso, 'speak not in this wise to your King. I banished the Cid only that he might see that my justice teaches all, and that no man may believe himself to be above it. Tell him that I punished his pride, but that I admire his prowess, and that he may return to my Kingdom and have back his lands. A great fighter is the Cid, he is stronger and nobler than any; but he bears himself too proudly. Embrace him in my name, and tell him that Castile weeps for him.'

Álvar Fáñez left the palace and made his way to the Jewish quarter. He beat upon the door of the den where lived Moses Roschil and Abel Vidas. With all the precautions of a prison or a refuge the door opened. Two Biblical noses and four eyes full of the Talmud peeped out.

'I am Álvar Fáñez; I come in the name of the Cid.'

'O my lord, enter; what brings you here?'

'I come to pay you the debt of the Cid.'

'The year is not yet up,' murmured lips of versicles.

'The Cid pays before his debts are due.'

'Here are the chests, ready for you to take away.'

'No. Take these four thousand florins for the two thousand you lent.'

'And the coffers?'

'The coffers? What should I want with the coffers, when there is nothing in them but sand?'

The Jews looked at each other aghast as in the presence of a landslide of prophecy, such a landslide as leaves not one stone upon another.

'What scares you? Have I not brought you your money?'

'My lord, if there was nothing in them but sand, they were worth nothing. And we had thought that we were guarding a treasure for security!'

'What say you? Does it seem to you that there is no worth in the good faith of a knight? Does the word of the Cid seem to you so small a treasure?'

'But, lord, if he had died?'

'We his vassals would have paid you. I tell you so—I, Álvar Fáñez.'

With a mien of righteous indignation and injured pride Minaya left the house of the Jews and returned to the heart of the city. Well he knew how to speak of the Cid to the heart of the city! With what passion did Álvar Fáñez recount to the burghers the great deeds of the Cid! A breeze of glory blew through all the homes of Burgos at the passing of Minaya.

That same evening he set out for the Abbey of San Pedro de Cardeña to salute Jimena and her children in the name of the Cid, and to bear her that great wine-butt full of gold and silver. The Abbot and Doña Jimena with her daughters and her ladies came out to meet him. They were all questions about the Cid. So many crowded in the throat of his wife that not one of them could win free.

Minaya smiled, and for the thousandth time that day he told the great tale of the hero's warrior deeds. But Doña Jimena was so used to hearing of the deeds of her husband that it seemed as if she knew them already. What interested her much more was his health. 'He is well,' said Álvar Fáñez, 'younger and stronger than ever; and if it were not that he is separated from you, he would be the happiest of men. While there are riches in the hands of the enemy he lacks nothing.' Doña Jimena pressed her hands to her heart to hide her sadness.

'He sent thirty horses to the King,' Álvar Fáñez went on, well pleased, 'he bade me pay the Jews twice what he had borrowed, and to you, Lady, he sends this wine-butt full of fine gold and good silver. He asks that a thousand Masses may be said for him, and that you keep what remains. He bids me tell you that, if God preserves his life, you will be rich and honoured as a Queen. He bids you take good care of his children, though well he knows that you have no need of this counsel. He bids you never be idle, for idleness is the same as death. And he bids you keep your rich attire until he returns or you come to his side; for a wife without a husband should go simply. And he prays that God may bless you as he blesses you every night.'

Doña Jimena raised from her weaving her eyes of waiting. 'When do you return to his side?' she asked.

'This very day,' and as soon as may be. Castile without the Cid holds no interest for us. I must hasten to overtake him; he should be already on the road for Barcelona.'

'Take him our greetings, our thanks, and our tears. Here we await his ordering of our lives.'

'Farewell, Lady; and to you, Abbot Don Sancho, farewell. Pray for us.' He set off, galloping hard, leaving the trail of a half-god in the Castilian air. Doña Jimena stood watching that trail that led from Cardeña towards the Cid. The children, tugging at her skirts, drew her from her dream. 'Where is Father? Where is Rigo, Mother?'

'He is following his destiny, my children; he is making Spain great.'

ZARAGOZA

Hard galloped Álvar Fáñez back on the tracks of the exiles. Asking news of them here and there, he caught up the host of the Cid not far from Barcelona. A great clamour greeted his return. To all he brought news from their homes and their families. The Cid embraced him in high content, and that night a gay feast was spread. They toasted Álvar Fáñez and they toasted themselves, for none had any misfortune over which to weep.

Two days of marching brought them to Barcelona. The people received them kindly, and the Cid presented himself to the Count Berenguer Ramon II to offer his services. But as the Count would not accept his offer or use his services, the Cid lost no time in shaking from his feet the dust of the city of the Count.

'My lord Count,' said Martín Antolínez, drawing himself erect in pride, 'I suspect that tomorrow you will think again. You know not what you are losing.'

'To Zaragoza, friends,' exclaimed the Cid, 'to Zaragoza!'

Álvar Fáñez approached him. 'Tell me, my Cid, how can you offer your services to the King of Zaragoza, who is a Moor?'

The Cid smiled and he stroked his beard. 'What matter that he be a Moor, if I can make use of him for the Christian cause? Have faith in me, Álvar Fáñez. I have made my plans, and time will tell them.'

At a gallop that host, led by a vision, set forth again, with their souls full of sorcery, leaving in the air a cloud like a dust of stars. Those fields still resound to that gallop of a thousand years ago, and God alone knows for how many centuries they will continue to hear it. Banished from Castile, spurned from Barcelona, the host of the Cid followed their unbroken march, with countenances full of confidence and hope, and with such easy minds that none could have guessed in them reverse or banishment. Singing and laughing, the exiles followed their march towards glory under the secrets of the stars...

At their last camp before they reached Zaragoza, the leading knights of the Cid met in his tent to take counsel on their course in what might lie before them.

'Do you not know,' Álvar Fáñez asked the Cid, 'that al-Muqtadir, the King of Zaragoza, is a man versed in politics, skilled in plots and pacts, such as few even among the Moors? Do you not know that it was he who had his brother Modafar killed so that he might seize the throne of Lérida himself?'

'There are Christians who have done the same,' said Per Vermúdez. 'Did not Berenguer Ramon II, Count of Barcelona, slay with his own hands his brother Ramon Berenguer the Towhead?'

'I do not deny it,' answered Álvar Fáñez; 'I would merely warn the Cid against all that may menace him among these people with whom he has now to deal.' The Cid listened in silence, but in his eyes could be read his pleasure in his knights' anxious care for his interests.

Martín Antolínez agreed with the others. 'Álvar Fáñez is right. We shall be among people of whom to beware, traitors, assassins, false and, what is most dangerous of all, subtle exceedingly. The Cid will need to use all his wisdom if he would not see himself embroiled in conflicts.'

Serenely the Cid rose to his feet. 'With the help of God,' he said, 'and with the strength of our arms we shall find here as good an issue as we have found elsewhere. Let us keep our eyes wide open and pursue our plans.'

By the side of the Cid Muño Gustioz and Galín García laughed at danger. Álvar Salvadores, like Álvar Fáñez, was for prudence. The Cid Campeador smiled, and his eyes seemed fixed on some far-distant point, at the edge of the sea.

In Zaragoza al-Muqtadir received the Cid with every mark of friendship and with a pleasure quite sincere. The fame of the Campeador had come to his ears, he knew what manner of man he was and what were his deeds, and he realised of what inestimable worth the aid of such a vassal might be to him, a King powerful but encompassed by enemies.

But, despite this, the Cid was not to spend long in the service of the Moorish King. Soon after the arrival of the Cid at Zaragoza al-Muqtadir died, and at his death he made that grave error of politics which was so common at that time: he divided his Kingdom among his sons. The King of Zaragoza had two sons, al-Mutamid and al-Mundhir. The first inherited the throne of Zaragoza, and the second Dénia, Tortosa and Lérida.

This partition was to open a new era of war and revolution. The Cid remained at Zaragoza in the service of al-Mutamid, who held him to be a factor essential to the maintenance of his crown. Al-Mundhir for his part made alliance with Sancho Ramírez, King of Aragón; with the Count of Barcelona, Berenguer Ramon; and with the Count of Rousillon, the Count of Carcassonne, and the Lord of Vich. The stage was set for war.

Al-Mundhir and his allies advanced and laid siege to the castle of Almenara, an old fortress which had been dismantled, but which the Cid had counselled al-Mutamid to fortify again. So close the allies drew their besieging lines that the besieged began to run short of water. The case seemed desperate. Al-Mutamid summoned the Cid, who was at Escarpe, a castle which he had lately taken from the allies.

The Moorish King and the Christian leader held counsel together at Tamarit. 'It would be well,' said the King, 'for you to attack the enemy and make them raise the siege.'

But the Cid, who had studied the position well, would not accept this proposal. 'I cannot commit my host to a battle in which they would be overwhelmed by the immensely superior numbers of the enemy. The unconquerable and admitted valour of my men cannot achieve miracles.'

'Then what do you counsel me?'

'Buy off the besiegers.'

Al-Mutamid offered ransom to the allies, but they rejected his offer, holding that the city was already as good as in their hands. When the Cid learned that the allies had refused with scorn to accept the ransom proposed by the King of Zaragoza, he summoned his troops and nerved them for battle in a short harangue.

'Soldiers, we are about to fight against an enemy a hundred times more numerous than ourselves. We are going to rescue from hunger and despair the valiant men of Almenara, who are holding out fearlessly against a great army. Never have you had an occasion such as this to demonstrate to Moors and Christians your unequalled heroism. Forward: from the heights of Parnassus forty poets are watching you!'

Without delay the soldiers of the Cid tightened their horses' girths, armed themselves to the teeth, and with faces frowning in determination set out to seek the foe. Marching down the coast, they saw the forces of the enemy encamped around Almenara. They had no sooner seen them than the attack was launched. There was no time even for a verse in the furious speed of that assault. Before such impetuous audacity confidence fled from the allies, and they fell into dismay and disorder, with mouth agape.

Into that open mouth drove the Cid, lance in rest; and riding between God and the Devil, he reached the heart of the enemy. It was seized with a syncope, a mortal syncope. The allied army was a great greenish corpse, stretched on the ground with clenched hands and mouth twisted in a horrible grin under the sky.

So the Cid, he of Vivar, won this battle, to the great honour of his beard. The Count Berenguer himself was taken prisoner; and when, five days later, he was set at liberty on the condition that he made a pact of peace with al-Mutamid, he went back to his own lands with this sentence dancing in his head: 'My lord Count, I suspect that tomorrow you will think again. You know not what you are losing.'

For all the triumphal reception that they gave him at Zaragoza, where the people came out to meet him full of enthusiasm and clapping their hands in their jubilation; for all that his feat of Almenara gave him such ascendancy that he came to have more authority than al-Mutamid in his own Kingdom, the Cid did not feel himself at ease. Homesickness for his country and his own family exercised imperious mastery over his heart, and in those days of joy his was the only face of sadness.

He had shown himself not only a great warrior, but also a great chief, an excellent leader of men; and not only a great chief, but also a man both skilled and prudent in politics. Yet at this time of his life the Cid passed for a space along the Way of the Cross. Secret struggles were fought out within his soul, and for the first time it seemed that doubt ate into the breast of this man decided and unused to hesitations. On the one side his family and his land called him. The King Alfonso had summoned him back to Castile. But on the other side was the hidden plan which for some time had taken shape in his brain unknown to any but himself.

He raised his eyes to the sky, and the sky, overburdened with enigmas, shining with destinies, gave him no sign. 'Courage, heart! One man decided is worth a thousand lukewarm.' The Cid stayed on in Zaragoza.

Throughout the lands of al-Mundhir he raided, attacked Morelia and laid waste all the territory from Alcalá to Chisbert, to the great content of his lord al-Mutamid. Al-Mundhir besought aid from the King Don Sancho of Aragón, who assembled a great army, ready to give a *coup de grâce* to the terrible Castilian, and led it into camp on the banks of the Ebro. From this camp he sent a message to the Cid: 'Cid Rodrigo de Vivar, I give you two days' grace to quit all the lands belonging to my ally al-Mundhir of Dénia.'

The Cid replied by return with another message: 'To the Kings Don Sancho of Aragón and al-Mundhir of Dénia: Pray tell me frankly if you would continue your journey, so that I may send you an escort.' Infuriated by his irony, the two Kings made up their minds to punish the mocker, and, with exasperation driving them forward, the Moor and the Christian rushed upon the host of the Cid.

Terrible as a bursting of dykes was the shock. But the Cid, swinging his two-handed sword, that Tizona hewer of heads, charged like a rogue elephant into victory. Miracle followed the man like a domestic animal.

Victory loved him like a woman whose honour had been saved. Who could withstand you, Campeador, who from some source unknown drew a mysterious power?

He who joked at death, he who conquered thirst, he who mastered hunger, he who crossed deserts and spanned mountains with the ease of a fairy tale, did not seem to be a being of this world, nor did his history belong to the history of men. The Cid was Deed; in him was prowess personified and incarnate. Of the enemy who set himself against him it might be said that he had made a pact with Rout, or been enchanted by that beautiful nymph with hair streaming in the wind whom they call Panic.

Pursuing the Moors and the Christians, the host of the Cid took two thousand prisoners, and among them were the King of Aragón himself and sixteen of the nobles of his Court. A magnificent booty fell into the hands of the Cid. That night in the tent of the victor, the King Sancho of Aragón paced thoughtfully from side to side. The Cid watched him in silence. Suddenly the King, as if all the ideas that assailed him had found their rallying-point, stopped for a moment. 'What the Devil had your father eaten the night that he made you?' he exclaimed.

The Campeador could not restrain the volcanic laughter that streamed like lava from his mouth. In the depths of his being this man, terrible, phantasmagorical, had kept much of the child. His soul had preserved itself pure, primitive and clean as a precious stone fallen from another star. Nothing was more extraordinary about him than that he should have kept his soul fresh, in all its intrinsic worth, unsullied by contact with a life tumultuous, a life of matter and of blood.

In the midst of the most awful battles he had raised his soul on high above the seething mass, so that nothing could reach it, as the bard of Portugal bore his poem above the waves of shipwreck. An ardent faith, a flame invisible, raised his deeds much higher than simple feats of arms. Faith held the man on a plane so lofty that his soul was ever ready to soar above the body and dwell in the upper ecstasies. There was something of a mystic in the Cid, as in all exalted men. He was a visionary with his feet planted solidly on the ground.

Such was the irresistible power of attraction that radiated from his person that when, after this battle, the Cid, ever generous, was ready to set his prisoners at liberty, they refused to accept their freedom, and preferred to remain at his side. So it was that the King and the noble lords and all his prisoners entered Zaragoza with him. Even more magnificent than that which it had given him after his battle against Berenguer Ramon was the reception which the city offered the victor; and strangest of all in this triumphal entrance was it that even as warmly as those of his own side the enemy applauded their conqueror.

The King al-Mutamid and his sons came forth to meet him and embrace him, and to bear him to the Royal Palace they made a litter of their crowns. In Spanish and in Arabic thousands of shouts acclaimed the hero; in Spanish and in Arabic thousands of inscriptions on streaming banners and hanging tapestries told of his victory; and in Spanish and in Arabic hundreds of furtive eyes of women addressed to him the dream of all their dreams, the most ardent of their desires. They loaded him with presents; but they could not give him the one for which he longed—his own country.

INTERLUDE

The heart of the Cid felt the call of his own soil and was sick for his own home. So, when the King Alfonso summoned him again, he could restrain himself no longer, he could master his heart no more, and with all his vassals he took the homeward way.

The homeward way ran downhill, even when the slopes were steepest to climb. From Zaragoza to Castile the roads cradled him soft as in a hammock. The host trod upon poppies. From branch to branch the birds cast him fragments of their hearts in fervent song. The sky was broidered with triumph. The rivers changed their courses to follow the Campeador, like a faithful leash of hounds. Clouds and birds, wind and waves, companioned him to Burgos, chanting victory.

There the people exiled from heroism flocked out to greet him, with all the hunger for glory, all the thirst for Epic, that in the expectation of this moment they had so long restrained. The soul of Castile rose from its bed, overflowed in enthusiasm, and in the wildness of its flood almost drowned the hero who came home. The bells melted in sounds of joy and dissolved into roses of happiness.

Borne by the current of his people, the King Alfonso welcomed him with palms and festivals. Castile was a crown of laurels upon his head. The King of Castile gave him the castles of Dueñas, Ibia, Eguña, Campo, Langa, Briviesca and Ordeyón. Also he gave him a charter, signed and sealed, that he might keep for his own and hand down to his descendants all that he might conquer in foreign lands. The Fairy Godmother of Spain smiled and wept for happiness in her grotto. Jealousy crept into a corner, biting her lips in her rage. How long would last the triumph of the Fairy?

The stars shone over Spain, and in the heights of space illusion weaved to and fro in sport. All was peace and the calm of life at home. The giant reposed with his feet to the fire. He was rocked in the heart of his wife, and he smiled on the lips of his children. But something was working in his head, something was growing in his brain, was not this a wave that ebbs only to surge in with renewed strength?

There were tremendous battles in his soul. He felt the noise of arms and the clash of swords in his breast. Then there were silence and peace. And then again there was uproar, and fascinating images defiled before his eyes. There passed great charges of cavalry who leapt from their horses before his beard. The rush of victory carved bas-reliefs on his brow and statues in his memory; and suddenly from the foot of his too-comfortable chair all the Moors fled from Spain and in one great white bound leapt from Tarifa to Africa.

The Cid rose to his feet and paced nervously to and fro. It was as if a ruby had burst in the night.

Three days later the Campeador with a great host marched once more over the roads of Castile towards the frontier. Home-keeping Eclogue mourned, and turbulent Epic exulted. All his friends, all his vassals and relations, companioned him again. What joy was painted on those visionary faces covered with hair and prowess! And how their numbers had grown! How many had been tempted by the stories of those who had come back rich and now went forth poor again!

They returned to their element like breasts recovering from asphyxia. They went eagerly from calm to tumult, from hearth to battle, and the very horses marched in vanity and pride. Babieca leapt for joy, as if she were going to her lover; for the love of such steeds is war.

Early Álvar Fáñez had warned the Cid that he could not long endure the Court, and even less endure inaction. He had made him see that the friendliness of the King would soon change to coldness, and that he would suffer himself to be influenced once more by his courtiers and the jealous rivals of the Cid. And the Cid himself was warned by some sense of premonition that mastery would be won again by those felon intriguers who cling to thrones as close as limpets; and he preferred to go before he broke with the King.

Nothing very definite had he said, but once he had been heard to say: 'I hate the Moor because he is an invader, an intruder in our lands; but even more than the Moor I detest the traitor, the false courtier of the palace. In any country he is the man most mischievous.'

Perhaps we may read in this sentence a betrayal of that close-guarded mind of the Cid; and even more might we ponder these words, which he kept on repeating from the moment when he was on the march: 'I am for action, and not for useless words. Repose has for me more peril than a hundred ambushes. There is danger in words.'

Be that as it may, it is the truth that the Campeador could not endure to remain even two years in Castile, and that during that time which was for him a period of calm he seemed smaller, weaker and of diminished lustre. But now he was hardly on horseback before he breathed as if he had four lungs, and he grew in stature with every step of Babieca. He marched in exaltation towards his destiny, more full than ever of love for his country. The trees that he was leaving behind him held all the warmth and colour of its soul.

The country which we leave for ever is more beloved than the country to which we return; but when this country is the stamping-ground of our chimera, the land where our dreams come true, then it is clothed with every kind of fascination and draws us with the force of magnetism.

At the passage of the River Duero all the horses of the host of the Cid bent their necks to the water, and stopped to drink the river in great gulps, deep draughts of aspiration; and then they followed the road towards Calamocha. The sun declining over some distant sea breathed a last sigh and plunged into the waters....

At Calamocha there came to offer homage and tribute the Lord of Albarracín, who had heard that the Campeador contemplated attack upon his lands. The Muslim ruler declared himself his tributary—tributary to this King without a Kingdom, this vagabond hero, this sublime nomad who dominated so many cities and made so many thrones tremble, though he had no city which he could call his own, nor any throne from which to issue his decrees.

From Calamocha the Cid went on to Zaragoza, whither al-Mustain had summoned him. Even more ascendancy to the Campeador this monarch yielded than his father al-Mutamid. For Zaragoza the Castilian had become a kind of fetish. Al-Mustain would have the Cid aid him to compel the King of Dénia, the restless al-Mundhir, his indefatigable rival, to raise the siege of Valencia.

At the mere name of Valencia the eyes of the Cid sparkled with the light of spears and shields—Valencia, the city desirable, that place which drew the eyes of five Kings and the hands of a hundred chiefs, the focus of a thousand intrigues. Gladly the Cid accepted the pact which al-Mustain proposed to him—accepted it as an ally, since now he was no vassal, and recognised only Alfonso VI as his King. Between Álvar Fáñez and Martín Antolínez, followed by Per Vermúdez, Muño Gustioz, Galín García, Álvar Salvadores, Gil Ordoño and many other nobles, the Cid Campeador marched towards Valencia at the head of his host of three thousand men.

With every step of his steed he drew closer to the last phase of his glorious life. He was forty-and-nine years old. He had a host idolatrous and brave, he had Babieca, he had Tizona. He was as strong and as active as in the flower of his youth. Nurtured on saws and sirloins, he was as ready as ever of mouth and arm. With every step of his steed he came closer to the most difficult phase of his Olympian life. He marched towards Valencia, he came closer to Valencia. Now he must bring into play not only all his gifts as soldier and leader, but also all his skill and talent for politics.

In the midst of battles, wars, revolutions, diplomatic intrigues, alliances and counter-alliances, complexities of all kinds, assassinations, treasons, the Cid went his way safe and sound, with his eyes fastened upon his fixed idea, and in the end he was to triumph over all his enemies. A demon for restlessness, always he kept himself serene. He leapt to the right, he leapt to the left, he went forward to the attack, he retreated, he went forward again, he slipped to one side lashing like a shark, glided to the other side, and slid between the hands of his adversaries.

The shark became an eel, the eel became a lion, lurking in the forest and craftily biding his time, or climbing to the highest peak to watch the enemy, awaiting the moment to seize and squeeze him like a bindweed. The lion became a fox, the fox became an eagle. He alone was all the fauna and flora of the world. Nothing could match in marvel the life of this winner of battles—a life which was a zigzag across Epic from prodigy to prodigy.

He was forty-and-nine years old, and I see him marching towards Valencia upon Babieca at slow, majestic pace. At the feet of this man, imperturbable and headlong, serene and restless, Time unrolled, and Eternity marched to the rhythm of his host. Arrows whistled, there were routs like stampedes of herds, crowns fell to the accompaniment of the sardonic laughter of men. He and his host passed before God. Spain defiled before the eyes of the world behind the Cid, in a column long and fascinating as a snake.

There came the men of Galicia, Celts of moonlit souls and origins mysterious. There came the men of the Asturias, cousins of them of Galicia, dreaming that they still followed Don Pelayo. There came the men of León, with the bearing of lions and the pace of the Duero. There came the sturdy men of Castile, seeing in the troops of the enemy herds of butcher's meat and in the castles windmills. The men of Vivar stood out for their eyes of faith and their faces of ardour; they were the veterans of the host of the Cid, the favourites of Song and Ballad. There came the men of Navarre and of Aragón, many of them types of pure Iberians, square-headed, with brains of stone, muscles of rock, nerves of steel—men impervious. With the Christians marched al-Mustain with four hundred Moorish soldiers. They marched towards Valencia behind the stirrups of the Cid, passing before God, before Chronicle, before the word, before me and before you. At the news that the Cid was approaching, al-Mundhir, who held the city beleaguered, raised his siege and shut himself up in Tortosa. Unaware that al-Mundhir had abandoned the field, the Christians marched on, making ready for battle. There before them arose Valencia, there suddenly appeared the city, unsullied, cleansed of besiegers. The column halted a moment to contemplate it. The eyes of that serpent glared towards the place, and its fangs fixed themselves in the midst of the hypnotised camp. Valencia sensed the bale and the poison and trembled.

Al-Qadir, King of Valencia, felt a chill which ran in long arpeggios up and down his Muslim spine. Knowing the Cid and all that the hero of Castile was like to do, al-Qadir realised that it would not suit him to adopt a warlike attitude, but that rather he must seek to conjure away this new danger with a show of friendship. So al-Qadir, that man who every day made and unmade alliances and pacts to save Valencia, went out to meet the Cid and thanked him for having saved him from al-Mundhir. He loaded him with embraces and with presents, and bade him set his camp in the orchards of Villanueva.

In the midst of all this hospitality to the Cid al-Mustain saw that he was left on one side, and he guessed that the Cid had no less interest in the city than himself. So he withdrew to Zaragoza, feigning to leave the hands of the Christians free.

'Bravo!' exclaimed the Cid as he saw him go; 'now we have scared away all the pretenders to Valencia and our rivals retire.'

'And what must we do now?' asked Álvar Fáñez. 'We must wait, and while we wait I am going to make some raids upon the subjects of the King of Dénia—a matter of taking the rust off our swords and winning some booty for our troops.'

So they did. The Cid attacked the Moors of Africa and made a foray through the countryside, levying tribute and taking the rust off his swords. But the problem of Valencia was not so simple. He had succeeded in thrusting away from it two of his competitors, al-Mundhir of Dénia and al-Mustain of Zaragoza; but there remained a third, and he the most important of all, since this was his own King Alfonso, whose vassal he still held himself to be.

The Cid assembled his knights and seized them of his plans. 'I have decided to return to Castile, that I may discuss with the King this matter of Valencia.'

'Do we need his aid to take the city?' asked Martín Antolínez.

'No; but since I propose to take it in his name, and not in the name of Moorish Kings, I must consult him and take counsel with him so that he may support us once the place is ours.'

'The Cid is right,' declared Álvar Fáñez; 'we must not forget the powerful Almoravids, who will surely try to snatch Valencia from the hands of the Christians.'

'The city is a rare prize, and all who pretend to it today will make alliance tomorrow against him who succeeds in winning it.'

'To Castile, then!' thundered that booming voice of Per Vermúdez.

Hardly had the Cid left Valencia on his way to Castile when al-Mustain made alliance with Berenguer Ramon of Barcelona and came back against the city. The two allies took the castle of Cebolla, made it their base of operations, and laid siege to Valencia. Al-Qadir sent messengers to overtake the Cid and tell him what had passed, assuring him that he would hold out until he could return with his troops. With all speed the Cid came back at the head of an army now swollen to seven thousand men; and when the Count Berenguer learned of the Cid's return with this much more numerous array, he raised the siege and retired without offering battle.

At the sight of the approaching host of the Cid al-Qadir went out from his city to meet him for the second time. He made a pact with the Campeador by which he engaged to pay him a monthly tribute of ten thousand dinars, on condition that the Cid compelled the submission of the lords of the castles and cities which had rebelled, pacified his lands, protected him against his enemies, and did not himself leave his territory. The Cid should have his mart and his stores of grain in Valencia, and there he could sell the booty which he gained in his raids.

Now Valencia was tributary to the Campeador. The serpent was closing upon the object of his fatal regard like the Devil's shears.

THE BALANCE-SHEET OF GLORY

In the soul of the Cid there were two supreme desires—the friendship of his King Alfonso, and the possession of Valencia. What had the indomitable man left undone to win that friendship? But ever between him and the King there stepped in an occult power; and whenever it seemed that the two hearts were to be sealed with a kiss of loyalty, again there was division, again there rose between them a wall of misunderstanding.

As for the possession of Valencia, the Cid could have made himself master of the city when he would. If he did not, it was because reasons of State counselled prudence. Those last months of the year 1090 the Cid spent in raids about the territory and in incursions into the lands of the rich and powerful al-Mundhir. He took the castle of Polope, he took Miravet, and he ranged in triumph from Jativa to Orihuela.

His name alone sent a chill of terror through all the West. Its provinces trembled on the map like leaves upon a tree. He had fashioned an army demoniac in its strength, a phalanx of invincibility which obeyed like a machine the least flicker of his eyes. 'What more could the King Alfonso wish,' Álvar Fáñez asked with good reason, 'than to have at his service this matchless host which does not cost Castile one farthing?'

But al-Mundhir did not sleep for an instant. Watching with startled eyes the raids of the Cid through his lands, he feared that at any moment he might fall upon Tortosa and rob him of the most precious cities of his Kingdom. So he decided once more to approach Berenguer Ramon of Barcelona, whom he knew held rancour against the Cid. He offered him money and advantages of all kinds to make alliance with him and rid him once for all of the nightmare of the terrible man of Vivar.

The Count had only bided his time until he could avenge himself upon the Cid, and he raised a great army and set off at once to confer with al-Mundhir. He established his camp at Calamocha, and there he agreed with al-Mundhir that they should propose an alliance to al-Mustain of Zaragoza and to King Alfonso himself, so that all the princes together might undertake a great campaign against the Cid.

But the King of Castile was a man shrewd in politics, and in the depths of his soul he knew very well on which side it suited him to play. He was sure of the loyalty of his vassal; and so, despite his old animosity, he rejected flatly all proposals that he should enter the league. Al-Mustain, fearful of the final issue of the campaign, would not join it either; but, if he did not lend his troops, at least he aided his former rivals with his wealth. On the other hand, that he might not alienate the friendship of the Cid, who might well survive this test as triumphantly as he had so many others, he sent him secret news of what his enemies were plotting against him.

The Cid was encamped among the mountains in the pine-clad valley of Tevar. When he received the letter of al-Mustain he sent him back by the same messenger the following reply:

'**To al-Mustain, King of Zaragoza**: I thank you for the news you send me; and, as I do not fear my enemies, you may tell them that here in the pinewoods of Tévar I await them, holding myself entirely at their disposition. Perhaps they will not dare to come. That would be a pity, for this year as yet has been poor in fine battles. Tell Berenguer Ramon in my name that he and all his are cowards, liars, and braggarts, and that they are not men, but women weak of arm and boasting of tongue. I salute you.

RUY DÍAZ.'

Without waiting to be asked, the crafty al-Mustain showed this letter to Berenguer; for well pleased he was to be able to foment discord between the two Christian leaders and weaken in war three powerful rivals. The Count in his anger replied directly to the Cid:

'**Ruy Díaz**, you have said that I and mine are no better than women. If God aids us, I shall soon show you that you lie. We know that the ravens of the mountains, the crows, the kites, the eagles—in a word, all the birds, are your gods, and that you have more confidence in their auguries than in the help of the Almighty. We, on the other hand, believe that there is but one God, and that this God will avenge us upon you and place you in our hands. Tomorrow as soon as the sun rises you will see us approaching, and if you then leave your mountains and come to measure yourself with us in the plain, we shall hold you for Rodrigo called the Warrior and the Campeador; but if you do not come we shall hold you for a traitor. We shall not let you rest until we have taken you dead or alive, and we shall treat you as you would have treated us.

BERENGUER RAMON, COUNT OF BARCELONA.'

At once the Cid replied:

'**To Berenguer Ramon, Count of Barcelona**: I shall not answer your accusations in the matter of my supposed superstitions. Beautiful are the birds when they fly in the air, and some are pleasant on a platter; but only your head could confuse the natural admiration of a man for the things of Nature with a religion.

'Yes, I have heaped insults upon you, and here are my reasons: When you were with al-Mustain in Calatayud, you told him that for fear of you I had not dared to penetrate into his lands. Some of your followers, such as Raimundo de Baran, have affirmed the same to the King Alfonso himself, in the presence of various knights of Castile; and you yourself, in the presence of al-Mustain, told the King Alfonso that you would have expelled me from the country of al-Mundhir if I had dared to await you, and further that you had not wished to fight against a vassal of Castile's King.

'That is why I have spoken ill of you; I loathe lies and boastings. Now you have no excuse for failing to attack me. On the contrary, you have made al-Mundhir promise you a great sum, and you have agreed with him to drive me from his lands. Keep your word, then. Come and attack me if you dare. I am in a plain, the largest there is in this country, and as soon as I see you I shall settle your account as ever.

RUY DÍAZ DE VIVAR.'

Berenguer was a bold man, and he could count upon a host great in numbers and his own match in bravery. He had no sooner received this letter than he set out on his march to the valley of Tévar. The Franks, as they called the Catalans then because Barcelona had been a fief of France, advanced in silence through the night, and taking advantage of the darkness, they occupied the mountains which surrounded the camp of the Cid. At dawn, before the sun rose, the Catalans fell upon it by surprise like an avalanche. The soldiers of the Campeador had barely time to seize their arms.

'They would surprise us unarmed!' roared the Cid, leaping on Babieca and hastening to marshal his men in battle array.

'Up, men!' shouted Álvar Fáñez on the other side of the camp, seeking to hearten his men. 'Courage, courage!'

The war-worn troops of the Cid had no need of such rallying cries. They were not men easy to dismay.

'Charge!' bellowed the Cid, and himself setting the example, charged first against the enemy vanguard.

'Forward, forward!' yelled Muño Gustioz.

'Fear not!' sounded the trumpet voice of Per Vermúdez. 'Let us give a lesson to those who thought to defeat us by surprise!'

The Campeador and his lieutenants flung themselves in all directions into the opposing ranks, fighting with a frenzy such as even they had never shown before. Tizona went mad in the hands of her master, who dealt death-strokes until his head nearly reeled, leapt over dangers, and balanced on the edge of abysses Hinging to his star, that star which is the godmother of the predestined. His host, charged with lightnings, let loose a rain of blood upon the field. The two armies were one wave which ebbed and flowed, carrying a wrack of death which floated lost in its gleaming surge.

Suddenly, in the midst of the thunderous tumult, Babieca stumbled on the stones and rolled to the ground. A shudder ran through Olympus, and the Cid felt a spear pierce his back. His rich blood gushed from the wound and drenched the ground. That piece of earth is today a reliquary of Poem. His blood fell upon Spain, fell drop by drop upon the memory of men. The miracle of transubstantiation was accomplished, and Spain was converted into a Host of Epic.

My pen is red with the blood of the Cid. In a second his knights had rallied around him to protect him. I myself turn my pen into a spear, and I would face ten Moors; but the hero was already afoot. Babieca stamped her foot with anger against herself, and Tizona was welded more solidly than ever to that powerful hand.

The wounded Cid felt anger rise in his breast, and it rose, too, among his men. A great wave of indignation shook their hearts, and flung them forward, a legion of demons uncontrollable. The thirst for vengeance doubled their strength, tripled their energy, quadrupled the swiftness of their blows. No longer did the Cid feel his wound. He struck, he razed, he obliterated. Babieca burst through all foes with her powerful breast; Tizona was a machine drunken with its own rhythm. Uncontrolled by the hand of her master, she seemed to fight of herself, delirious, electrical. In her proper fury she obeyed no orders but those of her own fever. Tizona had the very devil within her.

Before that onset the enemy bent and broke and were undone. Slowly at first, then more rapidly, they began to retire, the rhythm of retreat quickened its beat, until suddenly there came a *sauve qui peut* through the pine-woods and the mountains. The field was left to the Cid. Five thousand men his host took prisoner, and among them once again were the Count Berenguer Ramon and many of his nobles.

The night fell on a carpet broidered with slain. In the midst of it the blood of the Cid bloomed in a great poppy of Myth.

These were the fruits of that victory:

1. The road to Valencia remained clear.
2. The Count Ramon Berenguer and the Lord Guerau d'Alamany paid the Cid eighty thousand marks of gold as ransom for their freedom.
3. Al-Mundhir died of a broken heart, and his successor, rather than war against the Cid, preferred to place himself under his protection and pay him a yearly tribute of fifty thousand dinars.
4. Berenguer Ramon did the same, and placed a part of his dominions under the protection of the Cid and paid him a yearly tribute of forty thousand dinars.
5. The Cid won the sword Colada, almost as magnificent as Tizona. That night, in the tent of the Cid, while the Campeador walked the Heavens, Álvar Fáñez and Martín Antolínez reckoned up the tributes:

	Dinars a Year
Count of Barcelona	40,000
King of Tortosa	50,000
al-Qadir, King of Valencia	150,000
Lord of Alpuente	10,000
Lord of Albarracín	10,000
Lord of Segorbe	6,000
Lord of Murviedro	6,000
Lord of Jérica	4,000
Lord of Almenara	3,000
Lord of Liria	2,000
TOTAL	281,000

Without throne or crown, the Cid was a potentate. He who had gone forth banished from Castile with a meagre column of valiant followers reigned over one of the richest and widest regions of Spain, thanks to his genius for arms and policy.

He had an income which any sovereign in Europe might have envied: 281,000 dinars a year, without counting all his treasure in jewels, precious stones, tapestries, embroideries, and the like. He was the Rockefeller of his epoch. But what a Rockefeller!

He was the Rockefeller of his epoch; but there were many times when he had not enough to eat. His coffers full of gold often went companioned by stewpots that were empty.

This day, the second day of March, they were fighting before Liria. A great part of the Muslim army was encamped outside the place, under a hundred half moons fallen from the sky on to its banners. Hungry and weary after the skirmishing of the day, the Cid and his knights came back to their own camp, and sat down to sup around a long table made of four beams laid on tree trunks—a rustic table of adventure. Opposite, in the enemy camp, the Moors also were dedicating themselves to the pleasant business of filling their bellies.

One of the servants of the Cid approached him and murmured almost into his ear: 'My lord, there is little to eat, for supplies are running short.'

'Serve what you have, my son. Tomorrow will be another day, and we shall find a means of augmenting them.'

Somewhat bashfully the servant presented a great dish of lentils, and when all were served he could do no more than come back and tell them that there was nothing else.

'You mean to say there is nothing else?' exclaimed Per Vermúdez. 'And you tell us at the last moment, idiot, when every one of us is more ravenous than ten wolves.'

'And it makes it harder, sir,' said another of the servants, 'to have nothing but bread and lentils, when one can see the Moors over there preparing chicken and lamb for their suppers.'

The Cid shot a glance like a flash of lightning over his companions. He rose to his feet, and he smiled. 'My friends,' he cried, 'this is for shame. You have heard: the enemy are stuffing themselves with good fare before our very beards. I propose that we throw ourselves upon them and exchange our lentils for their chicken and lamb.'

'Exchange our lentils be hanged!' amended Per Vermúdez amid general laughter; 'let us add their chicken and lamb to our lentils!'

'Bravo, Per Vermúdez; agreed!' cried Martín Antolínez.

'Bravo, bravo!' repeated all in chorus, and ran for their horses. 'Hurrah for the chicken and the lamb!'

At full gallop they rode into the enemy camp. They burst among the Moors, scattering tents and dealing blows with such appetite that the chief and his men fled as if they were swept away by a wind from the sea, and were lost in the distances of flight. Nobody thought of pursuing them. The Cid and his captains laid hands on everything there was upon the regal board, and back they went singing, with the chicken and the lamb held high as glorious trophies for the bellies which rumbled in anticipation into bursts of laughter. Every chicken and every platter was a banner.

Before the lentils had gone cold they had won a battle, a famous battle of the belly, and a leg of lamb flanked by a wing of chicken set on the still-steaming plates bore witness to the lightning rapidity of that glorious feat of arms.

How those mouths gobbled! The noise which the teeth of Ugolino make in Italy was nothing to it. A hornet passed to and fro above the dishes droning like a siphon...

Sovereign in fact of all the West though he was, the Cid, despite his triumphs, obstinately held himself to be the vassal of Alfonso, and he stood ready to prove his loyalty at all times. So, when the King of Castile informed him that he was making ready a great expedition against the Almoravids, and would gladly have him take part in it with his host, the Campeador raised the siege which he was laying to Liria for its default in payment of its due tribute, and set forth at once to join the Royal army.

Midway between Martos and Jaén the Cid met the troops of Alfonso. The King went out to meet him and lavished on him marks of friendship and goodwill; but his heart was ever ready to doubt the greatest and most faithful of his vassals. Alfonso had pitched his camp on the slopes of the mountains. In proof of his amity and to show how zealously he watched over the interests of the King, the Campeador chose for his host the more dangerous position, and pitched his tents in the plain in front of those of the King.

This gesture of deference and affection was taken by Alfonso as an arrogant piece of insolence. 'See the affront which Ruy Díaz offers me,' he cried in a fury to his knights; 'when he arrived I told him that I was weary from long riding, and now he blocks our way and pitches his tents in front of ours.'

'The proud Campeador would ever cast a shade,' the Count García Ordóñez was quick to answer, making no effort to conceal his ancient grudge. After so many years he had not yet forgotten the tweaking of his beard at the Battle of Cabra! 'The time has come,' he added, 'to teach him a lesson.'

'Well he deserves it!' exclaimed the King. 'Is there no means of breaking the pride of this man of Vivar?'

Battle was joined, and victory was already inclining to the Christians when fresh forces arrived to aid the Moors, and Alfonso, overwhelmed by numbers, was forced to retire. At this crisis the military talent of the Cid saved his fellow-countrymen from complete rout, and his energy stayed the retreat. Nevertheless the King, infuriated by the failure of the expedition and urged on by his courtiers, blamed the Cid for the issue of the battle. He must seize the Cid and punish him. Poor King, seize the hurricane and punish the storm!

The Cid boiled with indignation when he learned the intentions of Alfonso, and he summoned his lieutenants and told them of the King's plans. Need it be said that, faced with so flagrant an injustice, all these men who adored him counselled him not to tolerate such an outrage? And there were even among them those who would have him rise against the King and attack his camp.

That the Cid would not do, but neither was he disposed any longer to endure the repeated affronts of his sovereign, who would not see the honesty of his acts, and was ever ready to interpret them crookedly. He would not attack the camp of the men of Castile and León; but in the silence of the night the Campeador and his own men stole away, furtive as a fox, and returned to the lands of Valencia.

The next morning the King Alfonso saw that the hated man of Vivar had slipped between his fingers. Furious that his plans were thus made a mockery, he took counsel with his captains, and resolved to punish him, cost what it might, through that which most could hurt him. Alfonso decided to wrest from him Valencia—Valencia the dearest dream of the Cid; Valencia which he could already consider as his own, since its King al-Qadir paid him tribute and obeyed him as a vassal.

Profiting by the war that the Cid was waging in Zaragoza in defence of al-Mustain against the men of Aragón, the King of Castile marched with a great army against Valencia, made alliance with the men of Genoa and of Pisa, who aided him with four hundred ships, and laid siege to the city by land and sea.

When the news of what was passing at Valencia came to the Cid, indignation schooled him at the last that the time for temporising was gone, and that he was forced to teach a lesson to his King. Enough of paying court to a man so blind and arbitrary; enough of seeking a friendship as difficult as it was dubious! He would punish. But above all he would punish the Count García Ordóñez, that sower of discord. Him would the Cid show that he knew well whence issued all the injustice under which he suffered; him would he show that, if the King was blameworthy because he let himself so easily be deceived, still more culpable was the Count who wrought so steadfastly at his labour of hatred.

He would punish the King and his evil counsellor. He would reply to the affront with a greater affront. He had no need of long thought before his talent for politics revealed to him what he must do. He left the lands of Zaragoza and marched with all his host into Castile. He passed like a whirling water-spout through the fields of Ndjera and Calahotra, over which the Count García Ordóñez ruled. The lightning emptied its wrath upon the very lands of its own enemy. He attacked the cities of Alberite and Logroño, which surrendered before his onset, and laid siege to the fortress of Alfaro.

With the fortress taken at the first assault, Muño Gustioz counselled the Cid to press on to Burgos. This would be the punishment exemplary, the buffet resounding, the slap in the face which would re-echo backwards to the first day of the world and forward to the last minute of creation.

'No,' said the Cid. 'I have shown them that I could do it if I would. Now I would have them see that my vengeance is aimed most at García Ordóñez; and I would have them feel that even my patience has its limits, and that I am vassal of Castile because it pleases me, and that I may cease to be so when I choose.'

'You have more reason than enough,' burst out Álvar Fáñez, stung by the words of the Cid; 'you have fought for your King, you have neglected your own interests for his, and he does not even thank you; he lends ear to the basest intrigues, as if deeds did not clamour in your favour.'

A sentence sprang from the depths of the Cid's soul: 'Ah, if the King had but understood me; if the King had but supported me!'

'God, how good a vassal! Would that his lord were as worthy!' murmured Martín Antolínez.

'If the King had not sent you from his side,' declared Per Vermúdez, 'with all his armies under your command, by this day there would not remain a single Moor in all the peninsula.'

'I will not march on Burgos,' said the noble Cid; 'I will remain here at Alfaro and wait until García Ordóñez comes to liberate his lands.'

And despite a secret voice that whispered in his ear how easy it would be to enter Burgos, and that if he would he could even proclaim himself King in the midst of a people that idolised their hero and the legend of his deeds, he went no step further. He waited.

He had not long to wait. The King in alarm raised the siege of Valencia and hastened to defend his own lands. Did he fear perhaps that he who had defeated so many Kings and conquered so many Kingdoms would wrench from him even his own? Two things the Cid had wished: to compel the King to withdraw from the city of the West, and then to meet face to face the Count of the tweaked beard. His plans worked well.

All his hopes were realised, for García Ordóñez informed him that he was on his way to attack him, and sent a messenger to bid him wait only seven days more in his lands until he should come to join battle.

'At last!' cried the Cid. 'Tell this Count that I will wait for him not only seven days, but three times seven. At last I am going to meet him in the open field, in the free air, this courtier insidious and vile. Praise be to God!'

The hour of justice and of punishment had come. All Spain eagerly awaited the moment, Chronicle fixed anxious eyes upon it, Legend raised its head. With what gusto are we about to watch and to describe the battle in which the Cid once more plucked another good handful from the beard of his mortal enemy!

Unfortunately we cannot describe that battle. That intriguer García Ordóñez has disappointed us. He set out on the way with his troops; and he turned back without presenting himself anywhere near where the Cid awaited him. In vain my pen is dipped in rose water and rubs its hands at the thought of giving a few good pricks to the poor Count, taking him prisoner, and rubbing his face in a manure-heap. He does not present himself. The term passes and three times the term—not a sign of the Count. He leaves me with my pen in my hand, he snatches the honey from my lips, he robs me of the joy of vengeance.

You dare not come? Very good; let you be pilloried as a coward, a courtier insidious and vile. Here I pillory you before the world, I lock you in this page, and I myself tweak your beard—you dirty dog!

DIARY OF ABEN ALI

There lived at that time in Valencia a famous Arab poet by name Aben Ali, cousin of that other writer no less celebrated, of mixed origin, half Christian and half Muslim, whom they called Aben Aben. Aben Ali kept a diary which may serve us to make clear many points of doubt, for in it we find jotted down day by day not only the most important events which happened within the city, but also, in short and summary fashion, his own opinions and even people's conversation.

1. Yesterday walking on the shore I heard some merchants say that the Cid Campeador had been seen near Segorbe. It seems that he is coming to Valencia with an army even more numerous than last year. It is incredible how the mere name of the Christian leader makes brave men tremble and faces pale. His name alone inspires more terror than a hundred legions. Why has Allah not willed that such a man be born among us? Why has Heaven not given us another Almanzor who would avenge us and save our culture, which is the only important culture in the world, from these rude and ignorant barbarians; and save our faith, the only true faith, from the Christian heresy? Inscrutable are the ways of Allah!

2. They say that the Cid has many soldiers. They say that before entering the provinces of the West he sent messengers through Aragón, Navarre and Castile, summoning all who would ride with him. He bade them join his host, for he was going to lay siege to Valencia. They say that the Cid announced that he would halt three days at Canal de Celfa, and that armed men rode in by every road. What a spirit of adventure these Goths have!

    They say that the Cid Rodrigo comes full of wrath against the Cadi Ibn Djahaf, who surrendered our city to the Almoravids, killed poor al-Qadir, who was under his protection, and sought to seize Al Faradi, who was his representative in Valencia. Ibn Djahaf is a vain and stupid tyrant, but Faradi is a traitor, and from the point of view of our race his conduct is more to be execrated than that of the other.

3. This morning Ibn Djahaf received from the Cid Campeador a letter full of menaces, in which he said: 'You have committed a base deed in throwing the head of your King into a pond and burying his body in

a dunghill. Apart from this account which we have to settle, I demand that you restore to me the wheat which lies in my granaries in Valencia.'

I like the energetic tone of this letter. What would I not give if there were such a man among us! It is said that there are times when the gods forbid certain peoples to produce great men.

4. Ibn Djahaf has replied to the Cid: 'Your wheat has been stolen and I cannot restore it to you. The city is now in the power of the Almoravids; and, if you swear obedience to the Emperor Yusuf, I am ready to be your friend and ally.'

     Much I fear that a letter so imbecile, so utterly lacking in diplomacy and common sense, will produce ill consequences.

5. There we are. The thing has happened. Good reason had I to fear that that luckless Djahaf would drag us all to perdition. The Cid Campeador has answered in very few words: 'I swear in the name of God that I will come and avenge the death of my friend al-Qadir.' So it is war. Discontent is growing in the city, and it is even said that there have been riots in the lower quarters.

6. The Cid has ordered the lords of all the castles of the district to provide supplies for his troops.

7. The Cid has laid siege to Cebolla. They say that, while part of his host besieges the city, another part is making raids through the countryside, carrying off quantities of provisions and cattle.

8. Here inside Valencia the situation grows complicated, and nobody knows exactly what is happening. Some say that Ibn Djahaf would rebel against the Almoravids. Others hold responsible the intrigues of their chief, Aben Nazir; and others again lay the blame on old Abderam, ex-King of Murcia. In any case it is not to be denied that hatred of Djahaf is growing among the people, and that it is justified by the attitude of the fool.

9. Today there set out an embassy composed of five worthy but pretentious nobodies to take magnificent presents to the Emperor Yusuf.

10. Great consternation in the city. The party which was on its way to visit the Moorish Sultan had hardly left Valencia when the Cid fell upon it, and wrested from it the enormous sums of money and all the other treasure destined for Yusuf.

11. Today there came to see me a friend of my childhood much given to occultism. He told me that yesterday he was present at a *séance* of wise men and wizards who called up spirits with magic incantations and foresaw the future through shapes in the smoke of incense. According

to these diviners great disasters are about to fall upon our race.

All day long I have been thoughtful and sad. I have written a poem about our race that dies after having fulfilled its noble mission among the barbarians and the infidels.

12. The Cid Campeador is the obsession of this city. All day I have heard men speak of him and discuss his deeds with gestures of discouragement. They say that he has destroyed the mills in the region and burned the boats on the Guadalaviar, and that the fortress of Cebolla has yielded to his attack and fallen into his mouth like a piece of pie. A great panic reigns among the chiefs, for it is certain that he will soon present himself at our gates.

13. That has happened which was bound to happen. Today at dawn the great Campeador appeared before the walls of Valencia. He is fighting to master his old camping-ground of Villanueva. Valencia is besieged. How short a time it takes to write down so grave a matter!

14. He has won Villanueva.

15. Today he launched an attack against the suburb of Alcudia. The wounded who have come in say that the fighting is terrible. They report that in the midst of the battle the horse of the Cid, the famous Babieca, fell to the ground; but on the instant her master was up again and shearing heads with greater energy and fury than ever. The Christian dragon drove his way through breasts and spears like a ship at sea.

The advance guards of the Cid are attacking the walls beside the gate of the bridge of Alcantara. A deluge of stones rains upon them, but they do not give way. They retire for a moment and return to the attack in a wave that pounds more heavily than before.

16. Alcudia has fallen into his hands. Panic grows every minute. People walk the streets with eyes starting out of their heads. The notables of the city have met and sent an embassy to the fateful Campeador asking for peace.

17. The Cid Campeador has replied with the haughtiness of a man very sure of himself. He demands the immediate evacuation of Valencia by the Almoravids, the payment of the tribute of ten thousand dinars a month accorded him by al-Qadir with all sums in arrear, the restoration of the wheat which he had stored in this city, and the setting of his encampments in Cebolla and Alcudia.

This last clause implies that the peace refers only to Valencia itself, and that he has no intention of giving back any of the suburbs which he has wrested from us by force. Ibn Djahaf has accepted these conditions.

18. The Campeador appears to be satisfied, and is organising his conquests like a shrewd man of politics and a practised proprietor.

19. What a Babel this city is! Nobody knows what he wants.

20. There is good news: they say that the Lord of Albarracín and Morviedro, the famous Ibn Razin, has bought the alliance of Sancho of Aragón, and that they will undertake together a campaign against the Cid. Praise be to Allah!

21. During the night the troops of the Cid have disappeared from our sight. What is happening? This morning there was not a single tent to be seen in all the neighbourhood. They have vanished as if by magic, as though they had flown away in the night.

22. No news. Nobody knows anything about the Cid and his host. The earth has swallowed them.

23. Since the tents of the Cid flew away in the night like great birds of destiny nothing more has been heard of them.

24. Ibn Djahaf has sent to the Emperor Yusuf to ask for the return of the Almoravids. This seems to me a grave error of politics, and I foresee that its consequences will be serious.

25. The cat is out of the bag. This Cid is a man of secret magic, he senses events beforehand in the air, and resolves situations with such speed that he baffles all his enemies. He has fallen by surprise upon the lands of Ibn Razin, and put them to sword and fire. Here is the explanation of the mystery of his retirement from Valencia. Ibn Razin is completely routed. The Cid is master of an enormous booty of cattle, horses, and sheep, and he has separated Sancho of Aragón from Ibn Razin and made alliance with him.

26. The Cid has sent to Yusuf to tell him that, since his own alliance with the King of Aragón, the Emperor will have to reckon with eight thousand knights if he dares approach Valencia.

27. It appears that Yusuf has not paid much heed to the warning of the Cid Campeador, for today there is news that his army is marching through Murcia.

28. They say that the army of the Almoravids has reached Jativa, but it is not under the command of Yusuf himself, who is ill, but of his son-in-law Abu Ibrahim. The number of his soldiers increases as he advances. From all sides flock Muslims eager to rid our race of the terrible Christian.

29. In spite of the news which reaches here, the Cid does not retire. The

Almoravids are now at Alzira. Does not the man guess that, if he offers battle to our allies, we shall sally out to attack him in the rear, and that he will be crushed in less time than it takes a cock to crow? Or is he so sure of his strength and his military genius that he is afraid of none, and not dismayed by the enormous advantage in numbers of his adversaries?

30. The Cid has destroyed all the bridges over the Guadalaviar and has flooded the plain. Now I understand. The wily strategist has left only a strip, narrow enough, for the Almoravids to traverse. Doubtless he plans to attack them there.

31. The army of the Almoravids is encamped at Alcacer. The whole population has climbed the towers to see the spears of the army of liberation. I climbed up too, but all I could see in the distance was a cloud of dust going up to heaven. The Cid had not budged from his ground, and he shows a calmness quite incomprehensible.

32. The night is dark and close. The sky hurls itself down in thunders and lightnings and falls in a deluge. From the top of the walls we can see the fires in the camp of our allies.

  Tomorrow the great battle will be joined. Here we are pressing forward our preparations for welcoming the Almoravids in triumph, and also for sallying out and falling upon the Christians at the most favourable moment of the battle.

33. What a disappointment! Nobody can understand what has happened. The troops of the Almoravids have not come to give battle. They are in full retreat towards the South. Is it possible? Without even attempting to succour us?

34. The Cid has heard of our intention to make a sortie from the city and attack him in the rear while he was fighting with our allies. His soldiers have come up to our walls and heaped insults upon us, shaking their fists at us. They shout incomprehensible words at us, calling us sons of whores, cowards, sons of bitches, cuckolds, milksops, and many other things which I cannot remember, but which must be foul obscenities.

35. The Cid is an implacable enemy. We did ill in seeking to attack him treacherously. Today, master of the field, he draws his lines closer around the city.

36. We are beginning to run short of food. With the approach of hunger appear menacing faces, and there is talk of plots. Ibn Djahaf is at his wits' end, he is afraid, and fear makes him a cruel tyrant. He has ordered

three alleged conspirators to be beheaded without trial or proof.

37. Today another conspiracy against the Qadi Djahaf was unearthed. They say that Ibn Mochich was at the bottom of it.

38. Ibn Mochich has been arrested, and his confederates have paid with their heads.

39. What a pitiless enemy is the Cid! Today he has compelled to return to the city all those who had escaped from it for fear of famine, and he threatens with burning at the stake any who try to leave it. The wily man would swell the number of hungry mouths among us. As if they were so few already!

40. The assault today has been frightful, indescribable. The very air grew hot with the friction of millions of arrows from crossbows and stones from catapults. The walls of the sky creaked, and Heaven itself trembled. Swarms of men clambered like lizards up thousands of scaling-ladders. Great battering-rams beat upon the gates so deafeningly that here in the centre of the city, where I live, I have had to spend the whole day with my ears plugged. Even now I can hear that awful pam ... pam ... pam ... pam.... Pray Allah that the gates do not yield! Javelins whistle through the air, and they are so many that at times they make an actual curtain over the sky.

    I hear a voice outside my window which says: 'We are lost; that fool of an Ibn Djahaf is to blame for all.'

41. The assaults go on—assault after assault, ferocious, pitiless. What could be more horrible than the siege of a city? All my philosophy falls to pieces in the presence of the terrible scenes which I witness every moment. And that deafening noise which echoes in the sky: Pam . . . pam ... pam...

    A smell of blood fills all the evening between screams near and screams distant. Shouts in divers tongues mingle in the firmament. All the mosques resound with prayers, and waves of supplication beat against Heaven.

42. Pam . . . pam ... pam... The deafening noise goes on from dawn till dusk. There are shouts and screams; blows and flights of arrows and of javelins. From the tops of the rolling towers the soldiers of the Cid shoot into the streets of the city, sowing death. O Valencia, Valencia, how tumultuous a centre are you on the map of the world shining under the sun! If it continues thus we cannot hold out much longer.

    The Cid and his captains are monsters out of fable come to life again; they are everywhere at once, animating their soldiers by their example, fighting with indefatigable fury. Every one of them is worth a hundred men.

43. The city can resist no longer. The one thing in the thought of the taking of my beloved Valencia that consoles me is that I shall see the Titan of Castile close. May Allah pardon me! I have an unwholesome curiosity to contemplate this terrible Cid, and see if he be a man made like other mortals.

44. Ibn Djahaf is at the end of his tether. Hatred grows against the person of this vulgar tyrant, there are riots everywhere, and today the people even dared to shout at him accusations of regicide and of robbery and concealment of the treasures of al-Qadir.

45. The assault is general, and more furious than ever. The wounded drag themselves along the streets, leaving trails of blood. All the city is an uproar of pain and death. Resistance is already hopeless, and they say that at five o'clock this evening the gates will be opened to the enemy. But what is that? What was that deafening din, that infernal outcry? I must go and see what is happening.

All is over. Farewell, Valencia; see how my tears stream! I can hardly make out what I am writing. At three o'clock this evening the Cid Campeador entered the city. I saw him, I saw him; and, now that I have sated my curiosity, I can only weep for what we have lost.

He came in at the head of his men on a proud horse that seemed to tread upon the clouds. He came covered with dust and beard and blood. He carried in his hand a naked sword that gleamed like a verse of Epic. His eyes shone as if they were the one luminous point in history, and his enormous shoulders seemed to hold up a world. Behind him, mounted on fine horses, rode his captains, and behind them marched the whole column of demons. They passed through the multitude of our people, who looked at them in silence with open mouths. They went singing a song in honour of Valencia, of its beauties and its women. Easy to see that for long years they have desired our city and dreamed of her! And they have good reason.'

LORD OF VALENCIA

It was natural that, as he entered Valencia, that city for so many years desired, the Cid should feel a stir of gladness in every atom of him. It was natural that his eyes should shine with a sheen of History and of Glory. And it was natural, too, that this boundless satisfaction should infect all his soldiers, since it is known that the electricity of the hero circulated its current through his men.

The Cid entered the city on a pedestal of high content, and behind him his host marched singing *Valencia,* forgetful of all the pain and blood that its conquest had cost them:

'Valencia! Land of orange groves and sweet content,
    You called me from afar;
Valencia! Where a lover croons his sentiment
    Upon a light guitar....

Valencia! Where there's passion in the songs
    A lover sings beneath the moon.
Valencia! I am waiting in my garden
    For a lov'd one to come soon.'

Master of the city, the Cid ascended the highest of its towers, and there, looking over the past and the future, he surveyed his long-desired conquest with eyes of love. Up there, on the pinnacle of his life, his heart beat in the evening and his lungs drew in all the air in the world. The sea, with the noise of a thousand drums, chanted victory at his feet. The rolling of its waves silenced Poem, and flowed over *Geste* and Ballad.

His eyes swept the fields, and the earth wafted him its blessing in perfume of fruit and flowers. All this panorama of sea and land, with its ships and its men and its horses, was his. All these landscapes and these seascapes were his, before they became the property of any painter.

Up there, on the pinnacle of his life, he who had been unworthily banished from his country; he who had vanquished every man who came against him; he who had overthrown Kings Moor and Christian; he who had made nations and Legend tremble, looked over the lands that he had won with his arm and his brain—the richest Kingdom of Spain! The evening waxed pregnant with pride. And when the Cid Campeador began to descend from the tower his tread resounded through the universe. He was coming down from Heaven to Earth...

His first act in his new-won lands was to bid his men respect the property and the customs of the conquered; his second to order the execution of the despicable Ibn Djahaf; and his third to retire to the Alcazar, which he made his home, and there take his repose. Then he set himself to place in due order the administration of the city. He expelled from it all those who showed rebel leanings, and had Christians come to take their places.

When he was solidly installed in his new conquest and all was ordered to his liking, he summoned his knights. This is what he said to them: 'You, Per Vermúdez and Muño Gustioz, go to the Saracens and care for their wounded and bury their dead. Assure them of my goodwill, and tell them that, terrible as I may be in war, in peace I am gentle. I will not take their goods or their daughters, and none has aught to fear of me while he shows himself loyal and peaceable.

'You, Álvar Fáñez and Martín Antolínez, go to Castile and take to the King Alfonso, that ingrate, a hundred fine horses richly caparisoned, a hundred Moorish slaves to hold their bridles, and a hundred keys of the cities and the castles which I have won. Go to San Pedro de Cardeña and bring to me Jimena and my daughters, and take with you thirty marks of fine gold for their journey to Valencia. Take another thirty marks to the Abbot Don Sancho for the adornment of his altar, give him my thanks, and tell him that he has but to ask of me what he would. Ride with an escort of two hundred men for the protection of my wife, my daughters, and their ladies.'

Still was the Cid obsessed by his King, still had he not abandoned hope of wooing his friendship. It would seem that even in the flush of his triumph, when he had conquered the city desired by so many powerful Kings, and when he might have proclaimed himself its King, he yet sought so to show himself the loyal vassal *par excellence* that none could call his fealty in question.

Once in Castile Álvar Fáñez and Martín Antolínez parted outside San Pedro de Cardeña—Antolínez to fulfil his mission to Doña Jimena, and Minaya to follow his road to Burgos, bearing to the King the captives and the horses, the treasure and the presents, as the Cid had ordered.

In the presence of the King Álvar Fáñez bent a knee to the ground and kissed his hands. 'Powerful King Alfonso,' he said, 'Your Highness receives here the goodwill and the offering of a banished knight. Rodrigo de Vivar, expelled by jealousy from his home and his lands, has won these riches from the Moors at the price of his blood. In a few years the Cid has conquered for you more lands than your father left to you. Do not accuse him of pride if he sends tribute to his King with the tributes of other Kings. You, his lord, deprived him of his own, and he pays you with the goods of others. Have confidence in him. So long as he has in his hand his sword Tizona and between his knees his horse Babieca he will increase your power.'

A Count rose to his feet. 'Do not believe these words,' he told the King. 'Rodrigo is proud and rebellious. Tomorrow, perhaps, he will come himself to Burgos to mock at you.'

'Silence all!' cried Álvar Fáñez. He cocked his hat over his ear and he spluttered in his rage. 'In the absence of the Cid I am the Cid, and his strength sustains my weakness. Listen to me, King who feed on lies—make a wall of these lies, and see how they will serve to defend you! I ask your pardon, Don Alfonso, for the anger that makes me forget the respect due to your blood. Give me the beloved pledges of the Cid, Doña Jimena and his daughters. See, I offer you their ransom as if they were your prisoners.'

'Calm yourself, Álvar Fáñez. You do right to defend the Cid, and I recognise that I have ever suffered myself to be deceived about the greatest of my vassals. May God forgive me, and may History and Song and Ballad forgive me too. Let us go together to San Pedro de Cardeña to visit Jimena and aid her to make ready for her journey.'

How well content were Doña Jimena and her daughters, those beings so beloved of the hero and of heroic verse, those beings who clothed in flesh the warrior legend! With what joyous hearts did they set out on the road towards the Cid! Every single year of separation had been as if five, and the days and the weeks had multiplied through the working of some evil spirit. At last there was an end of separation, an end of solitude! Dear God, how endless seemed the way to the side of that so long absent beloved!...

The Cid had bidden his guards advise him as soon as Doña Jimena should appear on the horizon. So, when they told him that she was coming, he leapt upon his horse and sped towards the horizon to meet her. The countryside was left gaping as Babieca scudded over it like a cloud. In an instant the Cid was together again with his own.

Doña Jimena flung herself into his arms. 'My thanks, Campeador. You have guarded me from all shame. You have protected me with the shadow of your name. I bring you your daughters. With God's help and yours have I reared them well.'

Enchanted, the Cid gazed at his wife and his daughters, now grown to womanhood. 'Dear and honoured wife, and you, daughters of my heart, enter with me into Valencia, your city, the heritage that I have won for you.'

Mother and daughters kissed those hands that knew not only how to slay, but how to pray to God, and on the carpet of the rejoicing and applause of the multitude they entered Valencia. The Cid took them up to the tower of the Alcazar, and there, tracing with his hand in the air around them a circle, a great circle that sank to the earth like a ring of magic, he exclaimed proudly: 'All this is yours!'

The beautiful eyes of the ladies looked at the city spread at their feet. On the one side was the sea; on the other stretched into the distance the orange groves in blossom. Winter was gone, and spring knocked at the door with its great blowing of flowers and bursting of fruit. Before that marvellous spectacle the three fell on their knees, and joining their hands, gave thanks to God.

All the time that Doña Jimena and her daughters had free from the ordering of their house they spent in visiting the sick, helping the needy, doing charity wherever they passed, and leaving behind them a murmur of blessings. The people worshipped them. They reigned in the souls of Moors and Christians, they stormed all hearts in the city. For the second time Valencia was won.

* * *

See where a Moor came along the road, riding upon a bay mare. He had buskins of Morocco leather, spurs of gold, and before his breast he carried a buckler, and in his hand a spear. He looked at Valencia, and he cried in a loud voice: 'May the fires of evil consume you! Yesterday you belonged to the Moors, and the Christians have won you. If my lance does not lie, you will come back to the Moors. As for that dog of a Cid, I will pluck him by the beard, his wife Jimena shall be my captive, the most beautiful of his daughters shall be my concubine, and when I tire of her I shall throw her to my soldiers.'

A verse sprang out of Ballad, and ran and told the Cid what it had heard. The Cid called to the elder of his daughters. 'Come here, my daughter. Put on your Easter robes. Hold me here that Moor, that son of a bitch, until I saddle Babieca and get me my sword.'

The beautiful girl showed herself at a window. 'Allah guard you, Lady,' said the Moor at the sight of her.

'God guard you, my Lord. You are very welcome. For seven years, seven long years, have I loved you, O my King.'

'There will be as many years, Lady, that you will reign in my heart.' He had hardly spoken when the Cid approached. 'Farewell, farewell, my lady, my well beloved; farewell, farewell, I hear the gallop of the Cid.'

Wherever the bay mare sped Babieca was on her tracks. They went like the wind. Seven times they circled around a corral. But the mare was light and she had a good start; and she reached the bank of the river, and there was a boat. Overjoyed at the sight, the Moor trumpeted a summons to it across the valley. In three strokes of the oars the boat had reached him.

The Cid reached the bank to find the Moor aboard, and he tore his beard with rage. The Moor set his hands to his mouth as a megaphone, and shouted to the bank: 'Long live Mohammed!'

'Son of a bitch!' roared back the Cid, quicker than echo, and he flung his spear with all his strength. 'Take this, dear son-in-law, take this spear! Perhaps you will value it.' The spear sped through the evening and sank in the heart of the Moor sweet as the Muslims' Paradise....

The next Sunday, in the great mosque turned into a Christian church and dedicated to the Virgin Mary, the Cid installed Don Jerónimo of Périgord as Bishop of Valencia—Don Jerónimo, that warrior cleric, that faithful friend, loved by the Christians, more of a knight than any knight, more of a soldier than any soldier.

He, too, deserves his stanza, Don Jerónimo who loved his Masses and his battles with an equal love, who fought with prayers and oaths, shearing the heads of Moors with his stout two-handed sword, giving them absolution as he sent them to the other world, rounding up enemies with his rosary, a great rosary mystical and military.

Two tongues of fire shone in his eyes. The corsair in whom he dwelt wrestled day and night with the saint. There was a mortal struggle within his breast. The people loved him, the host adored him, and they hailed his designation as their Bishop. As cleric he had fought beside them, and as Bishop he would go on fighting at their side.

As soon as the coming of the enemy was announced he was ever the first to hasten to arm himself. He flung away his breviary and he seized his sword. He abandoned his office to rush into battle: and he abandoned battle to rush back to his office.

Hurrah for Don Jerónimo, the new Bishop named by the Lord of Valencia! Hurrah for the warrior Bishop, the Bishop warrior! At the noise of the shouting Don Jerónimo rose up, aflame, shining, burnished like a mirror. He raised his head, strong and stately, and upon it there was no tremor in the noble architecture of his mitre.

YUSUF

The drums beat upon the horizon. Against Valencia marched the desert of Africa with thirty thousand lances and a hundred thousand mirages. For the Emperor Yusuf had not resigned himself to the triumph of the Cid, and at the head of his Almoravids, warriors and fanatics to a man, he came to dispute his conquest. Turbans flowed in a river over the beaches and the fields, and came to rest before the city, where tents were pitched with every emphasis of war and siege.

There was Yusuf, Sultan of Morocco, as who should say: 'From here no man shall move until he dies of hunger.' At the sight of the hostile host an immense joy took possession of the Campeador. He laughed like a child with a new toy, his heart expanded, and as it swelled his breast dilated in such measure that it took on something of the cosmic.

'Praised be the Creator!' he cried in a voice that rang among the planets. 'All that I possess is here in front of me. With great labour gained I Valencia, and today I hold it for my heritage, and while I live I will not let it go. Praised be Saint Mary that today my wife and my daughters are with me! From beyond the sea fortune comes in search of me. At last I am going to take up my arms while my wife and my daughters watch me fight, and see for themselves how life is lived in foreign lands and how their bread is won.'

He led his wife and his daughters up to the tower of the Alcazar, and showed them the tents of the enemy lying stretched like a herd of cattle in the sun. At the warning of the sentries the bells were tinging in the city. In the distance could be heard the drums of the enemy beating for battle. Doña Jimena and her daughters felt fear clutch at their hearts at the sound. 'Heaven preserve us, Cid, what is that?'

'Be not alarmed, honoured wife. That which frightens you is riches which come to seek us. You are but lately arrived, and already they would make you presents; here are the Almoravids bringing you as a gift the dowry of your daughters.'

'I fear for you, my Cid.'

'Fear nothing, my wife. Remain here watching with your daughters and your ladies. Be not afraid because you see me doing battle. With the help of God the field will be mine, and my heart swells with pride because I shall win it before your eyes.'

An immense carpet of burnooses spread and swayed at their feet. It was the hour of prayer, and the Berbers were down upon their knees, with their heads bending forward almost to touch the ground. As far as the horizon was to be seen nothing but one vast white prostration. There, making ready for battle, were the Almoravids, the Moors of Morocco—more valiant because less cultured than those of Spain, less used to pleasure and softness. They bore upon their camels the burning madness of the desert, the land of mirages and of whirling magic. Their eyes were dark with the resignation of fatalism. Their chants rose up in spirals like long-drawn groanings heard by night, and sent an Oriental shudder through the Valencian air. An elixir of mystery was wafted by a breeze of enchantment across the fields.

The drums beat louder than ever. Full of glee, the Cid turned to his wife. 'This will be a great day.' But Doña Jimena felt a terror which laid heavy hands upon her heart. Her daughters and her ladies felt it too.

'That awful beating of the drums...'

The Cid stroked his epic beard. 'Have no fear,' he said; 'I swear to you by my beard that before three days are out I will bring you those drums and you shall see how they are made, and then we shall give them to the Bishop Don Jerónimo to hang up in the Church of Santa María.'

He saw that the ladies were reassured by his words, and he came down from the tower to marshal his men for battle. It was time, for the Almoravids were to horse, and they were entering the suburbs in defiance. The host of Ruy Díaz was ready. He passed them in review for the last time, and, armed to the teeth, they rode out of the city. Babieca walked upon the air. A poppy bloomed upon her brow, and her great eyelids flickered faster than a butterfly in flight.

'What tactics shall we use?' asked Martín Antolínez, riding up to the Cid.

'None' answered the Cid; 'at the charge and forward. At the charge, at the charge, forward, forward! In this first sortie we must strike hard; then we shall see about the others.'

So they did. The men of the Cid went forward to the charge in serried ranks. The Moor who met them was one less dweller upon earth, one dweller more in Paradise. Forward, forward they went, driving off those bold ones who had invaded their irrigated lands. Doña Jimena turned her eyes away so as not to see the battle. At the close of day more than three hundred Moors lay dead upon the field, and the pursuit had been carried as far as the camp of the enemy itself. They had achieved enough. Prudence counselled a retirement to the city.

'Hear me, knights,' said the Cid, well pleased with his men; 'today has been a good day; tomorrow will be a better. Do you all take your rest now, and tomorrow before dawn let every man be armed. The Bishop Don Jerónimo will give us absolution, we shall get a Mass, and then we shall ride out again to attack them even more vigorously than today.'

'Willingly and with a good heart shall we do so,' they answered as one man.

Then Álvar Fáñez asked leave to speak. 'My Cid,' he said, 'entrust me with another mission. Give me a hundred and thirty knights for the fight, and when you fall upon them I shall appear from some other quarter. On one side or the other God will aid us, or on both together.'

'That is well thought of, Minaya, and so will I do.' The Cid strode into the Alcazar and embraced his wife. 'You see, Jimena, you had no need for fear?' 'God be praised, Campeador, and may He protect you as well tomorrow.'

When half the night was gone, but long before the dawning, the second crowing of a cock served as a bell to summon them to church. All was mystery in the half light. The church was full of indistinct forms of faith, of shadows indomitable. Don Jerónimo said Mass, and for blessing he gave them the major absolution. 'Him who shall die this day fighting in fair fight I absolve of his sins, and may God receive his soul. And of you, Cid Rodrigo, who in a good hour were girt with the sword, of you I ask, in return for the Mass that I have said for you, that you concede to me the striking of the first blow.'

The Cid, kneeling at the altar, raised his head. 'Agreed,' he answered. Restraining his warlike ardour, disciplining his energy, Don Jerónimo went on with his Mass. The *Ite Missa Est* was barely said when he tucked up his cassock and hurried down the central nave, jostling the soldiers who hastened towards their horses, himself most warlike of the warriors. His Mass done, he leapt from the altar on to his horse, seized his arms, and galloped ahead of an advance squadron full speed towards the enemy. The Cid smiled with delight at the sight of him.

Under the towers of Cuarte the host rode forth, and the Cid rode among them giving orders and counsel to his men. At the gates of the city he left guards well provided. Doña Jimena climbed the tower again to watch them as they went. Today she did not fear as yesterday. A strange sense of security possessed her soul and beamed from her eyes. 'The Campeador is invincible. Blessed Virgin, is he not invincible?'

She saw him ride proudly upon Babieca, fair with destiny and heroism. At every step of his horse assurance grew and overflowed her soul. She saw his standard go forth to war. How strong was the hand that bore that banner! Courage sprang out of all the soil beneath its shade. All those who saw it felt themselves electrified. How had that piece of fabric stored up so high a voltage?

The men of the Cid were five thousand and the number of those against them was thirty thousand. But not for a single moment did it occur to any one of his soldiers so much as to think of this disparity. Blindly they launched themselves to the attack. Yusuf laughed, and his laugh rang round as a cooking-pot; but it was soon to turn into grimace over a seasoning of aloes.

Doña Jimena watched the battle, and all its scenes were mirrored in eyes that grew round to give that far-flung tumult entrance to her field of vision. She saw Don Jerónimo dealing episcopal blows. It seemed that all the motive force of Heaven inspired his arm. The Moors flew into tatters before him, and heads dropped easily as rotten fruit.

Her eyes followed the Cid as he plunged, lance in rest, into the ranks of the enemy. She saw his spear shiver to atoms, and she saw him lay hand upon his sword. What blows he dealt, and how his sword darted from side to side! Tizona was a flying thing maddened by blood, delirious with movement. The enemy swayed back and forth in an enormous wave, and she saw her Campeador lost in that wave, vanished from sight, and then reappear again far away under the gigantic milling of his two-handed blade. It seemed to her that an angel of death rode in the air before her husband, clearing a way for him and aiding him in his task. Such were the energy and the fury with which her man sowed havoc upon the earth. He scattered death with the wide gesture of one who scatters alms.

There on the other side she saw Álvar Fáñez and his hundred and thirty men swaying to that same movement like the sea of swords that rose and fell, of horses that reared and plunged. This man who attacked with shouts and jeers upon his lips was Per Vermúdez. That other further away who gripped his lance burning with the heat of his arm and frowned and bit his lips at every blow was Muño Gustioz; and that other again who leapt and rose in his stirrups as if he would stand upon his horse's back was Martín Antolínez.

Forgetful of all else in the world, Doña Jimena before that spectacle, deadly and dynamic such as she had never seen before, seemed to be suspended out of Time. A thread of saliva began to drip from her open mouth, and even fell upon my head. Let it fall, illustrious saliva of that illustrious lady!

Babieca kept on trampling Moors, the hours kept passing, and Time itself would weary of striking them before the Cid would weary of dealing blows. Blood streamed to his elbow. In the centre of the battle he met the Sultan Yusuf. There they were face to face, Christian and Arab, the West and the East. Three blows the Cid aimed at Yusuf, and Yusuf fled the field, giving his horse free rein, and sought to hide himself in the castle of Cullera. Thither the Cid pursued, and there he caught up with him before he could take refuge. That was where Babieca showed her worth from her head to her tail. The flight of the Moors was a white flurry of birds that vanished under the eyes of Doña Jimena.

An immense booty remained in the hands of the Cid. His host collected the spoils. They found five thousand marks of gold and silver, and the rest they did not count. Merry was the Cid, and no less happy were his vassals. Laughter sprang from one mouth to another, a hundred times back and forth it ran between them. Never was there seen a greater gladness. The Cid left Álvar Fáñez in the field to marshal the treasures and the captives, and rode back to Valencia with a hundred knights. He had doffed helm and hood and he rode bareheaded. Radiant he returned on Babieca with Victory in his arms, stroking her long tresses of dream come true.

The waiting ladies welcomed him. 'Ladies, I bow to you, said the Cid, reining in his horse, but staying in his saddle.' A great booty I have gained for you! While you held Valencia for me I have won victory for you. Look at my sword Tizona, stained with blood—look at my horse, dripping with sweat. So are battles fought and won.'

So spoke the Cid, and then he swung from his horse and wiped his brow. Doña Jimena, his daughters and their ladies knelt on the ground before him. 'May God preserve you a thousand years!' With him they went into the palace and sat down around him on benches of price—benches for which the antiquaries of Epic would give all their fortune. With what pride and veneration they looked at the Cid, these women who had heard tell of his deeds, but had never until now been able to witness them!

'Doña Jimena, wife of mine,' said the Cid, 'I would that we should marry to some of my vassals these ladies whom you brought with you and who have served you so well. I will give them each a dowry of three hundred marks, so that they may know in Castile in whose service they have been. As for your daughters, let us take our time.'

The ladies rose together, and one by one they kissed his hand in gratitude. There was a scent of happiness in the air of the palace.

Meanwhile Álvar Fáñez was still in the field, writing down the tally of the trophies: tents, arms, fabrics and stuffs of price. It was not possible to take a count of all the horses of the enemy which ran riderless and could not yet be caught. All were well rewarded, and the friendly Moors as well had their recompense. To the Bishop Don Jerónimo the Cid gave a tenth of his own fifth share.

'Take what you will, my knights,' said the Cid to his captains. 'What ails you, Minaya, Martín Antolínez, that you have taken nothing? Help yourselves, Per Vermúdez and Muño Gustioz, and be quick about it!'

How well content were those excellent outlaws! Hands of generosity were stretched out in the light of day, while hands of rapine scrabbled empty in the shadows. Beyond the horizon, far away where flight had stopped to take breath, Yusuf was weeping....

The most redoubtable of his enemies was routed, and the Cid had leisure to make sure his conquests and lay his power in the city on strong foundations. To win the affection of the Moors of Valencia he relieved them of many of their taxes, leaving only such as they had been wont to pay when the Moorish Kingdom was at its peak of prosperity. About all things he was diligent, and nothing was too small for his care. He let it be known to the Muslims that twice a week he would hear and judge their pleas.

'Come to me when you will,' he told them, 'and I will hear you, for I am no man to go apart with women and sing and drink, after the manner of your lords, whom you could never approach. I, on the other hand, would know all your complaints, and be your comrade and your protestor, like friend to friend and cousin to cousin.'

Not for a moment did his activity falter. While he made himself loved within his city and gave it peace, he extended his dominions with the taking of Olocau, Sierra, Almenara and Murviedro. Then news came to him that the indefatigable Almoravids were assembling another great army near Jativa. Hereupon the King Don Pedro of Aragón offered him an alliance defensive and offensive, which the Cid accepted with goodwill.

The King of Aragón came to Valencia, and there the pact was signed, and there together they made ready their expedition. From Valencia they set out to take supplies to the fortress of Benicadell and make it their base of campaign. Difficult was the enterprise, for under the orders of Ibn

Ayesha, nephew of the Emperor Yusuf, the army of the Almoravids was raiding through the district.

But at the news that the Cid had issued forth from Valencia with his host and that of his ally, Ibn Ayesha deemed it prudent to retire towards the South, partly by reason of the fear which the name of the Cid inspired, but mostly to seek a favourable position for offering him battle. Rapid and resolute as ever, the Campeador accomplished his hazardous enterprise, and stocked Benicadell with wheat and supplies for many days. When this was done, with their united hosts the hero and the King marched southwards down the coast.

They reached Bairén to find the army of the Almoravids awaiting them, posted in an excellent position on the slope of a mountain opposite the sea; and, as if their immense superiority in numbers were not enough, supported by the Muslim fleet.

Nothing daunted by that was the Cid, but he saw that his men seemed to hesitate as they found themselves hemmed in by land and sea. So he went among the ranks of Castile and of Aragón heartening his soldiers and inspiring them by his words with the ardour which was on the point of deserting them at this critical moment. 'Courage, my children, courage! You are going to show these infidels of what stuff you are made. I vow to you that I am going to hack them in pieces like butcher's meat.'

All hearts were lashed into bellicose fury by his words. Now none hesitated, and none was afraid. A miracle was accomplished, and a great current of energy infected all the host like a fever, from the first of his men to the last. It was dawn. A cloud of burnooses moved upon the mountain, and in the sky a crescent moon sank like a secret ship of the other side. It seemed as though it would disembark reinforcements for the enemy. Even the moon favoured them.

But in the presence of the peril that confronted them through disadvantage alike of numbers and position, not a single heart was dismayed among the host of the Cid. Their beards bristled with heroism, and a strange light shone in their eyes.

Erect between earth and sky, Ibn Ayesha dreamed of Mohammed. If victory would not come to him, he would go to victory. But he had no time to put his decision to the test; for the Cid, as though he had guessed his thoughts, hastened in irresistible attack to bring him rout.

If the soldiers of the Cid had ever been worthy of wonder for their potency of perdition, never were they more so than on this day. With the speed of meteors, with an energy astronomical, they launched themselves against the enemy. It was something never seen before, a cosmic convulsion, a shock of planets, a war in the firmament.

At the sight of their coming the Moors laughed loudly through teeth of triumph. But their laughs were cut short and their eyes started out of their heads before the edges of the swords and the points of the spears. Without time of transition roars of mirth were transmuted into hiccoughs of agony. The echo of many jokes still rang upon the air when those who cracked them were in the other world. On every side laughter fell decimated.

Incredulous the Sun rose over a mountain where two armies out of Myth hewed each other to pieces. Such was the butchery that the Sun doubted if it saw aright and rubbed its eyes that still seemed foil of dream. Babieca had a legion of archangels under her skin. The volcanic horse erupted in rearings and tramplings, cleaving a way like a flash of lightning. Tizona had a legion of demons within her steel, and dealt such hammer-blows that she changed the course of History at her will.

The mountain groaned and seemed to crumple like a camel too heavily laden. An irresistible current surged through the earth. The phalanx of madmen of the Cid erased whomsoever stood in their path. A sinister vapour was exhaled over the labouring ground. That great throbbing of two serpents locked in furious embrace swept over the valley and the mountain up to infinity.

Before the avalanche of that rush of wild beasts let loose, the Almoravids felt the earth crumble beneath their feet, and it seemed that their bodies fought in the air transfixed on the points of the spears. Everything vanished before their eyes, and the earth began to revolve with such speed that they did not know whether they were downside up or upside down. Everything whirled and whirled until all capacity of thought deserted them. The living did not know if they were dead, the dead did not know if they yet lived.

Then came that instant of horror, that instant of suspense above the abyss, that precise moment than which there is nothing more terrible, when an army is transformed into a horde. It was flight, every man for himself, a desperate race of chaos to save its skin. Once more Victory raised the Cid in her arms and held him up above the centuries to the admiration of men.

At his feet the field of battle was an immense white burnoose rent in tatters, and exposing fragments of flesh, gaping wounds, dead mouths, and eyes of beyond the grave. Death passed over it drinking deep draughts of souls, mistress of the world, in the midst of arms cleft away with cuirasses, heads still helmed rolling on the ground, and horses that ran riderless. The very sky was bespattered with blood.

Back to Valencia the victors took their road, that road beneath a canopy of roses. Babieca marched in time to a mazurka. The making of a nation hung upon her saddle-bow, and she knew it. The Cid looked at his heroes with eyes of love. 'My thanks, my children; you have fought like lions. My Ballad will not forget you; and he doffed his helm to them.

Then he resumed his march, and as he marched he sang into the infinite:

> 'Spain was lost by Rodrigo one;
> By Rodrigo two shall she be re-won.'

A fresh breeze passed, restoring the world, and the firmament with sweeping swathes of cloud wiped the sweat from his brow.

PARENTHESIS

Beneath a mantle of bells and flowers they welcomed the Cid Campeador back to Valencia. History, Chronicle, Legend and Poem flung him wreaths of laurel, and Glory crouched like a greyhound at his feet.

He could take his rest. It was a parenthesis of repose. The Cid made use of this parenthesis to marry his daughters. Greater than a King, Lord of Valencia, and lord of battles, he could choose at his will; and he rejected the suit of the Princes of Carrión.

'No, my friends,' the Campeador told them, 'even though your suit is proffered with the support of the King Alfonso, I cannot accept your hands for my daughters. My wife, Doña Jimena, has no great liking for you, and besides she has had a strange dream about you; she saw you treat her daughters ill one night in the pine-woods of Corpes. That is an evil omen.'

'You forget our lineage; we are Counts of Carrión. And we have spoken with your daughters, Doña Elvira and Doña Sol…'

'Pardon me. You do not even know the names of my daughters. Their names are Doña Cristina and Doña María. I see that that which most interests you in them is their dowries.'

'Think, sir, that we could marry Princesses if we would.'

'Marry them and welcome. Here feelings towards you are none too friendly; and, further, it is said that you are not conspicuous for your valour, and I need sons-in-law who can second me.'

'We are as valorous as any of your vassals.'

At that very moment, as if Destiny had been listening to the conversation behind the door, a sound of shouting thundered through the Alcazar of the Cid. 'Have a care! The lion, the lion! The lion has escaped! Have a care! The lion has broken out of his cage!'

Flying feet were heard on every side of the startled Court. The men of the Campeador rallied round to protect him. As they heard the shouting and the roaring of the lion the Counts of Carrión ran like rats. Fernán González, the elder, squeezed himself under a settle, and there he hid himself and coiled himself up and made himself so small that he vanished completely. The other, Diego González, stampeded and hid himself behind the closet, where he left his cloak and his tunic.

Brushing aside his captains solicitous to defend him, the Cid rose to his feet and, with his mantle streaming behind him, so that he would make a fine figure for a popular print, marched straight upon the lion. At the sight of this monument of calm and majesty coming towards him, the lion was seized with such dread that he lowered his head and flattened his muzzle on the ground. The Cid took him by the scruff of the neck, and, as though he were a dog on a leash, put him back in his cage with the serenity of a Franciscan monk.

All the spectators were round-eyed with wonder. Then the Counts of Carrión issued from their hiding-places, and shouts of laughter greeted them. 'Ah, my men of valour!' said the Cid; 'get you back to your own lands; these are too perilous for you. Go back to anonymity, my lords the Counts of Carrión; and, if anonymity bores you, you must find some other way out of it.'

At the end of three weeks the Cid had chosen for his daughters two husbands to his liking and their own. The elder, Doña Cristina, was wed to the Prince Don Ramiro of Navarre; and the younger, Doña María, to the Count of Barcelona, Ramon Berenguer III, son of Cap d'Estopa and nephew of Ramon Berenguer II, who had slain his father and fought so many times against the Cid. The sons-in-law of the Campeador welcomed his daughters to their hearts, and kissed the hands of Doña Jimena and their glorious father.

In the Church of Saint Mary the Bishop Don Jerónimo said Mass, and then he blessed them and addressed them: 'Daughters of the hero, of the man who will walk in the love of his race until the end of time, never forget what duties this imposes on you. In the eyes of the world you are higher than Queens. Learned men of all countries will come to pry into your lives and make excavations in your souls. Therefore beware! You are the daughters of Spain and of its Epic, and your blood bids you give your country Kings and conquerors.

'And you, my Lords, who have the honour to be united to these most excellent ladies, watch over them with all your love and all your care, as if you watched over the dearest dream of the hero who begot them. May God give you happiness, and grant you a long line of descendants.'

Amidst the applause of the people and the whisperings of women they left the church. The Cid had made ready a Royal festival, and all the company rode to the arena of Valencia. There the Cid and his vassals fought in friendly tourney with such address that no critic of feats of arms was other than enchanted. How glad was the happy father to see that his sons-in-law were admirable horsemen! The Count Don Enrique, who was a guest at the wedding, was eager that the Cid should put Babieca through her paces. 'Great Cid,' he said, 'do us the favour to race your horse whose name is on the lips of all Spain.'

The Cid drove spurs into Babieca, and launched her at top speed from a standing start, swung her round, drove her forward again, and stopped her dead. 'By Saint James,' exclaimed the Count as he saw the marvel, 'there is no other such horse in all the world! Babieca inclined her head in acknowledgment at his words. The Cid patted her neck, and she arched it in her pride like a cat.

After the games the knights and their ladies rode back to Valencia, and there in the Alcazar the nuptials were celebrated with a magnificence never seen before, with a pomp such as no Court could display. The Cid had ordered seven tables to be spread, and they all but collapsed under the weight of the fare. Fifteen days lasted the festival, and then the nobles took their leave. The Cid gave his guests presents of more than a hundred beasts: palfreys, mules, and horses of speed, and a countless quantity of furs, mantles, fabrics, vesture, and tapestries of great price. Well content, his guests went their way, and all along the roads of Spain there ran an endless murmur of praise of the Campeador.

Even to the confines of Persia had reached the fame of the Cid, and the Sultan, hearing of his prowess, resolved to send him presents and seek his friendship. A long caravan of camels, laden with garnet and purple, with silks, gold, silver, incense, myrrh and precious stones, set out to cross the world on its way to the Campeador. Admiration extended him the hand of friendship from the other end of the earth.

A hundred horizons that caravan had to cross, and ever as it advanced across the world it grew more heavily laden with all the diverse wonders that the name of the Cid inspired. As leader of the embassy came one of the brothers of the Sultan.

'Tell the Cid,' the Sultan had bidden his brother when he set forth, 'that it would give me much pleasure to welcome him to Persia, or at the least to hear from him. Tell him that I would give all I possess to see him in my land, and ask him to accept these humble presents in token of an admiration and a friendship which will last all my life long.'

When the ambassador reached Valencia the Cid went out to meet him, and entertained him with that magnificence which he was wont to use. 'Very welcome are you to my city of Valencia,' said the Cid. 'Thank your noble King in my name for his rich presents. On your return you will bear him my salutations, and with them some humble presents which I would send him.'

So he did. After he had paid the ambassador of Persia all the honours of his palace for three days, the Cid loaded him with splendid offerings for the Sultan, his new friend. The caravan went back from the West to the East weighed down with the presents of the West—presents which perhaps held for those far-off men the same aureole of mystery, the same lure of fascination, the same exotic savour as their presents hold for us. For kilometres clothe with prestige like years; and distance is the verge filled with liberated dreams.

VICTORY AFTER DEATH

There was the Cid upon his bed, stricken with illness. That miracle of dynamic energy, the man made for movement and for action, lay helpless and disarmed before Death that was coming by forced marches against his heart.

He who so many times had leapt over it with a jest in battle, he who had offered his breast with a smile to all its threats, there he lay, a poor ghost of himself, suffering but resigned. He was on the pinnacle of his fame, lord of a great city and a wide and wealthy Kingdom, the terror of the enemy, wedding his daughters with Princes, naming Bishops, founding cathedrals, changing governors, destroying Kings and receiving homage from all the horizons of the world; and suddenly he fell from the summit of his glory to his bed of agony.

Bitterness against Destiny overwhelmed creation and mankind. They felt that some nameless evil was taking shape in the infinite. There was a lamentation of stars in space, and chaos was full of wailing. Long shudders ran through the veins of the universe, and a lump rose in the throat of the world. Endless waves of pain beat upon all hearts. Spain was a prey to portents, and she could not stay the leaping of her nerves. In the night, alone in her habitation in the world, alone in the darkness, she burst into a sobbing inconsolable.

The Cid heard her sobbing. He opened his clouded eyes, and his pale lips murmured: 'Do not weep, Spain; you have before you many days of sun and laurel.' Wearied by his labours, wearied from so many wars, he reclined upon his pillows, and Death began to bind his tireless muscles with cords of ice.

But an ailing child was now the Titan invincible. Yet even now he had not lost all that great fund of vigour of his. They told him that the Almoravids were seeking once again to assemble a great army to march against him and he called up all his strength. As though the scenting of the coming battle lent him wings, he raised himself upon his bed and issued his last commands.

He bade Álvar Fáñez set out at the head of his men to attack the Moors at Jativa, scene of his last triumph and now to be the base of his campaign; and his mind had no ease until he knew that his host was on its way.

Bedridden, mortally stricken, on the edge of agony, not for a moment did he cease his care for his conquests.

Then, in the presence of Doña Jimena and before the Bishop Don Jerónimo, he made his testament: 'I, Rodrigo de Vivar, known as the Cid Campeador, conqueror of the Moors, commend my soul to God, that He may admit me to His Kingdom, and my body that is dust I render back to earth. I would that after I am dead I should be embalmed and mounted upon Babieca. Behind my standard let me go forth to the field and be presented to the enemy.

'I leave Valencia and all its lands to my wife Doña Jimena, and I bid my captains, my cousins, and my friends aid her and serve her as they would myself. To the brotherhood of Saint Lázaro the Poor I leave Vivar and all its dependencies. Furthermore, I ask that there be no paid mourners at my burial. The tears of my Jimena will suffice me, and there is no need to purchase others.

'I bequeath Babieca, Tizona, and Colada to Song and Ballad, and to all those poets who are capable of understanding and loving these three beings so deservedly beloved of my soul. Furthermore, I order that to those two good Jews, whom by force of circumstances I deceived, my debt be paid a second time, with the weight of the sand in the coffers reckoned in silver. I name the noble King Alfonso, the good Bishop Don Jerónimo, and my faithful Álvar Fáñez as executors of this my testament. All else that I possess I bequeath to the poor, who between God and man are protestors and intercessors.'

When his testament was signed, the Cid had them bring him his banners, and he kissed them. How they wept now, those banners which had streamed in his battles upon all the winds that blow, streamed like the tresses of Victory, those standards so well beloved! He had them bring him, too, all the memorials of his past triumphs. How he fondled Tizona and Colada, those good comrades! The Cid Campeador, the terror of battles, brought low upon his bed, ran his weakening fingers along those blades of steel, and the blades trembled and broke into a lament like the strings of lutes.

Then he had them bring him Babieca, whom he would see once more. Sorrowful and silent, hanging her head, the mare came in, and with her tail between her legs she approached the bed as if she were shod with silk. How weak was Babieca! For days she had eaten nothing, and there had been no means of inducing her to swallow a mouthful, for all fodder choked her. She opened wide her great, dreaming eyes, and let two tears fall upon her master The Cid stretched out his hand to her, and she nibbled it with her lips; and behind the banners Doña Jimena broke into sobbing convulsive and unrestrained.

Doña Jimena wept, and with her wept Don Jerónimo and Babieca, and the banners and the swords. The whole earth was a sheath of sobs. In the midst of all that despair only the Cid remained serene, with his head thrown back and his face towards the sky. As they led from his side the cause of all these tears, Babieca turned her head round and looked back at her master.

Suddenly the eyes of the Cid shone, and already almost reaching from the other world, he caught the hand of the Bishop. 'When they speak against Spain, he exclaimed with lips radiant as if God spoke through them, 'pay no heed. Spain, despite all her misfortunes, will be the greatest country on earth. I who am dying tell you so. Spain will enlarge the world.'

The next day on the haggard face of the dying man there shone a strange splendour. Life still strove in him, and his thin fingers grasped the hand of his beloved Doña Jimena, who knelt beside his bed. Today, as every other day, they had brought him the Sacrament, and Don Jerónimo had blessed him and given him plenary indulgence.

Suddenly there was a noise in the next room, and he thought he heard the voice of Martín Antolínez. His knights were talking excitedly. The soldiers of the Cid had been routed by the Moors. That host inured to war, accustomed to conquer, that army lion-hearted, had lost a battle for the first time. Without the Cid at their head they lacked the spirit that made them unconquerable. His host was the same, the same men veteran in victory; but this day there had failed them that electric current, that motive force that streamed from the eyes of their terrible leader and multiplied their power a hundredfold.

The Cid raised himself up as he heard the murmur of voices, and asked what was happening. His knights entered, and Álvar Fáñez, with, all frankness, blurted out the truth: 'We are beaten. Your men are routed!

His head sank back upon the pillows as he heard the words. His pale face flushed to the ears, his hands clutched the sheets, and the hero breathed his last sigh, a great sigh like a mountain gust across the centuries, and his spirit fled to hide its shame beyond the clouds. After the first routing of his host he could live no longer. The beacon of his eyes was extinguished for this life and flashed upon Death.

It was a morning of the month of July in the year 1099. He was fifty-and-nine years old. Slowly the bells tolled in the depths of the centuries. A flight of birds that were singing his praises ceased their psalm as at a blow. The earth of Valencia perfumed the continent with the fragrance of its fruit and flowers. The planetary system felt a shudder that ran through it, and laid a finger upon its lips. The Eleventh Century reeled on the edge of the abyss, stricken at its heart with a stroke that re-echoed from all the clocks of the stars. Time stood still for a moment of silence and of recollection.

Rodrigo Díaz de Vivar was dead, the Cid Campeador was dead. Legend entered a limbo void and cold, and History was a wrack on the shores of darkness. There was anguish in the air of all the earth, and upon mankind fell a weight of desolation that would never lift for all eternity. There would be no more tales of deeds? And of prowess to pass from mouth to mouth, to lure imagination in a magic leap up to the spaces of the stars, to make eyes round and fascinated by the lodestone of miracle.

For long years the Cid had been Spain, and Spain had been the Cid. For long years the Cid absorbed all the nation and all the race. Its sap, its hopes, its thoughts, its pulsing, its blood, its history, its legend and its songs all flowed into the Campeador. Ruy Díaz de Vivar was a great river of a thousand affluents. The Cid flooded Spain—flooded and fertilised her. Spain and the Cid made love together upon a thousand fields of battle, and they ennobled blood and love and set them on the sublimest heights of passion.

Destined since the beginning of the world to be the incarnation, the spear-point, of his race, over the Epic of the Reconquest, from Don Pelayo to the Catholic Sovereigns, the Cid shines and stands pre-eminent at the zenith. And when the last tear of Boabdil started and dropped into History, within that tear stood up the Campeador, clad in all his armour; for that tear crystallised and was transformed into a jewel of the ages.

The Cid was the tempest launched by the vengeance of a race, he was the sword of a people, a sword that found a formless aspiration and gave it substance; a sword that flickers like a flash of lightning over the Dark Ages. Across Time that divides us I launch myself with heart aflame and pen in hand in search of him, and we meet in the night of eternity. Father of our race, who art in Heaven, take this offering of my pen of love!

The Cid was dead, and all the passion and zest of life were dead with him. So shattering was the idea of the end of that sublime adventure that the world could not believe it. But we must bring ourselves to believe it. The Cid was dead. Do you heat what I say to you? There is a drumming in my ears, an emptiness within emptiness, a chaos within chaos; and my pen is broken.

Spain fell swooning into the arms of her sister nations, but there was none of them that could console her. Her poetry, her exaltation, her most vibrant chord, her life peerless and glamorous, her superman strong and generous, her vital essence, her living symbol, was dead. There was the sound of a tear that slid into the infinite; and then a profound silence fell upon creation.

* * *

Emboldened by their victory, the Moors came up to the walls of Valencia and besieged the city. The hour had struck to fulfil the last commands of the Cid. His servants embalmed him, set his features in repose, and combed his hair and his beard. It seemed that Death had not touched him. For the last time Álvar Fáñez, Martín Antolínez, Per Vermúdez and Muño Gustioz attended their lord. They mounted him upon his horse. One prop between his shoulders and another at his breast held him upright in the saddle. Three days had the Cid been dead when his host made ready for battle. Álvar Fáñez ordered the bells to be rung in summons to the combat. The soldiers were duly marshalled, and then his captains set the Cid, mounted upon Babieca, at the head of his host.

The dead man rode as if he were alive. His right hand held his sword Tizona, and the sword was merry as a cricket. The eyes of Babieca shone with a strange light of decision. Silently they issued from the city and advanced. On one side of the Cid rode the Bishop Don Jerónimo and Muño Gustioz, and on the other Álvar Fáñez and Martín Antolínez. Per Vermúdez bore the standard, with a bodyguard of four hundred gentlemen. Behind them, valiant dame, marched Doña Jimena herself with six hundred knights.

At the sight of them the Moors made ready for battle, and loud was the beating of their drums. Babieca heard it, and as though her master had driven home his spurs, she broke into a mad gallop and flung herself upon the enemy; and after her sped Álvar Fáñez and all the knights.

Like a thrust from the other world the dead man drove into the battle. Babieca pressed steadily forward, trampling the world, splitting the plain, sowing panic in the ranks of the enemy. At her heels attacked the soldiers of the Cid, startled themselves at the doubling of their vigour that they felt in their muscles and that came they knew not whence.

Many hours the battle raged. The spectre of the Cid was tireless in attack, and at the sight of him an awful dread paralysed his enemies. 'The Cid, the Cid!' they shouted; 'the Cid has come back more terrible than ever! The Cid! The Cid!' and they broke into headlong flight. Through the midst of all the tumult Babieca galloped on, unrestrained, with free rein.

Look; down on your knees and marvel at the last miracle of the hero! The enemy were in rout, the Moors were in flight; they fled in all directions, they flung themselves on the ground, they burrowed into the earth, they sought refuge in the trees, before the passing of that horse of the Apocalypse. Babieca galloped on with free rein.

In vain the knights sought to overtake her. The mare sped further and further away from them, and she was lost in the distance. She gave a great leap over the horizon, and she galloped on with free rein.

The field was a desert sown with dead. The host of the Cid could no longer follow that strange, swift race of the Campeador, who passed far beyond the camp of the Moors. Wearily they reined in, and the mare galloped on with free rein.

Horse and horseman of History were now a knight and a steed of Legend, a memory which galloped across the fields of Poem, through the air of Image. They galloped on and on in that last ride of Epic and of Death.

They galloped across this world, and leapt its limits, and rode on through the sky. For a moment that career through space hid the light of the Sun. The girths of Babieca creaked in eternity. Night fell, and eyes looked deep into the distance, but there was no trace of that heroic horse and that heroic horseman. Babieca galloped on with free rein.

Darkness came, and silence, and there, leaping from world to world, the mare with free rein and her dead rider crossed the universe like a presage, rode in a shimmering vision through the gates of Paradise, and burst into the presence of God upon His Throne.

They lie who say his body rests in Burgos. That was the end of the Cid Campeador, the true end of the Cid Rodrigo Díaz de Vivar.

AFTERWORD
TO THE SECOND EDITION

The English and American editions of Wells's translation of *Mío Cid Campeador*, under the title *Portrait of a Paladin*, appeared relatively soon after the first Spanish edition and hard on the heels of the author winning a substantial award for his film-script (later reworked into a novella) *Cagliostro* in New York. It had been intended the latter book be turned into a silent film, but the Talkies came along, and the plans evaporated. Huidobro did however walk away $10,000 the richer.

The Cid novel was Huidobro's first foray into fiction, although he had already dabbled with essays and stage plays in addition to the poetry which had made his name. He claims in the dedication that it was his discussion with Douglas Fairbanks—an ideal candidate to play the role in a movie version, one would think—that encouraged him to write the book, and this may well be the case, as he certainly met Fairbanks when the latter visited Spain, and then again in New York. On the other hand, the mention of one of the world's most iconic movie-stars would certainly help the book get noticed, and Huidobro was good at the publicity side of things.

I would like to think that the novel's origins also have something to do with the author's new wife, Ximena, whose name coincides with that of the Cid's wife—the spelling is slightly different, although the same as in old Spanish, and the (modern) pronunciation the same. Given Huidobro's own somewhat tongue-in-cheek claim to kinship with the legendary hero in his introduction, this extra level of overlap with the subject was fortuitous. The actual source material for the book would have been mainly Menéndez Pidal's work on both the life of the Cid and on the 12th-century epic poem, *El cantar de mío Cid*. Another old work which had served to build up the myth was the *Mocedades de Rodrigo* (ca. 1360), which has gone under several titles in modern editions. Period sources also include the 12th-century Latin-language *Historia Roderici*, a story of the hero's life which is held by scholars to be generally reliable, and Ibn' Alqamah's eye-witness account of the Cid's capture of Valencia.

The translation appeared in London in 1931, the work of an experienced Irish translator of literary Spanish, and Wells did a good job with it. The text retains a slightly antique flavour, but in a historical novel, I do not see this as a defect.

In this new edition, I have amended a few things which jarred with modern taste, or were at least infelicitous, as well as the transcriptions of Arab names where I could identify the characters in question. Wells followed Spanish orthography in these cases and, as there is today clear agreement on the ways in which these names should be transliterated into English, I have opted for versions which the reader can look up in English-language publications, or online sources. In the cases of Spanish names, I have mostly left them as they were in the first edition, and, indeed, in the original, with accents intact. The only exceptions are Navarre, Castile and Catalonia, for Navarra, Castilia and Cataluña, respectively, as these states are well-known in English under their anglicised names. I agree with Wells's retention of accents as it enables the reader to come close to the correct pronunciation; if the reader doesn't care about this aspect s/he can just read *past* the accents. An accent in a name marks the point at which the stress occurs. Thus Álvar is AL-var, Jerónimo is Her-ON-ee-mo, Martín is Mar-TEEN, Díaz is DEE-ass and Fáñez is FAN-yes. (Note that at this period, the Castilian quasi-lisp did not exist, and nor does it in the author's native Chile. In modern Iberian Spanish, Díaz is DEE-ath and Fáñez is FAN-yeth.) Names with no accents should generally be pronounced intuitively: Rodrigo is Rod-REE-go; Fernando is Fer-NAN-do, Lozano is Loz-ANo.

The novel is of course a retelling of one of the great stories of Spanish literature and Spanish history, albeit in the latter case, somewhat encrusted with legend. El Cid, as Rodrigo Díaz de Vivar became known, was a historical figure, one of the greatest military commanders of his day, and—let us be honest here—a mercenary or, less pejoratively, a *condottiero*. He occupies a position in Spain akin to that of King Arthur in the anglophone world, with the difference of course that the Cid actually existed, even if he did not do all that was claimed for him. Not only did he actually exist, he was also the subject of the greatest surviving early epic poem in the Spanish language, generally known as the *Cantar de Mío Cid* or *Poema del Cid*, a work that was composed within 50-100 years of his death. The position of this poem in Spanish literature may be compared to that of *Beowulf* in England, the *Nibelungenlied* in Germany, or the *Chanson de Roland* in France.

It really does not matter that some of the events of the legendary life of the Cid did not actually happen, or did not happen *exactly* as described here, or in the old legends: they make for a splendid tale, just as the even less plausible deeds of King Arthur and his knights live on because they enthrall audiences even many centuries after they were first told.

Huidobro's take on the tale is respectful, and is related with some gusto. I rather feel that he would have enjoyed Anthony Mann's 1961 movie, starring Charlton Heston, which in turn takes a number of liberties with the source material. Again, it really doesn't matter that this was the case, because Mann produced one of Hollywood's best historical epics. I saw it at the age of 11 and was carried away by the ending: the legendary ending of the tale, of course, which actually never happened. But it *should* have, because that ending is a perfect storyteller's dénouement.

Tony Frazer

GLOSSARY

Abdallah, King of Granada: 'Abd Allah ibn Buluggin ibn Badis (reigned 1077-1090). Defeated by the Cid at the Battle of Cabra (1079).

Abderam: referred to here as ex-King of Murcia, a city which was under the control of the Taifa of Seville from 1078 to 1091, when it fell to the Almoravid leader, Yusuf. Abderam's name may well be that of the man history refers to as 'Abd ar-Rahman ibn Tahir, who had declared the independence of Murcia from the Caliphate in 1063. Given that this identification is not *absolutely* clear, Huidobro's spelling has been retained. One should also clarify that he did not declare himself king (*malik*), but minister (*hajib*), presumably to disguise the degree of his insurrection against the caliphate.

Aben Ali: it is unclear who this might be, although the correct name is likely to be *Ibn Ali*. There is however no trace of a poet by this name at the right time, although there *is* a famous Arabic poet from Alzira, a city near Valencia, whose full name was Abu Ishaq Ibn Ibrahim Ibn Abu Al-Fath Ibn Khafaja (1058-1138). He is known to history as Ibn Khafaja, and wrote a praise poem in honour of Yusuf after the latter recaptured Valencia for the Moors. There is also a long eye-witness account of the Cid's conquest of Valencia by the historian Ibn 'Alqamah (Abu 'Abd Allah Muhammad ibn al-Khalaf Ibn 'Alqamah, 1036-1116), the original of which has been lost, but a partial copy of which has come down to us via the later historian Ibn 'Idhari, whom modern commentators regard as trustworthy. It is possible that Huidobro's choice of name reflects, in corrupt form, 'Abd Allah Ibn 'Alqamah, even though he was no poet.

Aben Nazir: Possibly the Abenalhazis from the *Cantar*, and in turn *possibly* cognate with Abu Bakr ibn abd al-Aziz, King of Valencia 1075-1085. Previously governor of Toledo, he took advantage of the weakness of King Yahya al-Qadir to become *de facto* ruler of Valencia with the aid of King *Alfonso*.

Abenamic: identity unclear.

Alcobiella: probably modern Alcubilla del Marques, Alcubilla meaning 'small tower'. The *Cantar* in fact refers to *Alcoçeba*, but this has been assumed to be a copyist's error, although it could simply be an attempted transcription of *Alcazaba*, meaning citadel, deriving from Arabic *al-qasbah*, a walled fortification within a city. Other commentators have suggested that the location of this is now a ruined castle, probably added to a watchtower from the time of its Moorish occupation, at Atalaya de Vadorey in Soría.

Alcolea: modern Alcolea del Pinar, in the province of Guadalajara.

Alfonso, Don (c. 1036-1072). Son of Fernando. Became Alfonso VI of León after Fernando's death.

Alfonso X, 'The Wise', King of Castile (1221-1284). As Huidobro observes, he was a direct descendant of the Cid, via the latter's daughter, María, who had married into the Catalonian ruling house. Alfonso was a fine writer of troubadour-style verse, collected in the *Cantigas de Santa María*, which he wrote in Galician, although the language of his court was Castilian.

al-Mamun: Yahya ibn Ismail al-Ma'mun, King of Toledo 1044-1075. Protector of Don Alfonso during his exile, and father of King Yahya *al-Qadir*.

Almanzor: Abu 'Amir Muhammad ib 'Abdullah ibn Abi 'Amir, al-Hajib al-Mansur, 938-1002), *de facto* ruler of al-Andalus under the Umayyad caliphate. He was in fact Vizier (first minister) to the Caliph of Córdoba, but sidelined him. Al-Mansur is an honorific title meaning 'the Victorious'. And he certainly was.

Almanzora, town in Almería province. The name derives from the Arabic and means 'place of victory'.

Almoravids: a Berber dynasty from Morocco, which espoused an austere form of Islam and which established an empire that covered both Morocco and a substantial portion of the Iberian peninsula. The empire collapsed after defeat by the Almohads in 1147. The name by which they are know in Europe is a corruption of the Arabic *al-Murabitun*.

al-Mundhir, King of Lérida, Dénia and Tortosa. Also known to history as Mundhir al-Hayib.

al-Muqtadir, or Almuqtadir (Ahmad ibn Sulayman al-Muqtadir), King of Zaragoza (?-1081, reigned 1049-1081), son of al-Mustain I, first Banu Hud ruler of the city, who ruled 1039-1049. Succeeded by al-Mu'tamin.

al-Mustain (Al-Mustain II, Ahmad ibn Yusuf). Member of the Berber Banu Hud family, and fourth of that dynasty to rule Zaragoza, Reigned 1085-1110.

al-Mutamid: Muhammad ibn Abbad al-Mu'tamid (1040–1095; reigned c. 1069–1091), the third and last ruler of the *Taifa* of Seville. Father-in-law of *Zaïda*.

al-Mutamin: see *Yusuf*.

al-Qadir: Yahya Ibn Ismail Ibn Yahya, al-Qadir. King of Toledo, 1075-1085. King of Valencia, 1086-1092. He was a vassal of King *Alfonso*.

Ansúrez, Count Per: cousin of Jimena. Pero [Pedro] Ansures in the *Cantar*. Chief counsellor to King *Alfonso*; a knight of the old Ansures family, Lords of Monzón, near Palencia. Monzón was captured by the Cid in 1083.

Antolínez, Martín. In the legends, one of the Cid's most faithful knights. Ranked third amongst the company, he was from Burgos and served as Head Steward to the Cid.

Beltrán Massés, Federico (1885-1949). Born in Cuba, he was a very successful portrait painter, now rather out of fashion.

Berenguer Ramon I, Count of Barcelona (c. 1005-1035, reigned 1018-1035). the county was split three ways after his death, with his son Ramon Berenguer I (1023-1076, reigned 1035-1076) taking over the county of Girona, and part of the county of Barcelona.

Berenguer Ramon II, Count of Barcelona (1054-1099, reigned 1076-1097). Ruled jointly with his twin brother, confusingly named *Ramon Berenguer II*. The latter died in a hunting accident in 1082, and the surviving twin was accused of orchestrating the incident. It was subsequently agreed that he would continue in power but that his nephew Ramon Berenguer III, son of the slain twin, would take over when he came of age. Berenguer Ramon II was twice captured by the Cid in battle.

Boabdil: Abu 'Abdallah Muhammad XII (1460-1533), the last Moorish King of Granada, ruling from 1482-1492, and the last Muslim ruler in Iberia. Legend has it that, after leaving the city for the last time, he turned to look one last time upon it, and shed a tear of regret. The name by which he is known to Christian Spain is a corruption of Abu 'Abdallah. He went to Morocco after his departure, and lived in Fez until his death.

Calahorra: ancient city in the Rioja region.

Calamocha: town with Roman origins, some 70 kms from Teruel.

Calatayud: the name of this town, 86 kms from Zaragoza, derives from the Arabic Qalat al-Ayub (Ayub's Castle). A Moorish chieftain built a castle on the site, the ruins of which still survive, in order to control a pass on the road between Zaragoza and Mérida. A town grew up around the castle.

Calvo, Laín. Castilian warrior, and an elected judge in the County of Castile.

Cantar de mío Cid: name by which an anonymous medieval epic poem on the subject of the Cid is known, the earliest such work to survive into modern times. Thought by *Menéndez Pidal* to have been composed around 1140, but ascribed by most later commentators to a date around 1200.

Carrión: town some 40 kms from Palencia, on the pilgrimage route to Santiago. There is a monastery in the town dating back to the Cid's time. An important feature of the *Cantar* because of the story of the Outrage of *Corpes*, but the latter tale is left out by Huidobro as he explains in his Introduction.

Castejón: now Castejón de Henares, Castrejón in the Cid's time. Town on the Henares river.

Castle of the Moon: Castillo de La Luna; no trace remains of this castle, located on the River Luna, some 80 kms south of Oviedo.

Castro, Guillén de: Guillén de Castro y Bellvis (1569-1631), Spanish dramatist and writer of a play, *Las Mocedades del Cid* (The Exploits of the Young Cid).

Cebolla: castle in Valencia province now known as El Puig. It fell to the Cid in 1092.

Cervantes, Miguel de (1547-1616), novelist, poet and dramatist, author of *Don Quixote*.

Chisbert: Alcalá de Chisbert, today known as Alcalá de Xivert, a town in Castellón province. Founded by the Moors who had a castle here; *Alcalá* derives from the Arabic *al-qalat*, 'castle', and is found in a number of Spanish place-names.

Cid: the name derives from Arabic *sidi*, or *sayyidi*, an honorific meaning 'My Lord'. The Old Spanish pronunciation of the word then spelled Çid was *Tsid*. The name bestowed upon Rodrigo 'Ruy' Díaz de Vivar (1043-1099)

Coimbra, ancient university city in Portugal. In the Cid's day it was reconquered by the Christians, under King Fernando I, in 1064, but fell again briefly to the Moors in 1112.

Corneille, Pierre (1606-1684). French dramatist who wrote the play, *Le Cid*, first performed in 1637; this was partly based on **Castro**'s *Mocedades*.

Corpes: *The Outrage of (Afrenta de Corpes)*. This part of the legend was left out by Huidobro. In the **Cantar**, the story goes that the Cid had married his daughters to the princes of **Carrión**. These princes turned out to be cowards, and being ashamed that their cowardice had been discovered by the Cid's troops, they beat and humiliated their wives. To salvage the honour of the Cid's daughters, the Cid's men challenged the princes to duels and duly defeated them. The marriages were dissolved and the two young women married instead into the royal houses of Navarre and Barcelona. Given that the **Cantar** also has the wrong names for the Cid's daughters, it is as well that Huidobro jests with this episode, for which there is no historical evidence, employing it as a bad dream of the Cid's wife. As a dramatic device in the poem, it performs a valuable role however.

Cortes: ancestor of the modern legislature, it was an advisory body of nobles in the feudal state. The Cortes of León was the first such body in Europe.

Dolfos, Vellido: a knight who murdered King Don Sancho in a surprise attack. His name is also recorded as Bellido Dolfos and Vellido Adolfo. There is no documentary proof that he is anything other than a legendary figure, apart from one possible listing of his name in 1057, as Vellit Adulfiz.

Duero: river running from northern Spain to Porto in Portugal, more commonly known in English under its Portuguese name, the *Douro*.

Duro: a coin worth five pesetas.

Ebro: second longest river in Iberia, running from the Pyrenees to the Mediterranean in Tarragona.

Echegaray, José (1832-1916), leading Spanish dramatist of his day.

Elvira, Doña (1038-1101). Daughter of *Fernando*. Ruler of Toro, within the Kingdom of Castile.

Fáñez Minaya, Álvar (?-1114). The historical figure was a nobleman and military leader under Alfonso VI, and ran Toledo under Doña *Urraca*. In the legends he was vassal and military commander under the Cid in the latter's final years, but there is no documentary evidence of this. Minaya means 'my brother', being a conflation of Castilian *mí* (my) and Basque *anaia* (brother).

Fernando, King: Fernando 'the Great' (1015-1065), Count of Castile from 1029, and King of León from 1037. Became the pre-eminent Christian ruler in the peninsula.

García, Don (ca. 1041-1090). Son of *Fernando*. Became García II of Galicia after Fernando's death, Galicia being carved out of Asturias for his benefit.

García, Galin. Lord of Estada, and vassal of King Pedro of Aragón; in the legends he was one of the Cid's main followers.

geste: epic poem or saga in Old or Medieval French, from the word for 'exploits' or 'deeds'. Also *chanson de geste*.

Golpejares: the Battle of Golpejera, was a battle amongst Christian kingdoms fought in January, 1072. King Sancho II of Castile defeated the forces of his brother *Alfonso* VI of León near Carrión de los Condes.

Gómez de Orgaz: see *Rodríguez, Diego* under which name he is known today.

Góngora: Luis de Góngora y Argote (1561-1627), a Spanish baroque poet, renowned for his complicated style. Comparable perhaps to John Donne.

González, Count Fernán: first Count of Castile. Defeated the Moors at the Battle of Pedrahita.

González, Martín: champion of the King of Aragon, and regarded as the finest knight in Spain.

Gonzalo, Arias (ca.1025-?), knight of Zamora, and foster-father of Doña *Urraca*. Lost three sons at the fall of Zamora. His involvement with Zamora and Urraca is not attested in the historical record.

Gormaz, Castle of: Moorish castle, originally built in the 8th century, in the Soría province of Castile, which was the largest fortress in Europe after its 10th-century expansion. Now known, like the nearby town, as Burgo de Osma, the name of which derives from the Celtiberian Uxama settlement nearby. Pictured on the cover of this book.

Guadalete, Battle of: (711 or 712 AD). Battle at which the Visigothic King of Spain, Roderic (*Rodrigo*), was defeated by the invading Muslim forces of the Umayyad caliphate under Tariq ibn Ziyad. Roderic died in the battle, along with many of his nobles, and his capital of Toledo fell to the invaders shortly after.

Guerau [d'] Alamany II de Cervelló (d. 1097) Lord of Cervelló, and vassal of *Berenguer Ramon* II of Catalonia. His name suggests German origins.

Gustioz, Muño: brother-in-law of Jimena. After the Cid's death he continued to serve Jimena. His name is a corruption of the historically attested Munio (or Muño) Godestéiz, who married Aurovita Díaz, Jimena's older half-sister. His surname appears to be Basque.

Henry, Emperor: this is Henry IV (1050-1106), Holy Roman Emperor. Crowned as King of the Germans in 1054, he ruled as Emperor 1084-1105.

Holy Roman Empire: a political entity centred on the German lands, but also including Italy, Burgundy and Bohemia, founded by Charlemagne in 800 AD, and finally dissolved in the Napoleonic wars. The emperor was an elective position, with the electors being a group of three German nobles and three bishops; upon election, the chosen man would be crowned by the Pope. Despite its status as an Empire, it was never a unified state, remaining a patchwork of small kingdoms and principalities.

Ibn Djahaf: *Qadi* of Valencia, who murdered King al-Qadir, with the political support of the invading Almoravids. Brutally killed by the Cid after surrendering the city, but not completely complying with the terms of surrender.

Ibn Mochich: identity unclear.

Ibn Razin: Abd al-Malik Husam al-Dawla, King of Albarracín (1044-1103). One of a long line of the Banu Razin clan, Andalusian Berbers of the Hawwara tribe that had ruled the kingdom since 1012. The town's modern name comes from the clan's name.

Ite Missa est: the concluding words of the Latin mass.

Játiva: Xátiva in the *Cantar* and Xàtiva in modern Valencian. A town 56 kms south of Valencia, ruled in the Cid's time by a King referred to as Abenmazot in the *Cantar*. This is likely to be an attempt at Hispanicising a name such as Ibn Massud. The city fell to the invading Almoravid forces in 1095.

Jimena: born Ximena Gómez, she became the wife of the Cid, and is today known as Jimena Díaz de las Asturias (1055-1113). Daughter of *Diego Rodríguez*. Ximena is the old Spanish spelling; the name derives from Basque. Modern pronunciation is harsher; in the Cid's day it would have been closer to Shih-MAYna. This older pronunciation is preserved in the French versions of the story, where her name is transcribed as Chimène. The historical Jimena ruled Valencia after the death of the Cid until the Almoravid takeover in 1102.

Jerónimo, Bishop Don: Jérome de Périgord, a French Cluniac Bishop who came to Spain to oversee reform of the monasteries. He was named Bishop of Valencia in 1098 at the Cid's instigation. He converted the great mosque of Valencia into the Cathedral of Santa María. When the city was retaken by the Moors, he left and served as Bishop of Zamora and Salamanca until his death in 1125.

Laínez, Diego (d. ca. 1059) Father of the Cid. An alternative spelling of his family name is Flaínez.

Lozano, Count: Jimena's father according to the *Cantar*, but actually her godfather and Count of Ormaz, according to Huidobro. Jimena was in reality the daughter of *Diego Rodríguez* of Oviedo.

Menéndez Pidal, Ramón (1869-1968): Spanish philologist and historian, who produced the first modern annotated edition of the *Cantar de mío Cid*, with full analysis of the language and style. He was also the main historical adviser to the makers of the 1961 *El Cid* movie. Other significant publications include studies of medieval Spanish minstrel poetry, and of the origins of the Spanish language. He and his wife spent their honeymoon tracing the locations of the places mentioned in the *Cantar*, and he later composed a biography of the Cid (1929) which runs to almost 1,000 pages. President of the Real Academia Española (Royal Spanish Academy) 1925-1939 and 1947-1968.

Modafar: mentioned here (p.168) as the deposed King of Lérida, but this is a misattribution. The King of Lérida at the time was al-Mundhir (who was also King of Dénia), and Modafar (or al-Mudaffar) was a previous King of Badajoz, whose reign ended in 1067.

Morviedro: Medieval name of Sagunto, 30 kms north of Valencia.

Montes D'Oca: Montes de Oca, a *comarca* (administrative area similar to a British shire) to the east of Burgos, which was border country in the Cid's day, where previously the dominions of Castile and Córdoba had met. Disputed territory, it changed hands between Castile and Navarre more than once.

Moses Roschil: Jewish pawnbroker who took the Cid's chests when the latter was exiled. In the *Cantar*, his name is Rachel (pronounced Ra-KHEL, *Raguel* in modern Spanish). Huidobro is playing a game here by calling him Roschil, a name in which one can clearly hear *Rothschild* (pronounced ROTE-shilt in German, ROTT-shil in Spanish). In the story, he and *Vidas* regularly paid the Cid cash for his spoils of war.

Nuncio: a Papal ambassador, usually of at least archbishop's rank.

Núñez de Arce, Gaspar (1832-1903), Spanish poet and dramatist.

Oña: an important monastery town, 68 kms from Burgos. It reached its height in the Cid's time, when the court of Castile was based there.

Ordóñez, Count García (d. 1108), ruler of the Rioja region, with his seat at Nájera. Great rival of the Cid, and vassal of Alfonso VI. The historical record is silent on whether his legendary enmity with the Cid is true.

Oviedo, capital of the Kingdom of Asturias. Founded in 761.

Pelayo, Don, also Pelagius (ca. 685-737): a Visigothic noble who founded the Kingdom of Asturias, which he ruled from 718 until his death. His victory over the Moors at the Battle of Covadonga is regarded as the beginning of the *Reconquest*, the struggle against the Moors which was to take several hundred years. Covadonga is notable for being the first decisive Christian victory against Muslim forces in the Iberian peninsula.

Pepe-Hillo, Lagartijo, El Guerra, El Gallo, Gallito and **Belmonte**: names of famous bullfighters.

Pope Victor: Presumably Victor II (1018-1057), a German Pope who reigned 1055-1057. The only other candidate is Victor III, whose reign lasted only a year, from 1086-87, but this does not fit Huidobro's chronology. Victor II excommunicated Ramon Berenguer I, count of Barcelona for adultery.

Puerta del Sol: a central square in Madrid.

Qadi: Arabic word meaning *judge*. The position in Moorish Spain was not simply a legal one, as it also carried with it an administrative role.

Raimundo de Baran: in the *Cantar*, his name is Ramón de Bajaran. No information available.

Ramiro I, King of Aragón (before 1007-1063). Illegitimate son of King Sancho the Great. Although referred to as a King, his status is debatable. He did however expand the county of Aragón, with the holdings he acquired becoming the eventual basis of the later Kingdom of Aragón. Died at the siege of Graus.

Ramon Berenguer II, Count of Barcelona (1053-1082), nicknamed the 'Towhead' or 'Cap d'estopa', referring to his thick head of blond hair.

Raymond of Savoy, Duke: alas, there was no such person. Huidobro *may* be referring to Raymond IV, *Count* of Toulouse (ca. 1041-1105), leader of the First Crusade. Savoy was ruled by Counts in the Cid's era, none of whom were named Raymond. It only became a Dukedom in the 14th century. Another possible origin of the name is Raymond of Burgundy (c. 1070-1107), who ruled Galicia from 1090 until his death. This Raymond seems to have arrived in Spain with the army of Duke Odo of Burgundy in 1086, and he then married Urraca, daughter of Alfonso VI – not to be confused with her aunt *Urraca*. If this is the origin of the confusion it will lie with Raymond and his Lord, the Duke, being conflated into one.

Rodrigo, King: Roderic, last Visigothic King of Spain; died 711/712.

Rodríguez, Diego, Count of Oviedo (fl.1020-ca.1046), father of *Jimena*, the Cid's wife. Second cousin to Alfonso VI.

Saint James the Apostle: patron Saint of Spain. Legend has it that he is buried in Santiago (=Saint James) de Compostela, which is why the latter is a great pilgrimage destination.

San Pedro de Cardeña: a famous monastery (not an abbey, as the text here has it) dating back to the 10th century. The Cid, and later Jimena, were buried in a chapel there until their remains were moved to Burgos. His horse Babieca is buried in the grounds, with its own tombstone.

Sánchez, Fortun: Son-in-law of King Don García of Navarre.

Sancho, Prince Don (c. 1036-1072). Son of *Fernando*. King Sancho II of Castile after Fernando's death, King of Galicia (1071-72) and King of León (1072).

Santa Gadea: the Church of Santa Águeda (Saint Agatha) in modern Spanish, in Burgos, where the Cid forced *Alfonso* VI to swear an oath that he had had nothing to do with the death of his brother at the siege of Zamora. There is no historical evidence that such an oath was required, or made.

Sierra de Miedes: thought to be the modern Sierra de Pela.

Tagus (*Tajo* in Spanish, *Tejo* in Portuguese): the longest river in Iberia. Its source is in the centre of Spain and it runs to the Atlantic via Lisbon.

Taifa: an Arabic word, meaning *faction*. Refers to the multiple individual successor states that arose after the collapse of the first Moorish state in Spain, the capital of which was at Córdoba. The Taifas can be thought of as city-states of a kind familiar elsewhere in Europe, but they did tend to coalesce, with weaker ones falling to neighbouring stronger states.

Tarifa: one of the southernmost places in Spain, south of Cádiz, and an embarkation point for North Africa. It is named for Tarifa ibn Malik who attacked it in 710.

tercian hour: presumably 9 a.m., by analogy, as in the Catholic church *terce* is the service said at the third hour of the day, or 9 a.m.

Teruel: Lovers of (*Los amantes de Teruel*). Huidobro refers here to the famous story of Isabel de Segura, a wealthy woman of the city, and Diego de Marcilla, a poor man who fought in the Crusades so as to earn enough money to enable him to win Isabel's hand. They came to a tragic end, and their mummified bodies are in a mausoleum, *El mausoleo de los amantes* in Teruel's church of San Pedro.

Urraca, Doña (1033-1101). Daughter of King *Fernando*. Ruler of Zamora, within the Kingdom of Castile.

Vermúdez, Per: follower of the Cid. Also known as Pero [Pedro] Bermúdez. In the legends, he was a nephew of the Cid, and his standard-bearer, and was second only to Álvar *Fáñez* amongst the Cid's followers. Although his name appears in some 11th-century documentation, there is no direct evidence of his involvement with the Cid.

Valle-Inclán, Ramón del (1866-1936), Spanish dramatist whose work is modernist in style.

Vidas, Abel: Jewish pawnbroker and business partner of *Moses Roschil*. The name is likely to be a Spanish translation of the Hebrew *Hayyim* ('lives', *vida* being Spanish for 'life').

Visigoths: Germanic tribe who ruled Spain and parts of France after the collapse of Rome. Toulouse was their capital, but they were defeated by the Franks under King Clovis in 507, and thereafter were sovereign only in Spain, until their defeat at the hands of the Moors, after which they were confined to Asturias. The Visigoths gradually merged into the local Hispanic population.

Vivar: a village some 7 kms from Burgos, which legend claims as the birthplace of the Cid.

Walí: Arabic word usually meaning an Islamic saint, or alternatively 'friend', 'protector'. Here it is uttered by Moorish soldiers attacked by the Cid and his men, and thus on this occasion it is presumably a cry for help from higher powers (akin to guardian angels or patron saints) when facing what appears to be a demonic onslaught.

Yusuf: Yusuf al-Mu'taman ibn Hud [aka al-Mu'tamin]: third Banu Hud monarch of Zaragoza, he reigned 1081-1085; also a leading mathematician of his day. El Cid fought for him but broke off relations with Zaragoza in 1086.

Yusuf, Sultan: Yusuf ibn Tashfin (1009-1106), a Berber and prominent general of the Almoravid empire. He invaded Iberia and united the warring Moorish kingdoms under the Kingdom of Morocco; he was Emir of the captured lands and was regarded as the western Caliph, owing allegiance to Baghdad.

Zaïda of Seville (ca. 1070-1100): a refugee Moorish princess, daughter-in-law of al-Mutamid of Seville, who lived in exile at the Court of Toledo, and who became the mistress and possibly later the wife of King *Alfonso* VI of Castile.